the
OTHER SIDE
of NOW

ALSO BY PAIGE HARBISON

Anything to Have You

New Girl

Here Lies Bridget

the
OTHER SIDE
of NOW

A Novel

PAIGE HARBISON

ST. MARTIN'S PRESS
NEW YORK

First published in the United States by St. Martin's Press, an imprint of St. Martin's Publishing Group.

THE OTHER SIDE OF NOW. Copyright © 2025 by Paige Harbison. All rights reserved. Printed in the United States of America. For information, address St. Martin's Publishing Group, 120 Broadway, New York, NY 10271.

Designed by Jen Edwards

ISBN 978-1-250-35807-3

To Emily and Hartner. To Taryn and Jean.
To Elaine and Beth and our Greg.

To everyone else who lost their best friend.

I know what you must be thinking. "Poor little rich girl, what does she know about misery?"

—ROSE DEWITT BUKATER, *TITANIC* (1997)

PROLOGUE

⌒

fifteen years ago

I pull the trigger over and over and over as the increasingly feeble stream of water fails to propel my tiny horse as fast as I want it to go.

"Come on, come on!" I say, baring my teeth, which are still sore from today's orthodontist appointment, not taking my eyes off the bullseye for a moment.

Aimee's horse lurches ahead even farther, and that's when I notice that she's doubled over beside me, cracking up, her finger not even on her accelerator gun.

"Mine's broken!" she says between laughing gasps, and points at her ghostly horse, racing on speedily without her assistance.

My jaw drops and I yell, "This game is rigged!"

The finish-line bell sounds as Aimee's horse stops at the end of its track, leaving mine far behind.

"You win," says the bored, older teenager working the booth. He then gestures at the prizes. She picks a white teddy bear; he yanks it down from where it's clipped by the ear and tosses it to her, then sets up the horse game for another couple of suckers.

"It's rigged," I whisper to the girl taking over my old position. "The game is rigged."

"I don't think she got it," Aimee says as we walk away.

"Kids."

It's the end of summer and as hot as it gets in this part of muggy Florida. At home, the air-conditioning is broken, so I've been aching hot for weeks except for the nights I've been allowed to sleep over at Aimee's. Even our pool is hot. My parents keep reminding me what a whiny, ungrateful complaint that is, but it sucks, and it's not my fault they don't get that having something that *should* be nice that *doesn't work* is annoying.

Somehow, Aimee's pool is always cool. Aimee's *house* is cool. I know I don't live in some terrible, broken home or anything. It's nice. I'm lucky. But I always like being at Aimee's house more. Even when her parents make me do chores, I like it more. And they do. All the time. I know where the Comet and backup sponges are and that trash night is Wednesday, recycling is Thursday. Aimee and I are fifteen now, and her parents say that when we get our driver's licenses we're going to start doing the grocery shopping. They say it like a joke, but I wouldn't mind. As long as I get to go over there all the time.

Even though tonight is hotter than an oven, I'm happy. It's the annual End of Summer Carnival, the one super townie thing we really have around here. There's a Ferris wheel and some little roller coasters, a funhouse, lots of games, and—the part we like best—a ridiculous amount of junk food.

Funnel cake, ice cream, turkey legs, the good kind of chicken tenders with an array of dips, deep-fried Twinkies and Oreos, nachos, hot dogs, cheeseburgers, popcorn so salty it stings the tongue, soft pretzels with cheese dip that I can only find here (my mom eats them with mustard, gross), corn dogs, pizza, weird soda, root beer floats, snow cones (always disappointing), cotton candy, and then a bunch of stuff our moms like and we don't, like chocolate-covered bananas, cheesecake, onion rings, and chili cheese dogs. The air smells like fry oil, salt, sugar, and some other cheap neon smell I can't put my finger on but that practically intoxicates me every year.

Best of all, our moms come with us; they sit and drink pink wine from plastic cups and listen to the live music, and we get to run around with a twenty-dollar bill each and do anything we want with it.

Like get ripped off by a stoner in a tie-dyed shirt with a broken horse game, for example.

Aimee and I walk through the candy-colored stalls to the sound of the old-timey jazz band playing on the stage off in the distance.

"This reminds me of that scene at the beginning of *The Notebook*," I say. "Ooh, we should watch that tonight!"

"Oh . . . actually, um . . ."

I turn to look at her, thinking she's doing a bit. "Oh what, you don't want to?"

"I'm actually going over to Theo's tonight."

"Wait, what? Tonight?"

"Yeah. He didn't want to come to the carnival but he invited me over after. His friends are watching like . . . Tarantino movies or something all night and they invited their girlfriends." She says the syllables of *Tarantino* with unfamiliarity that she is clearly trying to pretend isn't there.

I stop walking. "Are you and Theo boyfriend-girlfriend now?"

She shrugs. "I don't know. I know you hate him."

"I don't hate him. He's . . ."

The worst. He smokes cigarettes and weed constantly and completely ignores me whenever I'm around. Worse than that, he acts like Aimee is a supporting character in *his* story. He talks over her and doesn't ask her questions and doesn't seem proud of her in front of his friends. He literally stands a little bit in front of her all the time, which I have recently learned is actually called *upstaging* in theatre. He walks into rooms and has full-on conversations without introducing or acknowledging that Aimee is even with him so then she's left to trail behind him like overlooked punctuation. Then she ends up explaining away every little thing he does that's weird. I guess that if she's a punctuation mark, she's an asterisk.

Not to mention the night I don't talk about. Not even with Aimee. It's the one secret in our friendship. I keep trying to find a time to tell her about it, but then I wimp out.

"Okay, well . . . you and I are hanging out right now! I'm not going to his place until later." Aimee keeps walking and I feel my heart completely sink as she pulls ahead.

I'm always afraid of her leaving me behind.

It was Aimee who grew out of playing pretend first, Aimee who was the first one to like boys. Now she's the one who goes and watches Tarantino movies after the carnival instead of what we usually do, which is watch a movie we've seen a hundred times, talk through it, giggle and gossip until a parent stomps in to say we need to lower our voices, and then sneak more junk food from the kitchen once our parents are sleeping.

"I wish guys still dressed like that," Aimee says when I catch up.

"Like what?" She can't mean Theo and his skinny jeans, chain wallet, and pre-distressed band tees.

"Like in *The Notebook*."

"Oh. Yeah. Same."

"And that we did too. It would be so fun to wear those cute dresses and do the hair and everything. Mrs. Harper talked about doing an older play soon, didn't she? Maybe it'll be from that era."

I don't get a chance to answer before we hear a raspy, accented voice on the wind.

"*Young ladies. . . . Get your fortune told.*"

We turn—me sucking the last sticky remnants of a caramel apple off my thumb, Aimee elbow-deep in a bag of white-cheddar popcorn, prize teddy bear under her other arm.

"Do you wish to know your fortune?" asks the woman. With her very cool, very chic accent, it sounds more like *D'yu wij tnoh yohr forchoon?*

She really looks the part, and I start making involuntary mental notes to re-create her as a character.

The woman has heavy eyeliner, emerald eye shadow, and tattooed eyebrows that have turned blue. Her thin lips are painted dark maroon, and her old skin looks unsettlingly soft and papery. Coiffed copper curls peek out from under her headpiece. Aimee's mom has the perfect scarf for me to wrap around my head like that.

She has a deck of ornately designed cards neatly stacked on her small table, which is draped in a velvet fabric that matches her eye shadow. A small tea light emits a gentle light from inside a scarlet glass.

Aimee and I look at each other, and I'm surprised to see that my friend, usually the most relaxed girl in the world, has gone a little pale.

Aimee nods for me to go first.

"Okay," I say to her. To the woman, I say, "Hi."

"Hello. Sit."

I do as I'm told. She's so commanding, I'd probably tap-dance if she told me to.

Let's be honest—if it seems like it'll get me some positive attention, I'll tap-dance for anyone. And I'm not even good at it.

The woman stares at me for a moment and then holds out her hands. "Your palm."

Like the skin on her face, her hands are ivory and seem silkier than they should be.

She stares at the lines on my palm and smiles. "You're going to do great things. Loved by many. Famous."

"Oh! That's nice."

"For a while."

"Oh. Okay, well." I look to Aimee and roll my eyes.

The woman studies my palm more closely, lifting a pair of tethered glasses from one of those necklaces that only older women and some weird men seem to wear, resting them on her narrow nose. "This is strange."

I don't really believe in anything she's saying—in fact, I don't want to, because she said I'd be famous but only for a while—but when she inspects more closely, I still start to get nervous.

The woman laughs, shaking her head. "Your life goes in two different directions. It divides. It's almost imperceptible, but undeniable. Look, you with your young eyes. Look for yourself."

She points a long, unpainted fingernail along a line between my thumb and my forefinger, going toward my wrist. Diverging from it, there's another.

"Okay . . ."

"Usually, there is only one line here. You have two." She stares hard at me, as if I'm supposed to understand the significance of this. "Two lives, girl."

I run my tongue along the braces at the back right of my mouth like I always do when I don't know what to say. "Oh . . ."

She tuts and releases my hand. "Two destinies. Two lives. You will know when the time comes to choose which life is for you."

I open my mouth to ask two lifetimes' worth of questions when she flaps her fingers wildly in Aimee's direction and says, "You, come." Then to me, "You, go."

My friend takes a slow step toward the woman, handing me the bag of popcorn, then dusts her hands off on her jean shorts. "Sorry. Cheese."

"Comes with the territory," the woman says, gesturing at our surroundings. As Aimee sits down, the woman reaches for her. "Show me."

Aimee hesitates. I wrinkle my eyebrows at her. She doesn't believe in this kind of thing, does she? Why is she being cagey about it?

She puts the teddy bear between her knees and gives over her palm.

The woman looks at it for a long, silent time. Too long, too silent. You know when it's someone's turn to talk and then they don't? And then they don't again?

The silence stretches on for probably only two or three minutes in real time, but in a context like this it feels like a very, very long time. And Aimee doesn't look at me once. Neither of them do.

Aimee stares at the woman.

The woman stares at her palm.

I stare at both of them.

Around us, the world spins. The jazz plays on, a song my dad likes called "Where or When." The crooning voice singing, *Oh the tricks your mind can play* . . .

The golden string lights cast a glow on future memories of hundreds of sugar-high kids as they laugh and push each other and hold hands for the first time. The old rides creak and spin and rotate as they've done countless times before and will do until they break. Corn pops and cotton candy is spun; apples are dipped in salty, sticky caramel or molten hot, toxically red sugar. Our moms sit at some splintery picnic table somewhere with that wine I hate the smell of, chatting about who knows what.

And then there are the three of us, locked in an endless moment that feels altogether different in a sudden and dark way I cannot describe.

You are smiling, you were smiling then, but I can't remember where or when . . .

The candle on the table flickers violently, growing double in size, and I see Aimee's and the woman's eyes jerk in unison toward the flame.

The woman releases Aimee's hand, abruptly but kindly and without a word. Her sudden benevolence is somehow more unnerving than the curtness of before.

Aimee gives a small shake of her head, like, *well?*

The woman responds with a sad, sorry sort of smile, her eyes tenting into an empathetic expression that makes no sense.

"What does that mean?" I ask. "Um, excuse me? What's going on?"

"Be well, little girls."

My skin rises in goose bumps.

If Aimee was pale before, she is a ghost now. I can see her heartbeat in the pulsing of her uplit jugular. Even so, as if in a trance, she pulls a five-dollar bill from her denim pocket.

"No," says the woman, closing Aimee's fingers on the money. "Be well."

Aimee stands up.

"Come on, let's go," I say. "This is creepy."

She comes to my side, putting a sweating hand in mine, and we quickly leave. Once gone, I could swear I hear the woman's voice far off in the wind saying, *"Drive safely, girls."*

Or maybe that's just how I remember it.

CHAPTER ONE

present day

The gun feels cold and hard where I hide it against the small of my back.

I lean on the rolltop desk and watch Kim cross in front of me, her chiffon pantsuit hanging loosely around her frame. I will the tears to come to my eyes. It'll be better if I look upset.

"It wasn't my fault you left. That was your choice," I say. I try to sound strong, but I don't hide the sadness and anger either.

"You couldn't accept that you were wrong; you *forced* me to leave. It was your fault and you couldn't *stand* that you made such a huge mistake!" She puts her hands on her hips and stares me down, the massive fake diamonds around her neck catching the light. I allow my eyes to be drawn to them only momentarily before I lift my gaze back to hers.

"No," I say, exuding calm, despite my voice shaking a little.

"You were too damn proud to listen," she says, a humorless smile playing at her lips.

"Proud?" I scoff, blinking the tears away, and underplay the next words where someone else might scream them. "If there's one thing in my life that I'll look back on with pride"—I pull the gun out from behind my back and aim it squarely at her exposed, ample cleavage—"it's this."

I pull the trigger. Kim falls back against the grand piano. Her underweight body drapes against the keys, sounding a discordant crash before she slides down to the ground.

I walk over to her, and before her eyes go blank, I yank the necklace from her. "I'll think of you every time I wear it."

She struggles to speak, and I lean closer to hear her say, "You . . . bitch."

I laugh. A little. Then a lot. Maybe too much.

"*Cut!*"

The grin falls from my face and I clear my throat and stand. "Did we get it?"

The director, Devon, bursts out of the control booth and comes over, tearing his headphones off. He puts his hands on my shoulders and his voice echoes through the cavernous studio. "Lana. You knocked it right out of the park. I'm not kiddin', you knocked it right out of the city!"

There is a massive cheer from the crew, all of whom are *beyond* ready to wrap for the season. The firearm-safety guy comes over with great caution and takes the fake gun.

Devon pulls me toward him, then drags me over to video village, saying, "I gotta show you that last take. It was absolutely mesmerizing. You're such a talent. I'm so glad Martin introduced us, and that I got to be the one to discover the great Lana Lord all those years ago."

I am desperate to get the hell out of here—the stage lights, which have the heat of the surface of the sun, and the many bodies in here have made this place a sauna—but I go with him, ignoring the way his hand has drifted down to my lower back. He seems to assume that since he's gay, I won't mind.

I sigh, too worn out to bat it away like I usually do.

"Take it back to right after Velma's monologue," he says to the camera operator. "Yeah, right there, right there."

He hovers two fingers in front of the monitor, and between them I notice where his spray tan has settled into the webbing. Then he hands me a pair of headphones and I hold one ear to mine and watch.

I never get used to it. Seeing myself this way. The blazing lights make my eyes look bluer and clearer than they are, and the waist cincher beneath my dress gives me an impossibly angled silhouette. Not to mention the fake eyelashes, the big-hair wig, the intense contouring, and the actual nose job I might never fully adjust to.

In post, they'll retouch us all to death, giving us that soapy, perfect look. It's good that they do, because it'll make a Botoxer out of anyone to see themselves this close up, unedited. No line or pore can hide from these cameras.

Falling for the hyperclear image myself, I wonder if a *little* more Botox wouldn't hurt. It's such a slippery slope. Once you put it *here* you need it over *there*, and suddenly you're getting injections in your earlobes and don't know what happened. I talked to someone at a party once who said she got her knees injected after seeing someone on Instagram say that they looked like angry hobbits.

I saw the picture and they weren't totally wrong, but frankly *everyone's* knees look stupid when you stare at them long enough.

"You look good, kid."

I sigh deeply and give Devon a loaded look. "Thanks."

He juts his chin and gives me a look back. "I know this isn't exactly what you had in mind when you made your deal with the Hollywood devil," Devon says, his voice low. "Hell, it's not the deal any of us thought we were making. But it worked."

I nod and say, "Well, I didn't have a functioning car when I started and now I'm here, so I guess you could say it's working."

He considers me for a moment, looking like he has something to say, but isn't sure he should.

"Just say it, Devon."

"I do have a bit of unpleasant news. Some words from up top."

I tilt my head, braced. "What?"

"They want you to lose another"—he drops his voice to a whisper—"ten pounds."

"*What?*" I ask again. I heard him. I can't believe him.

"I know, I know," he says.

"Devon, are you serious? They *already* had me drop ten pounds this season. I've basically been eating lemon water soup as every meal for three months."

"It's the evil twin storyline. I don't make the rules, baby. I'm sorry."

"This is insane. Another season and there won't be any of me *left*."

"Actually, hon, the truth is . . ." He comes closer again, close enough that I can smell his veneers. "I'm not sure there'll be another season. They're hoping, so you have to be prepared, but it's not a sure thing."

"Wait—what? The show is huge! The ratings are—well, obviously they're not great but that's kind of what we are. Bad and everyone likes us."

"I know."

"Is it because of that *New Yorker* article?"

"Shh, shh, you cannot tell anyone else. Not a soul. I'm not telling anyone but you. Don't worry, I've already got some backup plans lined up, and I promise I'll take you with me wherever I go if we get . . ." He drops his voice to an inaudible level, basically mouthing, "*canceled*."

I stare at him in shock, but then nod slowly and say, "Okay, I guess I'll . . . go ahead and lose those ten pounds though, just in case."

He does a *what are you going to do?* shrug, not quite getting my ironic tone, then says, "I know a guy over at *Love Is Blind*, rumor has it they're looking for a new host. What do you think?"

"I've got to go. Let me know if my career is over when you get word."

I turn on my Louboutin and leave.

After changing and having my fake eyelashes ripped off and my makeup removed for almost an hour, I walk to my ride while checking my phone. As always, I have several missed calls, a few voicemails, almost thirty missed texts, and a flurry of emails. I scan over them.

Hey Lana! Checking in that we're all good for the Gillian dress tonight? Spoke to Lisa Michele, and she said you weren't sure if—

Hi, gorgeous! We've sent along a FREE collection of our NEWEST
and most coveted lip stains. If you could post about it, that would be
great! Please be sure to include these in your post—

Lana, circling back after last week's call. Have you given any more
thoughts to a collab? SPOT—The Best Period Underwear. Period.—
would love to have you as a spokesperson—

Hi, sorry but Grayson told me to text you and ask if you knew where
his Bulgari Octo Roma watch is, he's supposed to wear it tonight and
get a picture—

I feel my blood pressure rise as I look at them. It's like a self-propagating
to-do list every time I open up my phone.

I get into the back of the waiting G-Wagon, handing my phone to Lisa
Michele, my personal assistant.

"Oh, ew, there's so much here. Okay, I'll forward these on over to myself." She pokes at the screen, then hands it back. "So annoying that they
keep contacting *you* instead of *me*."

I pull down my Dodgers hat so far that I basically can't see, a signal that
I'd like to be left alone.

Lisa Michele doesn't get it, and starts scrolling through her own phone.
Chaotic bursts of noisy video start and stop as she jumps from one clip to
the next. It's one of her worst habits. She looks up my hashtag and then
watches all the videos about me.

"This is so great," she says. "Literally everyone loves you, I'm not even
kidding. Like all the old people on Instagram especially for some reason,
but also like everyone my age."

I let my head loll to the right to look at her. She's an impossibly perky
twenty-two-year-old with vocal fry and upspeak, a piña colada vape pen,
and a degree in Social Media Management from Northwestern. I'm only
eight years older than her, but whenever I listen to anything at all that she
says, I feel like the old version of Rose in *Titanic*.

Not least of all because that is the reference that comes to mind first.

The car jerks as someone cuts into our lane and I grab the bar on the door, gripping so hard I think I might crack one of my Gel-X nails. My heart pounds in my throat.

"Oh, well actually, lies, not everyone loves you," Lisa Michele says, reacting to her phone screen but not the jerking of the car. "Some of these comments are . . . real cringe."

I take a few deep breaths.

To understand my career as it stands, all you need to do is read the six-page think piece written about me and the show I'm on, *Brilliance,* that was recently published in the *New Yorker.* The article was called "The Era of Eras Has Ended."

The writer, who probably lives in a perfectly nice apartment in Brooklyn but still complains about the entitled bourgeoisie, wrote an article about how *our times* are best reflected in the *bewildering, if not troubling, churning of briefly surging cultural fads so intense and so fleeting that they cannot even be gathered into something as amorphic and ephemeral as a zeitgeist.*

He went on to say that *Brilliance* is *at its core an unconscious parody of its predecessors and itself.*

He's missing the fact that it's *not* unconscious. *Brilliance* is an over-the-top primetime soap opera made for the streaming era. It's like *Dallas* or *Dynasty,* but intentionally camp. Devon once described it as *Succession* for the gay community.

The show plotlines include amnesia, resurrections, family secrets, love triangles, and—apparently next season—an evil twin.

An evil, problematically thin twin.

But people have been obsessed with the show. It's like the world all of a sudden got sick of cool shows, great writing, and nuance. It's all the drink-throwing and opulence of *Real Housewives* without the tricky real-world ramifications. It's all the betrayal and twists you want out of Shakespeare, but without the labor of Elizabethan English.

And I'm the lead villain. Daphne Gwenn, the new-money bitch everyone loves to hate.

The show is a sparkling, champagne-fueled, high-drama shitshow that everyone has watched, even if just to stay in the conversation. But ever since the *New Yorker* article, the headlines have started to get more critical.

Perhaps in part because of the article that predicted it, the phenomenon of the show must have a time limit. And after what Devon told me, maybe my success does too. I mean *Love Is Blind*? That's not even *Love Island*.

I mean. Of course it can't last forever. Nothing in Hollywood does. Famously.

My mind reels back to a summer when I was a teenager, the sound of old jazz and the smell of kettle corn.

For a while, she had said. I'd be famous *for a while*.

Lisa does not stop reading mean comments from internet trolls for the rest of the drive, even once the car is parked in the driveway. I say *the driveway* because no matter how much I actually live here, it still feels like Grayson's house. Not ours. Not mine. His, and I live here.

As we climb out of the back seat, she tells me that someone thinks I look like I am my own Madame Tussauds wax figure, and that's when I lose it.

"Lisa Michele," I say, rounding on her and raising my voice to a firm, angry-mom level. "My dude. You have got to shut the fuck up."

She blinks several times, her fresh eyelash extensions flapping. "Wow. That is so not professional."

"I can't—" I look beyond her and see that a gardener is filming us, and leave without another word.

—

"Okay, okay," I say, then, "Whoa!" as I almost fall backward off the piano bench. I laugh, so everyone else knows it's okay to laugh. I kick off my Amina Muaddi slingback pumps, saying loudly to the party fray, "It was the shoes, it was the shoes!"

I run my hand through my hair, which is now no longer neatly parted but raked through and swept to the side.

"Okay," I go on. "I'm terrible at toasts *but* I want to thank you all for being here for my thirtieth birthday, and say that I can't wait to have you all over next year. For my thirtieth birthday."

I lift my glass once more as everyone laughs at my joke, then down the rest of my champagne. I look around for Grayson but don't see him anywhere.

Tonight, I am playing the role of the charming, charismatic hostess who is wildly at ease and deeply clever. If this personality were a cocktail, it would be one part Zelda Fitzgerald, one part Serena van der Woodsen, and a few dashes of each character Kate Hudson has ever played. I'm serving it shaken, strained, and straight up.

It's a persona well-aided by the fact that all I've eaten today are some undipped crudités and a pearl spoonful of caviar, having only glanced at the crème fraiche and blinis.

"Happy birthday!" someone yells, and everyone else chimes in.

Another bottle of champagne gets popped and I lift one hand to point with approval at the guy who opened it.

This party was supposed to be outside, under the amber lanterns in the backyard with a big band playing. Usually LA evenings are cooler this time of year, and it *never* rains, as the song "It Never Rains in Southern California" is there to remind you. Even if that song was actually about the disillusionment of people with dreams in this city, I think of it every rare wet day. Like today, because seemingly out of nowhere, it began to pour. I hadn't looked at the forecast because we never have to in June. And I guess somehow *no one else did either*.

The catering crew had scrambled to bring all the bottles and glasses indoors as the rain began. Some guests left, because there are *always* people who give up the second there's a location change, even if it's by twenty yards. Everyone else made their way inside, some covering their hair, others rescuing bottles of wine from the tables.

It's so warm that I decided to open the accordion window walls that face the yard and then leaned against the column between them to watch the frenzy. Rain-drenched Barry Keoghan lit a cigarette and walked leisurely across the backyard with his shirt mostly unbuttoned, stopping in the middle of the lawn to look up at the sky.

I was still watching him when the party planner came up to me, mortified, clearly worried I was one of those punitive celebrities who would end her career because of a mistake. She didn't know that I honestly do not fucking care.

So now, instead of a fancy fete on a breezy June night, attended by guests with perfect hair and makeup, my party has devolved into this. The house smells like the sweaty cloud of Le Labo left over after a hot yoga class at One Down Dog. But the heat and the rain have lent a fun comradery to the evening: Women have put their Nine Zero One Salon–done hair into messy buns off their shoulders and the guys have rolled their sleeves up. Everyone's drinking too much wine, so the vibe is actually better than it probably would have been.

It should be lovely.

Maybe it would be, if I didn't give up on finding Grayson on the main floor, go upstairs, burst into my own bedroom, and find Grayson there with the costar of his latest Marvel movie.

I don't even linger. I turn on my heel and leave, knowing he'll follow me.

I storm to the sunroom, which is on the opposite end of the house from the party. Rain pelts the panes of glass all around us. The humidity reminds me of Florida.

"Can you please admit that you're sleeping with Elsa?" I snap, as soon as the door is shut. "I don't even care if you are. I just don't want you to make an idiot out of me when I'm the last to know."

"I'm *not cheating on you.*"

"You are!" I raise my voice. "I know you are! I'm not dumb, Grayson! You're in the bedroom with her doing *what*, then? God. I mean, seriously, have a little respect for me."

"No, Lana. Will you lower your voice?"

"Lower my—no! It's my birthday and I can have a meltdown if I want to!"

"Lana."

"*Grayson*," I say, in a mocking, schoolyard tone.

"I'm Hitchcock."

"Ex . . . cuse me?"

"In Spielberg's new biopic, I'm going to play Hitchcock! I told you about it, remember?"

I stare at him blankly.

"I'm going to be Alfred Hitchcock. I got the part, babe!"

I blink a few times at the redirect. "What does that have to do with you in our bedroom with Elsa on my birthday?"

"I couldn't talk about it in front of anyone!"

"So . . . why wouldn't you have pulled *me* into the bedroom?"

He goes red. "Because they haven't casted the Grace Kelly part yet and I think Elsa would be good for it."

I roll my eyes at *casted* and then say, "You don't think maybe *I* would be good for it?"

Even saying it embarrasses me. It clearly embarrasses him too. "They're probably going to go with a big name, anyway. Like Margot or Saoirse or Evan. Maybe Lily. Someone who's . . . you know, done more."

"So if you were going to suggest—ugh, forget it. God." I shake my head. "How are *you* going to play Hitchcock?"

I motion at his CrossFit-keto-intermittent-fasting-sculpted body.

"I've got a freezer full of Van Leeuwen and a kegerator being delivered on Monday. My trainer has a plan too. Gotta pack on the pounds." He pats his hard stomach, and it sounds like he's banging on a marble countertop. "This is it, babe. I'm going to kick my career into hyperdrive."

One would argue that came when he did the remake of *The Outsiders* as a teenager, played Sinatra in the Luhrmann Hollywood Canteen movie, or, yeah, when he got the lead role in the newest chapter of the limitless Marvel Cinematic Universe, a film that grossed the most since *Avengers: Endgame*.

Grayson Gamble is not just famous. He's nepotism famous. Hollywood royalty famous. His grandmother was in movies with Bing Crosby.

His mom was a producer on most of the erotic thrillers of the nineties. His cousin headlined the last Coachella. His whole family tree is hyper-linked.

"I wanna be taken serious, you know? I'm over going to like, Kardashian Christmas parties and doing collabs. I want to be . . . like . . . eating dinner at Vespertine with like . . . Joan Didion."

I shut my eyes with desperate patience. "Grayson."

"Is she dead too?"

He says *too* because he is constantly making this kind of mistake. So many women on this earth would do anything to be with this guy and they have *no* idea the labor it takes. I am, in fact, simply impressed he even got her name right.

"Yes, Grayson. She's dead."

"Why?"

"*Why?* Do you mean *how?*"

I've confused him. "Well. You know what I mean," he says, shaking his head like an Etch A Sketch. "Look, this is really important to me. Can you not ruin it?"

I gape at him. "Are you being serious?"

"Yeah?"

I let out a deep breath. "When our agents hooked us up, and we decided to go for it, we swore we'd be honest with each other if something needed to change. We're supposed to help each other, not make things worse."

"I didn't cheat on you."

I stare at him for a long moment and then say, "Okay. Then I have no choice but to believe you."

He closes his mouth and nods slowly.

Grayson rejoins the party with ease, and I take to floating around the place like a barely remembered ghost.

The house is full of somebodies and wannabes, delirious from the tidal downpour that has drenched and inflated the heat wave that's been puls-ing outside for the last few days, ending twenty weeks straight of per-fect weather. No one here has eaten a carb since 2019, but a bottle of champagne is popped every five minutes because drinking carbs is different.

In the kitchen, someone has produced a bottle of Sotol from some apparently *magical* town in Mexico and is talking about its aromatics.

On the couch, two people are getting the idea to write a script together, saying, *Wait . . . are we doing this?* over and over.

One girl keeps taking ostensibly subtle pictures of the goings-on, but I don't get the feeling she's planning to sell them. More likely she's gotten here by some series of mistakes and is texting them to her mom or best friend with a lot of *omg*s and skull emojis.

It's regular, run-of-the-mill Hollywood Hysteria.

I take an unopened Bollinger from an ice bucket, deciding to say *fuck it* to my caloric allocation and to the former service industry worker inside me who still thinks she needs to be the consummate host at all times.

I go upstairs to hide.

The noise from the party muffles when I close the bedroom door.

My eyes catch on something sparkling on the duvet. I go closer and find that it's a diamond earring. Not mine.

I arch my eyebrow at the multi-thousand-dollar clue and consider throwing it off the balcony. But my formerly bank-account-always-in-the-negative heart can't do it. I place it on Grayson's nightstand.

Asshole.

My black Lab, Dido, stretches as she awakens from a deep sleep in her bed. I go over and collapse onto her, sighing deeply. It's very melodramatic to say, but sometimes I feel like she's the only real thing in my life. Dido, with her sad little backstory of abandonment that had been written up on the rescue website alongside several photos of her adolescent, spindly frame. Already not a puppy anymore by the time I found her.

She always follows me around the house like I'm the only real thing in her world too.

God, I really am being *very* tragic. I don't even know why it's hitting me so hard tonight.

Maybe it's the insult of catching Grayson with Elsa. Maybe it's the fact that *Brilliance* might end. Maybe it's because it's my birthday? I know some people get emotional on their birthdays, but that's never been me. Though it is my thirtieth. That's a pretty big deal.

I decide I'll feel better, and perhaps less like a damsel in a Christopher Nolan movie, if I get out of this horrible dress that makes me look like Mermaid Batman.

I strip out of it, with great effort, and change into a baggy T-shirt and my favorite sweatpants. Gray, full of holes, and soft as a cloud. Down one leg they say *Burchell*; down the other leg, *Hawks*. My high school gym pants. They're soft in the way only well-made, decades-old cotton can be.

I wipe off every ounce of makeup, which takes about half a pack of Clinique wipes, then double cleanse my face, deciding to skip most of the fourteen-step regimen of serums and acids by which I usually abide. I put my product-laden hair into a ponytail, leaving the extensions in a creepy pile on the side of the infinity tub like a scalped Barbie.

I take my phone, headphones, and champagne out onto the covered balcony. The heat has gotten even heavier in the air, and I plug in the fan and lie back in the macramé hammock, looking out at the wet, starless sky. Well. Stars are there. You just can't see them in this city.

Deciding to lean into my misery, I put on Phoebe Bridgers and let the melancholic notes enrapture me, the Vornado blowing rainy mist onto me every now and again.

Phoebe sings *Jesus Christ, I'm so blue all the time* and it resonates so deeply that I feel guilty.

I know I have no right to be this miserable. I can't even say it out loud. I can't say it to my parents, who would think I'm ungrateful for my success. I can't say it to Grayson, who thinks the cure for unhappiness is, under every circumstance, a good workout. I can't say it to my friends because I don't really *say* anything to them at all. They know me as I was most of tonight: boisterous and fun, charming and spontaneous. Not this version of me, who thinks all of this is kind of, somehow, bullshit.

No one has sympathy for you when your life looks this good from the outside. It's like complaining that your enormous boobs make it hard to find clothes that fit properly. Or whining that you're afraid of heights when you're at the top of an ivory tower.

No one wants to hear it. And no one believes it, even if it's true.

I feel like my life is an illusion and even I can't see quite through it.

I did tell my therapist about my discontent, though honestly, I didn't fully open up. And yes, of course I have a therapist. An Angelino without a therapist is like a Taylor Swift song without a story. It simply does not exist.

My therapist told me to search my past. To find when I last felt truly happy. I admitted that I genuinely couldn't think of when that would be. She said to go back through my photos and videos. See which ones made me feel happy, not shitty.

I've made the hunt a nightly ritual. So far, I've gone back about ten years, and I still haven't found anything that brings me pure joy.

How depressing is that? Especially considering that *during* that time, I was *desperate* for the life I have now, and I'm still not happy?

Obviously, *it's me, hi, I'm the problem, it's me*. But then . . . what?

I scroll now through the years of my life in my phone. Past the Getty Images of me on the red carpet in dresses I starved myself to fit into and then had to return after each event; past the unflattering before-and-after photos from the rhinoplasty, the brow lift, and the buccal fat removal. Past the photos of my first LA apartment in Miracle Mile, which was a few blocks from the neighborhood Italian restaurant called Met Him at a Bar where I used to bartend. Past the Red Bull Vodka–fueled pictures of me partying in West Hollywood when I first moved to LA.

I scroll a little too far and my thumb lands on a low-quality video. I immediately know exactly what it is, even though I haven't watched it in years.

I hesitate before pressing *Play*.

It's me and my best friend Aimee in my high school bedroom. We met at the beginning of middle school when we got very well cast as Rhyme and Reason (me as Rhyme, Aimee as Reason) in our fall production of *The Phantom Tollbooth*. After that we were inseparable. Not that our parents didn't sometimes try when we were shrieking at two a.m. during a Friday night sleepover.

In this video, we were that kind of slumber-party-girl drunk that comes from no alcohol at all, but a stash of candy, banana-yellow microwaved popcorn, and a friendship that is mostly based on inside jokes.

It starts on a frame of Aimee's arm pulling away from the camera, which has been propped up. "Is it filming?" She checks the back of what I remember to be a Nikon Coolpix camera from Costco. "Oh, yeah it is. Okay, Meg Bryan, how have you changed since coming back from Avalon School of the Arts?"

She is, of course, using my real name, and not the stage name I've assumed since then, Lana Lord.

She holds out a hairbrush she's using as a microphone.

I come into frame wearing a red wig, with a red moustache drawn on in one of my mom's Revlon lipsticks.

"Who, me?" I say in a bad Irish accent.

Both of us devolve into laughter. When we finally compose ourselves, Aimee puts the hairbrush in front of my face. "You're a famous actress now. Do you think the fame has gotten to you?"

She's trying so hard not to crack a smile that it makes me, the real me watching the video, smile so hard that it hurts.

"No, no, I don't think so," says teenage-me, still in the accent. "I'm the same as when I left America! Only now, me favorite food is potatoes!"

This is too much for us both, and we burst into laughter all over again. We're both laughing so hard that we've stopped making any sound. Our mannerisms are so similar to each other; we spent so much time together. Both our tongues are blue from, I'm sure, Pixy Stix or Baby Bottle Pops, and both our faces are spotted with pimples in part from, I'm sure, Pixy Stix and Baby Bottle Pops.

"It's so"—teenage-me gasps for breath—"not funny!"

Aimee shakes her head slowly, still cracking up.

I didn't think so at the time, but hearing our voices now, we sound so young. Goofy and unselfconscious. High pitched and silly.

"Okay, let's never show this to anyone, ever," teenage-me says, turning off the video. It freezes on my phone as it ends.

You're a famous actress now. Do you think the fame has gotten to you?

It's strange that this fantasy came true. For me. I am a famous actress. Has the fame gotten to me?

Not in the way people mean.

In that video, I was seventeen years old, and I was about to get into the college of my dreams. Avalon School of the Arts, a small but highly renowned art school in Ireland, known for its theatre program. Hence the borderline-insulting stereotyping in the video.

Aimee and I had fallen in love with the school together, and we had both applied at the same time, with the same expectations: that we'd both get in, live there together, succeed together, and then be famous together.

But that wasn't what happened.

I got in. Aimee didn't.

We had sworn that if one of us got accepted and the other didn't, then whoever did wouldn't go. We'd attend our backup school together, which we'd *definitely* get into (and we did). But once Aimee got wait-listed for Avalon, she insisted I go anyway, tearfully telling me she couldn't live with herself if I didn't.

But we'd promised each other. So I stayed in Florida with her. I stayed, and we went to college twenty minutes from home.

Staying in Florida, not going to Avalon, was probably the biggest mistake of my life. Which means that this video of Aimee and me, which I know to be about three days before we found out she didn't get in, is possibly the last time I was truly happy. Except for the moments between finding out I got in and that Aimee didn't. It was delusional to think both of us would get accepted, but at that age and time it just felt like really shitty luck that we didn't.

Three days before we got the news that changed our lives. Instead of going overseas to a cute little school in a misty village, we would be staying in Florida, going to a charmless state school and living in awful dorms.

I shut my eyes now, unable to think about what happened later.

I inhale deeply and put a hand on my chest and try to keep a potential panic attack at bay. Breathe in and out. Everything's fine.

But it isn't. I know, in my heart of hearts, that I was supposed to go to Avalon, and since I did my part wrong, I'm living out the wrong version of things. That's what it feels like.

I scroll through more pictures and videos, skipping around and coming to one from college. I don't recognize it.

I'm holding my phone up in the mirror, showing my own reflection in the video.

"Okay, Aimee is in a mood, so we're going to try and see if this works."

College-me points the camera at my feet as I walk, laughing to herself as she does so.

Oh God, I do vaguely remember this.

With my iPod plugged into a portable speaker, I walk into Aimee's room blasting "Who Let the Dogs Out" by Baha Men.

Aimee looks jarred and shakes her head, gesturing to turn it off.

I do, and then say, "Okay, so like I said, Aimee's in a mood."

"Are you filming right now?" She looks exhausted with me. "I *don't* want to be *filmed* right now. I mean it—*stop*."

I hear a meager *sorry* and then the video ends.

It may as well have been a slap.

I feel so embarrassed that I'm actually nauseous. I hate seeing myself on camera. It's an oddly common affliction for actors. I can't watch my own stuff without feeling itchy. But it's way worse in a video like this, when I was actually myself, not even a character. Young and unselfconscious, hadn't learned tact or social caution. My voice was loud, unbraced for rejection; I was *uncool* in every sense of the word.

Why had I even kept that video? Why would I ever want to revisit that feeling?

I sit up, tossing my phone aside and taking off my headphones. The hot, fabricated breeze ripples over the porch.

I need to do something. I don't know what, but I need to do *something*.

I pop the bottle of Bolli and take a big swig.

Then, as the bubbles foam over and spill down my front, I am struck with an idea.

Maybe I need to get out of here for a little while.

I used to dream of discovering new places, and yet now all I do is work in LA, with only the rarest work trips to Georgia and Vancouver and the occasional weekend in Palm Springs, Joshua Tree, Big Bear, or Lake Arrowhead. I hardly ever go farther than a few hours, and I rarely even go to the beach. Which, to be fair, is something that can be said by most Eastside Angelinos. It takes *forever* and the traffic-jammed trip back sort of eclipses any seaside relaxation.

But seriously. I need to think bigger; I mean, I've never even been off this continent.

I open my phone and pull up the Airbnb app.

Number of guests? One.

I'm not bringing Grayson. I need a break from Grayson.

Duration of trip? Uh . . . one week.

My heartbeat quickens at the idea of getting away. Far away. To really change the scenery.

Destination?

I hesitate. Then I select *Anywhere*.

I browse for a while: an Airstream in Santa Barbara, a beachside casita in Rosarito, a hut in Bora Bora, a tree house in San Jose, a city loft in Lisbon, a high-rise on Bondi Beach. Then I do what I was always going to do. I change *Anywhere* to *Avalon, Ireland*.

There is only one result. I've got flash-sale fervor as I scramble to get it before someone else does.

It's a little white cottage called Surrey House with a red door and green vines. There's soft-looking grass in a gated front yard. It has old, warped pane windows and a crooked mailbox. Inside, there are exposed wooden beams and a high-arched ceiling. There's a stone fireplace in the living room and a stack of magazines on a coffee table (when was the last time I even *saw* a magazine?) in front of a plush love seat draped with blankets. The kitchen is cramped, with a miniature gas stove and fridge, a huge copper sink beneath a window, and a wide wooden butcher-block island in the middle.

In the bedroom, packed built-in bookshelves surround a bed that looks like an absolute cloud with a fluffy duvet and pillows. There is another fireplace at the foot of the bed.

This place is a dream. Maybe not to everyone. Maybe someone else would look at this and see a drafty old cottage with no modern appliances.

Not me.

I don't even look at the total before I press *Book*.

CHAPTER TWO

I awaken abruptly to a voice I don't recognize.

"What?" I say, confused.

"Looks like you fell asleep, miss."

I sit up, remembering where I am. I'm in the back of a cab. In Ireland.

"Sorry," I say. "I never fall asleep in cars."

He says nothing but gives a good-natured laugh and opens his door.

I blink, my contacts dry from all the travel and, apparently, a nap. I look outside and see that it's dark and foggy. But through the thick, blue-gray haze, I see it.

Surrey House. I can even see the little sign that says the name by the porch light.

I tumble out, shutting the door behind me, and then lean against the warm metal to take it all in.

There's a welcoming halo around the front door from the house's porch light, and the flowers that wind around the facade are all in full bloom.

It's even more adorable in person.

There are other sleepy houses down the lane and I can see the glow of life coming through some of the old windows.

It smells different in Ireland. Like dewy green grass and fresh, unfamiliar flowers, burning peat, and salty air that's traveled a long and verdant way.

When I look up, I can see stars. The last time I saw this many, this clearly, was on a glamping trip to Joshua Tree. But that experience was somewhat sullied by the fact that it was underscored by a Polish DJ on a comedown from DMT trying to explain why we needed to get to something called Giant Rock in order to commune with aliens.

I actually did it. I got here. My gleeful inner child can't believe it.

I feel so far away from my life, from my problems, and from the people who know me. I could be recognized here, but I doubt it. I'm not that kind of famous. At very least, I assume not *everyone* will know me like they seem to in LA.

Last night, after impulsively booking Surrey House, I bought my flights to and from Ireland, making *one trillion* percent sure they were for the right dates and without stops—and still, somehow getting it wrong and needing to cancel and rebook. I then spent an hour looking for my passport while the party raged on downstairs, then another hour packing, at which point Grayson came in and fell asleep on top of the duvet, wasted and reeking of rare Sotol. He didn't even ask what I was packing for.

I hugged Dido and kissed her a hundred times. To be honest, I did look into bringing her with me. But I would have needed a note from her vet saying she was up to date on shots, and I didn't have time to make that happen.

I can go a week without seeing her. I'll survive. Probably. And she'll be in good hands, I remind myself. Grayson has so much staff running around that she's always taken care of—probably given too many treats, if anything.

But I'm paranoid, so I shot a text to Lisa Michele and to Grayson's assistant, asking them to make sure Dido is cared for.

I then left Grayson a handwritten note explaining that I needed to get out of town for a while, and when I'll be back. He'll get it in the morning, likely after returning from a forty-mile run or something equally nauseating. He never gets hangovers.

For some reason, I was compelled to wear an outfit entirely comprised of old staples I've had in my closet for a decade. A pair of leggings from Nordstrom that have somehow survived since early college, a sweatshirt my mom wore in the eighties, and a jean jacket I borrowed from my dad and never gave back. My closet is filled with outfits I've been sent from Instagrammy brands; one matching two-piece of expensive cotton fleece was even called *the jetsetter*. Maybe it's nostalgia, but something has me wanting to dress like the real me.

A few hours later, I was through security, then boarding. It didn't feel real, all going by in a tired haze.

Yet it took forever to fall asleep on the plane because the only seat I could get was a middle seat in coach between a Chatty Cathy and a guy who spent the first two hours of the flight trying to figure out the Wi-Fi in order to call a girlfriend who had dumped him and whom he was on the way to winning back. He kept asking, "Does it work for you?" And I wanted to respond morosely that nothing seemed to work for me. Instead, I just told him my Wi-Fi was also not working.

Eventually I put on my noise-canceling headphones, took half a Xanax, and managed to fall into a frequently interrupted sleep.

"Miss?"

I startle to attention now and say "Oh, thanks so much" when I see that the driver has taken out my suitcase and carry-on and put them onto the dusty road.

I scan the portable credit charger he holds out, but there's no option for tip. I reach into my pocket for the cash I put there—euros I'd taken from the stash of international currency Grayson keeps in his closet, and which I'd never understood until I was leaving for another country on a whim—but can't find it. "One sec," I say, patting myself down all over. "Sorry, I—I had some cash for you—"

He says, "Don't give it another thought. Have a good night, miss."

"No, really, I—one sec, one sec."

I look in the back seat to see if I dropped it, but no luck.

I rustle through my carry-on on the street, but as I do, I hear the car start up and drive off.

"Hey!" I call after him. "Do you have Venmo?"

But of course, he doesn't hear me and doesn't stop. I exhale in frustration. I *always* prioritize being a good tipper. It only takes a few instances of clawing someone's used tissue out of the bottom of a Collins glass, or being tipped zero percent by table twelve even though you gave them your most charming personality, to appreciate everyone who works in service. I hate the idea that he probably thought I was stiffing him. But then I wonder if tipping is even a thing here. I'll have to look it up.

I stare at the house as the sound of the cab engine grows quieter and quieter, still standing there when it vanishes completely, reveling in the absolute silence.

I go through the wooden gate, up the path, and to the front door. The Airbnb information said the key was in a lockbox in the firewood box. I look around to find it. I do, and then put in the passcode sent to me in the app: 0619. I don't even have to double-check my texts, as that happens to be a number I remember.

The trap opens and I take out a tarnished brass key, then open the front door with it.

The house smells like vetiver and sandalwood, which is *exactly* my favorite combination. I've bought dozens of perfumes because I loved the scent and then found that the scent notes include those two things. Aka, I've bought the same perfumes over and over again.

I roll my suitcase inside and soak up the feel of these new surroundings. It's like being transported into a Nancy Meyers movie. How can a place be this cute and not be curated by set designers? And be *available?*

The stone fireplace is smaller in person, the way things in real life almost always are, and there's a pile of wood in an iron cradle beside one of those hanging racks for fireplace tools like a poker, tongs, and a little broom. There's got to be a name for every one of those things that I don't know, but despite the few weekends I've spent in Big Bear, I hardly know cabincore jargon.

I mean, the fireplace at Grayson's turns on with a remote and may as well be the Yule Log channel.

I run my hand along the couch and feel its soft, well-worn fabric and plush upholstery. There are two blankets thrown over the back, and the cushions are wide and deep and seem as though they could swallow you whole. The living room couch at Grayson's is an ivory-white leather sectional that's really more of an art piece with cushions; it's as hard as a horse saddle.

I want to take in every detail, but when my stomach grumbles, I realize all I've eaten today is an Auntie Anne's pretzel with plasticky—delicious—yellow cheese product dip. The one time on the flight that I managed to truly sleep was also the time food was being served. I need to eat something substantial. More than that, I *want* to. I've been living off of poached salmon and undressed broccolini for longer than I can remember, only sometimes allowing myself to have something like salted cucumber as a little treat.

I want something fried, I want to dip it in something fatty, and I want to drink something bloaty. I'll work it off when I get home. I know Devon said to lose more weight, but . . . no. If the show *might* get canceled, it probably *will*. Hollywood is getting more and more fickle as time goes on. And if they really need me to lose the weight that badly, I'm sure they can get their hands on a few syringes of Ozempic. Though the thought makes me feel weird.

My phone, as it turns out, is dead. I'd been watching the old Hayley Mills *Freaky Friday* on it in the cab and must have drained the battery. I look through my carry-on and find my loose debit card, but not my charger.

Well, I looked at Google Maps before coming, and I know I'm only a few minutes' walk from the center of town. When I looked it up at the airport, I actually found that I remember some cursory knowledge of the village layout from when Aimee and I pored over the map, memorizing the whole area. Not that it's that hard. It's pretty much one strip of businesses that have been there for ages and then a circle of houses around it. It hasn't changed much in the last decade. Unlike most of the world. Unlike me.

I leave my suitcases behind, make sure I lock the door and have the key, and bring my phone with me even though it's dead.

There's almost always someone at a restaurant with a charger.

I keep up a quick pace on the walk, but feel a little dreamy as I go, and I keep stopping to stare up at the sky. There really are *millions* of twinkling stars up there, and it's so clear that I feel like I can see them all. The sky is a velvety indigo with a dense dappling, and a moon that seems too big and bright to be believed.

I am tempted to take a picture but know that it'll look how the moon looks in every layman's photo—like a tiny, uninteresting, usually blurry sphere. I also resist because I feel that this trip should be far more about disconnecting.

I roll my eyes at myself. Another Los Angeles resident, traveling, not using her phone, and making internal proclamations about wire cutting, feeling proud of how analog she is. How original.

Oh, and my phone is dead anyway.

The little village road takes me around a bend, where old streetlamps light the way.

It's late enough that most of the businesses are shut. A knife sharpener, a little grocery store, what looks like a very cute wine shop called Dinner Party. I'm noticing a bookstore when I see an old woman coming out of its door.

When she sees me, she says, "Have a good night, love."

"Oh—goodnight," I say back.

She locks the door behind her and bustles off down the road in the direction I've come from.

It strikes me as odd, but then I remember that things are different in different places. People in LA don't talk to each other. LA is basically a bunch of private residential pods strung together by freeways, and no conversation between strangers isn't tinged with the unspoken puzzle of each person trying to figure out who has more power and if they'd be willing to share some of it.

I hear the place before I see it. I wind around the corner and see

Cairdeas, a pub that is open and cheerfully busy. I'm glad to have found it, as I'm getting a little too chilly. It's June, but it's nearly midnight and the air is cool and crisp. My jean jacket and crewneck are barely enough to be comfortable.

When I pull open the door a gust of sound washes over me, resting on my cold cheeks like hands that have been warmed by a fire. It's a lively atmosphere—people are chatting and talking, possibly arguing, and everyone has pints of beer or cups of coffee.

In a corner, sitting around a table, there are musicians with different instruments, playing what I can only, ignorantly describe as *extremely* Irish music.

I squeeze through the crowd to get to the bar.

There's only one bartender, a tall, lean guy with dark blondish reddish hair. He's in a black T-shirt and blue jeans. He nods to take someone's order, then reaches up to a high shelf at the back bar; my eyes travel of their own volition to the sliver of bare abdomen that's exposed when his shirt lifts. He's got that lean, V-shaped muscle that disappears into the unbelted band of his jeans. I happen to know that's called an Adonis belt.

As in, *Oh, no, I can't have truffle butter, not if I want an Adonis belt.*

That is a direct quote from Grayson Gamble to the server at Nobu Malibu whom I would go on to tip an extra hundred dollars after he also requested a new, chilled glass halfway through his martini.

The bartender at this pub looks serious, but there's something gentle and endearing about him, even from afar. He moves with an unfrenzied efficiency and—*my God* those ropey muscles in his forearms.

There's a small gaggle of girls hanging out at the bar in front of him, all trying to look tall and thin, messing with their hair and leaning toward him. Of course a guy like this would have a fan club. I'm not surprised at all.

A girl with long chestnut-brown hair says something that makes him smile a little, and I see that he's got those Heath Ledger dimples. I feel equal parts a heady, crushing admiration for how appealing this guy is and a bizarre, delusional jealousy that I'm not the one charming him.

It's kind of a crazy feeling, as I'm *really* not the *wow, that guy's so hot* kind of girl. Maybe it's the fact that, in LA, every hot bartender is constantly scanning the crowd for people worthy of attention—i.e., is there a well-known producer waiting to order a mezcal who might like a slice of orange with that and possibly to discover the next Harry Styles?

I wait my turn at the bar and examine the taps, deciding to have the red ale. But when the horde thins, he still doesn't come over to me.

Eventually it becomes obvious that he's ignoring me.

"Excuse me," I say.

He sighs deeply and then comes over. "What do you want?"

It's softened slightly by his Irish accent, but the words still startle me. Cool, he's hot *and* he already hates me. Maybe people do know *Brilliance* over here. The show *is* streaming in other countries, but I don't know which ones.

I'm suddenly shy. I always get shy when people seem annoyed with me.

"Um . . . can I please order a beer? And maybe some food if your kitchen is still open?"

"Kitchen's closed." He turns from me, taking a glass over to the tap. My stomach gives a familiar, hungry yawn.

I open my mouth to tell him which beer, but he fills the glass with the red ale, which is what I wanted anyway.

"That was a good guess; that's exactly what I was going to order," I say with a self-conscious laugh.

"You want it, or don't you?"

I flush with embarrassment at his brusque tone. "Well, yeah, I do." I accept it with a tight-lipped, awkward smile. "Thanks—hey, do you have a phone charger back there? By any chance?"

I give an apologetic grimace.

He looks, I'm sure now, *irritated* with me before holding up the tail end of a white cable.

"Thank you," I say, then plug my phone in and set it on the counter behind the bar where I can reach it.

"Did you forget to eat today, then?" he asks.

"What?"

"Did you forget to eat today?"

His question is so weirdly personal, and actually sort of accurate to who I am—and have always been—that I laugh. "Oh—oh, no, I didn't forget to eat. I didn't have a chance."

"What've you eaten?"

"I—well, I had a pretzel." Then, because it's only fair, "Why, what did you eat?"

"Fuck's sake. Go sit down, I'll rustle something up. Here, take this water; you probably forgot to drink that too."

I am completely bewildered by this. Listen, I was a bartender too. I often *felt* this annoyed with everyone, no matter how reasonable their requests, but I didn't show it. At least not like this. Is this what it's like at bars in Ireland?

"You don't have to," I say. "Really, I'll—"

"Go," he says, pointing at an empty table.

"Jesus Christ," I say to myself as he disappears into the kitchen. I go sit down where he told me to.

Unfortunately, his bossy, gruff manner has made him all the more attractive. On a surface level. Of course, I'd never want to be with a bossy, domineering man, if that's what he is. But I meet so many himbos in LA that it's nice to meet a *guy*. And kind of nice not to be sucked up to.

I take my first sip of the beer and actually groan out loud with how delicious it is. I've always heard the beers are better over here, but I didn't think they could be this different. This makes the beer back home taste like carbonated, penny-filled gutter water. That might be a bit extreme, but at least in this moment of relief, that's how I feel.

A man comes by, laughing at something his friend said, and pats me on the back.

"'Night, doll." Then he keeps walking, without waiting for a response from me.

I'm still relatively new to the whole *getting recognized* thing. In LA it's usually something like: I'll glance up from my hand roll at Sugarfish to see that there's an entire table of people taking turns pretending not to see me.

Or I stop by a Pressed Juicery for a lemon cayenne ginger shot, choke on it, and only then realize that I'm surrounded by a sea of rectangles filming me, and that a bunch of shitty kids are going to spend an afternoon making fun of me on the internet.

Then of course, there's the *nice* kind of recognition: the pretty moms in Alo Yoga sets who come up to me at Erewhon and apologize for interrupting, but they have to tell me how much they love the show. And sometimes I get a free drink or a discount on something from someone I'll never see again who wants me to like them. More often than not, the people who recognize me don't say anything, they just send anonymous updates on my whereabouts to Deuxmoi.

"Bye, Cillian!" says one of the girls who was flirting earlier. "Love you!"

They all crack up, doing that *oh my God you're being SO crazy!* thing drunk girls do together.

The bartender—Cillian, I'm guessing—gives a good-natured shake of the head and then a wave.

They go through the doors, and as they do, another girl soars in past them. She pushes through the crowd and sits right down at my table.

"Christ on a bloody knitting needle, you'll never believe the night I've had," she says.

She has shockingly blue eyes, long dark hair, and porcelain skin sprinkled with freckles. She reminds me immediately of Aisling Bea, and I feel certain she gets that all the time. Even without the accent, she's a dead ringer.

"I went on that date, yeah," she goes on, "with the guy me mam set me up with, the one from her work? Well, she failed to tell me that he's in his *fifties* and is, and I quote, *in the pre-separation stage* of leaving his wife. I need a bloody drink. As if I'm not locked already."

She gets up and goes to the bar, now emptier and absent of the hot bartender. She reaches behind the counter, fills her own beer from the tap, and comes back.

I don't know who this girl is, but just as I felt an immediate attraction to that Cillian guy, I instantly find her endearing.

Is everyone just drunk? I mean, I've gone into bar bathrooms by myself on nights out and come out with girlfriends I swear I'll keep for life. Sometimes it's like that when it's late and you're tipsy. Especially if you've been on some awful date. Maybe she saw a female person around the same age as herself and thought, *why not?*

"I mean, when I was in school," she goes on, "if I brought over a boyfriend who was even a year above me, Mam treated me like Lolita. Now she thinks Arthur from the accounting department might be the treat? Kay Donahue, the world's most insane mam. I swear it."

"Yikes," I say, at a loss for anything but cartoon words.

She gives a derisive spike of laughter. "Tell me about it."

A plate is set loudly down in front of me, and a bowl set down beside that.

The girl and I both jolt back at the abruptness.

"What's your problem, then?" she asks him. "I know it's a touchy time, but no need to be so rude."

"Nothing at all," he says.

"Can I get food too?" she asks.

"No."

"Why's she get it then?" she complains.

"She forgot to eat."

"I didn't forget to eat, I—" I interject, but they ignore me.

"Oy, come on, Cillian, just a bit! Enough for a wee mouse."

He looks away, shaking his head, and then goes off.

"Yes," says the girl. "I knew he'd cave."

He's made me a grilled cheese and tomato soup. One of my all-time favorite comfort meals. One I haven't had in as long as I can remember.

I'm starting to think I fell asleep in the cab and never woke up. Like I'm in a dreamworld. Or dead.

"To be fair," says the girl, "it is a bit mean of you, showing up here, no?"

"Mean?"

"I can never keep up." She reaches over and takes one half of my sandwich, has a big bite, and puts it back on my plate. "Are you pretending you're friends today, sleeping together today, or pretending you hate each other today? Last I heard it was . . ." She dragged her thumb across her throat.

He returns then, plopping down a plate. It's a wedge of white cheese and a butter knife stuck in it. "For a wee mouse."

"She gets a whole meal, and you give me this?" she asks.

"I can take it away, Kiera," he says.

"No, no, I'll take it." She protects the plate. "It's that class cheese, hey."

I down some water. Feeling confused is a common symptom of dehydration. One time, in Palm Springs, I was so dehydrated I could hardly understand the words everyone was speaking around me. They all sounded like they were far away, trapped in a well somewhere. That must be what's happening now, because everything feels unknowably off.

I take a few more huge gulps of water. I'm hesitant to eat the sandwich. I'm conditioned by years of withholding food like this from myself.

I gather the nerve, take a big bite, and *oh my God*.

It's unbelievable. One of the best things I've ever eaten. "Wow. Wow, this is good," I say with my mouth full.

"I know, he makes the best," says Kiera. "But of course, I must still act like it's shite to his face. All right, I've got to run. I texted Nial. *I know*, I know what you're thinking, I know I shouldn't have, but honestly, if I don't have sex soon, I think my legs will glue together like Ariel and I'll be stuck like that." She stands, folding the cheese into a napkin and putting it in her purse. "Talk tomorrow, Meggie, love ya."

She kisses me on top of the head and goes.

I almost choke. "Meggie?" I ask after her. How—

I set down my food reluctantly. Something is definitely off.

The music ends and the musicians start putting their things away. Apparently this is an indication to some of the clientele that it's time to go, because people have started collecting their coats and taking their last sips.

She called me Meggie.

Most people don't even know that's my name. When I moved to LA and started auditioning, there was no question that I had to come up with a stage name. My real name is Meg Bryan. Not Meghan, not Megan, not Margaret. Meg, and then, affectionately, Meggie. And while it might be easier for casting to remember a name like Meg Bryan, since it sounds like Meg Ryan, it's not worth the earworm similarity. Not when you have to do the, *no, I said Bryan, yes, I know, it sounds like that, ha ha, yes, I know, yeah* conversation over and over again.

So, I came up with Lana Lord. In retrospect, it's a little more showbiz than I wish it were, but whatever, it has worked.

I never think about my real name unless I'm talking to one of my parents. Even Grayson calls me Lana.

Does my Wikipedia even *say* my real name? It must, but I don't know for sure.

I reach for my phone, but then remember it's plugged in. I get up and go over to the bar.

Cillian doesn't look up when I approach.

"Can I grab my phone?"

He dries his hands on the rag from his back pocket, and then hands it to me. But it's not my phone.

"Um . . . sorry, no, no it's—it's an iPhone, but it's got no case on it, and . . . I mean I had it . . ."

"Meg, this is your phone. You've made me hold it a million times, I think I'd know."

I freeze. Look up at him. He doesn't seem like someone who's trying to mess with a celebrity by saying her childhood name or withholding her things. He's acting like someone who knows me well enough to be comfortably exasperated with me.

I think about everything that girl Kiera said. How she seemed completely at ease sitting down at my table. And then her questions about Cillian?

Wait, what the *hell* is going on?

Cillian loses patience holding the phone out for me and sets it down on the counter. He then walks away. With a booming voice, he tells the room at large, "*Hold your whisht*, get the fuck out, you're not stayin' all night like last night."

I stare at the phone on the counter. It's one generation behind mine and despite the sage-green silicone case, there's a hairline crack down the middle of the screen.

There is a grumble from the remaining customers at Cillian's closing time call. The crowd has thinned considerably, and they all seem pleasantly buzzed, making a lot of happy, late-night noise about the fact that they've got to go. Some people seem to think or know that the call doesn't apply to them.

I pick up the phone Cillian gave me and go, helpless, back to the table where my beer and food are sitting.

Some older women walk up to the bar and start telling Cillian how much they love him, how he's got to give their daughters a chance.

He's very popular.

The phone screen background is an auburn golden retriever in a little red bandana. The dog has also been put in a pair of tortoiseshell Ray-Bans. I used to have the same pair but lost them at a karaoke bar in a Korean mall in downtown LA.

According to this phone, since it's after midnight, it is June 25, like it's supposed to be. Two days after my birthday, technically, given the time difference and the flight.

I slide open the phone and it asks me for a passcode. I give a shake of the head, feeling like I might actually be going crazy. It scans my face, and opens.

I set it down with a clatter. I have another gulp of water, a swig of beer, and a big bite of soup-dipped sandwich.

In my experience, anytime I think I'm sick, dying, or losing my mind, I need rest, food, and water. I'm always behind on at least one of those things.

I pick up the phone again and open the browser. I type in my name. Not my real name. The one the world knows me by.

Lana Lord.

Unfortunately, it's not my first time googling myself and so I know that usually, a knowledge panel pops up. It says "American actress." It lists the things I've been in. It has my age and where I'm from. It says that people also search for Jennifer Lawrence, Emma Stone, Sydney Sweeney. There is usually a slew of images of me, good and bad, and whatever recent articles have been written about me or about *Brilliance*.

But not this time.

This time, I don't come up at all.

CHAPTER THREE

I drop the phone on the table again, this time pushing my chair back, away from it, my ears ringing and my heart pounding. It has always been a latent fear of mine that I might one day lose my fucking mind. That the super normal *call of the void* thoughts I have might one day take over and I'll lose control to them. That instead of sitting on a fifteenth-floor balcony over Park Avenue and idly thinking, *What if I jumped,* I'd actually do it. Or that I might fill the silence of a movie theater with some horrifically offensive word, all because my mind thought, *You know what would be the worst thing to do right now,* and then a synapse misfires and I actually scream it. Or what if, on a walk with Dido, I come upon a teacup-sized kitten and valiantly bring it home only to present it and have a loved one shriek, *That's a rat!* and then look down and see a panting rodent in my bare hand.

It's why I could never do peyote or ayahuasca, no matter how many *totally legit* gurus Grayson knows, and why even the legal THC/CBD bath bombs I use can sometimes send me into a spiral. I'm afraid that something will loosen in my psyche and I will simply cease to have power over myself.

It's why I get so uncomfortable and heartbroken when I see the many unhoused people of Los Angeles, walking around with signs and bare feet, talking to themselves, so often in anguish, especially when you can tell that they were once good-looking and were probably told by all the townies where they came from that they ought to give Hollywood a try.

It freaks me out.

I've told my therapist and she reminds me that it's very normal to have fears like this. That it doesn't mean it will happen. That our brains actually do the whole *call of the void* thing as a way of stretching limbs and considering all options available in order to make the safest choice.

I don't share these fears with anyone else, however, lest I either seem more troubled than I am or even worse, more inconsiderate than I am. As if I'm actually saying I'm afraid of mental illness. When in fact, I'm actually afraid of being safe one second and in irreversible crisis the next.

So the fact that I feel like I might *very* well be losing my mind right now is making me more than uneasy. Angry at my therapist even. *You said I'd be fine! You said nothing weird or fucked-up would happen!*

I breathe in deeply, trying to keep the panic attack from taking hold, even though I can feel my hands starting to shake and my heartbeat becoming particularly hard and irregular. The voice in my head saying, *No, this is worse than usual—this might* really *be a heart attack.*

The pub has now completely emptied out, and the music has been changed to something quieter. I can hear the clinking of empty glasses and I see Cillian stacking pints with one hand and taking the rag out of his back pocket and wiping down a table with the other.

I look away.

He did seem like he knew me. Didn't he?

I don't know, maybe not. I am practically a professional rationalizer. I blame myself for any and all bizarre interactions. Someone could push me into an elevator shaft and on the way down I'd be saying, *Oh no, whoops, I'm sorry!*

Another surge of adrenaline.

I block one nostril and breathe in for four seconds, hold it, switch sides, breathe out for four seconds. Box breathing.

I want to do grounding techniques, but it's hard to ground yourself while falling endlessly in an unfamiliar hoistway.

I feel eyes on me and glance back up to see Cillian coming my way.

I get self-conscious and try to give a polite smile, but I'm sure it comes off as more of a grimace.

"Meg," he says, crouching down beside me. Now that he's not yelling over a bunch of rowdy people, I hear that he's got a nice, soothing, slightly raspy voice, and that *accent*. Aimee used to tease me that the only reason I wanted to go to school in Ireland was because of the boys and the accents.

"Yeah," I say. Another surge; my lungs feel devoid of oxygen and unable to regain it.

"You all right? Are you having one? Meggie, look at me, it's okay. It's all right."

He sounds so sure, so certain that it's all going to be okay, that it comforts me. Even though I feel like my world is inside out right now, I know he can be believed in.

Somehow, it cuts through. My heartbeat steadies.

I finally lift my gaze and look into his eyes. A soul-rocking wave runs through me—a sudden magnetic pull that seems to go from me to him and back again. I see the tiny scar in his eyebrow and the short stubble on his jaw and I want to reach out and touch him. I feel a deep fondness for him that warms me as effortlessly and completely as desert sun on my skin, transcending and eclipsing logic, confusion, panic, and anything else I can imagine.

"Um." I pin my tongue between my teeth.

"You haven't had one of them in a long time." His hand is now on the back of my arm. My elbows are on my knees; my heart is in my throat. He squeezes me gently. "It happens when you feel out of control, remember. That's what we've learned, yeah? And it almost always happens when you haven't eaten and then you eat. It's because your blood sugar is rising back to where it belongs. Right?"

That's not what *we've* learned. That's not even what *I've* learned.

"Right," I say anyway, trying to catch my breath, too distracted to ask him what he means by *we*.

"Is it all the stuff with Aimee or is it . . . the other thing?"

My head shoots up. "Aimee?"

"Yeah, last I talked to you, you were upset about the Aimee thing again. But I can understand if it's—"

"How do you know about Aimee?" I furrow my brow and stare into his flawed, beautiful, strangely familiar face.

No one in my life now knows about Aimee. I haven't been around a soul who knows her name in over a decade, except my parents.

"Well, you told me most. I heard the rest. You know how this town can be. With bloody Kay Donahue running around unchecked."

He gives a small hint of that smile again, and I can see that it is rare and only earned. Unfortunately, the mention of Aimee has changed everything, and I cannot be distracted by his gritty beauty.

"I don't know what you're talking about," I say, more muddled than ever. "Why are you acting like you know me?"

The hint of dimples fades completely, and he takes his hand off of me. His honey-gold eyes bore into mine and he says, "It's going to be like this, is it? It wasn't my fault what happened, you know."

I shake my head. "No, no—"

"Forgive me, Meg," he says, standing. "Thought you needed some help, that's all."

He flips the rag over his shoulder and walks back to the bar.

I stand too. "Do you watch the show or—"

He holds his hands up. "Meg, I think you should go home. I don't know what you're playing at or what it is that you need, but clearly it's nothing I have to give. So do me a favor and let me close up. I didn't mind you coming in here—it's a business after all—but if you're going to be like this, then I don't need that, I really don't."

Suddenly my overall confusion gives way to the embarrassment of the moment that's actually happening. I clear my throat and nod.

"Right. Um. Yeah, of course, sorry 'bout . . . thank you again for the food. Oh shit—how much do I owe you?"

I check my jacket pocket for my debit card and find that it's missing.

"We're square," says Cillian.

"What? No, I can pay, I—I can't find my card."

"That's why people carry wallets." He grabs something from behind the counter and comes over with it. "I found it on the floor. Again. But there's no charge."

Again?

"Oh, that's not—"

I take the unfamiliar card, about to say that it's not mine when I see that it has my name on it. Meg A Bryan. It's even got the right middle initial.

It's a debit card for a bank I don't recognize. It's clearly well used, with an expiration date only a year from now. I look on the back and see my own signature there in the little white box. I haven't seen it in a while—I usually sign *Lana Lord* these days. But it's definitely mine.

"Goodnight, Meg. And hey, bring back my bloody dog, will you?"

He goes behind the bar, through a swinging door, and into what I assume to be the back kitchen.

Did he learn my name from the card? No, that doesn't explain anything, because I don't *recognize* this card. It's not mine. Even though it really, really appears to be.

I take another bite of the sandwich as I put my coat back on, then grab the phone. Cillian comes back out with a scratched black bus tub and starts putting the Guinness and Jameson branded bar mats into it.

I shut the door behind me, seeing a last glimpse of Cillian before I go. He's not looking at me, but I get the feeling that he was.

I hightail it back to the house.

I consider that maybe I somehow got canceled and now the world hates me. Then, because of this, I *had* lost my mind, time passed Rip Van Winkle–style, and now I've actually gotten my mind *back*. There was an old William Powell movie about that: he hits his head and, instead of getting amnesia, it turns out he *had* amnesia and he's gotten his memory back. Maybe it's that.

Or what if I was in a coma?

Oh God, what if I'm in my fifties or something, having lost decades of my life?

I open the phone and look at the calendar. No, it's the year it's supposed to be. And of course, if it was decades later, this phone would be an absolute relic.

I'd wonder if I'm dreaming, but of course I'm not. This isn't what dreams feel like. They aren't tangible, with buttery bread and cold walks in the middle of the night. At least not for me. My dreams never immerse me like that.

My mind goes to an old episode of *The O.C.,* the rain episode where Ryan hits his head and then finds himself in an alternate universe. One where he never moved to Newport.

I inhale deeply and remind myself that I am not in an episode of *The O.C.* or *Brilliance* or a William Powell movie. I'm in reality. Where things like that simply don't happen. There's an explanation. There has to be.

I get the door of the cottage open, throw on the lights, and toss the keys on the entry table without looking.

I hesitate for a second, feeling like something strange happened, but unable to put my finger on what.

I need something a little stronger than that beer I had at the pub. My nerves are rattled and my mind is racing.

I go to the kitchen and then directly to the middle left bottom cabinet, open the door, and crouch to reach to the back for the good bottle of whiskey. Then I stand and reach up to the right cabinet above the sink and get out a rocks glass—

"Oh my God," I say, dropping the bottle. It lands on the rug beneath the little kitchen table and miraculously does not break.

I slowly set down the glass and put my palms to my temples and step backward, looking at the open cabinets and the bottle on the ground, its agitated bubbles pooling at the side-turned-top.

How did I—how did I know that?

How did I know that's where the booze would be? How did I know where the *good* whiskey would be? Somewhere in my absent mind, I knew that I was reaching for the bottle of Green Spot hidden there.

And how did I know where the rocks glass would be, much less which of the mismatched glasses I had in mind to use? Because I *had*. I'd known I was reaching for the cobalt blue one with the thin lip.

I stare at the glass on the counter. It's familiar and yet there is no reason in the world it should be. Much like how I'd felt looking into Cillian's eyes earlier or hearing about that girl's date. It didn't feel like the first time I had done it.

Okay. Okay. I can figure this out.

I pick up the bottle and pour some whiskey into the glass. I have a sip, then, over the rim of the glass, I see that I am not alone.

There is a dog sitting on the sofa, staring at me, sleepily wagging its tail.

I cough, choking on the hot, undiluted alcohol.

"Hello?" I call out, straining my ears for a response but afraid I'll get one. I'm suddenly self-conscious that I haven't been alone this whole time, or that I'm in the wrong house altogether. Like the owner of the dog might be around here somewhere. But then I recognize the dog. It's the same one from the phone background.

Bring back my bloody dog, will you?

At this point, I have to accept that *something* is definitely going on.

What if the person who owns this place looks like me or something? A doppelgänger? And that's why Cillian—no, but that doesn't make any sense, he called me Meg. So did Kiera. *Meggie* even. And before I can go down the road of thinking that maybe my long-lost twin lives in this house *and* she's named Meg, that credit card he handed me had my full name on it. And my signature. Maybe her name is *also* Meg Anabelle Bryan?

But then Cillian knew me well enough to know about Aimee.

I go over to the dog and its tail starts thumping harder, rhythmically and comfortably against the upholstery. There's a pink collar tucked beneath the fur, and this makes me assume, possibly regressively, that it's a girl.

"Hi," I say. "Are you the dog who likes to wear sunglasses?"

For some reason, her presence makes this all feel a little easier to digest. Some people would arrive to their Airbnb, see a pet, and be outraged that someone left it behind. Not me. And honestly, even if I'm losing my mind, at least there's a dog here.

I sit beside her, and she squints sleepily at me, her wavy-haired ears submissively back and flat against her head, making her look a bit like a dolphin. Her wet nose sniffs at me.

"Hi, puppy," I say. "You are . . ." I look on the collar and see the tag. "Maur—*Maureen?*"

She responds right away, perking her ears up now into pert triangles, so it clearly *is* her name. Who names a dog Maureen? I know there was that whole fad a million years ago where everyone thought it was high comedy to name their dachshund something human like George or their Weimaraner Bob, but . . . Maureen?

I scratch behind her ears and she gives me a lick on the cheek, wagging her tail happily.

All right, as long as the dog doesn't start talking, I think I can manage to stay calm.

I stand up, urgently deciding that the first thing I need to do is make sure I'm still me.

I see a door to what looks like the bathroom, so I go in, briefly admiring how pretty the wallpaper is—blue with red poppies.

Then I see my reflection.

Whoa.

I actually let out a small scream before covering my mouth. But I immediately remove my hand. I need to in order to look at my whole face.

It's me. It's *me* me. A version of myself I haven't seen in a long time.

When I was first cast in *Brilliance,* I was not-so-subtly urged by Devon to get some work done. Unprompted, he showed me pictures of Scarlett Johansson's nose job and casually mentioned the incredible power of a brow lift. Not once, but *over and over* again. I ignored it until finally he took me to Spago, bought us each a glass of the good champagne—like *really* good—and told me, *Listen, honey, you wanna make it in this business, you're gonna need to get some work done, there, I said it, I said I wouldn't say it, but now I've said it.*

Next thing I knew, Lisa Michele was making me appointments in Beverly Hills and I was making up stories about a frisbee-to-the-face incident to my parents. Who didn't believe a word of it, to their credit.

My natural nose wasn't particularly big, crooked, or objectionable. It was a little round at the end and slightly broader in the middle—not the manufactured, neat and tidy, narrow nose so common on today's celebrities. But I still had the work done. With encouragement, I also got a little Juvéderm in my lips and Botox in my forehead. Then, because I was already at it, I got my buccal fat removed and that little brow lift.

I didn't look *drastically* different. I looked like me on a good day in a good picture, but now it was every day and in every picture. The Juvéderm didn't give me big duck lips; it made them a little more pillowy and plusher. The Botox was a little weird because when I smiled, the wrinkles—which had to go somewhere—started creasing under my eyes instead of around them, so I got more Botox there. The buccal fat removal was meant to make my cheekbones look higher. And it does, but sometimes I tend to look a little gaunt and slightly older than I really am.

But paired with the good styling and expensive products, it equaled a new-and-improved me.

You know how reality stars and contest winners tend to just look a *liiiiittle bit* (to a lot bit) better after they get the money? It was like that.

But right now, I'm looking in the mirror at what I can best describe as my own *before* picture. Plus a couple years.

I raise my eyebrows and see the natural lines form, which are unfamiliar to me of late. I touch my nose and my cheeks, somehow returned to their slightly plumper former appearance. I smile and watch my thinner top lip almost disappear.

I take my hair out of the bun I had it in on the plane, first noticing that it's dark blond with highlights instead of the icy blond it was when I left. When I let it down, I find that it's also much longer, falling just past my shoulders with long layers. It appears not to have been bleached over and over, and is instead soft and healthy. I guess K18 and Olaplex can only go so far.

I can't help but notice that it looks kind of amazing. People always tell me I have the face for short hair, so I never let it grow. But it looks like I should have.

What the *hell* is going on?

Wait. Does that mean . . . ?

I tear off my coat and look at my body in the full-length mirror. My body, which has gained back the twenty pounds I've spent the last few years staving off by eating unsalted fish and calling an annual square of dark chocolate an indulgence.

I take in the softer stomach and sloping waist. I don't have the tightly snatched look I've grown used to. I even have boobs again. Maybe a full D cup, like I used to be before I started checking every nutritional label.

Huh.

If most celebrities I know looked in the mirror and saw the effects of their tireless hours on the Peloton vanish into thin air, they'd scream. Perhaps spontaneously combust. I feel fascinated. And for some reason, a little relaxed.

When you're "perfect," you never truly are. You don't cross a finish line of hotness. It's a constant battle of maintenance that involves constant failure, and the goalposts are perpetually moving. The filler fad is replaced by the newly chic *dissolving* of filler, but people still want to improve their natural appearance, so it's all plasma injections and red light therapy from then on out until they discover that red light actually speeds up aging, and then everyone moves onto an all-cigarette diet or something. *It did wonders in the nineties*, they'll say, forgetting why we weren't smoking.

Plus, everyone out there is watching for you to let it all slip. For fuck's sake, that time the paparazzi snapped the pictures where everyone thought I was pregnant? I had an underweight BMI and had been on a diet of room-temperature water and fermented cabbage for a week for a magazine shoot. Why did the water have to be room temp? I don't know. That was just the advice I was given. Despite the improvement in the realm of body acceptance, there is still a projection in our society of the internalized standards that have been imprinted upon us for generations. No celebrity can go from 118 pounds to 132 without it getting noticed—even if it's with a passive-aggressive headline like *Ana Di Armas Embraces Natural Curves!*

It's the noticing, the caring, and the commenting that's the problem.

I shake out of my stare and realize I'm freezing cold. When I can't find a thermostat, stare at the fireplace in dread. Fires are cute and all, but aren't they a lot of work?

Sure. Probably. But I'm in the middle of ardent denial that something spooky is going on, so I'm happy to distract myself with a new task.

I get the phone that isn't mine and type *how to build a fire* into Google. I follow along with a video of a man in a flannel button-down who warns me about the flue, recommends his favorite kind of wood but admits that any dry wood will do, and demonstrates the best arrangement for the logs and where to stuff the wads of newspaper. Luckily, there's a box of paper products beside my pile of wood. I check each one before balling it up, making sure I'm not burning tax documents—or worse, burning up any clues as to what's going on. Some article titled *World Goes Mad* or something.

Once the fire is roaring, I sit in front of it, finally warm. Thank God for the internet.

I take a sip of the whiskey, which really is good, and set it down on the stone hearth beside me. I then go back to the browser on the phone. I type in everything I can think of.

Lana Lord Deadline
Lana Lord Wikipedia
Lana Lord Canceled
Lana Lord IMDB
Lana Lord Brilliance
Lana Lord Meg Bryan

As any search brings up millions of pages, Google has answers. But none of them are right. None of them are me.

I delete and think for a moment.

Then I type in:

Brilliance TV show

It comes right up.

Brilliance is a primetime "neo-soap" that follows the glamorous lives of several wealthy families living in Napa Valley.

Well, that's correct.

I look at the cast list and see that Kim, who was playing the much smaller role of Velma last I checked, is now in my role.

What the *hell* is happening?

I google Grayson. His name comes up, and according to an article posted a few hours ago:

Real-Life Couple? Grayson and Elsa Have a Marvel-less Night Out at Musso & Frank!

It shows a picture of Grayson and his Marvel costar in one of the dark red booths of the Hollywood restaurant—the Chaplin booth, where we have so often sat together. They're staring adoringly at each other. I know this doesn't prove that he was cheating on me, but I still feel vindicated.

I clear the search box and instead, I type in my real name. Meg Bryan.

As used to be usual, Google says, *did you mean: Meg Ryan.*

No, I did not.

Where the hell am I? If I'm not even on the internet, I'm nowhere.

I shut my eyes and shut off the phone screen, letting my wrist go limp over my knee.

Okay, so, it seems that the life I know is not the one I'm in. I am not Lana Lord. There is no Lana Lord—that I recognize anyway. I'm not an actress on *Brilliance*. I'm a normal weight, I've had no plastic surgery done, and the people in Avalon seem to know me.

It's not a dream, I know that, but *can* you hallucinate this vividly? This thoroughly and convincingly?

Maybe you can, but probably not without feeling otherwise off. I feel completely normal, except for being entirely exhausted and a little buzzed. I didn't do any strange drugs; that half a Xanax barely scratched the surface and it's already the lowest dose. I don't think I've experienced any skull trauma.

Does international jet lag secretly mean *this* and no one ever mentioned it?

I got on a plane, I got off a plane, I went through customs, I got my bags, I got in a cab. I did all of that while feeling completely fine—if, again, drained—and then woke up outside of the cottage in Avalon, where I expected to wake up. The only thing that was unusual is that I fell asleep in the car. I *never* fall asleep in cars. Ever. But after that, the house was as I expected it before I set off for the pub. Wasn't it?

I seem to have woken up in a different world. One where I am not a celebrity but at least two strangers in Ireland seem to know me by my real name.

I get up, leaving the phone on the coffee table and taking my glass with me as I walk around the house, searching for clues.

The first thing that pops out is a piece of art above the bed.

It's a large print of *New York Movie*, a painting by Edward Hopper. It depicts a young blond woman standing in the dimly lit hallway of a theater, deep in thought, while a movie plays in the darkened room on just the other side of the wall.

I used to have a print of it pinned on my wall as a teenager. This one is framed, but mine had been thumbtacked over and over again as I rearranged my room. In fact, I still have it rolled up with a hair tie in the back of a closet somewhere at Grayson's house. I wanted to hang it, but Grayson said, "You don't need to hang a ratty poster of the thing, I'll get you the real one if I land the Marvel movie."

He did, of course, get the Marvel role, and he did not, of course, miraculously obtain the painting. Last I checked, it still hangs at the Museum of Modern Art in New York.

I step forward and look at the corners of the framed print. There are countless little thumbtack holes.

This sends a strange flutter through me, and I don't allow my mind to fully form the thoughts it wants to.

I notice more and more little familiarities of the place. The books on the bookshelf. *Rear Window;* an old, tattered copy of *The World of Pooh; Something Borrowed* and its other half, *Something Blue; Call Me by Your Name; Fleabag: The Scriptures; I Capture the Castle; The Thorn Birds*; and countless other spines I recognize inherently because I own them too. Or used to. I donated over half of my books when I moved in with Grayson.

I open the closet and see that the collection of clothes is all in my size.

Not my LA size, but my real size. But there's an old burgundy sweatshirt
I once got from Etsy, with the Seattle skyline from the opening sequence
of *Frasier*. There's a pair of leather boots that I feel crazy for recognizing as
the riding boots I had all the way through high school and college. Except I
donated them to Goodwill many years ago when my closet was too small to
hold them and no one was wearing knee-high boots anymore. I'd gone on
to regret getting rid of them, as they were well-made Fryes and they would
have lasted a lifetime and, as with everything, come back into style.

"*Okay*," I whisper to myself, trying to stay relaxed, even though my
heart and mind feel suspended in a state of . . . what, confusion? Dread?
Excitement? Fear? Insanity? All of that?

In a way, this surreality feels satisfying and relieving. As if I always
suspected that a moment like this would come. But the pragmatic, earth-
bound side of me knows there must be an explanation. Knows that you
don't get the letter from Hogwarts, knows that you don't wake up in Mer-
lin's court, knows that reality always hits. Even if something seems deeply
bizarre, it never really is.

And yet.

Throughout the house, I am stunned to see that there are more trinkets
I recognize but haven't seen since I had them in Florida. An old paperweight
from my grandmother's house. A weird jade bookend I got at a thrift shop
in Ybor City. An enamel mug from a Disney World hotel that says *Happy
Camper*. It's filled with pens, some stolen from restaurants and hotels, others
the Pilot G2s which I learned to prefer when I *worked* in restaurants.

None of these things are one of a kind. But, at this point, I'm starting to
feel like I'd have to be an idiot to not see that somehow, in some way, these
are my things. I mean, they just *are*. There's no chance in the world, at least
not the one I know, that all of these things end up in one place that is not
my own. Not even with the world's best stalker. I've systematically gotten
rid of most of these things or left them at my parents' house. Lots of them
should be long gone in unceremonious ways.

I finish the last of my whiskey and pull a wooden lidded box off one of
the bookshelves in the living room.

Inside is a collection of things that I understand immediately.

I have always had a sentimental-things box and it looks an awful lot like this one, only the things inside are different.

There are three Polaroids right on top.

One of Cillian—he's really so hot—behind the pub bar like he was tonight, looking annoyed but indulgent. For some reason this makes me smile.

One is of that girl Kiera flicking off the camera with an older woman laughing hard—she looks so much like her, and I think it must be her mom. Bloody Kay Donahue.

The last is one of . . . me. Holding a puppy. A little auburn golden retriever. I look at Maureen and show her the picture. "Is that you?"

She hops off the couch, comes over to me, then lies down and puts her chin on my knee.

I look happy in the picture, grinning cheesily for the camera with bright red lipstick, wearing a black turtleneck sweater and tiny gold hoop earrings. My hair is in a long, one-length bob. V French.

Also in the box, I find movie ticket stubs, and a place card with my name on it that, if I had to guess, I would say is from a wedding. With it, there's a matching place card with Cillian's name on it. Cillian Madden.

There's an old loose fortune-telling miracle fish, one of those red pieces of cellophane shaped like a Swedish fish candy that curl up if . . . something.

There's a bar napkin from a place called Èan, a coaster that says NOTE, the letters arranged to rise, crest in the middle, and fall.

There are a few bottle caps and champagne corks. There's a tiny, tiny glass frame with a flower pressed in it. There's a small pale blue book I recognize from my own life. *The Words of John F. Kennedy.* I don't even know where it came from or how I ended up with it, but it's one of those weird little things I've always had that I think came from my dad's side of the family?

There are stacks of photos and other pieces of paper in the box, but I set it aside, needing a minute.

I sigh and pet Maureen.

This house could literally not be more perfect for me if I had designed it myself. It could not be more representative of me if I lived here. It has far more of my taste *and* belongings than Grayson's house does; when I moved in with him, I brought very little, never wanting to seem like a bother and knowing he had everything we would need. I had also chaotically thrown out most of my own possessions anyway for emotional or unemotional reasons and then often regretted it, as with the boots. According to everyone in LA, this is because I'm *such a Cancer*. Apparently my moon is Sagittarius so that's why I dump everything, but I care later because my sun . . . rises . . . I don't know. I've never understood it.

I take a deep breath and center myself around one truth. I am in my own body. Even if it's different than last I saw it, it's still me.

I am me. I can see, breathe, touch, hear, and—God knows after that amazing beer and meal—I can taste.

Deep breath in, deep breath out.

I have always loved movies. And reading. I love stories. And I've rolled my eyes at the main character of every magical movie I've seen and book I've read when they buy into the fantasy world a little too quickly or when they aren't *getting it* fast enough.

Like, hello, Bill Murray, it's the same day again, catch on, duh.

Or, on the contrary: Wow, Owen Wilson, you sure bought into the whole *traveling back to the twenties every night* thing pretty fast.

But I don't know, man. I am seriously starting to think that's happening to me somehow, and I don't have any *clue* what to think or do. Or say. Or—anything. It's hard to react at all because it's confusing. On one hand it feels obvious: Something crazy has happened. But on the other hand: I know crazy stuff doesn't happen. And whether I believe it or not, this isn't a simple trip to Ireland anymore.

I experiment with the evidential truth. I am not Lana Lord. Not an actress on a show. I am myself, but kind of the old me. I . . . live in Avalon? Or at the very least, this house is filled with my things. Also, I appear to have a past that I don't remember living, like meeting Maureen when she was a puppy. I appear to be friends with Kiera. I appear to have some sort of past or friendship or, I don't know, rivalry, with Cillian.

That cracked phone is mine. And if that's my phone, then there are answers in there.

I scan my brain hard for these memories that should, I guess, be there, but the life I think of as my own is all I find.

I go back over to the unfamiliar phone and open the photos app.

Oh God.

There are answers, all right.

It's a treasure trove of answers that pose more questions. There's a selfie of me that I never took holding up a cup of hot chocolate I don't remember drinking. There are several pictures of food in nice, unfamiliar restaurants. A frankly staggering number of pictures of Maureen. There are pictures of me and Kiera together and of Kiera by herself.

The answers being, *Oh, this is what this life looks like.* And the questions all being along the lines of, *What the fuck is going on and who are these people?*

I press *Play* on a video of Kiera.

It starts and I hear my own voice say, "Okay, go."

Kiera skewers a sausage with her fork, takes a bite, and then says, "Please date me, I'm a grand time."

I hear myself burst into laughter and say, "You can't say *please date me*, you psycho!"

"It's a dating app, that's the whole point!"

I make a *pfft* sound, and then it stops.

It reminds me so much of the video of me and Aimee that I'd unearthed before leaving LA. Two friends having an embarrassing, funny, fun time and making fools of themselves.

It is undeniably my voice. These selfies are of me. The little freckle on my cheekbone and slightly crooked gumline above my right lateral incisor—I know it's called exactly that because I recently had an appointment with an oral surgeon to discuss correcting it.

It's me in these photos. It's also *like* me to take pictures of my drinks and my food, to record people I like, and it was my first thought as I *watched* it to think, "You can't say *please date me*, that's psycho," even before hearing my own voice say it.

I tap on the Favorites album, feeling a little breathless.

There's a picture of me and Cillian. We're sitting at a picnic table, a late-afternoon golden sun shining on us. I have my smiling mouth open and a hand up, and I can read myself well enough to know that I'm in a good mood but joke-mad, insisting something to him. He is holding a finger up, as if he's going to press it against my lips to tell me to be quiet. But he looks happy too, amused by me, tolerant and patient. I spread my fingers apart on the screen to zoom into the photo and I see a look in his eyes I've never seen in someone who was looking at me. My unfiltered, not-over-considered thought is that *that* guy looks like he is desperately, madly in love with *that* girl.

I zoom in on my own face and feel my heart plunge as I realize that girl sure looks a great deal like she's in love with that guy too.

I turn off the phone screen, feeling an overwhelming urge to go find Cillian and rope him into helping me solve my mystery.

No, *that* would be psycho.

I yawn deeply and collapse backward on the couch. It really is as soft as a cloud and I feel suddenly heavy under the drawing curtain of fatigue—the kind of tired that you know will take you away to the restful, dreamy land of unconsciousness the second your head hits the pillow, if not a few seconds before.

I squeeze my eyes shut and then force them wide open. I can't fall asleep right now.

I've always had a bad habit of falling asleep in places that aren't a bed. I've done it since I was a kid. My parents will laugh to this day about how I'd fall asleep in my high chair or in a sandbox with other toddlers. One notable time, I fell asleep while getting a haircut. There's a picture of my dad and me, me snoozing away in my little haircutting cape.

Except in a car. I'm usually never more awake than in a car.

When I was a kid and fell asleep, it was because I was ultra-relaxed, or as my mom says, *always ready to travel to dreamland.*

Now when I do it, on the couch or on a lawn chair, it's not because I'm relaxed; it's because I'm constantly operating on about four hours of sleep and living under the demanding undertakings of trying to be charming and *actorly* and not-anxious.

Right now, I'm jet-lagged *and* I've barely slept in over twenty-four hours.

My eyes drift shut as I scroll through more of the favorite photos. I literally cannot keep my eyelids open, but I keep trying. Who can sleep when their world is splitting in two? I roll over and try to open my eyes again, one last time, and they focus briefly on a picture on the wall beside the couch.

Sleep takes over, and I don't get a chance to think it's odd that there's a picture—a recent-looking one—of me, Kiera, and Aimee.

Aimee, who has been dead for eleven years.

CHAPTER FOUR

I wake up the next morning to the sound of birds tweeting outside.

How sarcastically idyllic.

At some point in the night, Maureen had curled up at the end of the couch by my feet.

She rouses when I do, stretching her paws out in front of her with a tremble.

For a moment, nothing feels weird. It isn't surprising that I am where I am. Then I remember that *everything* is weird.

First things first.

I make sure the gate outside is shut, then let Maureen out. She does a little circle around the yard, squats, then trots merrily back in the house. She goes to a dog bowl and I search for her food, finding it easily.

While she eats, I go to the bathroom and check my reflection. Yep, I'm still this version of me. It gives me a strange surge in my stomach, and it takes a moment to identify it as excitement.

Now that I've had a good night's sleep, I feel more equipped to take it all on. I look at a clock on the wall and see that it's a little after eleven in the morning. I haven't slept that long in actual *years*. I feel more awake than any nootropic, kombucha, bulletproof coffee, or HIIT workout has ever made me feel.

I get a glass of water and sip from it as I go back over to the couch to decide what to do next.

A memory niggles at the back of my brain.

Oh my God. Oh my *God*.

I look for the picture on the wall beside the couch. It wasn't a dream, a hallucination, or my imagination. Or maybe it is, but if so, I'm still in it.

The picture is of me, Kiera, and Aimee.

I take the picture off the wall and look closely.

What the *fuck?*

Like all the photos in the phone last night, it's a picture of me that I've never seen before of a scene I never lived. But this one, unlike all the others, has the added element of my old best friend being in my life today. Or at least . . . recently. Unquestionably too recently for it to be from my own reality.

I need to call my mom.

I scramble to the phone, look for her contact, and immediately press it to call her.

After a few rings, she answers, her voice urgent. "Meg, what's wrong?"

I realize with a pang of guilt that there's a time difference. I quickly do the math. In Florida, it's six in the morning. She usually wakes up at nine these days and she's a worrier. Of course she thinks something is wrong.

Which, I mean, I am possibly losing my mind, but other than that it's not an emergency.

I do what I always do and lead with, "Everything's fine." And then I have no idea what to say. I can't tell her what's happening—or what I think is happening, especially since I don't really *know* what I think is happening—or she'll flip out. I need to get information, that's all. I can't scare her. "It's fine. I'm sorry to wake you up. I can explain later, but can you tell me where"—I hesitate—"where . . . I live? I know it sounds— Can you tell me?"

"What are you talking about? Where are you, what's going on? Meg, are you hurt?"

"No! Not at all, I'll explain later. Can you please just tell me?"

She hesitates. "This is very weird, Meg. What are you—"

I hear my dad's voice grumble in the background.

"What's wrong, is it Meggie?"

"I'm fine, I really am. When I explain, it'll be fine, and it'll make sense, trust me," I lie. "It's a stupid . . . scavenger hunt thing at . . . brunch."

I come up with the fake story out of thin air, knowing that it'll incense her to have been awoken for a drinking game, but that as long as she knows I'm safe, she'll give me the answer.

My eyes go back to the photo of Aimee.

"Oh, for Pete's sake," she says, moving the phone microphone away from her mouth and telling my dad, "She's fine, she's brunch-drunk." She returns to the phone to say, "This is very uncool, Meg."

"I know. I'll apologize later."

"You live at 432 Effie Lane in Avalon. I cannot believe you called me with this at the crack of dawn, it's incredibly inconsiderate."

"I'm sorry," I say. "Go back to—"

"Also, I'm finally on season ten of *Vanderpump Rules*, and we have *got* to talk about the whole Tom Sandoval thing."

My eyebrows shoot up in surprise. I've been telling my mom to watch that show for years.

"*Oh my*—"

"But not right now. I'm going back to bed."

She hangs up.

Well, that settles it. This isn't a prank. My mom thinks I live here. In Avalon. In Ireland.

I look at the picture again.

The other two girls and I are set against a backdrop of candles and wine bottles and other things I can't quite make out on wooden shelves. It looks like a shop.

My hair in two longish braids, I'm leaning over a table, laughing, my hands keeping three empty wineglasses steady as Kiera, who is beside me, pours champagne into one of them.

On my other side is Aimee. Grown-up Aimee.

The baby fat is gone from her cheeks, and she has more freckles than she ever had. And there's something about her that looks more lived in. She doesn't have dramatic wrinkles or anything, but there are soft laugh lines around her eyes. She's holding a candle to her nose and breathing in the scent with her eyes shut and a placid smile on her lips. It's so weird to see her like this after not seeing her since we were teenagers.

A memory comes to mind—one I haven't thought about in years.

For my eighteenth birthday, almost exactly twelve years ago, Aimee and I drove to St. Augustine, a cute little historic town south of Jacksonville. It was only a few hours away, and we drove with the windows down, cranking our sing-along playlist. On it, there was a healthy dose of the best Beatles songs to sing with, some top-forty stuff, throwbacks like Britney and Ace of Base, the *Evita* soundtrack (the Patti LuPone one, *not* the Madonna one), the *Moulin Rouge!* soundtrack (the movie, *not* the Broadway show), and a smattering of songs from the *Twilight* and *Hunger Games* soundtracks, which anyone of our generation will tell you were actually *bomb*.

We stayed at a hotel on Vilano Beach and took a five-minute cab ride to dinner at Cap's on the Water. We ate fried shrimp and chicken tenders and a slice of key lime pie each, and drank virgin strawberry daiquiris. She did not tell the staff to sing me the "Happy Birthday" song, because there is nothing worse than that and we both knew it. I like attention, but the birthday song is . . . no.

After dinner we went to the historic district and ate fresh fudge and tried on ugly hats and sunglasses, even managing to stuff down some pizza later on. We got flirted with by some surfer dudes and then freaked out when they asked us to go to a party, so we ran away squealing.

We went back to the hotel that night and took a bottle of champagne my dad had given us out to the darkened beach, where we sat for hours getting silly and loud and laughing about nothing and everything, drinking straight from the bottle (never as easy as it looks with increasingly warm champagne), taking pictures with my digital camera, and talking about boys and TV as the ocean relentlessly reached for the shore and pulled it under, grain by grain.

It was the first night I felt like a real adult. I wasn't, of course—we were teenagers and we were acting like it. But checking into a hotel, paying a check at a restaurant, having a bottle of wine on the beach—it all felt so grown-up. Our childhood was in the rearview, more and more every day, and the future was looming before us.

I thought it was our beginning, but it was so close to the end.

I can't believe I had forgotten about that so completely. How had my brain been powerful enough to hide that from me?

I guess I hadn't wanted to remember. It was too hard.

I look down at the picture in my tight grip and turn the frame over to take the back off so I can look for a date.

There it is. The picture was *printed* only three years ago.

I don't even need that confirmation. It's obvious to me that this is a version of Aimee that I never knew.

It seems like I live here, in Avalon. And that Aimee does, or did live here too, or at the very least, visited. What if—

Oh my God.

It all comes crashing down on me, as hard and fast as a Florida thunderstorm in summer.

I suddenly know *exactly* what's happening. Suspension of disbelief fully engaged.

This is the other life. The one I would have had.

I feel like I've missed an entire flight of stairs when I remember the words of that night at the carnival.

Usually, there is only one line here. You have two. Two lives, girl.

I've spent my whole adult life fantasizing about what would have happened if I'd turned right instead of left, gone to Ireland for school by myself instead of staying in Florida. I've spent my whole life blocking out that memory, not willing to think about what the fortune teller meant by that, because how often and how hard can you consider the words of a fortune teller at a local carnival?

But . . . what if she was right?

I will never know what she saw in Aimee's palm. She never said it out loud. But when Aimee died, I felt a terrible, sinking certainty that maybe I did know.

And now, there is a deep knowing spreading through me, the kind that only happens when you are reluctant to believe what you already know.

I am in that other life.

Of course it's not that I don't want to believe it. It's that it feels very, very hard to accept it.

Because I'm not a psychopath who thinks, yeah, sure, that makes perfect sense, the sky is green, time is a bagel, the Earth is made of Jell-O, yahoo, let's all wear shoes on our hands now.

But I'm starting to think it's the truth.

Everything makes sense. I might have gone to school and then stayed on after, here, in Avalon. Providing I figured out how to stay in another country, which I've watched enough of *90 Day Fiancé* to know is very difficult. But if I'd stayed here, then I wouldn't have been at that party with Aimee, we wouldn't have fought, and so . . . she'd still be alive. If she was alive, I wouldn't have gone to LA, or at least not in the same way, and I wouldn't be on *Brilliance*. I wouldn't be on a diet for robots who don't need nutrients, I would probably not have succumbed to the pressure—or at least not been able to afford—to get any work done on my face. So, yeah, I'd be a normal weight and have my own nose.

I'm on the road not taken!

I feel a little hysterical.

God, I mean, what if this is the *real* road? What if the *other* life I know is the hallucination?

I need my phone. Or . . . the phone that is apparently mine. I have to see if Aimee is in there, and if she is, I have to call her.

I'm about to open the phone to look for her name when I'm interrupted by a knock at the door, sending Maureen into a frenzy of barking as she leaps off the couch and runs to the door.

I pause, not wanting to put another second between me and Aimee, but someone here likely means more answers. It could even *be* Aimee.

I almost fall on my face scrambling over to the door with that thought.

I pull open the heavy wooden door, and Kiera comes in along with a gust of cool sunny air.

I try not to be disappointed.

"Good morning," she says, then, "Oh, hello, Maureen. Yes, I know, I know, I love you too."

I gently pull the dog back by her collar. "Come here, come, come on. Good girl."

I grew up with dogs, and I have my own, so it feels like second nature to handle Maureen, even though I don't know her.

"Don't be mad at me," Kiera says. "I brought you a chai. One pump of vanilla with full fat milk. Like you like it. Cillian texted me you were a little off last night after I left, thought you might need a little extra care. You okay?"

"Uh—yeah, I'm good."

"Good. Here you go." She hands over a cup. "So. I'm a good friend, a smart friend. I'm deserving of your friendship. Even though I can't stop sleepin' with that useless scut."

I move aside to let her in and take a sip of the chai, which *is* exactly how I like it, though it's been years since I've had anything but sugarless coffee or some mushroom bullshit that's supposed to be healthier than coffee.

"Why exactly would I be mad at you?" I ask. "For the chai?"

"Well, I don't want to give you any ideas if you're not," she says, thinking I'm joking. When she sees I'm actually puzzled, she says, "Because of Nial?"

"Nial. Why would I care about Nial?"

"What do you mean?"

"I mean . . . why would I care?"

She squints at me. "Drink your tea. Clearly you need the caffeine."

In movies, when someone wakes up in a life that isn't theirs and they have to play catch-up, the other characters are always answering questions with tons of helpful exposition. Like in a Hallmark movie I once watched, where the heroine finds herself in a small town where everyone thinks she's her identical, long-lost twin. The heroine, with her conservative outfit and perfectly blown-out hair, asked things like, *And you are . . . ?* and the char-acters always responded with things like, *Darcy, you're so silly today! I'm your quirky, hopelessly single, nameless best friend who runs the local muffin shop! We've been friends since we were sixteen years old? You remember, we get together every morning for coffee and discuss things like how to help the mayor save the local firehouse?*

Kiera is not being as helpful. Instead, she's taken the lid off her drink, promptly spilled some on the table, and has begun dabbing it up with a tea towel.

Maureen has found a stuffed toy and is now milling in circles with it, hoping to be noticed and appreciated.

"Don't talk to me 'til I've had my coffee, am I right?" says Kiera, holding up the towel and then tossing it into a rattan basket with other dishrags. "Anyway, how you getting on?"

Even less helpful.

She sits down on the couch by the fireplace and waits on the update.

"Did you have a fire last night?" she asks, gesturing at the hearth. "Did Cillian come over?"

"No, I was cold," I say, though a dreamy, romantic image has come to mind of that gorgeous bartender here stoking my fire. Not a euphemism. Although—

"And you didn't turn on the heater?" she asks, gesturing at a metal object I can now see is very obviously a space heater. "You never use the fireplace."

I shrug, a gesture that feels wildly blasé for how strange everything is right now. "Thought the fire would be nice."

She gives me a look of confusion and says, "Who are you and what've you done with my best friend?"

Welp, I'm not gonna get an opening better than that.

I bite my bottom lip and then decide I can't do this completely blind. I need some answers. I need an ally.

I sit down on the couch across from her and lean forward, elbows on my knees. "Kiera, we're close, right?"

"Obviously."

"K, well, I'm about to say something, and I know it's going to sound absolutely insane. I want you to have an open mind, if you can. If you don't want to, that's fine, but—"

She gives me a look. "I hardly think you'll shock me."

"Ha," I laugh. "We'll see."

"What is it?"

Maureen gives up on being the center of attention and curls into a ball on the floor.

I get up the nerve to say it.

"I don't know who you are."

"Jesus, Nial's not *that* bad. What are you on about?"

"No, no, I mean, I don't know who you are at all. I don't know who that bartender was last night, though I understand his name is Cillian. I kind of don't know who . . . who I am, right now. I mean, I do, but—yeah. I don't live here. I'm from California."

"I thought you were from the one with all the alligators and crime. What's it—Florida?"

She's rightfully confused, and I know I'm being confusing, but I can't help it. I'm *also* confused.

"I am originally, yes. Okay. Look. I know this sounds like some weird joke or lie or, I don't know, a crazy delusion. And honestly, maybe it is. But the thing is, I live in Los Angeles. I'm an actress."

"What the hell are you— Are you *Truman Show*–ing me?"

"I had my thirtieth birthday party, all these people were over, Barry Keoghan was there."

"Did I tell you my cousin Marnie went to primary school with him? O'Connell in Dublin. She said he was a twat. But Marnie's a bit of a twat." She looks at me. "Sorry, go on, you had a party, ol' Barry was there. Where was I when you were having this party?"

"I don't know, I was in LA. Right, okay, so that night, I booked this cottage on Airbnb and a flight all on a whim. I flew here, I got out of the taxi, I walked inside, dropped my suitcase, and then I went to the pub to get food, as all I'd eaten all day was a pretzel from the airport. As far as I know, before last night, I've never spoken to you or to Cillian or—anyone here before."

"Oh, wait, is this a dream you had? You're supposed to start that kind of thing with, *I had a dream where this batshit thing happened.*"

"No, I'm telling you the truth. That's my real life."

"Are you concussed?"

"No! I don't think so. I know how this sounds."

"We should go to hospital." She stands up and makes her way to the door.

"No, no, I'm fine, really! It's—"

"If you don't recognize your friends, and you think you live in a place you never lived, then I think that's a cause for emergency. So come on, off we go."

I consider the number of tests I'd be likely to undergo—if a person comes in and thinks they have another life or that they've time traveled or they're from another planet, no one would ever believe them. I'd end up on some medication, maybe locked in a psych ward somewhere. I'm becoming increasingly unsure why I even expected Kiera to believe me. *Of course* she thinks I should go to the hospital, that's what I'd say if someone told *me* this.

She gives me a serious look. "If you really believe what you're saying—" When I appear, I guess, horror-struck at the idea, she says, "Well, we must at least go see Jim."

"Jim?"

She looks really troubled now.

I try to seem mentally stable. "Can I tell you what I think is happening?"

She hesitates. "You've got five minutes, and then we're leaving." She goes back to her chair.

"Okay, thank you."

I'm really going to have to make a good case for myself here.

"I got into Avalon School of the Arts when I was eighteen years old. I applied with my best friend—"

"Aimee, yeah, I know that."

It's thrilling and a little dizzying to hear this stranger refer to her.

I go on to tell her my version of what happened. The wait-list, the college dorms in Florida, everything. Everything but the big, important part, about how Aimee is dead.

She narrows her eyes. "This is mad, what you're doing. It's very unlike you to do an elaborate joke like this to make a fool of me."

"Yeah, I'm not doing that. I hate that kind of thing actually."

"That's true, you do." She cocks her head at me, suspicious. "Oh, feck, this isn't some weird method acting thing or something? You used to do this kind of thing in school, but—"

"No, it's not."

"The problem here is, you're a good actress."

I have the compulsion to google myself again, to use the internet to prove it. It's what you do if you're a hundred percent sure Harry Styles has four nipples, and you desperately need to prove it to someone.

But since the internet seems to be in on whatever charade this is, I can't simply look it up.

"Kiera, I swear on everything. I swear on my dog—I mean my dog back home. Dido. I met this dog last night."

We both look at the retriever.

"You're telling me you don't know Maureen."

"I can't even *fathom* why I or anyone else would name a dog Maureen."

"He named her after the actress didn't he? Maureen O'Hara? *The Parent Trap*? I thought it was your idea."

"He?"

She squints. "Cillian."

"Ah, right. He wants me to bring her back apparently."

She shakes her head. "You're telling me you don't know the dog that you've literally kidnapped every other night since she was a puppy?"

I look at Maureen, who is now using her toy as a pillow.

"She seems very sweet, but I don't know her," I say.

"Was it the breakup? Did it cause you to go daft? I mean, you two have broken up a hundred times, and you've never forgotten your entire life. Something did seem different about this one, though. I feel like you aren't telling me something about it."

A plunge of reasonless guilt goes through me and I shake my head. "I don't know. Cillian seems nice too."

She gives me a challenging look. "*Cillian seems nice?* I'm starting to feel a bit gaslit."

"Wait—breakup? Are you telling me I was *with* that guy?"

She looks puzzled. "You don't remember being with Cillian? For years on end? Off and on, over and over?"

I shake my head slowly. "No."

"You don't remember breaking up with him yesterday?"

"*Yesterday?* Oh my God, no wonder he seemed so annoyed with me being there."

The pieces of this new image start to fall into place. I was *with* Cillian. Or . . . some version of me was.

"To be fair, he's always a bit like that." She laughs, but then remembers what I'm telling her and looks seriously at me. "You're telling me you really don't remember any of this? You really believe you have a different life?"

"I swear on everything. You don't have to believe me. I mean, I wouldn't believe *myself* right now, if I hadn't looked in the mirror and seen"—I gesture at my face—"all this."

"What about"—she gestures at my face too—"all this?"

"In my life, my real life, I weigh like twenty pounds less and I've had some work done. Not a lot. But enough that I can say with one hundred percent certainty that this is not the face I had when I woke up yesterday."

She laughs. "In my real life, I too am about twenty pounds thinner." She then shakes her fists at the heavens. "God, won't you wake me up from this nightmare?"

"I—*ugh*. I need to prove this to you." I rack my brain. "Okay, okay, um . . . okay! I can tell you everything on the menu of this *amazing* Thai place in Silver Lake. There are actually several locations, but—okay, this restaurant called Night + Market. Google it."

She furrows her brows at me and then raises them and pulls out her phone. "Okay, I'll play your little game."

"Type in 'Night + Market Silver Lake.' It's the Song location. On Sunset."

She gives me a look, types it in, and then says, "Got it."

"Okay, find the menu. They've got something called Startled Pig, though they don't always have it. They have this um . . . oh, *larb,* they've got like two or three kinds of larb. They have a crispy rice salad—"

"I'm not sure what this is supposed to be proving, except that your obsession with food has started to stretch globally."

I let out a growl of impatience.

"I need something better. Oh!" I clap my hands together and point at her. "You know Grayson Gamble?"

"The one from that Marvel movie? So fit."

"Yeah, that's him!"

"I know you hate that guy."

"Do I?" I ask, feeling practically airborne with my eagerness to prove myself. Partially because I want someone else in on this with me, but also because if she believes me, she can help me to believe myself.

"You said he looks like a Disney prince that cries after sex."

This catches me off guard and I say, "Actually, he turned down an *Enchanted* spin-off and one time he cried *during* sex, so that was an excellent read."

"You said he looks like he sits sidesaddle on the loo."

I laugh at this. "That's very funny. I can't confirm it, but I wouldn't be surprised."

"Because you're so close, the two of you."

"I can tell you where he lives. You can zoom in on his house on Google Maps. I can tell you exactly what the house looks like. I actually live there with him. It doesn't really feel like my house. But that's its own thing."

"I'm not saying you would do this, you'd have to be barmy . . . although, at this point . . . but, Meg, you could have looked all this stuff up. Memorized some mansion in Beverly Hills, or—"

"Silver Lake."

"Whatever that is. Or looked up some random menu for a restaurant and memorized it. I don't know why you'd do that. But you could have."

"You're right, you're right." I pat my lips with my fingers, thinking. "We could call Grayson."

"We could call Grayson Gamble?"

"Yes!"

"Even that, while insane, still wouldn't prove you're . . ." She shakes her head and widens her eyes. "Are we really having this conversation, Meggie?"

"Actually, I wouldn't know his number by heart." I struggle to think. "Oh, God, I know—when he was thirteen, he burned his house down."

"Jesus!"

"Everyone was fine, but his parents were obviously miserable about it, and he never told anyone it was his fault."

She crosses her arms. "How'd he do that?"

"He"—I laugh, thinking of the story—"it's awful, I shouldn't laugh. He was pretending with his stuffed rabbit, Flip Flop, trying to cook with him, but it was a gas stove, and Flip Flop caught on fire and then Grayson knocked over the box of pasta and then tried to put it out with oil—"

"Terrible."

"He only told me because we were together. I mean, and he was also on peyote at the time."

"When he was thirteen?"

"When he told me."

"Ah. So you reckon," she says, "I should call up *famous movie star* Grayson Gamble out of the blue and suggest that when he was a little too old to be playing with dolls, he might have burned down his family home."

"Maybe that's too mean."

"There must be a way you can *prove*"—she puts air quotes around the word *prove*—"this, without retraumatizing a man."

"You're right." I breathe in deeply. "You must be right."

"As usual," she says quietly, fidgeting with her nails.

Then I think of it.

"I know what I can do!"

"Go ahead then." She takes a sip of coffee.

"There's this show called *Brilliance*."

"Duh. Love it."

"You've seen it?" So it does air here. Good to know.

"Have I seen it? I watched the first season twice. I thought you hated that show."

"*Do* I?"

The Me-Who-Lives-in-Avalon seems to hate all the things that make up my entire life back in California.

"You do. Anyway, carry on."

"The finale hasn't aired yet. It airs . . ." I glance at my watch. "Tonight, right?"

One of the soapiest aspects of our show is that we broke modern tradition and have almost thirty episodes a season, and when we shoot it, we air it almost immediately, like traditional soaps. It's one of the things that got people's attention. I know the inside scoop, which is that the writers wanted to be able to change the show if something was or wasn't working. Which has been hell for line memorization, but worked well for keeping the attention of our fans.

"Yes, it airs tonight."

"I know exactly what happens. I know every line. Well, all of *my* lines."

"Your . . . lines?"

"Right! You don't know. I play Daphne."

"Kim Wong plays Daphne."

"Yes, but in *my* world, Kim plays Velma."

"Jordan Levinson plays Velma."

"She does? The weird girl from those banned tampon commercials?"

"The *what?*"

"Never mind, it doesn't matter—this is the perfect thing. I can tell you my entire monologue at the end when—"

She plugs her ears. "Ah! Ah! No spoilers!"

"I'm sorry," I say. Then, "So you are starting to believe me."

She exhales, furrowing her brow at the ground. "Am I?"

Hope lifts within me.

"Look, I can't say this will work. I have no idea what's going on. I don't know if the monologue will be the same. Maybe without me, it's different." In fact, it probably will be. The writers change everything based on audience response. "But this is a good place to start. I won't spoil it for you. I'll write it down and give it to you and you can open it after you watch the episode."

"Shouldn't there be some wizard guiding you through this or something? Or like, Father Christmas?"

"I know, right? That would be nice."

She considers. "All right, fine. We'll do the finale thing. But will you do me a favor in the meantime?"

"Anything!"

"Let's get your head checked. I mean, you seem normal enough. You seem calm, sort of, and you don't seem like you've had a catastrophic cranial injury, but obviously everything you've said since I arrived is absolutely *mad*, so I think it's best we get you checked out."

"I really don't like hospitals."

"We'll just go see Jim."

Jim again.

"Okay," I say.

"Great, good, grand, okay." She starts to make moves.

I remember Aimee. Not that I'd forgotten, but the idea is so massive it's hard to hold it in my mind while I think, speak, or do anything else.

"And . . . you know Aimee?" I ask.

"Of course I do."

"Is she . . . is she here?"

"What, in the room with us?" She makes a face.

I breathe deeply. "No, I mean . . . I—does she live in Avalon?" I stumble a bit on the word *live*.

The moment between my question and her response is one of the longest of my life. Is she here? Is Aimee here? Is Aimee somewhere at all?

"Yes . . ."

Holy shit. Oh my God, oh my God.

"Can we go see Aimee? Now?"

I stand.

My heart skips a few beats as I stare up at the photo of Aimee, Kiera, and me.

"I don't know if that's a good idea, Meg. You two haven't spoken lately."

"What?" Bile rises in my throat. "Why?"

She stands too. "Meg, this is really worrying. You really don't remember anything that's happened?"

I let out a deep sigh. If I were her, I would have already called the men in white coats to take me away.

Part of me wants to tell her why it's so important and staggering that she's saying Aimee is here. But I can't do it.

"I don't know," I say, rubbing my eyes in frustration. "Maybe my plane crashed and this is my version of *Lost*. Maybe we'll all find out I'm dead in the finale."

Her eyebrows drop to a heavy line and she lifts her chin at me. "You know damn well I'm only on season three."

"Shit. See, I *don't* know that. And also, I'm sorry. And also, it's still worth watching, people give it a bad rap, but the ending is actually *not* what that show is all about. It actually aged into something more interesting."

"That is exactly what you said to me last month when I was looking for something to watch."

We're silent for a moment. I drink my chai, she drinks her coffee.

"Well." She stomps her feet and looks at me. "Let's take your positively broken brain to the doc, shall we?"

CHAPTER FIVE

W ell, it definitely isn't a hospital.

When we arrive at Jim's house, he is on all fours in his back garden in a feminine-looking sun hat, snipping herbs and collecting them in a basket.

Kiera greets him by saying, "Hiya, Jim! Half retirement suits you."

"Girls, what brings you two round?"

She explains that I'm being weird, and that we wanted to get his professional opinion.

He takes us inside, shedding his dirt-covered gloves and uncinching the string of his hat to remove it, telling me to take a seat at the kitchen table.

I'm not sure what Kiera or I expected him to do, but he merely looks at my head all over, poking it and saying, "Does that hurt?" while I say no again and again. As if there might be a gaping wound somewhere that I hadn't noticed. Like, *Oh, I didn't know the golf ball wedged into my skull was an issue.*

"Open up those baby blues for me, love."

I open my eyes wide, and he shines a pocket flashlight into each of them.

"Any nausea?" he asks.

"No."

"Does your head *hurt*?"

"No."

"Blurry vision?"

"Nope."

After about a hundred more questions, he sits back and says, "You look all right to me, Meg," and rolls his sleeves back down. Strange to hear this stranger say my name. "What *did* make you think something might be wrong?"

He's a nice man, and he's good-looking for being, I'd guess, in his seventies. He looks kinda like Sean Connery.

"I've had some . . . memory issues? I guess?" I say, understating the issue so much that Kiera laughs.

"A bit," she says.

He arches a silver eyebrow. "That doesn't surprise me; every time I run into you two, you're at Cairdeas."

"Does it seem like too much?" asks Kiera, a coy smile playing at her lips. "Answer carefully now, oul fella, because if you run into us *every* time you're down the pub, and you think that's a lot, then I guess what you're saying is—"

"All right, all right, no need to get so spirited, Kiera. So what d'ya mean by *memory issues*?"

"Some short-term memory stuff." I ignore Kiera's eyes on me.

"Are you hallucinating at all?"

"Uh . . . well, I guess I wouldn't know, would I?"

"You'd know. Do you feel dreamy? All your limbs feel like they move when you tell them to, things like that?"

I lift my arms and knees. "I don't feel dreamy"—not quite, anyway—"and my body moves normally."

"How do you feel?"

"Honestly, generally normal."

"Could be stress. Or something you ate. To quote Ebenezer Scrooge when he saw the ghost of Jacob Marley, *you may be an undigested bit of beef, a blot of mustard, a crumb of cheese, a fragment of underdone potato.*"

"Is that your professional diagnosis then, Jim?" asks Kiera, arms crossed. "Stress or a potato? You've never been more Irish. You may as well prescribe her a Guinness."

"Tea, loves?" A woman, I assume the doctor's wife, comes in. She's also very good-looking, with blond hair pulled back in a neat chignon, and fine lines and freckles on her face, neck, and arms. She's in an oversized white sweater and pleated periwinkle-blue pants.

"Yes, please," says Kiera.

"How are you, Meggie?" She's a little stiffer with me than with Kiera, I can't help but notice.

"I'm all right. Um, how are you?" I say.

"Mm-hm," she says, putting the kettle on and then leaving the room.

I look at Kiera. She exhales deeply and then says to Jim, "Marcia not so happy with Meg, I take it."

"Oh, she'll be fine. Always is. Upset about the breakup, that's all. I think she was really counting on it working out this time." He gives me loaded eye contact, and it seems as though I'm supposed to get something here that even Kiera doesn't know. But of course, I don't.

"Don't tell me you've forgotten Cillian, then?" he asks, clearly thinking he's making a joke.

My silence is confirmation enough. His smile fades and his brow furrows.

"Jim and Marcia are Cillian's parents, by the way," says Kiera, looking a little uncomfortable as she says it.

"Oh God." I slap a hand over my mouth. I want to apologize for the breakup, but then realize I don't know for sure if he broke up with me or I broke up with him.

Kiera steps toward us. "This is what I'm saying. She doesn't remember any of us, Jim. She says she's here from outer space or something."

"Kiera!" I say.

"What? Did you think you'd *Weekend at Bernie's* yourself around here, pretending everything was fine?"

I furrow my brow. I don't know what I thought. "I didn't say I was from *outer space,* I said California."

"Same thing," she says.

The kettle starts to whistle and Marcia comes back in. She pulls out four teacups and starts about making us all tea.

"California," says Jim, looking troubled now.

"She thinks she's a famous actress living in LA and that she never moved to Avalon."

"You might be leaving out some pretty key symptoms, Ms. Bryan. Can you catch me up?"

"Okay." I sigh, then, as I did with Kiera, try to explain what is going on even though *I* don't understand it.

Kiera looks nervous as I talk, and Jim listens patiently and without judgment. Marcia, on the other hand, has arched a perfect eyebrow so high it looks like it might float off into the air above her head.

"But I called my mom this morning and *she* thinks I live here. So I know it's not you all, like . . . messing with me or something like that." I blush, feeling embarrassed to even suggest something so self-centered. "And I feel fine, so I don't know what's happening."

"Any history of mental health issues?" he asks. "Any family history?"

"I have an aunt who thinks she's drop-dead gorgeous, but in reality looks like Rod Stewart."

"Ah, Aunt Cath," says Kiera. "Bless her."

She knows about loony Aunt Cath. How weird.

"No," I say, to be clear. "No real mental health issues. I get panic attacks sometimes."

"Right, you told me about those. Grandiose delusions are a symptom of several different psychological disorders," Jim says, studying me.

I laugh. "I mean, they're hardly grandiose. Being famous kind of sucks."

Kiera and Jim exchange a look. Marcia lets out a sharp *ha!*

I must have been the one to end things with Cillian. It's the only explanation for why this woman seems so mad at me.

"I thought it might be because of the breakup," suggests Kiera.

"True enough, but she's usually fine after the breakups," he says. "If a bit reclusive."

"How often do I break up with this guy?" I ask. "Or does he break up with me?"

"It's always you," comes Marcia's voice.

A guilty plunge goes through me and I say, "I'm sorry. I can't imagine why I . . . why I did that."

Jim gives me a kind look. "Meg, I really think you ought to go to Tralee and be seen by someone."

I stare blankly at him, then look to Kiera for explanation.

She glances at Jim and then says to me, "University Hospital."

I shake my head. I really do hate hospitals. They're a place for crisis and tragedy. And what could they tell me? I *know* this isn't my life. No number of MRIs or psychoactive drugs will change that. This is the kind of thing Netflix makes documentaries about, and don't we all watch them and think the people are crazy?

"No hospital. Please."

Kiera sighs.

Jim makes a firm line with his mouth. "I can't make you go. But if you're not having any violent tendencies or some such, no dizziness, then I think the best thing we can do is give it a few days. Try to keep her in her routine, if you can, Kiera, and let's keep an eye on her. I wouldn't let her out of your sight for a night or two."

Kiera snaps and does finger guns at me. "Sleepover time. Looks like you'll be watching the finale too, my love."

"I'd actually love to. I want to see how Kim does in my role."

"*Brilliance*," says Kiera to Jim by way of explanation. "She reckons she plays Daphne in her *real life*."

Jim keeps a straight face, but something lightens in his eyes. "I think Meg would make a great Daphne."

"I do!" I say, insistent.

"Seeing Meggie play a villain . . . oh, let me see if I can stretch the imagination," says Marcia, rinsing her teacup in the sink.

Kiera drops her lips into a dramatic frown and then mouths *savage* at me.

"That's enough, Marcia. It's none of our business what happens with the kids, you know that." Jim gives me an apologetic look.

She puts up a hand wordlessly and then drops it.

There's an embarrassed silence before Kiera puts down her mug and launches herself off the kitchen counter.

"Okay, stupid, let's leave the poor man to his gardening, shall we? We have work in an hour anyhow. Marcia, good to see you, even if you are in rare form today."

"Work?" I ask, but no one hears me.

Marcia smiles kindly at Kiera and says, "I could never be thick at you, darlin'," pulling her in for a big hug and a squeeze on the arms.

"Oh, it's nice to be the favorite," says Kiera.

"Did you say work?" I ask again.

"Isn't it grand," she says with a side smile to Jim. "She's doesn't remember she has a job, the breakup has completely slipped her mind, and she's forgotten she's not a movie star."

"TV star, actually," I correct. "I've never done a movie."

All three of them look at me for a moment and I want to die.

"If it's a delusion, maybe you don't want to wake up from it," jokes Jim. "But really, kid, if anything else crops up or if this doesn't clear up after a few days, come over. Anytime. Day or night. We'll make sense of it."

He rests a paternal hand onto my shoulder, and I feel deeply reassured by it. I rarely spend time with people who offer this particular sort of comfort. You don't meet a lot of paternal older men in Hollywood. Usually they're too busy trying to hold on to their youth or grab on to yours.

"Thanks," I say.

"Keep an eye on her," Jim says to Kiera.

"Sure look," she responds with a thumbs-up.

Marcia leaves the kitchen tsking, and we make our way out.

I've done so much work to release the strain of never being able to please everybody. The early reviews used to kill me. The comment section is a radioactive wasteland. That *New Yorker* article. The videos Lisa Michele forces me to watch or overhear. I have tried so hard to not care about what other people think. And yet here I am, a million miles from real life, and someone's mom is *mad at me*.

It's kind of my worst nightmare.

We make our way out, but as we get to the end of the front path, Jim stands in his doorway and calls, "And Meg?"

I turn. "Yeah?"

"Give him his bloody dog back, will ya?"

I glance at Kiera, then back to Jim. "I will."

"He's lost without her, you know. He's lost without you, too, but the dog—let him at least have her."

"I will."

"All right, love. Tell him his old man said hello. See you down the pub."

Then he goes inside and shuts the door behind him.

I turn to Kiera. "Good looks really run in that family."

"Feck's sake, even when you've lost your memory, you're lusting after Cillian."

"I mean, no, I don't even know him." We walk for a few seconds in silence, and then I say, "But he is pretty hot."

"This is turning into a porny version of *Cloud Atlas*."

I squint at her. "*Cloud Atlas*?"

"It's the one with—"

"I know, it's just such a bizarre thing to reference."

"Okay, well, get back to me with another interdimensional love story."

We walk down the path, back toward town.

Avalon is every bit as beautiful as I'd hoped it would be. There are sleepy green swaths of grass alongside the lazy paths, and the sun has hidden behind gray clouds. The cool breeze has been replaced with a slightly balmier one, the air swirling with wispy, violet fog.

"The fact that I'm even considering believing you is concerning," Kiera says. "Maybe I should have had *my* head checked."

I put my hands on her head and say, "Does that hurt?"

"No."

"Head check done, you're completely fine."

She laughs and it feels so strangely familiar and good. I know how pathetic it sounds, but to be honest, I haven't had a real *friend* in a while. Not like this. Not the kind you get paired with in sentences like *every time I run into you two,* or who feel comfortable enough to take a bite of your food without asking. It's an intimacy I've missed.

"To be clear," Kiera goes on, "what I believe is that *you* believe it. And if this is something you need to work through, I'll help you. But if it goes on too long, I'm going to have you admitted somewhere, all right? Put in a padded room or something. I don't really know how any of that works. But. I'm going to figure it out if I have to."

I think of Aimee again and realize that I'm now actually putting off the attempt to see her. As long as I don't try, I can believe she's alive.

Man. My denial skills are *kinda* stunning.

But if she is alive, I have to know for sure. Of course I have to know.

I stop and pull out my phone.

I swipe through. There she is. There's her number.

Holy shit. Holy fucking shit.

"Meg?" prompts Kiera, seeing the contact pulled up.

"I'm going to call Aimee."

CHAPTER SIX

A re you sure you want to do that?" asks Kiera, cringing. She's stopped
walking on the path. A breeze runs between us, bringing with it the
scent of honeysuckle from somewhere.

I stop too, the phone and Aimee's contact information waiting there.

"You said we haven't seen each other in a while."

"Not really."

"Why not?"

"I don't know all the details. I think it was sort of a slow falling-out.
After the wedding—"

"Wedding? Whose wedding? Is she *married?*"

Kiera nods.

Aimee was nineteen the last time I saw her, and we were in no way
talking about things like marriage. I know people get married at that age in
like, Utah, and wherever the NXIVM sex cult is still secretly operating, but
the idea of getting married was so *far* from our minds when I last saw her.

Well . . . actually, was it?

Aimee was always so much more traditional than I was. We wanted to come here. We wanted to be actresses, and we used to say we wanted to get famous and go down in history like the Cates/Kates.: Blanchett, Winslet, Hepburn. We wanted to be charming and funny, with a dash of serious acting mixed in.

But I guess I was really the one who talked about it the most. She loved doing plays, but she was usually in the ensemble and happy there. Or doing tech. I, meanwhile, either got lead parts or was furious at myself when I didn't, overthinking every weak syllable in my audition.

Aimee didn't crave the limelight like I did. She *had* talked about her future wedding. She even talked about having kids one day.

I talked about walking down the red carpet, and she talked about walking down the aisle. How had I forgotten that?

"What's her husband like?"

"You sort of hate him."

"God, it sounds like all I do is run around hating things. Actors, TV shows, husbands. I keep breaking up with perfectly nice-seeming guys."

I feel a little sick, wondering if that is how I am in LA too. Annoying and restless when everything is arguably fine.

"Just the one nice guy, really," she corrects. "And you've only broken up a few times. It's really more the fact that, even when you do break up, you can't stop being around each other, and you keep hurting each other that way."

"Tell me I'm not as bad as I sound."

"No! You're grand. I mean, you're always down for a good kippy chat, but you're not really a shite-talker or anything like that. I think your problem with Theo has more to do with your past—"

"Wa-wa-wa-wa-wait," I say. "She married fucking *Theo?*"

"So you do remember *him* of all people?" she asks, confused.

"I mean, they were together in high school and then they got back together in college. Yeah, I hated him. That's a judgment I can stand behind."

"Okay, so you remember everything up until being, what, like, eighteen?"

She swats at a mosquito; I pause to think it funny that mosquitos are part of this delusion, hallucination, whatever it is.

"No, I remember everything up to this moment. There are no gaps in my memory, it's just that the lives seem to have sort of . . . diverged when I went to college. Because you seem to think I've been here that whole time, right?"

"Since the first year of college, yeah. I mean, you visit home now and again of course, but yes, you're here."

I shake my head. "How did you and I meet?"

She hesitates, and then half sits on the wooden split rail fence behind her.

"We were in classes together. I was getting a degree in art. Painting, specifically, but we all had to take classes in the other disciplines, you know. I met you and Aimee in a basic acting class. It was *not* for me, let me tell you."

"Okay, and how did Aimee end up here?"

"She came in the second semester of your first year."

"How? She didn't get in, right?"

"Taken off the wait-list, I guess. Well, look, why don't you try to piece your life together for a day or so and then think about reaching out."

This is crazy. If I'm right that this is the life I would have lived, then it sounds like everything would have gone according to plan if I'd just come. It's almost too much to comprehend.

"Well, it doesn't matter that we're fighting, I'm going to call her. Is the whole Theo thing why we're on bad terms?"

My heart is pounding.

"That's where it started."

"Okay, that's fine. Theo sucks. That's on the record. But if she's mad at me, we can fix that. It doesn't matter. I can apologize for that."

"But Meg, you two drifted apart. You have different lives. You want different things."

"That doesn't make sense! You don't get it. It would never happen like that!"

"Well, what happened in your, eh, other life? What's your friendship like there?"

She gives me a steady look, the way a good therapist might speak into their patient's fantasy to get to the heart of things.

I clench my jaw to keep in control, unwilling to go all the way into it. I can't, I *never* say out loud that she died. And in this case I think it might sound off different alarm bells than I need to. Aimee might not even see me if I go around saying something like that.

"We're great," I lie, instead.

She narrows her eyes at me. "I don't believe you."

"I'm going to call her."

"Meg."

My blood runs hot and cold in equal measure as I hit Aimee's name.

"It's ringing," I say.

Kiera nods, accepting it. She looks almost as tense as I am.

The ringing stops. And for a moment I'm suspended in wait. I'm about to hear her voice.

Then . . . voicemail.

Hey, you've reached Aimee. Leave a message after the beep. I'll call you back as soon as I can.

The beep goes off, and my tongue feels tangled. I'm so anxious there's a pulse in my eyelids.

"Ah, uh, hi, Aimee, it's Meg. Call me back as soon as you can. It's urgent. And also, I'm sorry. About everything, ever. I don't want to be in a fight or not talking or—call me back, okay? Anytime. But soon, like right away. Okay. Bye."

I almost can't bring myself to hang up. It's the closest to talking to Aimee that I've come in over a decade.

I manage eventually, and then look at Kiera.

After a minute, I say, "I'm gonna call her again."

"No, no, no, okay. Let's put the phone down, let's, yeah." She takes it from my hand and locks the screen. "Let's give her some time to get back to you."

"Does she live nearby? Let's go over!"

"You ever seen *The Banshees of Inisherin*? It's like that. I don't think she'd chop all her fingers off if you show up, but nevertheless."

I stare at her, uncomfortable in my own skin. Now that I've called Aimee, I feel frenzied. It's like when I decide I want a haircut. Once I've made the decision, I become *desperate* to do it. If I don't get to a salon within hours, I'm going positively feral with a pair of kitchen scissors.

"Listen, we've got work in a bit. Let's get a bite to eat and then go over. It'll all be all right."

"Where do I work? And do I have to go? You'd think this would be cause for a sick day."

She gives me a look, then puts her arm around my back. "Come along, you poor, ill critter. You have bills to pay. Let's go."

⁓

We pick up a seafood chowder each and a hunk of bread to share with richly creamy, yellow, salted butter and take it over to the shop called Dinner Party that I noticed last night. Apparently, we both work there.

Kiera unlocks and opens the front door, which hits a bell that hangs above it, sounding a cheerful jingle.

She flips on the lights.

"Oh, this is so *cute*," I say. Then, when I feel her eyes on me, I turn and ask, "What?"

"Well, it's a bit trippy to arrive at work with you and have you act like a customer who's never been in before."

"I'm sorry, I don't—"

"I know, I know," she says. "You don't know."

"So it's like a little gift shop."

She hesitates and then says, "Yeah, so . . . mad, okay, so, the idea is like hostess gifts, for lack of a less nineteen-fifties-housewife way to put it. We sell chocolates and candies, some small-batch jams and things. Some wines and digestifs. Little gifts you might pick up when you forget your anniversary or go to meet your boyfriend's parents or something like that."

"Oh my God, that's *such* a good idea. This would kill in Larchmont."

"That's a neighborhood in LA, yeah?"

"Sorry, yes."

She goes behind the counter. "How's your wine knowledge?"

"I was a bartender, actually. Before the whole *Brilliance* thing. I'm not exactly a sommelier, but I know enough to think *Sideways* was actually a bad movie."

"Between the toxic buddy bromance and all the pinot noir chat, that movie should be deleted from all streaming services. Though I do agree with them about merlot."

She switches on the speakers, and Django Reinhardt starts playing. I look at the wooden shelves of wine and realize that this is where the photo on the wall was taken. The one of Aimee, Kiera, and me.

This is too weird.

Kiera walks me through the store, showing me what to do during a shift. Training me, essentially. Every few minutes she stops to ask, "Do you really not remember? I'll kill you if you're making me go through all this for nothing."

And each time, I assure her that I have no idea.

Eventually, though, she's shown me everything, and we're sitting there in the peaceful, quiet little shop, waiting for someone to come in.

Kiera is on the ground using a selection of chalk pens to draw on an A-frame. I wander around.

There's a selection of records, and I flip through to see *No Angel* by Dido (which is the Dido my dog was named after, if I'm honest), *The Rhythm of the Saints* by Paul Simon, the soundtrack to *Butch Cassidy and the Sundance Kid*, Caroline Polachek's *Desire, I Want to Turn Into You*, and an old, ratty version of Ella Fitzgerald and Louis Armstrong's album *Ella and Louis*. There are more, and all of them seem to be entirely a selection of things I listen to on a regular basis.

"This is basically all my favorite music," I say.

"Makes sense, you picked them out."

"Really? Oh, that's so fun."

The bookshelf is filled with books to give someone who might not read them but will at least like displaying them and therefore seem cultured and interesting. The orange edition of *Last Summer in the City* by Gianfranco

Calligarich, *Answered Prayers* by Truman Capote, *Hotel Pastis* by Peter Mayle, *A Little Life* by Hanya Yanagihara, *All Fours* by Miranda July, and a massive, clothbound Slim Aarons coffee-table book.

My mind cycles around Aimee. Disjointed visions of my life with her in it. Imaginings of her as an adult.

I keep looking through the store. There's a selection of match jars, a few ceramic vessels, incense holders, a handful of Moleskine journals, a curation of restaurant pens, vintage barware, candles.

"Ugh, I love this one," I say about the third candle I smell. Then, after the fourth one, "This one too."

Kiera sits up. "To be clear, you picked *everything* out. You do the shopping for the place."

"*What?* That's *so* fun!"

She smiles, furrowing her brow at me. "You're effin' and blindin' about it all the time."

"Does that mean I talk about how great it is?" I ask, knowing it probably doesn't.

"No, it means you love to *bitch about it.*" She says the last part in an American accent that rivals the insulting quality of my Irish accent.

"Why do I do that?"

"I've no idea. You literally get to travel on the dime of the owner, Fia. You go round to anyplace she thinks, picking up nice trinkets and bringing them back here."

I touch a tea towel, crisp linen with an embroidered crescent moon and stars. It says *Reaching for the Moon* in dusty blue thread and a mid-century font.

"That seems like a dream job."

"It is, trust me. Half the time I tow along with you. It's all been delightful, but for the one nervous breakdown."

"Nervous breakdown?" I ask, alarmed.

"A wee one."

"Mine or yours?"

She points at me.

Should have known. "Why?"

"It was in Italy. We went to an old movie theater where they were show-ing *La Dolce Vita,* and afterward you had a right fit."

"That's—what was the fit about?"

She sighs. "It's a bit hard to repeat now, considering everything you're telling me about how you're a movie star in your real life and all. But you were upset because you thought you'd given up. When I say upset, I mean you were yelling down the alleys of Rome. We were a little overspritzed, possibly. I think it was the heat that got to you. You were insisting that your life was too small, too . . . um. Provincial."

"Provincial—"

"Like in *Beauty and the Beast,* that's right."

"I wasn't singing though. Please lie to me and say I wasn't singing."

"No, no. Nothing as bad as all that. You thought you belonged some-where else."

I gnaw on my lip for a moment and then say, "Well, that's embarrassing. I mean, it wasn't *me* me, but still."

"Nah, it's not embarrassing. We're friends! You've seen me tear through three party-sized bags of crisps in one sitting and I've seen you lament your existence in front of an audience of Roman tourists."

"Eating a lot of junk food is hardly on the same level. Although that is a lot."

"Well, you were also there for me when I tried to squat and pee on a long walk home from a party once but filled my shoes instead of the grass. And the time I accidentally called my boyfriend *daddy,* not in a hot way, that was a fun one. Or the time I was at my other ex-boyfriend's mean parents' house and tripped, only to spill hot Bolognese sauce all over a chair that cost more than I've ever earned. I could keep going."

"And I could listen to it all day." I laugh.

"Did I tell you about the one who kept his toenail—"

The bell sounds above the door and we both turn and see a tall figure come in, sleeves of his sweater pushed up to his elbows, a bit of mud on his boots.

"Cillian," says Kiera. She looks to me, and then he does too.

I cannot explain the physical reaction I have when I see him. My chest feels hollowed out, my hands begin to tingle, and heat rushes to my face. It's all the feelings I'd expect when seeing someone I have strong feelings for, only I don't know him. And I've never had this feeling. Not ever.

"Hi, Cillian," I say.

He nods, his lips forming a straight line. "I need some of those crisps everyone's obsessed with."

"Speaking of the crisps in question," she says to me, then reaches for a bag on the shelf. They look expensive, with soft matte turmeric-colored packaging and a single graphic of a potato. Beneath the image, it says *Butter Cheddar Thyme & Sea Salt.*

"Is it for you?" asks Kiera, standing up.

"No."

"Who's it for then?"

At first I think it's a silly question, but then remember this is a small village, and she probably *does* know whoever it's for.

"Doesn't matter," he says. "I also need something to drink. Something with bubbles, I guess. Round thirty quid."

"Oh, big spender, suddenly," says Kiera.

She would die if she knew how much Grayson Gamble spends on bottles of wine. He doesn't even really like it, and yet he has a fully stocked, climatized wine cellar.

Kiera goes over to the sparkling wine section and grabs something, bringing it over to the register. Then, comprehension seems to dawn on her. "Tell me you don't have a date, Cillian."

He sighs. "Can you ring me out please?"

Her mouth falls open and she scoffs before saying, "That'll be fifty-five."

"I said thirty for the bottle—how much are those crisps?"

"Five."

"So . . ."

"Yeah, I'm putting on an arsehole tax."

"You're going to buy a bottle with my money later, aren't you?"

"Well, that's what you get, coming in here buying snacks for your date with someone else in front of our Meggie!"

He shakes his head. "There's nothing going on, Kiera. Not that it's any of your business." He glances furtively at me.

"None of my business." She shakes her head. "Would you be wanting a bag then?"

"Yes, please."

"Wasteful," she says, shaking her head again before handing it over to him.

"Thanks a million, Kiera." He looks at me, only briefly letting his eyes catch mine. "Meg."

"Cillian," I say, barely audible.

On the way out the door he stops and says to Kiera, "Last time I get you cheese after the kitchen closes."

And then he's gone.

"Miserable little pox," she says.

"You're a good friend."

"I know. It's hard because he's such a good man, but it's my duty as your friend to hate him."

"A great friend." I look in the direction Cillian went. "Poor guy. Can you tell me what happened between us? Cillian and me?"

I could do with a break from mentally obsessing about Aimee.

She lets out a deep breath and then reaches under the counter. She brings up two empty wineglasses. They look the same as the ones from the photo. I had noticed the slightly angular bowl and very thin stem. "I think it's time for some wine training at the cruvinet. We don't usually drink at work—not much, anyway—but if this doesn't call for it, I don't know what does."

She comes over and starts on the far-left end with a pinot gris.

"This one has notes of lemon cream, a bit of rosemary, goes well with delicate fish, blah blah blah." She hands me my glass and then we clink.

"Cheers," I say.

"Cheers indeed. Okay, so, Cillian. God, this is so odd that you don't know. I feel like I'm recapping an entire television series so you can jump in and watch when I *remember* seeing every episode with you and you deny it ever happened. All right, okay. So."

I sip from my small pour of wine. It's very good. "Mm. That's delicious."

"You and Cillian first met when you were in school. You got here, and you didn't know anyone yet, and you used to go read at the coffee shop. He passed by you all the time, and thought you were pretty. Then one Friday night, you went to the pub when the café was closed, and you started reading there instead."

"Sounds like I had a real wild college experience."

"Oh, you did, some, but you were a bit of an introvert before Aimee got here. And before you met me, of course, and I helped pull you out of your shell." She twirls her hair and then says, "You're welcome for it, by the way. Let's move on to the Torrontés. A bit dryer, notes of chili pepper and lime."

I've never been called an introvert in my life. But when I picture what I was afraid of when I stayed home in Florida instead of coming, it was that I would be too shy. That I am only confident in my comfort zone, but unlikely to thrive in a bigger pond.

As I often do, I tried to do things the easy way and found myself doing them the nearly impossible way. Don't get *off* the couch to fetch the glass of water on the table five feet away; bend inelegantly over the arm of the couch instead, tugging on the coaster beneath the glass and catching it before it falls. I could have gone to Avalon, instead I went to LA.

I take my sip. It's even better than the first. "Okay, so I was at the pub."

"You were at the pub, he was your bartender that first night—his mam, Marcia, owns the pub, by the way. You two got to talking, God knows about what—probably something about how Hemingway is overrated or some such pretentious shite. Anyway, you started up all innocent-like at first, you were both too shy to make a move. It took ages, my God, Aimee and I were dyin' for you two to get together. You both had these ridiculous puppy eyes for each other. You were always trying to get us to go to the pub instead of any parties or anything like that. You used to have him come fix things at Surrey House when you and Aimee lived there—"

"Aimee and I lived at that house together?" I asked.

"For years, yes. Fia owns it. Charges you nearly nothing. You both stayed there until Theo. But that's another story. Okay, so he'd come over and fix things. He'd ask for your help buying Mother's Day presents, you'd help him find shoes that didn't make him look like an old man. I've never seen two people more obsessed with each other or more blind to it. You were in complete denial about each other. It was madness."

"I mean, it's also kind of cute," I say.

She rolls her eyes and pours another splash of wine, this time the Chablis from the third spigot. "It sounds cute now, but for me as your overly involved pal, it was *exhausting*, I'll tell you. Anyway, so then you finally, after four *bleeding* years of this, you go out to dinner. It was him who finally made the first move. He asked you to be his plus-one at a wedding in Dingle and you shared a room. Believe it or not, you still didn't do anything, but you stayed up all night talking. I actually remember that you had some kind of amazing-sounding chicken fried rice and ate it in the backyard of a pub, oh what was it now—O'Sullivan's! Yes, and there was music that night, you said. Then you had espresso and beer from the hotel bar and sat outside until the sun came up."

"Aw, that's so nice." It sounds like something out of a fantasy. "But are you serious, four *years*? I mean, that's a little insane."

"It was like you both knew it would be the real thing when you got together, so you were both in conniptions every time it got close, afraid you might feck it up."

"So how did it finally happen?"

"Ah," she says. "Well, one day after he broke his collarbone—"

A shiver runs through me, involuntarily. Aimee broke her collarbone on a ski trip when she was twelve. The scar had always given me chills.

"I know," she says, "you can imagine what it did for his already gruff exterior. So he broke his collarbone and his dad, you know, being a doctor and all, was ready to take care of him, but then you said you would play Florence Nightingale for him. So he's lazing on your couch, absolutely banjaxed on painkillers, and then right in the middle of *The Notebook*, which you were so generously airing for him, he told you he loved you. He said you two were like Noah and Allie and that you ought to be together forever."

My mouth falls open and then I shut it in a pout. "That's adorable."

"Yes, but then he fell asleep about five minutes afterward and slept for fourteen hours. Woke up the next morning without any memory of it."

"Oh my God."

"But it was fine, because you told *me,* and I decided enough was enough after the donkey's years saga, and I told him what he'd said. You two finally talked, and then you were together for two good years."

"Two years? That's a long time." To someone like me, who has usually freaked out around that time.

"You had wee breakups in between, you'd bicker and then throw the baby out with the bathwater, be apart for a few days, and then go crawling back to him."

I hate hearing about myself. "And he always took me back?"

"He made you beg sometimes, just to keep a bit of his dignity, but yes. Always. Then around the two-year mark you broke up and it stuck. You freaked out."

Ah. "Okay . . . why did I freak out?"

I feel like I could guess.

"Oh, you know." She pours us more wine. "You were afraid of living some humdrum little life. You didn't want to become a wife and a mother and then forget you ever had dreams."

"Huh."

"Yeah. I mean, I get it. Lots of people don't want to keep a small life."

"What about you?" I ask.

"Me? I lead an almost delusionally contented life, me. All the rushing around, hustling and bustling—not for me. I want good wine, good food, and some good sex. Until I tire of sex in my old age, and then I'll care about some good orthopedic shoes and say endearingly inappropriate things to my young, fit masseuse."

"Sex right up until the orthopedic shoes, huh? Then no more."

"No more. I'll be tired then. Okay, so you broke his heart, and then about six months ago, you got back together. It seemed like things were okay. Great, even. Always the bickering, but in a cute way. And then out of nowhere, it seems, you broke up with him. Again. I don't think anyone thought it would happen again. Least of all him."

"Sounds like . . . I mean it sounds like a mess."

"It is. But I tell you, I've never heard one of you say a bad word about the other. You were and are obsessed with each other. Always taking up for each other, helping each other out. You're too scared. You're always threatening to leave, saying you want to move somewhere like London or New York or . . ."

I catch where she's going and say, "Or LA."

"Yep. Everything seemed perfect. Then suddenly everything was over. I don't know what happened. You'd been acting weird for about a month, anyone could see it. You told me nothing except that the breakup was for real this time. Cillian is a wreck, poor thing. Puts on a brave face."

"This is appalling," I say, my heart clanging in my chest for Cillian. For me.

A phone rings and we look at each other.

I run across the place, only barely managing not to drop the wineglass. I get to the phone and see the screen.

It's Aimee.

CHAPTER SEVEN

The phone almost slips out of my hand as I try to answer. When I do, I'm afraid it's too late, that she may have disconnected.

"Hello?" I ask, then glance at my screen to make sure I didn't press the *End* button.

"Hey," she says.

Holy shit.

That one word. That one syllable. Her voice sounds so familiar and so *the same* that it feels like a glass of water after a trek through the desert. Such a relief that I'm afraid I might choke on it.

She always had this cool, raspy voice that I envied. Whenever we filmed ourselves as teenagers or recorded for no reason on GarageBand, and we often did, she always came across like young Stevie Nicks and I sounded like preteen Kermit the Frog.

"What's up?" she prompts.

I can tell she's annoyed.

I glance at Kiera. She's chewing on her thumbnail and watching me anxiously.

"Can we meet up?" I ask.

She sighs. "What is there to say, Meg?"

So much. So, so much.

"To be honest, I don't know why we're fighting and—this would be easier if we got together and talked."

My nervous system is electrified. It's like I'm a teenager talking to the boy I'm crushing on, but a hundred thousand times more intense.

"I'm too busy to think about doing that right now. I don't have the energy. We've talked about everything and I don't want to go back through it again, I'm not . . . I . . . don't want to . . . yeah, I guess I don't want to."

Those words crush me, and I have to remember to keep breathing.

I'm torn. It will sound too fantastical to remotely try telling the truth. I mean, it's beyond belief to even me. But I can't accept not seeing her, obviously I can't.

"Meet me for a coffee or something. As soon as your mug is empty, you can go. I promise."

I cross my fingers for the lie, an old habit clearly brought back by the fact that I'm talking to my teenage friend for the first time in over a decade.

I would sooner tie her to a chair than let her go after only one cup of coffee. Especially with the way she drinks any liquid put in front of her. We once got Frappuccinos and snuck them into the movie theater, and her straw was sucking whipped cream off the bottom of the cup before the title credits had rolled. She was drinking a *venti*. I mean seriously.

"Fine," she says. "One cup. Tomorrow. I'll meet you at Joy's, yeah?"

"Okay, what time?"

So eager.

"Well." She sighs. "You'll probably want to do something like noon."

"I probably will?"

"Unless you've magically become a morning person."

I don't want to wait.

"There's no chance you want to come down to, uh"—I search for the memory of the name—"Dinner Party like . . . right now, is there?"

My stomach feels oily as I wait for her answer.

"Ah come on, Meg, I've got the kids and Theo will be home any minute. We have *very different lives*, remember?"

I don't know quite what she means, but she could not be more right. Even so, I'm a little stuck on the fact that she says it in a way like she's quoting *me* back to me.

Also, *kids?* I'm like a cartoon doing a double take way, way too late.

"You have *kids?*" I accidentally blurt.

There's silence on the other end of the line, and I see Kiera looking mortified for me.

"Okay, that's very funny, Meg, but—"

"No, sorry, bad joke." I shrug at Kiera who is blushing a hard Irish red at the secondhand embarrassment. "Tomorrow it is," I stumble, "and noon sounds good. Unless earlier is better. I can do whenever."

She's also right about the fact that I never used to want to do anything before noon. But to see Aimee I'd wake up at the crack of dawn. I'd do anything. Even if I wasn't used to rising painfully early and running on fumes these days.

Besides, I must be jet-lagged, but adrenaline or pixie dust or something else has me feeling awake and raring to go more than usual.

"Noon it is. I need to go to the market anyway."

"Okay. I'll see you then."

"Right, see ya."

I can't bring myself to hang up, so I let her do it, leaving the phone at my ear for a few seconds extra to linger in the moment.

Eventually I take it away and stare at the screen. The contact photo, as I noticed briefly when I saw her calling, is an old photo of us. One I do remember. Us in my bedroom in front of my collage wall where I'd pasted magazine cutouts of all the movie stars and characters I wanted to be. We're in our cast T-shirts from our high school's production of *Brigadoon* and I remember the night well enough to recall that it was when we developed our truly revolting habit of pouring melted cheddar cheese and butter over microwaved popcorn.

"What did she say?" asks Kiera.

"We're meeting tomorrow at Joy's? At noon? Where is that?"

"It's the coffee shop I mentioned. It's just that way." She points behind her, a left out of the shop. "You can't miss it."

I let out a breath I feel as though I've been holding since I answered the call. "I can't believe I'm going to see Aimee. I can't believe I have to *wait* to see Aimee."

"I thought you said everything's good with her in your *other life*." She puts quotes around the last words, blue eyes narrowing at me. "Why are you so eager to see her? Crippling codependence, or are you not telling me something?"

I hesitate a second too long and then say, "The codependence one."

"For a great actress, you're a terrible liar."

I roll my eyes theatrically, though flattered by the part that was a compliment. "The point is, I'm seeing her tomorrow."

She nods. "Well, that's good. I'm glad she was willing to see you."

"Why is she so *mad* at me? Was it really that bad, whatever I did?"

"I don't think you *did* anything." She shrugs. "I think you two don't get on anymore. I told you."

I want to tell her this is impossible, but know that strangely I have much less information than she does.

Kiera tuts and comes over to me, seeing my anguish, and puts a hand on my shoulder.

"Why don't you put on some music you like? That always makes you feel better, eh? Maybe have some chocolate?"

An uncharacteristic urge to cry gives way to laughter.

"What's so funny?" she asks.

"You sound like you're talking to your doddering old grandmother or something."

She nods stoically. "It does feel a bit like that, doll, yes."

I put on an old Nat King Cole album, reinforcing the role, and spend the next while wiping down every surface, cleaning all the glass, and re-smelling all the candles.

"Looking Back" starts up and I try not to listen too hard to the lyrics. If I do, I might feel like crying again.

"Do I have money?" I ask. "I seriously want to buy one of these candles."

Buying stuff has always been a good coping mechanism for me.

"Don't," she says.

"Why not?"

"I'll show you later. It's about closing time anyway, so I'm going to count the cash drawer, which should be easy since Cillian was our only customer today."

"Is it always this slow?" I ask.

"Sometimes, but it doesn't matter much. Fia's as rich as God and this is a fun little hobby for her. Plus we do lots of events in the back and we sell a lot around the holidays and weekends."

"Who works when we're not here?"

"A couple of college kids. Whoever needs a part-time job. There's always someone looking to pick up a shift. All those starving art students."

"Wait, did you say closing time?" I look at the clock on the wall. "I feel like we just got here."

"That's right. Why do you think I've worked here so long? Hours are longer on the weekends, but then everybody comes to the tastings and things and it's sort of a fun atmosphere, so it's all right. Sometimes Danny, my brother, comes and plays the guitar."

I can hardly see how I would ever complain about this job. Given where I come from and how busy and stressful my life has been lately, this has felt positively meditative. But I'm probably looking at it through Holiday Goggles. Seeing everything as if it's some sort of utopia, when in fact, it's simply a welcome break from the norm.

"Ah well. All right, the *Brilliance* finale is on soon and I have sweatpants to get into and snacks to put in bowls, so let's move it. I placed an order next door for some shepherd's pies, we can take them home and toss 'em in the oven to keep them warm. But more importantly, it's time to find out if you're really having a psychotic break, or if you truly are from another planet."

"Not another planet. Same planet."

"Time travel then."

"Same time."

"Another— Feck it, let's go."

CHAPTER EIGHT

I t starts raining on our walk back to the cottage, so we run-walk the last half mile, Kiera holding our bag of food gingerly, and then burst inside and turn on the space heater immediately. It may be June, but it is Ireland. A shady little house on an overcast day still gets cold.

Maureen reacts with enthusiastic tail wags and licks when we arrive, reminding me that I'm supposed to get the dog back to Cillian. But then she nuzzles my neck and gives us a sweet whine and I decide that one more night of kidnapping her can't hurt. I let her out, and she does her little routine before coming back in. I feel bad for leaving her home all day, and resolve to walk her in the morning.

It's very clear that Kiera has been here a lot. The first thing she does in the kitchen is crank on the old oven and put the pies on a tray. She then pulls down a large yellow porcelain bowl from a very high shelf and dumps the butter-cheddar chips into it. From another high shelf in one of the few cabinets, she pulls out a copper wine chiller and puts in the bottle of Pét-Nat she brought from the shop. From the selection of mismatched, clearly thrifted or inherited dishes, she picks out a small sky-blue plate, and shatters a bar of sea salt caramel chocolate onto it.

All the while she sings along with the Kate Bush album she put on.

"I'm going to build a fire," I say, not sure what else to do, and thinking it would be cute.

"Ooh, lovely," she says. "The new you, I suppose."

I have a pang of guilt and for a moment I can't figure out why. Then I realize it's because I'm secretly wishing that it were Aimee here. Not Kiera. Even though there's nothing wrong with Kiera. She's great, in fact.

It's just that I've missed Aimee so, so much. Aimee and I could change in front of each other, pee in front of each other, rage in front of each other, be excited in front of each other. I went to her for advice and to vent and she came to me for the same thing. It was never one-sided.

Another memory flashes in my mind, long suppressed.

We were fifteen, and I had gotten dumped for the first time. The boy was named Dickie, which I was somehow able to take seriously. He had bright green eyes and straight, post-braces teeth. He played baseball and wore the black-and-blue Burchell Hawks gear 90 percent of the time. We had been official for two entire weeks, and then he'd broken up with me because another girl said yes to homecoming *faster than I did.*

I was obviously heartbroken, particularly because he had called my house phone and done the dumping in a matter of ten seconds. My parents were out at dinner with some friends, so I ran to Aimee's house unannounced and rang the doorbell. Aimee answered and half an hour later we were in the backyard eating pizza ordered by her parents and drinking Sprite over lots of ice (she had a machine in her fridge, unlike us) from Tervis tumblers. I cried and cried, as I used to do so often, then she made me laugh, and I felt better.

It's so strange to imagine crying in front of someone so easily now. Unless I'm filming, I *never* do. I get the urge often, but I never let it happen.

I take a match to the newspaper I've put under the careful pyramid of logs and watch it erupt in flames.

I'm getting pretty good at this.

"Oh shit, the flue," I mutter to myself, remembering in time.

"All right, I'm going to borrow some comfy clothes. Cool?" says Kiera, walking into the bedroom.

"Cool!" I say with a little too much enthusiasm, making up for any involuntary unkind thoughts. "I'll change too." I dust off my hands and stand in front of the hearth, where a fire is now roaring.

I follow her and pull open the wardrobe, grabbing for a specific hanger.

Kiera pulls a big T-shirt out of the small dresser, singing, "*The hounds of love are hunting*" in a low Kate Bush imitation. She stops when she sees me. "What's wrong?"

I point limply at the wardrobe. "It's hard to explain."

"Give it a go. But I swear to God if you tell me Narnia's back there—"

"No, no." I laugh. "I was getting something to change into and somehow I knew exactly where these would be."

"You wear them constantly. I'm not surprised. It's muscle memory."

"Yes, but my muscles have *different* memories."

There's a silence between us as she decides whether or not to humor me and my wild story.

"Right." She looks at the ratty old sweatpants. "Did you still have them in your . . . other life? And keep them on a hanger like a psycho there too?"

"Yeah, that's what's so bizarre—the holes and everything are in the same places." I hold them up. "It's spooky. Like, what, no matter what I would have worn them in the same way? I don't know. It's weird."

The part of my mind that has still in no way accepted everything that seems to be going on screams, *NO SERIOUSLY, WHAT THE FUCK IS HAPPENING?!*

The other part of my mind, the weirdly chill part that has adapted and can't help but keep living, walking, breathing, eating, sleeping, says, *We Sliding Doors-ed ourselves, that's all; it's totally cool and normal. These things happen!*

"Well, if you've worn them in two different lives it explains why they look like such shite. They are comfortable, I'll give you that," she says. "Good to know that in any given world, you still wear those hideous things. No wonder you can't be talked out of them."

She reaches into the wardrobe and pulls a pair of bike shorts down from the top shelf.

She takes off her jacket and button-down, her side to me, undressing down to her bra. She's clearly not self-conscious in front of me. For a moment I think it's unusually comfortable, but then remember that she saw me three days ago, two days ago, yesterday, and today.

It's only me who's known her for a matter of hours.

It's funny, too, because I was just fantasizing about how perfect my friendship was with Aimee, and all the while it seems to be the kind of lived-in relationship I have with Kiera.

"It's available to stream in ten minutes," she says, shimmying into the shorts. "So if you've got some script you're going to write out for me to read after, you'd better get started."

"Oh, shit, I totally forgot. Yeah—paper and pen?"

"I'll get them while you change. Shall I pour you some wine?" she asks, walking out of the room.

"Yeah, that would be amazing, thank you," I call after her.

"You got it," she says from the kitchen. She starts singing along with "The Big Sky."

I put on a tank top, as I'm a little warm, the humid and rainy air feeling different now that I, myself, am dry and have built a fire. I flip more carefully through the clothes here, looking for familiarity. It's strange. There are few things I know—things I would never throw away and have in my other life as well. Some well-worn cast T-shirts from high school. An old *Jungle Book* nightgown I bought when I was unquestionably too old for it at age sixteen when my mom and I went to Disney World. My dad's old Levi's jeans from the nineties.

I touch the old, faded denim and shake my head at the bizarreness of it.

Seeing these things reminds me that I had meant to call my mom today in the waking hours. I consider doing it now, but I *have* to see *Brilliance*. I send her a quick text instead.

sorry about the early call!

I mean, at this point it seems pretty confirmed that these people fully know me and that no one is playing a weird, elaborate prank on me. Still. Calling my parents, having them explain in more detail what my life has been like up until now—it'll make it feel more legit.

"Eight minutes 'til showtime, and you're not saying a word *or* having the light on while we watch, so you'd better crack on."

I laugh. I love the way Kiera is willing to commandeer what is not her home for the sake of a TV show. I'm the same way. Whenever a new episode of something like *The White Lotus* is on, I need everything to be perfect. Snacks, drinks, vibey lighting—it all has to be *just so.*

"Thanks," I say, seeing the Moleskine journal on the table with a Pilot G2 pen. "You know, this is my favorite pen in real life too."

"This is real life to some of us, love, but yes, it's a very good pen."

I give an apologetic smile and she cheerfully blows me off.

I open the journal. "A whole new journal? Are you sure I should write in it? It feels sacred."

Now a look of kind exasperation flashes on her face.

"First off, it's *yours.* Second off, you've got a whole lot of them over there."

She points at a bookshelf, where there are at least twenty more.

"Do I keep a diary or something?" I ask, thinking that would be incredibly useful.

"As far as I know, you buy a new one every time you get a good idea or read something about gratitude journaling, then you either don't write in it until you think the idea is fully baked, not wanting to waste any pages, or you write in it for about seven pages and then never touch it again. Then you need a new one the next time you have a good idea, since the other one's already sullied."

My mouth curves in a weary twist. "I seem like a lot of fun."

"Oh, it's endearing," she says with a loving shrug. "The candles, on the other hand, are out of control."

She opens up a cabinet, and out pours the pungent—but nice—scent of about thirty candles. It's the source of that scent I smelled when I first arrived.

"What the hell?" I ask. "I'm like a hoarder of nice ideas."

"I don't know the story with those candles, exactly," she says. "You buy them because you love the scent, then you never want to waste them so you burn the cheap ones from the supermarket."

"Oh, come on," I say. "You're joking."

"Hey, you're preaching to the choir."

I stare at the candles. What is *wrong* with me?

But as I think about it, I realize it's not that far off from me in my real life. My therapist once told me I have a *scarcity mindset*.

"Here you are," says Kiera, putting down a glass in front of me.

"Oh."

"What is it?"

I flush a little, embarrassed by my knee-jerk objection. "Nothing!"

"No, go on, what is it?"

"I thought it would be in a wineglass. I usually . . . I'm sorry, this is great." I shake my head, truly baffled. "God, what's wrong with me? I've become a total asshole! In *every reality!*" I slap my hands onto my cheeks.

"You've a bit of a stick up your arse in your *real life* as well, don't ya?" asks Kiera, hands on her hips.

I have no words for what an idiot I feel like. I don't even *care*. I'm just *used* to it back home. Home where I'm used to agreeing with powerful producers that the *nose* on this *Sancerre* is *truly divine* and that it's *so much better out of a Zalto*.

I admire her for not getting activated. For not being sensitive. Instead, she manages to look amused.

"I'm sorry," I say.

"Not hurting my feelings," she says. "They're your glasses, after all. You used to have them fancy ones from the shop, but they broke. These are safer for us all, believe you me. The last time one of those nice ones shattered I was picking microscopic shards of glass out of my foot for— Okay, only five minutes left, get writing."

"Shit. Yes. I'm on it."

I'm suddenly going weirdly blank. I only have a few minutes. She's going to watch the whole episode either way. I'll do the end scene.

I scribble down a bit of the setting. The big rolltop desk, the ferns in the corner, the large velvet couch. The piano.

I write down the lines I remember, knowing that it might not match up completely, but hoping I can at least show a little insider's knowledge that helps me prove myself.

It wasn't my fault you left. That was your choice.

You couldn't accept that you were wrong; you forced me to leave.

I blank on the rest of Kim's line. I end it with a scrawled *etc.*

No.

That's my line. Well, that's not going to convince anyone. Why couldn't this have been an episode with one of my many indulgent monologues, instead of it being one of the *sneaky* ones, which had me lurking around corners and standing with dramatic lighting at the tops of staircases for the first twenty-five minutes?

Kim's next line: *You were too damn proud to hear me,* I write. That's not quite it, but I can't put my finger on why. I keep writing. To listen maybe? I put that too, in parentheses with a question mark.

Then me.

Proud? If there's one thing in my life that I'll look back on with pride, it's this.

I write out the direction then, how I shoot her right in the chest. How Kim—or her former character—collapses against the piano. Then I walk over to her and pull off the diamond necklace.

My line.

I'll think of you every time I wear it.

Her only line I remember for sure: *You bitch.*

Maniacal laughter, etc., etc.

We've filmed so many episodes that my brain has this—suddenly inconvenient—tendency to completely delete the past scripts to make way for the imminent new ones. It's lucky I remember this much. I probably would have come up empty on a monologue, ending up scribbling *something about revenge?* as the specific lines escaped me.

"Okay, pencils down," says Kiera, settling into the couch with her enormous bowl of chips. "Hit the kitchen light, if you will."

It's only when I do it that I notice that the room is slung with twinkling fairy lights. Behind the books on the bookshelf, with the tchotchkes, even in the kitchen. I used to decorate with them when I was a teenager. And it does make a room cozy. I'd *never* do that now. Grayson's house is all expensive lamps from Rove Concepts and retro-inspired, brand-new pendants from Schoolhouse. The mood lighting is mostly smart bulbs that are set to very specific timers and have very specific routines. He got a guy who does the Hollywood Bowl to do the lighting design. Sometimes they don't work, for some unknown reason, and I end up moving through complete darkness until I find a blessedly analog lamp.

I sit down on the couch. I'm actually excited to see the episode. Or maybe nervous is a better word. It seems unimaginable that it exists without me. Not because they can't or shouldn't make the show without me, but because I've been on it since day one. There's never been an episode of *Brilliance* that I wasn't on. Even those few episodes where I had no lines and only sat staring catatonically out a hospital window because I fell off of a sliding library ladder at the Montgomery mansion, only a white bandage wrapped just so around my perfectly curled hair to indicate some sort of injury. Kind of like now, where I have only *an entire other life* to indicate that something is wrong, but I seem generally fine. I don't even have a bandage.

The episode plays out now basically how I remember, but with some strange differences. It's Bizarro World *Brilliance*.

There's the first scene at the coffee shop with the teenage characters having their homework and hot chocolate flirtation. The character who plays my sister shows up at her husband's office and confronts him about an affair. Daphne—now played by Kim instead of me—stands in a hall, eavesdropping to hear her grandfather saying that the money is all gone. Daphne then runs off to tell her lover about the money when she overhears a conversation between him and her *sister*, who are having their *own* affair.

Then there are the filler scenes. The *Downton Abbey*–esque subplot with the middle-aged butler and his younger protégé and would-be lover, where they clean the tires of the vintage Rolls-Royce and try not to give in to temptation. The scene between the server and her boss, who both want the same woman but are *also* fighting temptation between each other.

The scene at the bank where the teller removes a safe-deposit box and admires the handful of diamonds within it before glancing surreptitiously around and putting them away again. I said that scene was stupid and served no purpose but to ham-fistedly remind the audience that there are diamonds at the bank, but I was overruled.

I try to tell Kiera this, but whenever I open my mouth to speak she glares at me.

At the first commercial break, she says, "I don't care if you're a time traveler or whatever, *I* have been waiting for this finale for ages and you will not spoil it for me, or I'll put those treasured pants of yours straight into the fire."

"I'm sorry! You can't imagine how weird this is."

She gives me a tolerant look, then does a zip-lip gesture.

I nod, mirroring the gesture back at her. And then in the next segment, I find myself speaking along with one of Daphne's sister's lines.

Kiera stares daggers at me, then at the next break says, "Bloody hell, this is like watching *Titanic* with you."

I refill her wine as an apology and then say nothing else as I sip my own.

It's funny—I'm remembering now that Grayson and I had a fight about wineglasses early on in our relationship. I was drinking some expensive Chablis out of a coffee mug and he called me a rube with no taste. He said it like a joke, but I really didn't ever do it again.

Huh.

I look back at the screen and see the slow camera zoom on the gun at the small of Kim's back.

"This is it," I say. Kiera inhales deeply through her nose beside me and I hold up a hand and whisper, "*Sorry!*"

Jordan Levinson is indeed playing Velma, Daphne's long-lost friend from equestrian camp. She crosses in front of Kim. Kim makes a different choice than I did—she doesn't get tearful. She looks villainous and deathly serious.

It actually sort of gives me chills. I always thought she was good.

"That wasn't my fault. You chose to leave." Her voice cracks.

Velma stands in front of her and stares her down. "That can't be how you remember it."

Dammit. Dammit *dammit.* The lines *are* different.

"I—" starts Daphne.

"You what? You could have stopped me. You wanted me gone."

"Oh my God," Kiera mutters beside me. She is quite literally on the edge of her seat. "I knew it."

"That's not what I wanted," says Daphne.

"Then what do you want?" asks Velma.

The camera shows the gun again. Daphne's fingers play with the trigger, shaking a little. Then—

She pushes the gun under the pages of an open book and steps away from the desk.

"No!" I say out loud.

This time Kiera doesn't shush me, because this time she also said, "Oh my God."

"I think you know what I want," says Daphne.

Wait a minute. Wait—

The camera moves to an angle between them, each of the women's faces on one side of the screen.

Daphne reaches for the necklace around Velma's neck, fingering the diamonds.

Then with the intensity of a jump off a cliff into uncertain waters, the two of them suddenly move forward, their lips catching each other's. There is then a hot and heavy make-out session.

The credit music starts as the camera moves off, showing that around the corner, the man who plays my—I mean Daphne's—lover lurks in the dark, watching them. His eyes shift to the gun on the table, and the screen goes black.

The credits roll as the muted saxophone theme song—a clear rip-off of "Careless Whisper" that has now become iconic in its own right—begins to wail.

"Damn," I say, my eyebrows up and mouth agape. "That was a much better twist."

"*Jesus,* I knew they were going to do that—there was all the weird talk about horse camp and— Wait." She shifts to me. "Better twist? I take it that wasn't the same as in, eh . . ."

"No. That was actually much better."

She goes over to the table to pick up the Moleskine.

"A lot of it is close enough, I think!" I say. "The setting of the room, all of it—the gun! But like I said, I guess they wrote it differently with a different actress. They were always changing stuff. I should have known it wouldn't be the same without me."

She starts to read and I start to think.

Why was it different with me? Maybe I didn't have chemistry with Kim or something. But that's not fair; I *would* have if I'd been told this was a possible storyline. Maybe in this reality, it's enough to save the show from the Hollywood guillotine. Plus, there are no major queer characters, all relegated to utility roles, an oversight that has been noted by everyone, including the cast.

I think over the two scenes. It's got to be close enough to the scene to prove it to Kiera, doesn't it?

The meaning of some of the lines, the words—they were close enough.

Watching the episode, more than anything so far, feels like the real, tangible proof that I don't exist. Meg "Meggie" Bryan exists, and she exists here in Avalon. Lana Lord is no more than fiction.

I set out to convince Kiera, but I think I really convinced myself. This is really happening.

"Wait, what time is it?" I say suddenly, looking out the window.

"Just after ten?"

"How is it still twilight?"

My heart starts to pound. I can't take any more strange details and right now *everything* seems suspicious.

She shrugs. "Always like that this time of year."

"Really? How have I never heard that? I knew it about—"

"Should I read this or not?"

"Sorry, yes, go ahead."

She laughs and shakes her head.

When she finishes reading she looks up at me.

"What do you think?" I ask. "Do you believe me?"

She sets it down. "Look. I told you back at the doc's house. I believe you believe it. I know we came up with this little plan so you could prove your story, but I don't need you to do that. You're my friend, I told you."

I get up and let out a frustrated groan. "Why did they have to *rewrite it*? I mean, I said the gun! The piano! The fact that the last scene *is* Kim and Velma?"

She makes a face.

"What?" I ask.

"I don't want to do this! It makes me feel like I'm quizzing you."

"Tell me why that isn't proof enough," I say, pointing at the journal where I wrote my lines.

"Well, you've hate-watched every episode with me, and frankly a monkey with her own G2 pen and a Moleskine could have predicted all that. It's my favorite show, sure, but that doesn't mean it's *good*. No offense to the other you, 'course."

"None—none possibly taken, because it would be way too confusing a rabbit hole to take that personally." I let out a sigh. "I really wanted to prove it to you."

"Well, to be honest, that's exactly what you said would happen in the finale when we watched last week's episode. What you wrote there? That was almost word for word your prediction."

CHAPTER NINE

I have a restless night's sleep that night. It's somewhere between the wakeful Christmas Eve feeling I used to have as a kid and the panicked, anxious feeling I get before an early flight or an audition. Any dreams I do have are about missing my alarm clock, but mostly it's the sort of semiconscious rest where I spend the entire night aware of the passing time.

It's not the worry over accidentally sleeping through our meeting time—even I can't sleep past noon, and I haven't since I had mono as a teenager. It's the fact, of course, that I'm going to see Aimee. I honestly don't believe it will happen. But the proof will be in the intergalactic pudding.

It's hard enough to believe I heard her voice. It keeps ringing in my head. Impatient and irritated, so the romance is a little marred by that. But still. It's her.

When I do wake up, I expect to see Kiera, who slept on the pullout mattress in the sofa with Maureen. She said usually we bunk in my room together, but since I'm *having the world's longest moment of confusion*, she decided to sleep out there.

Instead, there's a note on the table.

G'mornin' Crazy! Visiting round my mam's today, but I'll be back to-night. Doctor's orders. Maybe some Indian takeaway for dinner? Xx, Kiera

I set it down, feeling grateful that she's coming back. It's a little weird without her here. At this point it feels like it would be easy to float off into the clouds of Cuckoo Land, but her presence makes me feel tethered.

I look at my phone. It's ten.

I put Maureen's leash on, thinking I really ought to get her back to Cillian soon, and then take her for a walk.

Avalon is really gorgeous. I can't stop marveling at the power of the quiet. No shrilling emergency vehicles, no one shouting conspiracy theories punctuated with "and that's what they want you to think!" on a street corner, no metallic revving of power tools, no cars whizzing by at fifty miles an hour. The streets aren't littered with disused office chairs and mattresses. I'm sure there are times when these things (some of them anyway) might be heard, but it's clear that here it is at least rare.

I'm starting to feel like the city has been psychically draining my energy every day and I didn't know it. Not even to mention the pressure of my work and the scathing hatred of the internet. As I look up at the sky, smell the fresh nature around me, and walk down the winding roads, I feel like maybe this is what I need. That even if this is all a hallucination, it's because my mind is desperate for a break.

All I can hear is my own Reebok Club Cs (well, they're my other me's shoes, but that still counts as mine, I think) on the ground, Maureen's trotting paws beside me, the wind in the grass and trees. I haven't missed my constant stream of newsfeeds or podcasts. Of course, given everything, my mind is busy already and doesn't need the extra stimulation, but honestly it feels like *even* given everything, I am still more relaxed and untroubled than usual. What does that say about my quality of life?

I let Maureen lead me, it seems we have a path we like to walk, and eventually she guides me home, where I feed her and then glance at the time. No rush. As eager as I am to see Aimee, I can also appreciate the fact that I don't have to dash anywhere.

In LA, my routine is a dry, hurried, but boring part of the day, including celery juice and a slow scramble of unseasoned egg whites (if I'm not intermittent fasting), an upsetting number of vitamins and supplements, followed by an hour on the Peloton and sometimes a soak in the cold plunge tub (hell) or a few minutes in the sauna (better hell).

But here, I put on some music, find some Greek yogurt in the fridge, and top it with granola. I make a cup of coffee, add the fresh cream I find on the top shelf of the fridge, add a few pumps of vanilla syrup, and sit down to go through the pictures on the phone. My phone. The one filled with proof of another life I might have led.

It's strange. It's kind of like an ultra-curated Instagram feed of images guaranteed to catch my interest. Lots of food, drinks, and selfies. People and places I don't know but I can see why I took a picture. There are lots of Cillian and Kiera.

I click on a video. It was taken at the pub—the doctor might have been right that I am there too much—and it's a slow zoom on Cillian behind the bar. When he catches me filming, he looks irritated, but in that somewhat adoring way of his that I'm coming to recognize. "Cut that out," he says from the distance between us.

"What?" comes my voice, feigning innocence. He gives a casual wink and then takes someone's order. "He's so hot," I say.

Then I recognize Kiera's voice in the background saying, "You two, I swear."

I watch it twice more. I agree with other-world me. Cillian is *so* . . . ugh. Hot isn't even the right word.

I sit back, drinking my coffee and sliding through more pictures. It looks like such a good life. So warm and filled with love and friendship and laughter. And maybe I'm focusing too much on it, but *food*. Real food!

But where is Aimee?

I think for a moment, and then open the Hidden Photos folder. It needs my Face ID but then it unlocks. In it is a treasure trove.

It feels a little like invading someone else's privacy to look.

As I predicted, there are a fair number of nudes. Not that many, but some. I look pretty good, I decide, though I can see that I used some unfortunate photo editing in some of them. I mean, even in LA, my waist isn't *that* small. I inspect them all with strange fascination.

But it's not only nudes that I wanted to hide. It's also a lot of normal pictures of Aimee, of me and Aimee, of Kiera and Aimee. And then of a couple of kids that I assume must be hers.

It's a thrill to see her life go on past nineteen, but also terribly melancholy. This is the life she was supposed to live. I know it.

There she is with a toddler on her lap and a glass of champagne in her hand, a tray of chipped ice and oysters in front of her, water and blue sky behind her. Then another where she feeds the little girl a bite of buttered bread and she strains in her mother's arms.

They and several others from the same day are geotagged in Galway.

An odd feeling creeps in as I see the photos. It's not like a memory, but I can deeply imagine the sense of being there. The breeze from the water, the briny taste of the oysters and that cucumber mignonette. The warm bread with the soft butter. The weight of that kid on my own lap, the way her fingers would grasp at my hair and pull, but in a nice way.

Then there are a million pictures of that child and another playing in a grassy backyard. There's one of me with them both. I'm in loose jeans and a sweater, my hair up in a messy bun, and I'm smiling and holding my arms open as the little girl runs toward me. That one is from a few years ago. And it was taken nearby. It's probably at Aimee's house.

It's tempting to follow the map and go, but I can't do that. I know I shouldn't. It's only another hour and a half now. I can wait. I've waited this long.

Seeing Aimee and her family—and me—in a variety of settings I've never seen her in is like a strange dream. Snowy Avalon. Summery Avalon. Coastal Ireland. At the pub, in unfamiliar home kitchens, in a grocery store I've never seen.

When Aimee and I discovered the existence of Avalon, it was in a pretty unmagical way. There used to be this website where you put in all the things you wanted out of a school and then it gave you places that might be a good fit. I used to spend *hours* on that website, in a way I never have with dating apps. Fantasizing about who I might *be* has always been more interesting than fantasizing about who I might be *with*.

One weeknight, Aimee was over for dinner and to watch the most recent *Twilight* movie with our moms (we had already seen it, but they hadn't). They were downstairs drinking wine and making spaghetti and salad and garlic bread and talking about *Real Housewives*, par for their course. Aimee and I were in my room on my computer, dreaming of our future and playing on that website. We were debating, in important tones, the value we put on class and campus size, on- and off-campus housing, in versus out of state, whether we wanted to take on loans or not. In-state, each of our parents could pay for. But it also meant staying in Florida. Out-of-state opened up the whole world.

One of us said something about *the whole world* and that's when we realized we weren't even looking out of the country. And that's when, after factoring in small class sizes and a focus on acting, we came upon Avalon.

We did a lot of saying, *wait . . . wait . . . wait, this is perfect . . . wait . . . ohmigod . . .* and then we went downstairs to tell our moms everything we had learned about this place that was so perfect that if we didn't go then we would literally die, could we please go, please, please, please?!

The answer, like with any out-of-state college, was that if we were willing to get our own financial aid, we could do whatever we wanted.

We took this as practically being accepted on the spot and jumped up and down and hugged each other, then couldn't stop talking through dinner or the movie. So our mothers released us from girls' night, probably with some relief that they wouldn't have to ensure more lip-biting from Kristen Stewart, and we went upstairs to go look up everything the internet had to offer on the town and the school.

That's pretty much how it carried on for the rest of high school. Only, thinking about it now, I can see that Aimee's excitement tapered off after a while.

I shut the phone screen off now, closing the portal to all the memories I would have if this life were mine. I suppose there's a chance my *real life* isn't real, and Kiera and Jim are right—I lost my memories and replaced them with a fantastical story. That would explain why I know to find my sweatpants and the whiskey, and why I have such a deep feeling of fondness for Kiera and Cillian. It would also explain why, when I had come across a photo of Maureen begging happily beneath the table, there was a faint recollection or essence of a memory of how it felt to be sitting in this little front yard and playing cards late into that night with Cillian. The taste of the chilled red wine in my juice glass, the sight of his ropey-muscled arm reaching across for a salty olive from a glazed terra-cotta bowl.

Yet, isn't this the mental trick I use to act? Pretending has always been my best ability. I don't use the power for evil; I'm not manipulative. I don't lie. But I can fool people. It's what acting is. The problem is that I can also fool myself. It's why I can get so easily into character, building a world around them in my mind. It's why I'm so good at denial. It's why I'm afraid I'll pop my clutch and lose my mind one day. I feel as though—or I fear as though—the curtain between reality and imagination is whisper thin in my mind.

I put down the phone and coffee, rubbing my eyes and feeling a little drained by all the information.

I get up and go over to the journals to look for clues there too. But as Kiera said, most are empty. Some are empty with missing pages, and some have my scrawling handwriting. In one, I wrote the things I was grateful for each day—looks like I kept it up for about nine days. Some entries include:

1. *Cillian*
2. *Kiera*
3. *Butter*

1. *Maureen*
2. *Avalon*
3. *Having a TV*

1. *Short work shifts*
2. *New lotion*
3. *Meditation*

I roll my eyes. Not at meditation, but at myself for writing it. I feel absolutely certain the other me did it weakly for about ten minutes max, for a handful of days, and then wrote it here. Who is she kidding.

I know that because *same.*

Most of what I was grateful for were people and things. Some I completely stand by, like *not having to wake up for school ever ever again.* But some days other-me couldn't come up with a third thing.

I find myself wanting to fill all the empty journals with gratitude for this mysterious other life.

The intoxicating smoky green smell of the town, the way beer really tastes different, how young and real I look with the plumpness of my cheeks and softer curves, and my *God,* how incredible cream and butter and salt and sugar taste. How it feels to eat like a human. This cottage. The little totems of my past, proof that there is more to time than *now.*

Also, the friendships. I know the other me listed Cillian and Kiera, but how did she not exclaim at the miracle that it is to have them? And that they're so special! How was she not more specific, to not mention Kiera's patience or wit, her ability to set those around her at ease (I've not seen her around many other people, but I can tell it's who she is). How funny she is, what a serious blessing it is to have someone over who knows their way around *your* house? Her nonjudgmental way of talking about past moments of embarrassment.

And Cillian! How amazing the food was that he made. How he has to be a really good person to get dumped and then make grilled cheese and soup for the girl (he thinks) who dumped him. And then to go on being nice enough to walk her through a panic attack. Plus, how completely special it is for a guy *that hot* to not be a total fuckboy.

But I know why she didn't go into it. The same reason I didn't in LA when I tried gratitude journaling. Because it was too hard to see my world for its good when its bad was so much louder and more distracting.

There's nothing else much in the journals, only some disjointed ideas, so I put them away and realize with disgust that I haven't bathed since LA. I'm starting to be able to smell my own hair, and that's an emergency.

I'm amazed by the delightfully warm water and strong water pressure. There's fresh eucalyptus hanging from the shower head and all kinds of fun shampoos and conditioners and hair masks.

I kind of wish I could stay in here all day, not figuring out what's going on in my life.

In my lives.

I get out, blow-dry my hair, put on a little makeup, and spend about twenty minutes dithering over what to wear. I finally pick a pair of jean shorts, a clean white T-shirt, and a denim button-down over top.

I look at my phone again. Still too early to leave. I shoot Aimee a text.

Still on for noon, right?

She doesn't respond right away, and it reminds me that I want to call my mom, who also didn't answer my text.

I press her contact and sit on the edge of the bed with my foot tapping as I wait for her to answer.

My heart falls as the phone rings and rings. Then I get her voicemail. She sounds a little more chipper in this version than in the one I'm used to.

Hi, you've reached Char. Leave a message or send me a text and I'll get back to you as soon as I can. Thanks!

Char? My mom's other voicemail says, *This is Charlotte Bryan. Leave a message after the tone.*

It's so bizarre. I leave her a message.

"Hey, it's Meg. Everything's fine. Please call me back."

I then dial my dad. More ringing. Then his voicemail.

This is Kyle. A long pause. *Leave a message.*

That's the exact same voicemail. Somehow, that tracks. Same old Dad.

Why is Mom's so different? She seems happier.

I never think of my mom as *unhappy*. Neither of my parents. They go out to dinner more than once a week, see movies I can't believe they think they'll like and then call me on speakerphone to talk about how much they hated them; they save up to buy new patio furniture from Costco, and then post pictures on Facebook (hellscape) of it so all their friends with names like Nancy and Rod can leave comments like *Looks great! Love, Nance* and *That'll get the job done!*

I mean, maybe they're not exactly thriving. My dad has wanted to leave his job for over a decade and my mom is always booking vacations and then canceling them, deciding the money could be better spent on things around the house. New patio furniture, perhaps.

Who needs Cabo? We have a new grill.

I've been telling them to leave that old house for years. Telling them to get *out* of godforsaken Florida. I've offered to contribute financially, but the very idea offends my mother and no amount of arguing could change her mind.

I don't leave a message for Dad. He never listens to them anyway. He famously leaves his phone behind wherever he goes, defeating the entire purpose of having it.

Finally, it's time to leave for Joy's. I bring Maureen since Kiera mentioned that there's lots of outdoor seating at the coffee shop. Having a dog with me always makes me feel better. Even a dognapped one. Possibly *especially* a dognapped one.

But still, it's a tense five-minute walk for me.

I'm excited, of course, to see Aimee. It's been a long time. And the last time I saw her, things were ugly, and then things were catastrophic. But I'm also afraid. Afraid of letting her down. Afraid that she'll let *me* down. Afraid it'll feel weird and awkward. Afraid to tell the truth when it's so impossible to believe.

Maureen has no sense of the drama, however, and is just happy to be here.

Joy's is a little red coffee shop with an adorable storefront and open paned glass windows with boxes of flowers beneath them. My heart pounds as I scan the faces of the patrons, looking for hers.

She's not here.

A few people nod or wave at me in polite neighborly recognition. I do the same, then go up to the counter.

The barista is a nice-looking guy with double ear piercings and a broad smile.

"Hey, Meg!"

"Oh." I glance at his name tag. "Hey, Freddy."

I'm pretty proud of myself for my visual detective work, but then he laughs and covers the name tag. "Oh, I know. I forgot mine at home again, so I had to wear Freddy's. You want the usual?"

Damn.

I think Kiera was right to tell Cillian's dad the truth, that I don't know who anyone is. Partly because he's a doctor, and partly because it's ridiculous to walk around trying to fake it constantly. But it would also be a little absurd to lead a small interaction like this with, *Hi! I will not be able to engage in this conversation and meet your expectations of familiarity. Please treat me like a stranger! K, thanks!*

Honestly, I should get my own name tag that says all of that.

"Usual sounds great," I say.

"Three quid, love," he says. He has an English accent, not an Irish one, I realize.

"*Three?*" I ask. I'm suddenly afraid my *usual* is a glass of unfiltered tap water, which is about what that dollar equivalent would get you in LA.

"I know," he says, "they raised the prices a little. But it's temporary! Only 'til the cup dispute is figured out."

In this world, apparently I'm up on whatever *the cup dispute* is.

"No, it's fine," I say. "Here, keep the change."

I hand him a five. I found a little card wallet at the cottage, saw that it had my own identification in it, and not a lot of money, but some, tightly folded and slid in. If looking at my other me's nudes had felt intrusive, this felt like outright stealing.

He hands me back the change. "Keep it," I insist.

He gives me a weird look and I remember I didn't look up the tipping culture. "Ain't gonna argue, am I?" he says, pocketing it, then starting in on my drink.

While I wait, I turn around, checking that Aimee didn't walk in while I was ordering, and then go out onto the little flower-filled patio to double-check. My drink is ready when I come back, so I get it and then I realize that I should go wait out front—and that's when I run smack-dab into her, almost spilling my chai all over her white linen dress, Maureen's leash tangling between our legs.

"Hi, Meg."

CHAPTER TEN

———

"Aimee."

My ears ring. I'm dizzy. The sunshine is suddenly as blinding as the flashbulb on a paparazzo's camera and I feel clammy in the damp air.

Aimee. Here. Alive. And because I just bodychecked her, I know she's solid, real, and in front of me.

The samenesses of her feel like tiny, unexpected shocks as I notice them, rolling over me one after the other. Her height. Her hair color. Her eye color. Simple facts you'd put on a driver's license, and yet these are the things that strike me the most. She has loomed so large in my memory that it's odd to see her stand at merely five foot six. To see her hair color, that particular honeyed brown that feels specific to exactly her and only her. The color of her eyes that's somewhere between blue and green—a color our poetry teacher in college once called *the color of pond scum*, which made us laugh until we almost peed ourselves. Seeing her irises again for the first time in over a decade, I realize how true and darkly beautiful a description it actually was.

It's the humanity of her that catches me off guard. It's kind of how it feels to meet a celebrity in real life. Like a *real* celebrity. An icon. I've seen Cate Blanchett's face a hundred times, blown up to the size of the IMAX screen at the Chinese Theatre in Hollywood, so it felt strange when I stood next to her willowy figure on the red carpet and saw her narrow wrists and the little, almost invisible blond hairs on her arms.

Aimee, here. Now. Not only alive, but in perfect condition.

I understand nothing about how or why this is happening, but I am certain, in this moment, of one thing.

I will never leave this life.

Whatever the rules are, I don't care. There is no wizard or Ghost of Christmas Anything here to explain the lesson I'm supposed to be learning, much less to wrench me back to my life. Why would I ever go back? This isn't exactly a Sophie's choice. Everyone in my life is in this one, except, heart-shatteringly, Dido. I can't really think too hard about her; it makes me ache.

But there is no reason, no power strong enough on earth to move me from this spot. And by that, I mean Avalon. Because of course, I'm not going to forcibly sit in Aimee's lap whether she likes it or not, smothering her with the relief I feel. I can't be Lenny with the puppy here. I have to give her some space if I want to have her at all. But nothing is going to take me away.

"You okay?" she asks. "You look sick or something."

This brings me back to reality. Or as close as I can get right now.

"I'm fine. Did you order?"

My words come out rushed and mangled, like I've forgotten how to string the letters together to make words.

"No, I'll go now. Here, can you put this at the table?"

She hands me her jacket, an ease between us that has managed to stay despite her evident anger with me. Then she goes to the counter. Not-Freddy is there, chatting with some girl he's clearly into.

I take her in some more, now noticing the things that are not the same.

Her hair, tied up in a tortoiseshell clip, is long like always, but she has curtain bangs. Of course with her hair texture and natural wave she probably didn't even have to work for them to look that perfect. She's still lean and strong-looking, but I can tell somehow that she's had kids. There's a sturdiness to her, a sure-footed gentleness in her posture and her steps that feels more like that of a woman than of a young girl. Her body looks like it's endured time, lived through more. Like she may have nursed her kids, but also taken up running.

She returns after only a minute or two with a mug of black coffee and a packet of raw sugar.

"This is like my third cup today and I still feel exhausted," she says. "The kids have been a nightmare, so I've been up at five a.m. every day. Hi, Maureen."

She scratches the dog behind the ears.

"Does Theo help?" I ask.

"With the kids?"

I shrug, regretting the question. "Yeah."

"He's their father, Meg. It's not help."

"I didn't mean it like that, not like they're your responsibility and that he . . . you know, that's not what I meant." My whole body is hot. How is *this* where the conversation went? It feels like the kind of misstep you have on a date with someone you don't know at an overpriced cocktail bar in Echo Park while the server cringes and drops off your Negroni riff and you want to go home.

She takes a sip of her coffee and I notice the smile lines by her lips and eyes. She's always had those pretty, petite features. The kind that age well and keep you looking young unless you get up really close, and the age shows maybe a little earlier than on someone with fuller features but it doesn't matter because you're so damn pretty.

"So, what did you want to talk about?" she asks.

Nerves undulate in my core at this question. It's time.

I have thought a million times about what I'd say to Aimee if she were alive, but I always imagine the middle-of-the-conversation parts, where we're already fully in the swing of hashing things out. Never have I imagined the part where I have to get the ball rolling.

And until recently, I never pictured this conversation starting with a science fiction premise of interdimensional travel or whatever.

"Why aren't we talking?" I ask. Keep it simple, stupid.

She sighs. "What do you mean, *why*? Like I said on the phone, I don't know why we have to do this again. We've talked. It's over."

"What's over? Us? Our friendship?"

She looks away, and I can tell that it's a reluctant confirmation.

I feel sick.

"It's not that our friendship is over. That's not what I meant. Things are different now. And that's okay."

She's not getting clearer. I tap my teeth together, deciding quickly what to do.

Then I jump.

"Okay, I'm about to tell you something really weird, and you'll have to try to trust me for a few minutes. Can you do that for me?"

I have her attention. "Go on."

"As far as my memory is concerned, I haven't seen you since we were nineteen."

I start there and lead as slowly as I can into the reality of the situation, telling her almost the whole truth. I tell her about her not getting into Avalon, then me deciding to stay in Florida. I tell her about Grayson and Dido, I tell her about *Brilliance*. I tell her about my birthday party and booking the house. I tell her everything that's happened to me in Avalon since I got off the plane.

When I finish, she takes a long pause. I can see her wheels turning and I feel a pang of affection for her. I always admired how smart she was. She came up against any problem or question as if it was the start of a genuine mystery. Her hair straightener would stop working and she'd bite her bottom lip, furrow her brow, and consider, like it was suspicious instead of annoying. And, often, she'd fix it.

"That's not what I expected you to tell me," she says finally.

"Yeah, I know. Kiera thinks I've lost my real memory and that the whole LA actress thing is something I dreamed up. The doctor thinks I'm having some sort of disassociation and that I need to keep up with my general routine. And if it was as simple as not remembering where the local gas station is, or even as simple as not remembering anything about my life, then yeah, I'd assume it was some sort of bizarre amnesia. But it can't be. I'm telling you."

"That's really the only thing that makes any sense, though, isn't it? I mean, I guess people *do* get amnesia. It's insanely rare, but it's real. And you're sure you didn't hit your head?"

"No. I feel completely normal, except everyone here seems to think I live here, and I am completely certain I have an entire other life. There are actually no words for how sure of that I am."

Though my certainty is starting to weaken.

"You must be . . . I mean . . . you *have* to have had some sort of injury that you don't remember. And like, your brain made up a story?"

"Yeah, maybe," I say, to be agreeable. "But I am telling you, I know every detail of my real life. I remember boring days like when I had the stomach flu and stayed home pounding Pepto-Bismol and watching reruns of *Vanderpump Rules*. And how, actually, I've met like half the cast members. They're always at The Grove. And that, I mean, I know my way around LA. I remember making tacos like five years ago and forgetting to buy the tortillas and having to go back out to Trader Joe's and the parking at the one on Hyperion was a total mess as usual. I remember every rejection at every audition. I remember awful sunburns and bad haircuts and weird dates and—I don't think it's possible to make all of that up like this."

"This is really weird," she says.

My heart lifts. "Do you believe me?"

There's a very long pause in which she stares at Maureen, who has now settled onto the ground with her head on her paws.

"I mean . . . it would be really fucked up for you to lie about something like this. That doesn't seem like you."

She looks thoughtful, considering me. I am glad that for all my short-comings in Avalon, the people here don't think I'm also a liar on top of it all.

"I know it sounds insane. But I watched the finale of *Brilliance* last night, and it was so strange to see it because they changed some stuff, and in the end—"

She covers her ears and makes *la-la-la* sounds. "I haven't watched it yet!"

I actually laugh. The power of a spoiler is interdimensional, and yet still, after a huge HBO finale, *The Cut* will do a post with the twist in the headline.

"Okay, okay. But watching it—I mean, I know how cold that soundstage is when the lights are off and how boiling it gets when they're on. I know about the director's personal life. He has a secret boyfriend, and he takes the Rolls-Royce offset sometimes, which he is not supposed to do but he used to date the transport guy so he gets away with it. Also, that secret boyfriend is named *Bob* which is kind of the weirdest part of any of it. Bob."

There's a flit of amusement in her expression, but it's gone as quickly as it came. "I don't know."

"The only thing that makes sense is that I am in the other version of my life. The one where I went to Avalon instead of staying home with you when you didn't get in."

Her cheeks go pink and I scan her eyes. She drops her gaze and then clears her throat.

"There's a lot of quantum science stuff going on. I was listening to an episode of *Radiolab* about it this morning."

"Really?"

"Well, not exactly this—it was about how they're able to see molecules sort of do two things at the same time. It's complicated, but I think there's no limit to how unknowable our universe is."

"I forgot what a science nerd you are."

She laughs, and my heart breaks a little.

"I like learning." She takes a sip of her coffee. Then she gasps and puts a hand to her mouth. "Oh!"

"What?" I actually look behind me, thinking there's a man with a nail-skewered baseball bat or something.

"The fortune teller."

My heart rate slows again. "Yeah. *Usually, there is only one line—*"

"But you had two."

We had obsessed over that whole experience after it happened. I had been afraid to bring it up at first, since Aimee's reading had been so bizarre, possibly dark, but she wanted to talk about it too. We were bewildered, scared . . . and then eventually it became a big joke. Though I always suspected that we both knew it wasn't that funny.

I nod and then shake my head. "It's insane. You're the only person who might remotely get how weird it is, especially because of that woman."

"The way she was after I showed her my hand." She shivers. "It freaked me out. I thought I was going to . . . like . . . I don't know. Eat some bad sushi and croak or something."

I feel suddenly as though I'm skiing down a mountain, hearing the snow creak ominously, an avalanche threatening. I need to get off the hill.

I nod again as normally as I can and then pretend to think Maureen is eating something off the ground. When I come back up, Aimee is looking at me.

"Do you swear to me that this is true? To you, anyway?"

I feel such a heavy relief I am almost nauseous.

I hold up my pinky. Until now, I had forgotten about our pinky promises. How had I forgotten that?

"I swear everything I've said is true."

Her eyes dart between mine for a moment, searching for the lie. She's always been able to tell, but luckily, everything I've said *is* true. And her psychic radar for lying doesn't do as well on obfuscation.

"You're telling the truth," she says, holding up her pinky, sounding sure but also baffled.

As soon as she touches me, I feel an electric shock course through me at its strange familiarity. We must have hooked our pinkies together a million times for a million promises.

Pinky swear you think this outfit doesn't look ugly.

Pinky swear you'll call me after.

Pinky swear you really heard him say that.

Pinky swear we can leave the second it gets weird.

Pinky swear we'll never stop being friends.

She releases before I do, and then looks down at her mug. "I need another cup of coffee."

While she gets it, I work on breathing in deeply and trying to steady my shaking hands. It's Aimee. It's her. Walking. Talking. Being suspicious. Asking things. Drinking things. It is beyond surreal. Beyond weird. It's more than my feeble human mind was ever meant to comprehend.

Although, that's how losing her had felt too.

She comes back after a few minutes, this time with a frozen drink. "I need the sugar," she says.

I remember then how she has always been about sugar. It was always her comfort. When she felt sad or off, she would get a bag of Sour Skittles or a milkshake and then she'd feel better.

"So, what am I doing in this other life of yours?" she asks. "Am I famous too?" She smiles, teeth on her straw.

Everything comes crashing down. Like that avalanche was being held at bay by a twig, but begins to fall the second that it finally snaps. I feel my blood run cold and I wish that I could wade back in time to a few seconds earlier. Back to safety.

I've felt that way before.

I don't know what to say to Aimee.

How do you tell your friend she's dead?

CHAPTER ELEVEN

I take a sip of my drink, stalling.

"Oh, Jesus, I'm not dead, am I?"

The elderly couple at the nearby table pause in feeding their enormous Great Pyrenees pieces of muffin to look at us.

I'm so shocked that I choke on my drink, laugh, and say, "*No!*"

She eyes me and says, "Oh my God, I'm dead. Am I fucking dead?"

I don't know why I don't use the opening to tell her the truth. Maybe it's the panic in her eyes—she must really believe my story—or the fact that, as usual, I can't say it out loud. I am not only used to living in sunny California; I'm also used to living in denial.

Instead, I kick into acting mode and give it my best shot. "God, how morbid. No, you're not, you're fine. You live in New York and you're directing plays on Broadway. Not huge ones, some smaller stuff, but I mean, it's Broadway. I only acted weird about it because . . . we don't see each other all that much."

There's that difference between lying and acting. The distance between the two is a hair's width, but it's there. And right now, I am lying.

She narrows her eyes. "Like what? What am I directing?"

"You did *Three Tall Women* recently. That one was pretty boring, if I'm honest, but it was well done. My favorite one you did was *Death of a Salesman*. You had Jake Gyllenhaal and Scarlett Johansson in that one. That's probably the biggest . . ." I feign a scroll through the fictional repertoire. "Yeah, that's the biggest one you've done."

I watch her mental gears turn. "Okay. That's pretty cool, then. But that"—she drops her voice—"*fortune teller*. She said you had two lives. So that came true, right? But what she said to me . . ."

I will my cheeks to stay unflushed. "Well, to be fair, she didn't really say anything to you. We don't know what your palm said."

We look at each other and I know, just like back then, that we're thinking the same thing. That we do know. Only difference now is that I'm sure.

"Maybe she just hates theatre," I say.

Aimee snorts her drink at my joke. She nods. "Could be that." She clears her throat. "So why were you so frenzied about meeting up with me then? If I'm around in your real life, then it shouldn't be a big deal, right? Even if we don't see each other that much." She looks suspicious.

"When I found out that this version of me messed things up, I wanted to fix it. That's all."

I can tell that she's reluctant to believe me, but she acts like she does anyway. Maybe because it sounds nice and she *wants* to believe me. Maybe because she simply doesn't want to argue about it.

I wonder if it sounds intoxicatingly appealing to her, this life I've invented. If the mother of two who sits before me feels excited and wistful at the idea of a glitzy life like that. If she wishes she could trade early mornings with kids for late salons with the literati of Manhattan.

It's a lot better than the truth.

"So, what are we fighting about?" I ask.

Her face hardens a little again and I wish I hadn't asked.

"It wasn't one thing, you know? It wasn't like you slept with my husband and now we don't talk."

"Well. I mean." I cock my head briefly.

"What?"

"Well, if your husband is Theo, then definitely not." It's meant to be sort of a dark joke, but it comes off mean, so I add, "But I wouldn't do that, even if you were with a young Robert Redford."

"Who?"

My jaw drops. "Do not tell me Robert Redford doesn't exist here."

She smiles. "Kidding."

"Oh, wow. You know, that Kiera girl has been really nice about all the things I don't know."

"What are old friends for?" She leans back and sips from her drink. Somehow, she's already on the last sip. "*That Kiera girl.* It's funny to hear you act like you don't know her. You two hang out all the time."

"You're friends with her too, right? She seems to know you. I've seen pictures of the three of us."

"Of course, yeah, I mean everyone knows each other here. We're friends. It's more like you and Kiera are friends and therefore, she's my friend too. It's not like we spend time separately from you besides running into each other or at a party or something. Been a while since I've hung out with either of you, but that's been the dynamic. It was."

I shake my head. "So we really aren't close anymore here? Because I can't imagine any world in which we aren't."

Unless, of course, death is in the way.

"We drifted apart."

"Bullshit," I say. "That's literally impossible in a town this small. If we're not friends, it has to be on purpose."

Her cheerful energy fades a little. She looks at her phone screen and says, "Shoot, listen, I have to go. We can talk more, but the kids will be out of their playgroup soon and I still have to get groceries."

I almost want to ask her if I can come, but then the idea of trying to continue this conversation while winding around the islands of the produce section stops me. Also, if she wanted me to come, she would invite me.

But I have a trillion more questions. How did Theo end up here? How old are her kids? What is life *like* here for us? What is she lying about?

How did she end up *here?* I need the confirmation.

That one I ask anyway.

"Before you go . . . how did you end up in Avalon?"

She lifts her shoulders to her ears and then lets them fall. "I got taken off the wait-list."

Aimee gives me a weak smile, and I give her one back.

"Okay." She slaps her hands on her thighs. "Now that I'm way overcaffeinated, it's time to go pick up my hyper children so we can bounce off the walls together."

"Do they have little accents?" I ask, silently agreeing to lighten the subject.

A real smile stretches across her face. "They do. It's so fucking adorable."

"Wow," I say, with a breath of disbelief.

"No kids in my other life, huh?" she asks.

"No," I answer truthfully.

She nods, and then says, "Well. Glad I'm in this one then. They're really cute."

With that, she raises a hand in goodbye, hoists her mom-purse higher on her shoulder, and turns to go.

She hesitates and turns back. "Are you busy tomorrow?"

"I have no idea. Apparently I have a job here. But besides that, I don't know. Why?"

She laughs, and then says, slowly, "It's Clare's birthday."

"Clare is . . ."

"Oh—my daughter. She's turning five. If you want to come. If you're busy, it's fine, but . . . yeah. It's at eleven. Kiera's invited too, of course. I think she knows that. No need for gifts. We'll have food and drinks and some music. It should be a good time."

It's a hint of forgiveness. I'm well aware of the gravity of the moment, even if I do want to play it cool.

"Yeah, that sounds nice," I say. "I can't wait to meet her. See her. I don't know."

She gives a small shake of the head. "Right. Okay, well, I'll see you then."

And then she's gone. I can't believe I'm able to let her go, but I have no choice.

The magnificent weight of the encounter hits me as I sit there in the aftershock. It's so big, so unknowably peculiar to have seen her again that I can hardly believe I was able to do anything but rub my eyes and gawk at her.

It's how our brains work, I guess. We come up against the strange or unexpected, and we adapt. I got used to being famous. I got used to living in California. I got used to being without Aimee.

After she died, I would chastise myself. How had I ever gone a day without appreciating her? How had I gone a single Friday night without having her over? How had I sat silently on the other end of the couch while we rewatched *Moulin Rouge!* for the thousandth time instead of putting my arms around her and demanding she never leave the safety of that living room?

I pick up her empty cup, drained quickly as was always her way. I set it down and absently slide it over the condensation on the table from hand to hand.

The answer to how is unsatisfying. The truth is . . . we live. We can't spend every moment treasuring the things we love. We still get mad at the dog for tracking mud through the house even though one day, we would give anything to have her muddy paws back on our white carpet. We still roll our eyes at our parents' needy voicemails even though one day, those recorded moments will be all we have left.

My exceptionally depressing reverie about dead parents and dead dogs comes to a halt as the woman with the Great Pyrenees suddenly appears in the seat across from me.

"Dear God—hi," I say.

"It's nice to see you two girls patching things up," she says.

"Oh. Um." I smile. "Thank—thank you, yeah, it's nice."

"Were you two rehearsing for the new play? I didn't know you were going to be in it!"

"Play?"

"Isn't it this weekend?"

"Oh, no, yeah, the play. Right. No, I'm not in it."

She gives me a kind look, and then smiles and pats the table. "We'll see you tomorrow at the party. Say hello, Bernard," she says to her husband.

"Hello," he says.

"Now say goodbye, Bernard," she adds, picking up the dog's leash.

"Goodbye, Meg."

"Bye, Bernard." Then to her, "Bye."

"Bye," she says.

The dogs briefly acknowledge each other.

Once that exchange is finally over, I wait long enough to ensure that I don't end up going the same direction as them and having to say goodbye six more times. Then I gather my things to walk back to the cottage.

Once there, I try to call my parents again, but I still get no answer. What the hell? Isn't the *child* supposed to be the aloof, unreachable one?

To be fair, my dad never answers. But my mom almost always does.

I'm actually starting to get worried. Again, we worry in my family.

I look through my texts. Before I texted her apologizing for the early call, the last text exchange was four days ago.

Hey, thanks for that. I'll pay you back asap.

And her response:

No rush

I look back in the conversation, searching for clues about my life. Some links to Sephora for products she read about; a picture of avocado egg rolls and a wine I'm sure is sauvignon blanc at the Cheesecake Factory along with the comment *wish you were here!*; and a screenshot of a conversation with my aunt about the house that they grew up in having sold again. These texts could very well be from my real life. She's one of the few people I talk to regularly on the phone, so our texts are usually pretty insubstantial but constant.

I look at my texts with my dad.

Not a lot of back-and-forth, which is consistent with the dad I know. It's mostly me sending him songs and him saying *Nice!* or *thanx.*

I roll my eyes affectionately at this. Classic Dad. The last song I sent him was "The Melting of the Sun" by St. Vincent. His response: *cool song!*

Maybe I can see what their lives are like by looking online. Maybe Mom has posted a picture of, like, healthy crackers from Trader Joe's lately with a caption like *yuck!*

But I can't find her. Does the woman who, here, calls herself *Char* not do social media in this world? I mean, good for her if that's the case, but it's not very helpful for me. I need to stalk my parents, and even with the power of the internet, I'm getting *nothing*.

I give up, and then through the window I see a group of college-age kids walking toward the town. I decide to finally see if I can take a look at Avalon School of the Arts. I should have been curious, but the fact that Aimee is here kind of wiped away any other curiosities.

I know exactly where to go, if my memory serves (not a given). I leash Maureen again and after a breezy little walk, I see it for the first time in real life.

Wow.

There it is.

There's a low stone wall that breaks for the gated entrance, which is open. A gold plaque says AVALON SCHOOL OF THE ARTS, then beneath that, FOUNDED 1792.

I watch the students coming and going, and think, feeling unusually elderly at thirty, that they look so incredibly young. Like seriously. I see bad concealer amateurishly applied to cover up pimples and gawky bodies that haven't yet filled out. In LA, every teenager seems to have the anxiety, cut-crease eye shadow, and skin care routine of a much older person, but here, they look like real kids.

They look how Aimee and I must have looked on our trip to St. Augustine. Awkward. Cute. How we must have been when we were here, in this life.

I enter the courtyard at the front of the school. There's a fountain running in the center, and benches around squares of grass, a peaceful but enthusiastic energy around the place. I hear snippets of students running lines, complaining about professors, and passionately describing the costumes of a production of *Les Misérables* they saw in the West End on holiday.

Some people notice Maureen and point, saying, O*h, puppy!* and other things people say when a cute dog suddenly appears.

I expect to feel envy or relief that I had never been one of these kids, and in a way I feel both, and in another way I feel neither.

Growing up, I never spent time surrounded by people who all wanted the same things I did. Not until LA, where none of us could really support each other since we were all squeaking by. In my college, everyone was majoring in different things and in my classes, there was only vague passion. Students who had chosen theatre because they liked it, not because they were dedicated to it.

What would it have been like to be in a college atmosphere like this, where everyone was here for their art, had to be really *great* to get accepted? And yet where it seems safer? In Florida it had been high-key as fuck, an endless loop of red Solo cups being filled with Fireball, chugging warm Natty Light in games of beer pong, and general education requirements that made it all feel like *High School: The Sequel.*

Here, I could have focused on what I loved. Love. I'm sure there's a fair share of holding each other's hair back after five-too-many shots of the cheapest whiskey they can get their hands on. I think the drinking age is eighteen. But it seems so much more serene.

I didn't really get to be challenged by acting until I was in LA, going on auditions, getting burned in trials by fire. I lived in a crappy ground-floor apartment without AC, with old, slatted windows that blocked out *no* sound, and every *day* it seemed like they were dragging the dumpster as slowly and loudly as possible down the asphalt driveway right on the other side of the wall. It sounded like nails on a chalkboard amplified through a megaphone. But my little hellhole was around the corner from incredibly historic places that made the whole thing feel worth it.

I went to a million cattle-call auditions. Some turned out to be bigger than I expected, some smaller; some wound up being multi-level marketing scams, and some felt more like porn casting couch situations. I got pretty good at figuring out the difference before driving all over town. I tried to create a presence online but my attempts felt lame and uncomfortable.

I bartended late into the night and went out for things whenever I was off, getting shifts covered whenever something unexpected came up like a callback. I lived paycheck to paycheck, going negative more often than I ever had a surplus. And my eventual big break had little to do with my hard work or talent. The only reason I am where I am today—or, was where I was a few days ago, anyway—is that I was bartending on a slow Thursday night when a studio executive came in with his friends, got drunk, and decided to discover someone.

Yeah. Pretty ridiculous.

Old men in LA all pretend they have the power to make you a *star,* but of course very few of them do. And the odds of being discovered like Lana Turner at a malt shop are even lower. But I made him my signature Cherry Cola Vieux Carré riff (Michter's Rye, Carpano Antica, Peychaud's bitters, vanilla bean syrup, and a Luxardo maraschino cherry) and it caught his attention. I didn't ignore him like I would have if I'd been in a different mood. And then he gave me an audition you usually need a good agent for. He gave me an audition you usually need a good agent and a packed *resume* for.

It was his idea for *Brilliance* to come in hot with a completely fresh star. Me.

My screen test went well—that part I can take credit for—and I got the role. Then I got a little work done on my face and went on what was, at the time, the craziest diet and workout routine I had ever heard of. We did press, they set me up with a team of managers and agents and people to tell me what to do and wear, they took over my social media, they hired paparazzi to take pictures of me doing things in places I wouldn't normally be with celebrities I wouldn't normally interact with. Including Grayson.

We were supposed to go on a few dates, just to get a little buzz going—he'd been going out with too many models and was starting to look shallow—but we ended up liking each other. I think I was a little starstruck, I mean he was *Grayson fucking Gamble*. I was so pleasantly surprised that he was nice and fun and, I guess, human that it went a long way toward making me like him. He liked me too, which was no surprise, I was putting my very best self on display. Not only physically, as I had a new wardrobe and had been introduced to many beauty procedures I hadn't previously known existed, but also I was confident. On a blissful high that my career had started to take off.

So we decided to keep seeing each other. It wasn't pure romance; we always knew it made us look good. And then, like in lots of flawed relationships, we got used to it and stopped wondering if we actually wanted it. Until, I guess, he met Elsa.

And so that's how I *made it*. A star was born. In a lab.

It's funny. People talk about nepo babies, but they forget about the blank canvases the industry picks to Pollock all over.

Maureen and I drift up the stairs and into the rotunda of the college now: a two-story hall with grand, ornate floors and walls made of gleaming chestnut wood that arch at the top, where the beams support a jade-green glass dome. It's the kind of shit you can only really build in a century like the 1700s, when architecture like this was a priority and time must have stretched on endlessly.

Two girls breeze past me, laughing. One of them is saying, "If I have to do another mime routine, so help me *God* I'm transferring!" in a charming English accent. Of course it's impossible not to think of them as an iteration of what might have been for Aimee and me. Two girls happily loathing the requirements of our fun little major.

I spend over an hour walking the halls, waiting to be told dogs aren't allowed, feeling the strangeness of being in a place I'd imagined so often. When I was a teenager, I used to fall asleep imagining this place. Imagining my foreign life. Ever since I gave up my acceptance, and particularly since Aimee died, my wandering mind has come here, to this life, to this world—a dependable fantasy as intoxicating as dreaming of a crush.

I walk past classrooms and see some of the afternoon classes where students are engaged in history lectures, public speaking practice, and, in one particularly lively class, a deep dive on Lee Strasberg.

The big stage at Avalon Playhouse is locked, and I see it's empty and dark through the small window in the door, but I do walk past a black box theater where a guy and a girl are onstage in front of the rest of their class, both gripping books rolled open to the relevant page.

He steps toward her and puts a hand on his chest, saying, "You think this is easy for me?"

She shakes her head. "No, I don't, I—"

He doesn't come in early enough, so the interruption seems false when he says, "You think I *like* being this kind of man?"

"Of course not." She sounds tearful and intimidated.

I recognize the book in the girl's hand. It's a sleepy drama about an abusive husband and his battered housewife who murders him in the end. I used to practice these scenes when I was doing auditions. I played it differently than that.

I lean on the doorframe. It makes the door open farther, and everyone turns to me when they hear it.

"Oh, look who it is," says the teacher. I know from the ledger outside that it's likely to be someone named Professor Lehman.

For a moment, I forget myself and think she recognizes me as Lana Lord. But then I remember.

"Hi," I say, putting up a quick, apologetic hand. "I'm so sorry to interrupt. I was watching. You guys are great."

"Come on in, Meggie," Professor Lehman says. She tells the class, "This is Meg Bryan, she was a student of mine. And it looks like she's stolen Maureen again."

I hear a few of them snigger and repeat my name. I roll my eyes and take a moment to think the worst of them. The old *wow, your name sounds like Meg Ryan* bit. I guess it's nice that people still know who she is, her rom-coms living on.

"Meggie was good," says Professor Lehman, head moving to follow me as I walk a little farther into the room. "Untapped potential. She never let herself break through, and then she quit acting before she got there. A shame to see a natural talent go to waste like that."

I feel a little embarrassed, then remember she isn't really talking about me.

"What did you think of the scene?" she asks.

The students shift on the stage: The boy crosses his arms challengingly, and the girl looks a little hopeful.

"It was great. You guys are doing a great job."

"No, they're not," says Professor Lehman. "It's dead! The scene is dead. We all know it—that's why we're here today, we're workshopping. We're not here to congratulate each other on how amazing we all are. The scene isn't working. Now, I'm going to ask you again: What did you think of the scene?"

I don't need any psychic memories to suddenly know what it's like to be her student.

"Um . . ."

"We don't do *um* in this classroom, Meg, you know that."

"Right." I almost say *um* again but catch myself in time. I do wish I'd had her around when I started auditioning, because I made that mistake all the time. "I think there's a way to add some depth. It's easy to say he's the abusive husband, she's the shrinking violet. The wife is scared until the end when she snaps. But there's another way to play it, where both characters' anger is present onstage, so the audience doesn't know which of them is going to snap. Right now, it's a bully pushing until he gets punished, and that's not really very interesting."

The guy looks satisfied, as if the note isn't for him. The girl blushes.

"So, you"—I point at her—"bring up your confidence and sort of"—I look for the right word—"seethe a little more, and you"—I point at him—"bring a little more fear into your performance, because that's where your character's anger is coming from. Then you both meet in the middle and you'll find a more interesting story. Less predictable."

Everyone blinks at me and I shrug a little.

"Let's run it Meg's way, from the top," says Professor Lehman, spinning in her seat and crossing her legs as she watches the stage.

Both actors look more nervous now.

They do it again, but neither of them nails it.

"No, no, no," says the teacher. "Meg, why don't you go show them how to do it? You read as Isabel."

"Oh, no, I couldn't. That's—they're doing a good—"

"Now, Meg."

Yikes.

She holds out her hand, flapping fingers, and I realize she wants me to hand over Maureen's leash. I do, then see the girl is handing me her script, but I don't need it. I've heard the scene twice, and I vaguely remember it anyway. I hand it back to her, slightly bashful as I tell her I'm good.

She smiles politely, but I can tell she hates me on a soul level. I completely understand.

My knees feel weak. I haven't been on a stage in a long, long time and screen acting is completely different.

The scene begins with a short monologue from him, and then, as Isabel, I say under my breath, "There was another way. You didn't take it."

I choose to sit at the table rather than stand, adding dynamics to the scene. Making my character look more powerful in her certainty and stability and his character, Jason, looming and desperate.

He steps toward me, putting a hand on his chest and saying, "You think this is easy for me?"

Instead of shivering and stuttering, I smile up at him. It disarms the actor and he looks unseated.

"No, I don't," I say coolly, imbuing a subtext that Isabel thinks Jason is too stupid to find anything easy. I wait until he's about to speak, thinking I've forgotten my line, then I say, "I—"

It unseats him again. "Y-you think I *like* being this kind of man?"

There's a nervousness there now. It's better.

"Of course not." I drop my chin. I am saying: *Who would want to be a man like you?*

The scene ends as he does some stage business, getting a bottle of vodka out of the freezer and chugging it before storming off. But this time he's anxious; he almost walks the wrong way off the stage. It plays.

It's kind of awful dialogue. Exactly the sort of show that makes outsiders hate drama kids: acting for actors and no one else.

The room erupts in applause, and Professor Lehman stands. "Brava, Meg! Brava!"

I laugh a little at the use of *brava*. I've missed the silliness, the pretension of theatre.

I get off the stage feeling strangely energized. I end up staying another hour as they run the scene again and again, trying to nail it. Maureen lies at my feet, seemingly never unhappy with where she is.

I sit in the audience with the other students and watch as they take notes and try, hard, to break through to the other side. To try to find the reality of the story.

When they run it the last time, the girl playing Isabel does better than I did. I genuinely get chills when she smiles.

This is why I love acting. Because it's playing. It's learning. It's on-the-spot energy that changes and evolves.

I thank Professor Lehman, who thanks me back, and then I slip out before the class is over so I don't end up in a conversation I don't know how to have with someone who thinks she knows me.

The walk home feels good, and I realize that the Avalon version of me would have done that every day of college, then taken this walk back to the cottage. What a fun, quaint routine that would have been. A lot better than declining coke in the bathroom at every bar in WeHo for the first few years of my independence. College in Florida hadn't felt like independence since it was so close to home. It would have been nice to be here, in such an insulated place, while still taking such a big gamble on myself.

I get back to the cottage and put together a plate of cheese and crackers, then go through the house, familiarizing myself, with Maureen trailing loyally at my heel. I listen to Father John Misty on the Bluetooth speaker I found in the bedroom and wonder how I ever forgot how much I loved the feeling of being onstage.

While I'm snooping through my own life, Maureen suddenly howls and starts to bark her low, sweet bark.

There's a knock on the door, and I open it.

It's Kiera, like I expected, as it's after seven. But she looks sheepish when I open the door.

"What happened?" I ask.

"I think I fucked up."

CHAPTER TWELVE

W hat did you do?" I ask, allowing her to come in.

"I told Mammy."

It's funny to me that the Irish use the names *mammy* and *daddy* so much more commonly than Americans use the equivalent *mommy* and *daddy* in adulthood. It would have been nice if I'd done that, rather than the exceedingly self-conscious transition I put us all through when I turned sixteen. My daily use of *Mommy* shifted to the sober syllable *Mom; Daddy* became *Dad*. And they both teased me mercilessly about it, each of them still signing cards and things with their original names.

"Told your— Told her about what, me? About my . . ." I twirl my finger at my temple and she nods. "Why?"

"I dunno!" she says, tossing down her hoodie. Everyone here seems to travel with an extra layer, and even in the last few days I've started to see why. The chill sets in. "She was plyin' me with French onion soup. She goes through these cooking phases," she adds as explanation. "She's on soups now."

"That's fun."

"And she's getting proper good, too. Anyway. I was there, having a chat, and I cannot overstate how *good* this soup was. It was the right amount of cheese and onions and had such a *depth*—"

I do a *hurry up* gesture, needing to know quite how serious this is. I can't see why it matters that she told her mom, but I assume it's bad.

"Right. So. Somehow in the haze of it, I started telling her about how you didn't have your memory anymore and how you had this whole idea that you were a famous actress in Hollywood and all."

"All right," I say. "But what's the problem? I mean, it's your mom. I think that's fine."

She makes a tight face and says, "You don't know me mam. Apparently."

"Well, no."

"Did you ever see that old Norman Rockwell painting with the game of telephone and the gossip?"

"Yeah . . ."

"Right. Well, the one who sets it all off? That's Kay."

"Ah."

"My mother."

"She's a big gossip, then." I remember now from my first night, Cillian said something about *bloody Kay Donahue running around unchecked.*

"Yes."

"She's going to tell everyone?"

She shakes her head. "If she hasn't already, I'd be stunned."

"Okay. Huh." I put my hands on my hips and exhale. "Isn't that kind of fine? It's not like it's a secret. Cillian's dad knows. I told Aimee earlier."

She gasps. "Oh my God! The café with Aimee! I completely forgot. I'm a terrible friend. Was it all right?"

"Yes, actually."

She raises her eyebrows. ". . . yes?"

"Yeah," I say. "She believed me and everything."

"*Really?*"

"Yeah. I was kind of surprised too, but yeah. All good."

"That woman is like a human lie detector."

"So does that make you believe me too?"

"No."

"Why not!"

"Because! It's a batshit crazy thing you're walking about here saying. I'm sorry, but I'm not as easily sold as your old friend. She's the one who's always going on about UFOs and things. But I? Am a bit more practical than all that. It's never that I think you're *lyin'*."

I let out a frustrated sigh. "I don't think I'd believe it either, if I'm totally honest."

"But like I said," she says, "I believe that you—"

"Believe it," I say, filling it in. "I know. And I appreciate that."

She goes over to the kitchen and opens a drawer, then pulls out a paper carryout menu.

It's funny, because in some way, coming to this small village *is* a bit like time traveling. In LA it's almost impossible to find a tangible menu for carry-out. And everyone orders everything on Caviar and DoorDash anyway.

She hands it to me. "Pick what you like, I'll call."

After a few minutes of perusal, I say, "Chicken tikka masala with a side of basmati."

"Should have known," she says.

"That what I usually get?" I ask, hesitant still to buy into this, even after all that I've seen.

"That's right. I suppose you want some garlic naan as well? And some raita and lime pickle?"

"Ooh, yes," I say, "I forgot about naan, oh my God, I haven't had it in forever! Raita definitely. I've never had lime pickle."

She scoffs. "You have, and you love it. You haven't had naan in forever?"

"No. Before coming here, I think the last time I had bread was like . . . I can't even remember. The only starch I ever do is brown rice, and even that's rare. I basically have to be about to pass out to have something like that."

"Sounds like disordered eating to me, if I'm honest. Like Gwyneth Paltrow with her IV of nutrients."

"Not reall— I mean, sort of. It's part of the job. It's not forever. If I get successful enough, I can . . . well, I mean, I'll always have to keep it in check."

"It's what I've never understood about these actresses. They work so hard to get recognition. Then they do. Then they have to stay skinny and beautiful all the time. And if they don't, then they're constantly having to defend themselves. That's no life, in my opinion."

"You get money." I shrug. "And you get to be remembered."

"That's true. But that's the rub, isn't it? I feel like people get famous only so that they can go into hiding and get what they really want, which is simply to have a nice life. I don't even know if the money matters that much, except that it means you can relax. And what's the point in having all that money if you can't have a good pudding whenever you feel like it?"

I open my mouth to speak but find that I have no response. When *am* I going to really live? I'm withholding carbs from myself like there's a finish line, when I *know* there isn't. She's also right that celebrities often get famous, then spend their lives trying to go unseen. Is it really all about the money? No, I guess it is the notoriety too. But still, it all feels a little pointless when it's lined up like that.

I think of my walk earlier, how much I appreciate it after so many years in a chaotic metropolis.

"You don't have to worry about it tonight, anyway," she says. "All right, I'm ordering."

A moment later, she's on the phone—like speaking to a person. Another thing that never happens in my real life.

When she hangs up, I say, "So, Aimee invited me to Clare's birthday party tomorrow."

She lifts her chin dramatically as she says, "Ah, wow. That's good, isn't it?"

"I think so. I mean, she said she believed me about the whole . . . thing, and then she invited me over there. You too."

"If this is all a ploy to get a blank slate with her and Cillian, I'd say you're one down, one to go."

"It's not!"

"If it were, it's not a terrible idea."

"Well, it's not. Also, what's the play that's happening this weekend?"

"Did she tell you about that as well?"

"No. I met some woman at the coffee shop after she left. She had a huge dog and his name was Bernard? Or, no, the husband's name was Bernard."

"Ah, Bernard and Sara. She's a busybody, but she's harmless. Mae West is the one you have to look out for. You've never experienced anything like being surprise-humped by a female dog that's bigger than you."

"Gross."

"Pfft. You're telling me. That dog happens to like me quite a lot."

"So do I not act? Even though there's a theater here and plays going on?"

"Afraid not."

"Why not? Do I suck?"

"No! Not at all."

I can tell she's not saying something, so I ask, "What?"

She moves her head from side to side and then says, "You sort of act like it's beneath you."

"Jesus *Christ*. I'm the worst."

She nods tightly. "You're not as big a dick as you sound, I promise. And I mean, I get it. It's a little playhouse, that's hardly the same as walking the red carpet."

"I am an absolute brat."

"You're not a brat." She steels herself. "You're insecure, I think."

I get the feeling it's something she's never said to other-me.

I nod. "Sounds like it. Is Aimee involved in the play?"

"Yeah, she's the director."

"Wow." So I wasn't that far off when I came up with the other fake life for her. I mean, far off in that community theatre isn't the same as Broadway, but it was headed in the right direction.

"Yeah, the show this weekend is one of her own. There's some big critic coming in from *The Guardian,* so she's hoping for a good review. She's always hoping for a good review, obviously, but if she gets one this time, and from a critic like that, then it could make her career. I think she's really nervous."

"Wow. That's huge. And what does Theo do?"

"Theo recently got made redundant and he's having trouble finding a new job."

I laugh derisively. "That feels typical."

"It's not really his fault," she says earnestly. "He's not as bad a lad as you seem to think he is." Her phone rings and she pauses our conversation to answer it.

I go over to the fridge and get out a bottle of gewürztraminer, which will be good with Indian food. I open the cabinet and consider which glasses to use, then decide to go with the same ones Kiera picked the other night. A small act of contrition for my pretentiousness.

"I know, Mammy," she's saying in the bedroom. "I told ye, please don't tell anyone! Well, what do you mean it's too late, I told you before I left not to— Well, *why* would you do that? You know Sara's got a mouth the size of a bowhead whale." She lowers her voice further. "The whole town will know by morning, and now Meg's going to be at Aimee's party with every old geezer— I know, Mam. I know you're sorry. I know. But please, next time keep your mouth shut, won't you? I know it's a bit late now, I'm talking about next time!"

I walk over with a glass of wine and she gives me a grateful, apologetic look.

I mouth "It's fine" as I sit down to give Maureen some scritches under the ears.

"Look, Mam, I've got to go— Mammy, no, don't start in telling me about more gossip, that's— No way, serious? I thought the two of them didn't get on anymore? *Really?*"

Her eyes catch on me and my look of amusement.

"Ah, Mam, now you got me doing it!" she says. "I've got to go. Goodbye— No, goodbye, Mammy."

She hangs up.

"Sorry about that," she says.

"Really, I think it'll be okay."

A while later, we're sitting outside at a little table, string lights turned on and music coming through the open windows.

"So, she's directing the play? Who's in it?"

"Some of the college kids. I think she's having a lot of trouble with them though."

"Maybe I can help out," I say. "I don't know how, but I mean . . . I act. I know about this kind of thing."

"You two haven't worked together like that in years. I'd be surprised if she lets you in. Plus, it's only a few days away, I'm sure they're in final rehearsals, no? You know better than I would."

She's right, of course.

"I'll give it a shot," I say. "Maybe I can remind her why we used to be friends. I just want to help. Even if it's just as an usher or something, I don't know."

The food arrives and we set about arranging the feast on the table. Indian is always a highly aromatic cuisine, but this smells particularly good. It tastes even better. Every bite I take, I groan with amazement at how wonderful it is.

"I can't believe you waited so long to eat. You're awfully good at it," says Kiera.

Inside, Nancy Sinatra's "Lightning's Girl" plays and I bob my head to it and sing along: *Better stop your groovin' round another rooster's hen, if Lightning ever catches you he's got to do you in.*

"I'm so happy right now."

Kiera smiles and narrows her eyes at me. "It's nice to hear you say that. Most of what you talk about is wanting to get the hell out of here. Which I can only imagine is what you were saying in Alligator Land before you came here."

Kiera takes a big bite of naan and winks at me as I kick her under the table.

"Well, you're right," I say. "I was desperate to get out of Florida. And it sounds like I was desperate to get out of here. And I'm sure you can guess how I was feeling in LA."

She nods deeply.

A breeze lifts and bends the grass toward us, the smell of greenery I can't identify and lavender I can identify in the yard mixing with the cumin, basil, cinnamon, and garlic in our food. I stretch back over the old creaky chair and look up at the still-twilit sky.

My toes grab at the grass beneath my feet. It's starting to get a little cooler out and the blades feel chilly on my skin. "That's the thing, Kiera—whatever's happening right now, what you keep calling time travel or visiting from another planet"—I smile as she nods soberly—"I can't understand why I'd ever let it end. But . . . will this go on forever? I never get back to my other life? Why would I want to, when—"

She looks at me. "When what?"

I narrowly avoid blurting out the truth about Aimee. I don't want to tell her. Or anyone. Maybe part of me is afraid it'll become true again if I utter the words.

I wish I had someone shepherding me through this strange experience.

"I feel like I'm my own Christmas ghost," I say, aware that it sounds like nonsense.

She puts her fork down. "I completely understand what you mean. You're your own guide on this journey."

"Ohmigod, yes, exactly!"

"Go on."

"You really get me."

"Best friends for years for a reason. Carry on."

I really like her. Yet another person I'm beginning to fear losing. "I don't want to leave. There's nothing whatsoever in my real life that I'd choose over this one. I miss my dog. I can't think about her. I can't. But . . . nothing else is missing for me here."

"Maybe not yet, but you didn't seem completely happy to me. Not the Meg I know."

"But this life is better. It suits me better. I'm happier here."

"The Meg I know could very well say the same thing about a life in LA."

I consider this, tearing off another piece of bread. "I just have this feeling it's going to come to an end. That I can't simply choose this life because I like it more. Maybe I've seen too many movies, but it never works like that. Isn't that the point of every story about a genie? Every morality tale? Like . . .

the old love potion thing. You can make someone fall in love with you but it won't be real. This isn't real."

"I can assure you, this is real. It's my life, you know."

It's the first time I feel like I've come up against the edge of Kiera's patience. I don't blame her.

She's right. This is real. It feels like it anyway. As solid and firm as the reality I'm used to. More so, in some ways.

I've always had a vivid imagination. How far can that take a person?

"I'm sorry," I say to Kiera. "It's confusing. I don't know how to frame it. I keep having this terrible feeling that I'm going to wake up one day in my other life. Find I've been swept off like Dorothy, and all of you will be gone. Or maybe Oz is real, and Kansas is the dream. Something isn't reality, and I don't know which it is anymore."

She looks a little relieved, like my delusion is starting to loosen. Maybe it is. I don't know.

"It's okay. I know it's a mess."

I'm afraid to know what the truth is. I'm actually hoping I made up an entire life for myself, and that *can't* be good for a person.

Maybe Kiera's right. Maybe I should trust it.

The little voice in my head makes a doubtful sound and I wish I could kick *myself* under the table.

"Can I ask you a question?" she says, scooting back from the table and crossing her arms.

"Of course."

"Why do you hate Theo so bloody much? You've never told me, but I've always thought there's more to the story than you're letting on."

"Ugh."

"Yeah, that's what I mean."

Fittingly, the song inside changes to "Boy and Girl" by Unloved.

"Okay, well, I don't know what I've told you. But, so, before they started dating, I actually"—I shiver—"hung out with him one night at his house. He played in a band and, at least that night, I thought he seemed cool. Which he wasn't. We hung out in his basement and he and his friends smoked weed and got drunk and played video games." I cringe, thinking about how cool *I* was trying to seem to *them*. "Then I lost a bet and had to smoke hash oil. I had never smoked anything in my life and I thought I was going to die. I was lying on the ground, feeling paralyzed, and they had a dog that was crawling all over me while everybody laughed."

"*God*," says Kiera. "Vile."

"Yeah. It took like three days to feel normal again, but I still hated everything that happened that night. He actually tried to kiss me, and I didn't want to kiss him, and he was really nasty to me about it and then told me he'd fuck my friend."

Kiera's eyebrows shoot up.

"I didn't tell Aimee about it because I thought she was way smarter than I was and that she'd never fall for his bullshit. I was also way too embarrassed to tell her I'd tried drugs, which we were super not into, or about the dog walking all over me. It was so awful and saying it out loud would have been . . . like, impossible at the time."

I realize as I'm saying it that this was probably my first case of major denial.

"Surely once they started dating, though . . ."

I shrug. "I was a teenager. I told her way too late. By the time I did, she told me I was ridiculous for trying to insinuate their entire relationship was about me. Which I understand. At that point, it had been a few months. But still."

"Well, that's truly villain shite."

"It is, right?"

She nods. "I know him now. I can say he loves his kids. He loves her. He's sort of boring, if anything. A normal guy who seems like maybe he was cool to his mates once, but now he's some interesting woman's husband. If that makes sense."

I clench my jaw and shake my head. "Yeah." I bite my bottom lip and stare at the ground. "Still, she deserves so much more than that."

Kiera says nothing, and when I eventually look up at her she gives me an empathetic smile. "I'm sorry. That sounds like a terrible night and an absolutely horrid thing to carry with you. Especially once she started seeing him and you had to be around him all the time."

"That was the worst of it. Then I saw him treating her the same way he treated *me* that night. It felt like *insert girl here*, you know? And then after—"

I catch myself *again*. After not mentioning Aimee or her death in the last decade, I sure am champing at the bit to tell Kiera about it. Maybe this is what would have happened if I'd truly let someone into my inner circle at any point.

"They broke up in my life," I substitute. "And then he got with some other girl and that seemed the same too. Like he doesn't care who it is. As long as there's someone there."

There's a long silence, and then Kiera says, "Well, should be fun to see him tomorrow at his daughter's birthday party!"

CHAPTER THIRTEEN

I wake up the next morning to the sound of a metallic crash.

I shoot up in bed, my heart racing a million miles a minute, and rub my eyes until I can see clearly.

Kiera tiptoes into the doorway. "Feck, I hoped it hadn't woken you."

The sound would have woken Beethoven.

"It's fine," I say. Then, smelling the air, "Is something burning?"

Her eyebrows shoot up in alarm and she vanishes from my sight.

I walk into the kitchen and see that it's been completely overturned. The faucet is running over a steaming pan, the gas stove is on but unoccupied, there's a pile of cheese grated on the butcher block, and there's been an explosion of flour. It has settled onto most surfaces like a fine dusting of snow.

"This is nice," I quip.

"I'm so sorry," she says. She actually has a swipe of flour on her cheekbone, putting me in mind of the harried women of rom-com lore who run around in a frenzy until they find a boyfriend who reminds them to take things one step at a time.

On the ground, Maureen licks up some spilled sugar. It strikes me as funny but I pull her away from it.

"I don't care about the mess! It's more like . . . how the hell did you even *make* such a mess?"

"I'm not a very good cook."

"I'll say."

"I didn't want to show up empty-handed! Last time I went to a party at Aimee's, all the other lads brought somethin' and I looked like an eejit."

"Why don't you bring something from the shop?"

"I thought it might— Well, it doesn't matter now. I was *trying* to be thoughtful."

I look at the clock that ticks from the wall of the living room. "We've got an hour."

We both survey the kitchen.

"I'll clean it up. Could you nip over and get something?"

"Sure."

Kiera glowers at her mess. "Get a bottle of something and some of those chips. We'll pay for it tomorrow. And chocolate maybe, even though she'll hate us for bringing sugar over for the children. It'll be locked, don't forget."

"Do I have a key?"

"It's on your key ring. The big gold one."

She reaches under the sink and grabs a bottle of spray and a roll of paper towels.

I slip on a pair of sneakers, grab Maureen, and take off down the village road. It's a sunny, slightly dewy morning, and I muse that Ireland's reputation for unendingly miserable weather is another one of those foreign misconceptions, or perhaps a rumor perpetuated by residents who don't want the island overrun with tourists.

There is still a dampness to the air that somehow feels alive and fresh, liberating and refreshing. Florida's humidity feels like dog breath. Southern California is mostly very dry and monotonously temperate. But this is like wading through wispy rain clouds.

Thinking of Florida, I decide to call my mom again. I feel sure she won't answer, but to my surprise, she picks up.

"Hello?"

"Mom! Hi. You've been hard to get ahold of."

"Oh, sorry, babe. We've been so busy lately. But we're getting pretty good at pickleball, and then all the rigmarole of getting here."

I shake my head. This is so weird. How did *me moving to Ireland* at age eighteen change things in the butterfly effect chain enough that my parents picked up pickleball?

"Getting where? Can we Facetime?" I ask.

I can *hear* her eyes rolling. "You know how I feel about that. But fine."

I pull my phone away from my ear and press the button. My mom's face appears.

She's the same, and it makes me want to burst into tears. Good old Mom. I want to curl up in a ball in her lap and watch old episodes of *Frasier* with her while she makes me pasta with too much butter and cheese.

What is unfamiliar, however, is the setting behind her.

A mountain carved into a crystalline blue sky, speckled with candy-colored buildings.

"Actually I'm glad we're doing the Facetime because isn't this *gorgeous*? It's simply stunning."

I squint at the sight as she pans to a beach with red-and-white-striped umbrellas and loungers, calm water reaching out endlessly to a horizon. "Wait, where are you?"

"What do you mean? We're at the hotel. Just got in last night."

It looks like she's on the Amalfi Coast. "Two seconds, Mom."

I switch out of the call and into the Find My app. If it's anything like my real life, I am anxiously following all my loved ones.

There they are. Mom and Dad are in Positano. And Kiera, Aimee, and Cillian are all less than a mile away.

"Meggie?"

"Sorry." I go back to the call. "Positano! Looks nice."

"It's heaven. Truly. So what was the call about the other day? Some brunch game? We're getting ready to go to lunch, but I have time."

"Is that Meg?"

I hear my dad's voice, and then my mom turns the screen so I can see him.

He comes into frame and I feel a warm surge of affection for him. He also looks the same as ever. Maybe a little fitter.

"How's LA?" he asks.

My mom glares at him.

"I thought you gave her the money to—" says my dad.

She shushes him patiently and looks to me to answer.

"LA?" I ask.

"Did you change your mind? When I saw you were still in Avalon, I wondered."

God, this is a tight rope to tread.

I consider telling them the truth. Just as quickly, I decide I definitely can't. She has plans. She never goes out and does fun things. She never goes to Italy. Well, maybe this version of her does, but still. I can't dump all of this on her, because realistically, if I tell her, she's going to think I've had some kind of breakdown. Then my parents would probably end up hopping on the next flight to Ireland. And as much as I'd love that right now, I don't think that's what anyone really needs. If all this doesn't begin to make sense soon, I'll tell her. Maybe I am having a breakdown, but I need a little longer to make sure.

"Listen, I know I got a little protective when you talked about going. It's just, Hollywood, you know? It's got such a terrible reputation for taking talented people like you and ruining their lives. Even when it goes well!"

I'm starting to get it. I was going to LA. To move or to visit, I'm not sure.

"I was just going to scope it out," I say, tentatively.

"Right, and that's why I shouldn't have freaked out. It would be nice to have you back in the States, even if it is pretty far still. Maybe you'd visit more!"

Ha. Try *never*.

"Right," I say.

"Are you okay, Meg? You seem a little . . ." She makes a hand and head gesture I recognize of hers that means *topsy-turvy*.

"I'm about to go to Aimee's house for Clare's birthday party, so I'm a little frazzled. That's why I canceled the trip," I improvise. "Aimee finally wanted to patch things up so I had to take her up on it."

I gamble on the fact that I've told my mom everything, including that Aimee and I are not speaking. I brace for them to say Aimee's been dead for years.

They exchange a look and then I'm certain that's what they'll say.

"Really? Oh, that's wonderful!"

"That's great," says my dad. "Tell her we say hello, will you?"

"And give those sweet little ones a squeeze from us! Oh, they must be so happy to have their Auntie Meggie back."

My cheeks sting.

"Yeah, of course." I try to think of a way to ask a question, get some more information, that doesn't make me sound like I've traveled through space and time. "So how's Positano?"

"Well, like I said, it's heaven. There's no other word for it. When Jenny and Joe couldn't stop raving about it, we decided, let's do it!"

Jenny and Joe are Aimee's parents. In real life, they're still friends too, but my mom never mentions them to me.

"Oh, you should go to Grotta Fresca, everyone loves it." I stop myself, wondering if this version of me would say something like that. I know about Positano because every celebrity and influencer goes as often as possible and comes back talking about the *amazing* octopus they had that was fresh from the sea that morning. "Instagram," I say to explain.

This works for my parents, who nod. "Okay, we'll see if we can get a table. If you're sure everything is okay, then I guess I have to let you go. Jenny and Joe are on their way over, and I need to touch up my face before we all take off. Call me and let me know what happens with Aimee."

"Will do," I say, not mentioning how bizarre it is to me that Aimee's and my parents are in Italy together. Happy. Whole. Unmarred by tragedy.

"Love you."

"Okay, love you guys," I say. "Thanks, Mom. Bye, Dad."

Before she hangs up, I see her face light up at the sight of someone else walking into her vicinity and I hear her say, "Oh, speak of the devil, I was talking—"

The phone disconnects.

A moment later my mom sends me a text.

You seem stressed. Call me back if you need, anytime.

I send back a heart emoji.

Once I get to Dinner Party, I splash my face in the employee bathroom and pick out some chips and a bottle of wine. I grab a small bar of chocolate for myself and a big bar for Aimee, toss them in a gift bag, and close up.

Confusion having built up, I take advantage of being alone by shouting, "*What the fuck is going on?*" as loudly as I can. Silence answers me. Maureen stares at me.

As I walk back, I wonder about the ticket my mom mentioned. I go through the phone to see if I can find one, and sure enough, there is a ticket from Dublin to Los Angeles. It's for the same exact time that I took my flight to Dublin from LAX.

Something clicks in my mind and I stop walking.

Maybe *this* is what happened. The two versions of me made the same, opposite choice at the same time. And it caused my universe to split into two. Is the other me there, in my world? Is she eating steak tartare at Dunsmoor and looking through her phone's contact list, marveling at all the famous names? Is she using Face ID to log into Chase, looking at the six-figure checking balance and feeling free at last? I bet she'd be over the moon. I mean, waking up super skinny, famous, and rich would probably be a dream come true.

But what happens when she hits Aimee's contact and gets no answer? I've never deleted it. Couldn't. Even though, of course, calling it would probably reach someone else now.

How long would it take her to discover the truth? What evidence did I leave in that life, besides her absence, that she is gone?

And how much would she care? I want to assume it would devastate her, but that version of me sounds so self-involved that maybe it would feel like a worthy cost for her dream life.

I have a feeling that if she is there, she wants to come back to reality as little as I do.

My stomach does an uneasy turn as I think of my own impending return ticket. I never want any vacation to end, but in the case of this trip, I genuinely don't think I can cope if it does.

When I arrive back at the cottage, Kiera has completely finished cleaning the kitchen.

"When you make as many messes as I do, you get pretty efficient at cleaning them up," she explains.

I consider telling her about the ticket that Avalon-me had, and even mentioning my own ticket back, but when I see her happily getting ready for the party, I decide I can't talk about my drama all the time. I have to be better than the me I just privately considered to be self-involved.

I then speed into *getting ready* mode, rummaging through the closet for something to wear. I land on a long lace-and-cotton dress and a pair of strappy, well-worn leather sandals. I put on the same basic makeup I would do on any other given day, surprised to see that I have gravitated toward some of the same products in this reality as in my other. Same ILIA mascara and Rare Beauty blush.

When I come into the living room, ready to go, Kiera's jaw drops.

"What?" I ask.

"You look gorgeous," she says. "Cillian won't be able to take his eyes off you. Though he never can."

"Really?" I look down at the dress. "I feel very normal looking."

"It's the makeup—it looks so much better than usual, so pretty and professional looking. You look like a—"

I grin. "Do I look like a *mooovie star*, is that what you were going to say?"

"That is what I was going to say, and I'm glad I didn't, because it seems like it would have made you more insufferable."

"You know, in my old life, I had a glam squad made up of these four

Scandinavian guys named Rod, Ron, Rob, and Roy. I must have picked up a thing or two from watching them do my makeup constantly."

"Clearly."

"They had a podcast called *The Male Gays*. Spelled *g-a-y-s*."

"Cute."

"They were friends with Oprah."

"Christ." She then gives me a look. "Do you know you just called it your *old life*?"

I replay the scene back in my head and hear myself. "Huh."

"Don't know what it means, but it's interesting." We head toward the door and Kiera adds, "Cillian bought you that dress, you know. At some shop in County Kerry. You loved it but said you'd never wear it. He bought it for you anyway, and you were right, you never wore it."

"Why?"

"Said something about being afraid of ruining it."

"It's a miracle I don't have plastic casing on the couch."

I decide to leave Maureen in case Cillian is there and wants to steal her back. Or, I guess, repossess his own dog. I'll ask him if it's okay to keep her another night, and give her back if he says no.

Aimee lives only a ten-minute walk from the house, and after about seven minutes, we start to hear music.

She lives in a cute cottage not unlike Surrey House, but it's bigger and the backyard is enormous. There are tons of people there, and I have to assume it really is the entire population of Avalon.

As soon as I process this, I realize that this was perhaps a very big mistake.

"If it starts to feel weird, we can go," says Kiera, reading my mind.

"Okay," I say.

If Kiera's right and her mom did tell the whole town, then it'll be a lot of people with questions. It's the first time since arriving in Avalon that I feel the old LA sensation—the one where I get overwhelmed in a crowd of people because all of them know me and I don't know any of them. The good news is, I'm used to it.

The people of Avalon are nice, warm, and friendly. What I notice most is that everyone is comfortable. There's no posturing here. No preening or sucking in of the stomach. The women are all attractive in their way, if not in the cloney Hollywood way. It's interesting how the lack of vanity has made them all infinitely more appealing. The partygoers chat and throw their heads back in laughter and talk with loud voices over each other. The din is joyful and pleasant, everyone happy to get together.

Kiera drops our gifts on the kitchen table where other people seem to have done the same, then we each pour a cup of cider from a keg marked *Bulmers* in a bucket of ice, and I feel a little funny. In LA, before the fame, I spent most of my time auditioning and being very serious about making connections, and when I *did* go out, it was usually to wait in lines for Davey Wayne's, get my purse stolen at the Abbey, or sit in the nosebleeds for a Tchaikovsky fireworks show at the Hollywood Bowl. I only really attended parties in the last few years. I've been to weird hangs in Echo Park that served Funyuns ironically and where the guests were basically all former or current cast members of *SNL*, and I've been to fancy parties in the Hollywood Hills where there were security men at every door and everyone in attendance looked vaguely famous, very famous, or like they wished they were famous, like my birthday party the other night.

I haven't been to something like this, where it's normal people having a good time, not taking themselves too seriously, in as long as I can remember.

The band is vibrant and cheerful. Half the party attendees are dancing or chatting, and the other half are watching the music with happy, deferent silence.

More than one person comes up to me and says something like *Do you remember me?* or *Oy, tell Brad Pitt I'll leave my husband for him!*

But without a doubt, all of them are good-natured, looking to tease me. As if I had a funny dream about being a famous actress, and they want to get their digs in.

Kiera and I drink our ciders and laugh along. We watch some of the couples dancing and she tells me who is who, who used to be married to whom, who owns what local business, and who I apparently know and like best. All the while, I look around for Aimee, bothered by the fact that I haven't found her yet.

I'm learning about how someone named Timmy Kane once took me on a date to a falconry and an owl became obsessed with his hair and he'd been so embarrassed that he never looked me in the eyes again. I feel a warm hand on my shoulder.

There's a soothing, strange familiarity to the touch, and I already know who I'll see when I turn around.

"Cillian," I say.

"You're wearing the dress," he says as a greeting.

"I— Uh, yeah." I look down and smooth it with my free hand. "It's pretty, isn't it?"

He nods tightly and then says, "I hear you don't remember any of it."

CHAPTER FOURTEEN

———

D ammit, Kay," says Kiera, cursing her mother for her gossiping ways.

"Do you think we could go talk somewhere?" Cillian asks.

My heart skips a beat and I nod. "Yeah, of course. Kiera, I'll uh, I'll be back."

I gesture for Cillian to lead the way.

He's dressed up today, wearing a pair of light, perfectly draping wool trousers and a sage-green button-down that looks comfortably worn in. He's got the kind of physique that can pull off anything, I think. Some people can slip into Valentino and look ready for a premiere, and some people need to be tucked and nipped all over before looking right. It's nothing to do with attractiveness either; it's that some people have a quality that makes everything work on them.

Cillian has that quality. Effortless.

He leads me to a quiet part of the garden about twenty yards from the party and we sit down on a bench. I know I was in the fray only a moment ago, but stepping away from it, I already feel like an outsider.

Aware that it's not my life. Jealous that it isn't.

"So can you catch me up?" he asks, his voice low and patient.

Grumpy as he may be, I have a feeling all of our issues stem from me.

I do catch Cillian up, and his face remains impassive as he listens. He leans over with his elbows on his knees, his finger tracing the lip of his plastic cup. When I finish, he furrows his brow and lifts his gaze to mine.

"Don't take this the wrong way, but Meg, is this all about . . . well, I don't even want to ask. I can't imagine you'd make something like this up."

"No, I wouldn't. I promise you, I'm not messing with you or lying or—I mean, the only real possibility here is that I have completely lost it. But I feel fine!"

He shakes his head, looking overwhelmed, rightfully, by the information.

"You've been to see my dad?"

"Yes. He didn't mention it?"

"Of course not," he says. "I heard about your . . . condition from a couple eejits at the pub last night."

I take a moment to appreciate his dad for his discretion, fully aware that this should be a given with any doctor, but also a little too used to the frequency of mysterious leaks that make their way to Page Six.

"Your dad thinks I'm disassociating. Kiera keeps calling it time travel but doesn't believe me either way. I mean, she believes I believe it. Aimee is the only one who seems to understand that I've slid dimensions. Or something."

"You told Aimee? I suppose that's why you're here, then, yeah? You two put your stuff on hold in the wake of whatever this is."

"I guess so. She invited me after I told her. And look, I do get that if I wanted to wipe the slate clean with you and Aimee, this would be one way to do it. But I would never. I could never. No matter what. It's not me to do that."

He nods. "I know it's not, Meggie."

Hearing him say my name, my old nickname no less, makes me feel weak. "Good."

"Did you tell your mother? I suppose she said the same thing as my dad, then?" He says it with the slight tone of an inside joke.

I don't get it, of course, so I answer honestly. "I didn't tell my mom. You think she'd think the same thing as your dad though?"

He looks at me briefly, clearly deciding whether or not to play into my apparent amnesia.

"Sure look. The way they hit it off when your parents came over here. They spent the whole trip kindred spirits. Your dad and my mother as well. The two of them got on like a house on fire, talking about music nonstop. Your mammy and my dad talked about us the whole time."

"They did?" It gives me a strange thrill to imagine my parents here, hanging out with Cillian's parents. I've never brought my boyfriends around my family. Even if a relationship goes on for a year or two, I always sense that it won't work out so I don't want to waste everyone's time. Plus, of course, I barely see my parents myself. "What did they have to say about us?"

"Oh, you know." He takes a sip of his beer. "Same thing as everyone and always. Why aren't the two of us married, when are we going to stop fecking around and admit we're in love with each other. Admit there's never going to be anything else like this for us. Admit we wouldn't want it if we found it."

He avoids looking at me.

My heart blows up to three times its size at these words. It's a completely involuntary feeling and completely unfamiliar, at that. All those boyfriends I wasn't bringing home—it's also because I never felt anything like this.

How is it possible that I feel so much from his words? I don't even know him.

"I'm sure you can understand how difficult it is to believe. You don't remember anything?"

"No. It's really not a matter of *remembering*. I know my entire other life."

"The one where you're an actress."

"Yes."

"Right. It's a bit funny, is all, that you're saying it's your other life."

"What do you mean?"

"I think it has more to do with that fortune teller than you think it does," Cillian says.

I feel the ground fall out beneath me. "I told you about that?"

"We've told each other everything. You even told me about the time you sneezed . . ." One half of his mouth turns upward in a wry smile.

Then I realize what story he's talking about, because it happened when I was in high school.

"Oh my God, the pee incident? I told you about the *pee* incident?"

It wasn't a *lot* of pee, but still I never told *anyone* about the sneeze-and-pee. No one but Aimee, and it's only because she was there and I couldn't stop laughing and needed to explain myself. And borrow a pair of shorts.

I laugh now, and he cracks a smile too.

"I can't believe I told you about that. The . . . the fortune teller thing, I mean. The other thing either, but, uh . . ." I nod and look off into the sky. "I'm sorry. Everything I've heard since coming here . . . it sounds like I was kind of exhausting."

He shakes his head. "Never exhausting for me. I think you exhaust yourself at times. Like when Clare cries and cries until she falls asleep in the middle of the room, little fists still balled up. Which, as I understand, you used to do as well."

This makes me laugh again, and when I laugh, he does too.

God, his smile is beautiful. Straight white teeth, but a tiny, tiny gap on one side between his canine and molar. A perfect imperfection.

I'm not really sure what else to say, so I go with, "The music is fun."

"They're good." He nods.

"The extent of my experience with Irish music is the dancing scene in *Titanic*."

His head falls and he says, "God, you love that bloody film."

"It's so good!"

"I'll never understand how someone can find comfort in a disaster story about a tragedy that killed thousands."

"It's not *about* that."

"If you don't remember anything, and don't recall the millions of times you've made this case to me about this movie, then does it mean you also don't remember the ten to fifteen times you've made me watch it with you?"

I bite my bottom lip in response.

He exhales loudly. "What a right waste of time that was."

I tut my tongue and say, "Whoever you are, it seems like maybe you have no taste."

He drops his chin at an angle, giving me a challenging stare. "You certainly seem like the same old Meg."

"Really?"

He looks at me and then covers his mouth as he leans back and considers me. He lets his hand drop as he says, "You know, in a way, I sort of want to believe you forgot everything. To start over with you. We've made such a mess of things. I wonder if we would have been better off meeting now."

My lips part and I say, "I don't understand how we screwed it all up so badly."

"I'd need several years to tell you," he says. "And it wouldn't matter anyway. I don't understand it myself."

We both turn, then, hearing someone call his name. It's one of the girls who had been flirting with him at the pub, standing with her friends.

He gives them a tight smile and lifts his hand.

"You're like Gaston with your gaggle of milkmaids," I say.

"Ah, the Bimbettes." When he sees my look of impressed surprise, he says, "We googled them once. That's how they're credited."

They call for him again.

"You should go," I say, and then spot Aimee. "It's fine."

"I don't need to go," he says. "They're silly girls. I'd much rather talk to you, even if you don't remember me."

There's a micro-expression that comes with his words. Somehow, I believe I understand it, fleeting as it is. I think the look is about the grief of what's died between us, and the strange hope that maybe there's a way to begin again, even if it is something akin to magic.

It's a lot to translate from one little look, but I know deeply that I'm right. Either because I know him, somehow, or because I make my living conveying complex inner stories with something as minute as a flicker of an eyelid.

He looks and sees Aimee, sees that's where my gaze has gone, then stands. "Glad you two are making up."

I stand then too, smoothing the wrinkles in my dress. He fiddles with the now-empty cup in his hands.

"It looks good on you," he says, his eyes dropping for a moment to the dress. "I always knew it would."

Then he walks off, and I feel desperate to reach my hand out, grab his, and pull him back to me. What I'd do then, I have no idea.

Well, that's not true; I have several ideas.

Aimee has vanished by the time I get through the crowd, so I rejoin Kiera, who's now in a conversation with a lanky, red-haired guy with an intense amount of freckles. He's cute, with that boyish-charm-slash-fatal-flaw that makes it seem like he can probably never take a situation seriously.

"Oh, stop it!" she's saying, patting him on the chest. "Meg, there you are. Thought you two might not come back."

"Hiya, Hollywood," says the redhead.

I take a wild guess. "Nial?"

"Ah, see, she hasn't forgotten everything," he says, pointing at me.

"Is it starting to come back to you, then?" asks Kiera.

"No, I just had a feeling this was Nial." Over his shoulder, I spot her. "Excuse me one sec."

I set my drink down on a nearby table and then make a beeline for her. She's with her children.

Aimee's in belted, high-waisted, glen check trousers and a white button-down with the sleeves rolled up. It looks like vintage Ralph Lauren, and it's exactly the perfect style for her. With her tawny skin and brunette hair, she looks like old ads from the eighties in the magazines my mom had kept.

I walk up to her and she gives me a broad smile. "Meg. Ronan, say hi to Aunt Meggie."

A wave of *this is so fucking bizarre* washes over me, but I breathe through it. I can't simply sit in amazement at her very existence every time I see her or I'll freak her out.

"Do you remember her, buddy?"

He shakes his head.

"It's okay." I drop my voice to a whisper. "I don't remember meeting you either."

He smiles bashfully and turns his head against her chest, away from me.

Ronan has piercing blue eyes and thick, shiny dark hair. He can't be more than three, and he looks like he's overdue for a nap.

An unexpected wave of affection for the child comes over me. The way his small body wraps effortlessly around hers, the way his fingers wind through a lock of Aimee's hair.

I don't have a lot of kids in my life. I'm an only child without much extended family. I don't have a lot of adult friends with kids. I'm awkward around them. I say things like, *Been to any good movies lately?* Which is not even how I talk to adults, so I have no idea what's up with that.

"Oh, come on," Aimee says to her son. "Say hi."

"Hi," he says quietly.

"Hi, Ronan," I respond.

"Hi," he says again.

"That's good," Aimee says, then shrugs at me. "We take what we can get. Clare, come here, come say hi."

Clare comes over. She's in a floral dress with a fluffy little white cardigan on over top. She gets down into that full kid squat, picking at the little rogue flowers that grow in the grass by our feet.

"Meg. I remember Meg, yes," she says, a singsong little voice. She *does* have a little accent. Okay, again, there's no denying that this is a cute, cute set of children. "Auntie Meggie."

My heart blooms again. I feel like I could cry. For everything. For Aimee. For this life of hers. For these extensions of Aimee. Not only has she lived, but she's created *more* life. More Aimee in the world.

"Hi, Clare. Nice to see you."

I crouch down to her level.

"This is for you," she says, handing me a dandelion. "Make a wish."

I take the flower. Ordinarily, when a kid hands a wispy dandelion to an adult and tells her to make a wish, the grown-up usually politely says, *Okay, done*, not really thinking it makes much of a difference, except to keep magic alive for the little one.

But I have no idea what's real anymore, and magic is somewhat overwhelmingly alive for me right now, so the stakes of my wish feel like they could be catastrophic.

The wish goes out of my mind as a tall tattooed man appears behind Clare, and I look up from my crouch to see Theo.

Again, *ugh*.

I stand and say, "Theo."

He smiles a little, then says, "Good to see you, Meg."

"You too," I lie.

He seems to sense the residual bitterness in my tone, so he reaches for Ronan, and then says, "I'll take these two over to the other kids. Let you catch up."

He then gives a nod and walks off with the children.

"Are you still . . ." she asks.

"*Sliding Doors*–ing?"

She nods.

There's a distance between us that I long to close, but I know I can't do it right this second. I have to be patient. Even though I want it now.

Aimee shields her eyes from the sun and looks off at Theo in the distance. A softness appears around her eyes as she does.

I look at him too. He's accepted a beer from someone, and he's chatting animatedly with another man, both keeping half an eye on their respective children.

I can't even imagine what it feels like to gaze across a backyard and be looking at your family. The one you created. Kids who call you their mother. A husband who calls you his wife.

I've always chosen to believe my disinterest in all of this is because I'm modern—I don't need a wedding. I don't need to have kids. I want a *big life*. Which, I guess to me, means success, wealth, having a blue check, being remembered long after I'm dead.

Seeing Aimee with them—seeing the obvious joy in her as she watches them—it reminds me that there's a part of me that does want that kind of connection.

I'm having trouble reconciling past-him with the version I see before me.

Aimee always seemed to see something in him that I didn't. Aimee saw something so different that even when I *told* her who he was she still loved him anyway. Was she a fool, or was it love?

Is that the same thing?

Whatever the answer, it is one of my many beliefs about Aimee's death that if it weren't for Theo, Aimee would still be alive. In both worlds, not just here.

Though, it's harder to blame him for it when he's here and she's fine. But that night . . .

"How did Theo end up in Avalon?" I ask. "We all may as well have stayed in Florida."

I regret saying it as she gives me a look, and I give a cringey expression of *don't hate me, it's a joke*. She seems to choose not to give me shit for it, which I appreciate, settling on an eye roll.

She puts her hands on her hips. "Well. We broke up when I moved. But we never lost touch. He went to community college for a while and then ended up getting accepted to Cornell." She pauses for my shock, which I give her. "After he graduated, I asked him to come here. I said I'd go to him, but he said he'd rather see things outside of our broken country. I told him things are broken everywhere, but he came anyway. It took some time with the visa bullshit, but eventually we were both able to settle down here because his father is from the UK. We got married a little over four years ago."

"I heard he got fired. What was he doing?" I ask her.

"He wasn't *fired*, Meg, he was laid off. He's a plant breeding specialist. He works in genetics and plant biology to create new species."

I can't bring myself to look impressed even though I am.

"I guess that explains the weed he used to grow," I say.

"Eh, not really." She adds, "That was because he liked it."

I see that she's kidding, and I feel free to laugh. We both do.

Kiera comes over with two drinks and hands them to us. "I want to keep the conversation lubricated. Carry on." She then does a funny little bow and runs away.

"Kiera," Aimee says. "Funny girl."

"So, wait, tell me about your play," I say, remembering.

She blushes and I watch her smile fade. "Oh, it's nothing. Silly. Nightmare actually."

"I mean, you're directing it, right? And wrote it?"

"Oh, well . . . yeah."

When she offers no more explanation, I take a sip of my drink. "Okay, so what's it about?"

"Ah . . . friendship? I suppose?"

The way she doesn't meet my eyes tells me it might be in part inspired by *our* friendship.

"I can't wait to see it."

She looks suddenly stressed. "If it happens."

"What do you mean?"

"I mean . . . I don't have a second act. So."

"What? How? Isn't it—"

She gives me a deathly glare and I back down.

She relents a little and says, "I know it's ridiculous, but we got this chance to have the show seen by this critic. I met him at a writer meetup thing in Dublin. I mentioned it, he liked the general idea, and since he'd apparently heard good things about my past work, he said he'd come to my next one. I have these girls in it and they're not connecting with it, I can tell, and I've been rewriting, and then this weekend I detonated the whole second act. It's not that long, it's sort of experimental anyway, so the actors were down to . . . oh my God, I shouldn't even be out here. I should be inside working on it."

Aimee looks massively overwhelmed. And I don't blame her. Nuking the whole second act a week before performance night is, objectively, batshit. But I'm not surprised. Aimee never thought anything she did was good enough. She once threw away an entire Funfetti birthday cake we made for her mom because it wasn't good enough. How boxed cake could be anything but, ya know, boxed cake, I had and have no idea.

"Well . . . maybe I could help."

She flushes a deeper shade of red. "No, no, I'm fine."

For me, it's essential to spend as much time as possible with her. For her, I'm a friend from whom she's been estranged. I get that she doesn't quite know how to be around me. I probably wouldn't either.

"This critic thing sounds like a big deal."

"God, don't remind me." She takes a big swig of her drink.

"Look, I know you're mad at me. But let me help. I'm not saying I'm a savant or anything, but I've been in Hollywood awhile now. I'm also not saying anyone can write a script. But maybe I could be of some use. I've picked up a thing or two being there, you know. In LA."

"Yes, I noticed your makeup."

"Okay, how *bad* at makeup was— Forget it. Anyway, yeah, if it's about friendship, I mean . . . I've had a friend before."

She looks at me and then can't help but laugh a little.

There's a space between us, and I try to find a way to fill it in.

"I went over to the school yesterday."

"Oh yeah?" she says, nonplussed.

"Yeah. It was really weird. Seeing it in real life. Remember how we used to obsess about it? Looking up every image on Google. They're burned into my brain. I obviously never ended up seeing it, 'til now."

And neither did you.

She seems to remember then that it was my first time, and says, "Oh, right! So how was it? Did you see any teachers?"

"Yes, actually. Professor Lehman?"

Her eyebrows shoot up. "Ooh. Tough cookie."

"I got that vibe."

"What happened?"

"She asked my opinion on a scene between two kids. I made a suggestion and then . . . she had me act it out for them."

"How did that go?"

"It was fun! I actually stayed for a bit and watched. It made me even sadder I didn't get to do that. Go to school here, learn that way."

"This is so weird. Obviously *I* remember you doing it. We used to sit in the back of Professor Lehman's class and imitate her."

I think of her lilting English-Irish accent and say, "I can see that."

"*Do the scene again, but this time try to move less like an ostrich, yes?*" she says, in a perfect imitation of Professor Lehman. "*Once more please, try not to sound as if your mouth is full of ice cubes.*"

I laugh, and she does too. "Oh my God! Yes! I can totally see it."

She shakes her head, nostalgic. "She's something else."

There's a long silence.

"Come on, let me help with the show," I say, pushing her a little on the shoulder. "I'm good at this!"

"You really want to?"

"Yes!" Of course I do. And honestly it sounds like a shitshow.

"Okay. Sure. Maybe tomorrow? Or, no, the stage will be booked tomorrow. But we don't necessarily need the stage—"

"How about at my place? At the cottage?" If she used to live there, then maybe being back will shake up her positive memories of all our good times.

"Yeah, sounds good. Noon?"

"Perfect."

"Okay," she says on a long exhale. "I'm going to go reprieve Theo. Thanks for coming."

"Of course."

Of course. I mean. Where the hell else would I be, given the chance?

She goes off, running with open arms to her daughter when she gets close. Kiera is deep in flirtation with Nial. I go inside and ask someone where the bathroom is. They look at me like I'm crazy, and then point me down the hall.

I can't figure out why at first, but then remember that they probably think I ought to know where it is. In Aimee's home. That, or I forgot to call it *the jacks*.

There's a line at the bathroom, so I follow my instincts and go upstairs, looking for another one. I have a feeling there's one up and to the left.

I find a door shut with the light on. I don't know if I'm right that it's the bathroom or not, so I wait awkwardly for a moment. Right when I'm about to give up, the door opens and Cillian comes out.

"Oh. Hi."

"Hi," I say.

We then move past each other, swapping places. I'm about to shut the door when I see he's still standing there.

A muscle twitches in his jaw.

"What is it?" I ask.

"It's odd. We've had a whole life together, and you have no idea about any of it."

I shake my head slowly. "No. I wish I did."

"I could tell you things that would make your hair curl," he says.

I struggle to come up with a clever answer, managing to stop myself from saying something dumb like, *Well then, maybe you should curl my hair.*

"Do you want to know?" he asks.

There's a trill in my chest and I nod. "Yes."

"Okay," he says. "Let's go for a walk."

"Okay." I start to follow him, then say, "I'm actually going to—"

"Right. I'll wait downstairs."

Then I pee, check my makeup and hair, and take a few deep breaths before going to find him.

CHAPTER FIFTEEN

W hy is everything closed?"
We've walked back into the heart of the village, and it is a ghost town. Like being on the Warner Bros. backlot when nothing is shooting.

He gives me a look and then tilts his head back in the direction whence we came. "They're all back at Aimee's, aren't they?"

"Sure, but—I mean *literally* everyone?"

"Nah, there're a few old codgers on their farms probably getting ready for bed about now. The ripe old hour of six o'clock being a bit late for them. But there's no sense in keeping the places open when it's a big event like that."

I shake my head. "That's insane."

He points across me at Joy's and says, "That's where you were reading the first time I saw you."

"Oh, I went there yesterday. I didn't realize that's where we met."

"Not met. I saw you there. Didn't have the nerve to approach you yet."

"Right, I remember that now. Kiera sort of gave me the lowdown on our whole . . . thing."

"Ah, did she?" he says, putting his head back, walking with his hands in his pockets.

We're keeping a slow pace, neither of us in any hurry. The sun is turning the sky a golden orange and it's a strange feeling to know that it is hours from setting, unlocking a time between dusk and nighttime that I've never known before. A whole new time of day that has been spliced into the life I thought I knew. I know it's science, but it feels like magic.

I could stay on this walk for the rest of my life.

A cool breeze tumbles over us, and my arms are alight with goose bumps.

"Here, let's stop in here," he says, nudging our direction over to the pub. He pulls a set of keys out from his pocket and opens the door.

I follow him in, feeling strangely, happily nervous to be so very, very alone with him like this.

"Shut the door, will you?" he says, once we're both inside.

I do as he asks, and then look around the darkened, empty pub. There are no lights on except an old lamp by the bottles that burns with an amber glow.

"I'm going to run upstairs quickly," he says. "You can come if you want, but you're welcome to wait there, too, if you prefer."

"What's upstairs?"

He hesitates. It's clearly strange that I don't know. "It's my flat. I live up above the place."

"That's so cool," I say.

"It's cool until the lock-in goes on 'til dawn and your mam is up partyin' with the best of 'em."

"Your mom is mad at me," I say.

"You've seen her?"

I follow him up the steps and through the door at the top.

"When I saw your dad about my"—I look for the words—"mental collapse."

"She's not mad at you. She's mad at us."

He holds open the door for me and I go through. It smells comfortingly familiar, even though it shouldn't. Like smoky peat and dried autumn leaves.

Inside is a large, high-ceilinged room of dark wood that's been neatly divided into a bedroom and a sitting area. There's a closet and a bathroom, and one of the walls has three windows that look down over the street.

This little flat is so idyllic. When I moved to LA I wanted a huge glass-and-marble house with an infinity pool. I wanted space. I wanted money so I could buy myself some augmented reality. One of the allures of Grayson had been his house. But seeing this place reminds me of the draw I've always had to drafty old buildings with rippled windows and flaws in the wooden floors. I wonder how long it's been here. Probably a long, long time.

He's a neat guy, I notice, which endears him to me even more. The idea of him keeping the place tidy makes me feel disproportionately fond.

On his coffee table, I see that he's been reading *The White Album* by Joan Didion. I pick it up and look inside to see what I somehow knew would be there. An inscription from me.

> C—
> *Read it. Maybe you'll want to run away to LA with me.*
> —M
>
> *PS—I mean there's some dark stuff in here,*
> *but you'll see what I mean.*

I set it down, making sure to leave it open to the page he was on, and keep snooping around.

Some old *Playboy* magazines are stacked under the coffee table on the lower shelf. Clearly for the novelty, as they look old and well preserved. A few Bill Bryson and David Sedaris books are stacked on a bookshelf, along with *The Bell Jar*, *Strangers on a Train*, and *The Catcher in the Rye*, and modern classics like *Gone Girl* and *About a Boy*. No wonder we got along so well. I have things to say about every book in his house.

On the bottom of the bookshelf, I see the spine for *She Comes First*.

I arch an eyebrow at the discovery, then grab it to see if there's an inscription in that one too. There isn't, and it makes me think he may have bought it for himself. It's weirdly hot.

I put it back and keep looking.

There are framed photos of his family, Maureen the dog, and even one old photo of the bar itself.

I am struck by this sudden vision—a fantasy, a scene as if my life were a movie, or an interdimensional memory, I'm not sure—of Cillian and me here on the couch using chopsticks to eat out of paper Chinese food containers, listening to John Coltrane while snow falls outside. Him in a soft white cotton T-shirt and me in an oversized green sweatshirt. I can almost make out the words on the front.

I walk over to one of the windows and look outside. The sky has already darkened a bit, and I get the feeling it's going to rain.

"Here you go," says Cillian. He has come out holding something folded, forest green. I stare at it for a second too long, then take it. *Avalon Rugby Club*. It's the one from the . . . daydream. Whatever you want to call what just happened. Where I saw myself from outside my own body, and I was wearing this very thing.

"It's the one you usually borrow when you're cold."

I take it. "How did you know I was cold?"

He gives me a look like it was so obvious. "Ready?"

I nod, and then say, "Actually, let me run to the bathroom again really quick before we go. All that cider."

He gestures in its direction.

It's as clean as the rest of the house, which is nice, I manage to think as I lean on the sink and puzzle over what just happened.

Some things about this life, I seem to know. Deeply.

I put on the sweatshirt, and then look at myself in the mirror. I may not have my expensive new nose or lineless skin, but my reflection looks a lot happier here. Even now, when I'm so deeply confused.

On the way out of the bathroom, as I pass the closet, I catch a glimpse of another framed photo.

I flip on the closet light and go over to the dresser in the walk-in to see that it's that picture of him and me that I had favorited on my phone. The one of us at the golden hour, me in that dress, him looking at me like he sort of, probably loves me.

I pick up the frame and stare at it, feeling almost sick with melancholy for a life that isn't even really mine.

"Christ, you're nosy," he says from the doorway, startling me.

"Shit, sorry." I laugh nervously and set down the photo. "It looks like maybe you do still like me," I say, then regret my nervy comment immediately.

"Like you? I don't even know you."

His response embarrasses me at first, and then I see there's a playfulness in his stern expression as he gestures for me to get out of the closet. I go, feeling a little giddy and silly.

He shuts off the light as a clap of thunder crashes outside. The combination of the light turning off and the unexpected sound makes me jump. I don't exactly leap into his arms, but I do lay a hand on his chest in surprise. It's warm and hard and I don't want to take my hand back. But of course, since I'm not a psycho, I do.

"Sorry," I say.

"It's okay," he says. He looks past me toward the wall of windows and says, "Ah, fuck."

"What is it?"

"The hape'll be storming the place any minute now. They'll expect me to open up."

"The—who?"

"The partygoers. They'll be coming here now, to the pub, because it's raining out there. It's going to be a mess. It always is when I'm working alone and everyone shows up at once. My mam is out in Limerick at her sister's."

"I could help," I say.

"Not this again."

"What! I can!"

"You've never properly worked behind a bar a day in your life."

"Maybe not in this life. But I spent like five years working in the service industry in LA in my other life."

He gives me a look that says he has no choice but to give me a shot.

We go downstairs and he shows me the basics of where everything is. It's the same as any bar, really, so almost immediately I shrug and say, "I think I got it. Three-compartment sink, wonky ice well, kegs in the back but you're gonna get those . . . seems like the usual."

"I can't be up here the whole time if we're doing food. And if we don't do food, they'll get rowdier," he says, looking at me warily. "You sure you'll be all right?"

I wave off his worry and say, "I'll be great."

When the place doesn't immediately fill up, I wonder if his assumption that the party might relocate was wrong. But after only a few more minutes of cursory training, the place suddenly becomes alive with the sound of tipsy party guests cheerfully announcing their arrival with jovial hollers and laughter.

A circle of musicians have gathered at the big table and started playing traditional music, which adds an immediate festive air to the place. Some of them are the guys from the stage earlier, but some others have joined in too.

"You sure you got this?" Cillian asks me worriedly.

"You can trust me." I give him a small smile and then shoo him off. "I wouldn't say I could do it if I couldn't."

His eyes hold mine for a moment before he nods and goes.

It's *pouring* rain outside, and the entire crowd is sopping. Everyone hangs jackets on the racks by the entry and seems to be congratulating each other on surviving the trek from Aimee's to the pub.

Kiera and Nial are quickly entwined in a corner, his arms around her waist, her arms around his neck.

Aimee is nowhere to be seen. I have to assume she had to put the kids to bed, or at least start to wind them down. But I do see Theo laughing with a group of guys, dealing out a few hands of cards at one of the big round tables in the corner.

People come up to the bar and start ordering pitchers and pints of beer, glasses of whiskey. Thankfully, I'm not in the land of mojitos and Miami Vices, and it's easy for me to be fast, even out of practice. I roll up my sleeves and get started. Well, technically, they're Cillian's sleeves.

I'm surprised by how efficiently my old bartending skills come back to me. Within ten minutes, I've folded Cillian's sweatshirt under the bar and have a rag slung through the rope of my dress at my waist, a beer key tucked into my bra for easy access. I'm leaning over the counter and catching orders for beer, whiskey, and even food, managing to remember all of it and fulfill every order without a misstep. I always thought memorizing tens of orders at once was good practice for line memorization. In this case, all my *line* memorization has helped me stay sharp for *order* memorization.

We move around each other with the choreography of Olympic figure skaters to the pizzicato score of the fiddle player, Cillian taking orders out of the kitchen and me swiping them from his hands and replacing them seamlessly with dirty dishes. When I call to the back quickly to tell him we need one of the Guinness kegs changed, he doesn't miss a beat or require more polite words before he says, "Got it." The only hesitation comes a few moments later when he emerges from the back with the keg in his arms and I find myself overfilling a glass from one of the other taps, distracted by the sinewy muscles in his arms.

"Shit," I say, then, "Here you go," wiping down the sides of the glass then handing the cider off to Kiera, who saw me watching Cillian.

"You two, I swear it," she says. It warms me to see the look she gives us.

"Hush!" I say anyway, laughing and blushing, "I have guests!"

After the first big wave of food and drink orders, the place settles into a happy hum of contented revelers. The air smells like the fire burning in the hearth and the sweet, warm scent of fried fish and chips. Cillian brings me a small plate for myself and I take bites between customers. How did I *ever* go without good food? And how is Cillian's *this good?*

Around nine, two men approach the bar. They're each pink in the face from drinking, both smelling of pipe tobacco.

"Oy, isn't you that big famous actress?"

My peaceful mind ratchets into high-intensity mode as my heart falls. Is it over? Is the hallucination fading?

"What?"

They both burst into laughter, patting each other on the back, and then one of them says, "Two Guinness, Ms. Hepburn." They crack up again, reminding me of the old guys on *The Muppets*. He raps on the counter and then gets back into conversation with his friend, and I realize they were teasing me. They heard the gossip. It's as Kiera anticipated.

"Arseholes," says Cillian, who clearly overheard, after I give them their beer and they thank me. "That's Danny and Eoin though. Always a pair of eejits."

"They're fine," I say. "They're teasing. They probably think the whole thing is a lark." He nods and then stares at me. "What?"

"You know, you've helped me out behind the bar before."

"I have? Then why didn't you think I could do it?"

He laughs. "Because you were a disaster all the other many times you've insisted on trying to do this."

"What? How!"

"Well, one time you did okay, but after the rush, it turned out you'd forgotten to charge anyone."

I slap a hand over my mouth and stare at him with wide eyes. "Oh, shit. Oh, no . . . Cillian, was I supposed to charge people tonight?"

"You didn't . . ." he says, face falling.

I take my hand away from my mouth and reveal my smile. "Kidding."

"Christ, you almost gave me a heart attack. Took well over a week chasing the apes down to pay last time."

"Nope, everything's good. It's in the cash drawer. Big cash town."

"They know that's what we prefer."

"Doesn't every business?" I ask.

"They're an understanding bunch, them." He nods at the throng. "During particularly hard times, my mam will come in and charge everyone double, and if they don't like it they can leave."

"What happens?"

"Well, she's a bit of a force to be reckoned with, so they pay triple."

I laugh.

He looks unsettled and I feel sorry that I don't know anything about our life together or the details about him the way he knows them about me.

"Anyway," he goes on, changing the subject back. "You were a complete tornado every other time. It would have been easier to do it all myself."

"Wow. Rude!"

"I'm not trying to be an arsehole," he says. "You were just that bad."

"Ice cold, Cillian."

"And yet, tonight, you're perfect. You didn't feck anything up. How exactly is that?"

"I spilled a lot of beer. I always do. My mats were always full by the end of the night. It would be embarrassing if I wasn't also really quite good at the rest of it."

He squints. "You did the work of two good bartenders here tonight, and as far as I've ever known, you've been about as useful as a T. rex with a broken cocktail shaker in the past."

"Okay, okay," I say, unable to hide my amusement at the mental image. "I get it, I—oh, wait. Are you saying you believe what I've told you, then?"

"I'm saying that you were so shite at bartending last time that I can think of only one explanation for how you're that much more competent. It's literally easier to believe in magic than to believe you improved that much overnight."

I gnaw on the inside of my cheek as I watch him. He's kidding, I know that, and it makes me want to kiss him.

I can't understand how, in any world, I could ever dump this guy.

"Can I get a whiskey, darlin'?"

I turn to see a man standing at the bar. Bernard, I remember. He's the one with the big dog.

"Hi, Bernard, of course. The house?" I ask.

"That'll do."

I take the bottle out of the well, and without looking at Cillian, I do the one and only bar trick I know how to do, which is to flip the bottle and catch it on the back of my hand. It hurts like a motherfucker, I can only do it with nearly empty bottles, *and* I only manage it one out of every five attempts, but the stars align for me to show off, and I do it perfectly.

Magic truly is afoot.

There's an eruption of appreciation from the customers who saw me. I can hear snippets of people asking, "Since when can Meg do *that*?"

After pouring the whiskey and taking the money, I slide past Cillian to get to the register, as if I didn't do anything at all.

"Excuse me," I say as I pass, my entire backside making brief contact with his entire front as I move past him in the narrow bar.

"You think you lost your mind," he says into my hair as I go by. "I think I'm losing mine."

~

Cillian shuts the doors and says, "Thank God they wanted to leave, I didn't have a lock-in in me tonight."

"Okay, you said those words earlier and I didn't know what they meant then either."

He furrows his brow and then says, "Oh, a lock-in. It's basically when the bar is shut but no one leaves. The good'ns stay on a bit."

I nod. "We kind of have that in America. But not in an official sense."

He smiles and I get the feeling that anything that might occur to me to tell him I may have already said to him. Not in a bad way. In a cute way, actually. Like, in every world, I would want to tell him every stupid corner of my mind. And he's nice enough to not look tired of me.

I am filled with a sense of satisfied well-being. I never once felt at the bars I worked in LA. I was always counting the minutes until it was time to leave, hinting heavily to managers that I wanted to be cut early, or even sometimes feigning an illness to get out of the slowest shifts when I could see they were overstaffed. Working with Cillian tonight was totally different. It was *fun*. Now it's quiet, and we're listening to *The Rhythm of the*

Saints album by Paul Simon on the speakers. I'm running the mats through hot sanitized water, and he's picking up all the glasses from the dining room and putting them on the counter. I can't hear him but I can see that he's singing along with the lyrics to "She Moves On."

The last customers tonight were Kiera and Nial. She had barely disconnected from him all evening, except for the half hour she took to go walk Maureen for me. The two of them made out and played darts all night, beating all the old guys. They'd all celebrated every win and loss with a new drink order, and at the end, Kiera went off with Nial, arms around each other's shoulders, her singing *Meg and Cillian sitting in a tree.*

Soon all the work is done, our beers are almost empty, and I would give anything for another floor to mop if it meant being with Cillian a little longer. That *must* be love.

A morose, melancholy voice in my head says it can't last forever. I retool everything I learned in meditation about allowing thoughts to pass unthinked.

I can't think about home, or the fact that this might end. It's hard being away from Aimee all night, knowing she's nearby. It'll be hard to be away from Cillian when we lock up. I'm even sad to see Kiera leave with Nial, feeling certain she won't be having a sleepover with me tonight.

How will I live the rest of my life if I can't be near them at all? If they do not exist?

That sounds dramatic, but . . . *it is* dramatic. I mean, if this isn't high drama, what is?

If this were just the trip I thought it would be, and I had met all these people—except for Aimee and her subsequent family—I could have made the wild, impulsive decision to simply stay. I could have said, *These people seem nice, the town seems nice, I'll have a life here.* But if this ends, then I'll have no way of finding my way back to them. They'll be gone, as irretrievable as Aimee had been. There one day, gone the next.

Cillian flips off most of the lights, and I'm sure we're about to leave when he says, "Can I convince you to stay for one more?"

My skin flushes at the relief that we both want the same thing.

He holds up my pint glass and I nod, trying not to look too eager.

Without needing to ask what I want, he pours me a red ale, and then brings it over to the armchair in front of the fireplace. He tosses another log on the fire and it catches quickly, reigniting the enthusiasm of the licking flames.

"Can I ask you something?" I say.

"Go ahead." He sits in the chair beside me.

"Why *did* we ever break up? I know I don't know you, but I can't—I mean I know myself, and you seem like . . . well—"

"It's always because you want to leave."

"Kiera said that. But . . . really? That's it? I thought maybe she didn't have the whole story."

He nods. "We are, or were, that mystical couple who never fights. We bicker constantly, don't get me wrong, but never fight, really. We're always happy when we're together."

The silence that follows is punctuated by the sharp crackling of the burning wood.

"And then, what, I decide this isn't the right life for me, and I break up with you?"

"You get unhappy. Start getting restless. It's like you're embarrassed about your own life. You once told me that you feel like there's an audience watching somewhere, and your ratings are dipping. Suddenly you'll do anything to save the show."

I've used that analogy before.

My gaze locks on to the flames. "So, I try to burn it all down."

"I want you to be happy, Meggie. But I want to be happy too, is the thing. And you're what makes me happy. So we're constantly pushing and pulling in opposite directions. I've offered to come with you, wherever you want to go. But you always end up saying it would never work, even though sometimes you seem like you do want me to come. I guess the part that's most upsetting is that you always end things with me, but you never actually end up leaving. So it feels more like you actually don't want a life with me. Like I'm the thing you want to escape."

I think about all the pictures in my phone that I've saved of him. The snippets and notes and tickets in that box I found in the closet, things I have a feeling are related to times with Cillian.

"My mom said I borrowed money from her for a ticket. A plane ticket to LA."

He looks at me as the blood leaves his face. "When?"

"It was for last Thursday. Which is the same night I arrived here. I think whatever happened . . . I think it happened because I was coming here and then your Meg . . . I think she was going there."

He gives a small shake of the head. "That's a mindfuck."

"Tell me about it. Why do you think your Meg finally tried to leave?" I ask.

Something passes across his face but he says nothing.

"What is it?" I say.

Finally, he says, "I think it'll be because of the proposal."

CHAPTER SIXTEEN

⟶

The—what?" I prompt.

"Don't make me say it again."

There's a long silence between us as my mind reels.

"You . . . proposed to me?" I feel like I'm falling at top speed down a water slide.

"Yes," he says.

"Did . . ." I nonverbally communicate the question.

"You said a lot of nonsense words, turned as scarlet as a radish, and then said you had to think."

My mouth hangs open. "When was this?"

"Meg." He gives me a look.

"What?"

"If you really don't remember, then you should really be in hospital."

"Please tell me."

He leans forward and sets his beer down. His next words are said with patience, but I can tell that it's hard for him to truly believe I need this told to me.

"Few days ago. Then you told me you needed to have a big life and that you were sorry. You made yourself scarce, and the next thing I knew you came in acting like nothing had happened the other night."

"When . . . when I couldn't find my phone? And you made me soup and a sandwich?"

Aka, my first night in this reality?

"Yep."

The cringe is *bone* shattering. I rejected this guy's proposal and then, as far as he must have known, just showed up at his work. His family pub. I cringe even harder remembering that I'd said something like *Why are you acting like you know me?* that night. To him, that must have sounded so harsh.

"Why would I say no? To you."

"Well. Dunno exactly. You love me." He looks bashful. "You do, by the way."

I flush. "I had a feeling."

He lets that sit between us as our eyes stay locked for a few seconds too long. I feel myself go hot all over.

"But you felt like marriage would trap you into a life you weren't sure you wanted. I don't know where you got this black-and-white thinking," he says. "I've tried to tell you there's more than this or that. Not that I'm trying to explain to you how you should feel. But I've made it clear that I would make any compromise for you. Sometimes you get so binary on things."

His accent lends such a gentle lilt to everything he's saying. The word *you* comes out like *ya* or *ye*. When he says my name, there's a different emphasis on it, one I've never heard. Even Kiera says it differently.

"This is awful," I say. "So I guess I rejected your proposal"—the word sounds unfamiliar on my tongue, unowned by me—"and then freaked out and tried to go after the other thing I thought I wanted."

"I guess so."

"Wow."

We drink our beers in silence for a moment.

I have always felt afraid I'd never find someone to love enough to really *be with*. Why does it feel like, with Cillian, I could be that open? Like he'd only love me more for any love I'd show. Kiera too, now that I think about it. I can just tell.

The friends I *do* have in LA are all snarky. We make fun of the same things. We roll our eyes at the same people. We don't connect on anything real. I always thought that was fine, feeling like any more authenticity would be a drag. Like if I got real, it would be tragic and dull. Forced. Keeping things light seemed better.

But here, I'm having connection and it *still* feels light. It feels simply good.

"So, I think that's why you broke up with me. If I had to guess. World closing in on you."

"I've never been proposed to. You know, if I'm honest, I have . . . these feelings for you that I can't quite figure out. And I feel like a fraud, because this isn't actually my life. Even if no one truly believes me, even if you want to but you can't completely. I know this isn't my life, but I am so drawn to you. And to Kiera. Not in the same way."

He gives a small laugh at the delineation. "You're not a fraud."

I let out a deep, unsteady breath. "I never feel like this. Ever."

He stares at me, that muscle going in his jaw again, and I breathe through a chill of desire.

"Me neither."

I actually shouldn't be as mystified as I am by how badly I want Cillian. I've had one-night stands with less context. It's the *intensity* of the desire that's surprising, because I've always felt more apathetic than I've wanted to in the past. It's also the fact that it's more than mere desire.

Whatever I feel for him has a heavy base to it. It's kind of like the first time I held an Academy Award. I never won one, of course, but I've held one and those fuckers are *heavy*. Nothing like the hollow, plastic trophies given to every participant in my recreational basketball league when I was a kid. An Oscar is dense, heavy, and hard to knock over.

Like that, there's an unexpected solidity, a satisfying density to how I feel about Cillian. All the fakes before the real thing have been hollow and the seams have shown. The real thing is undeniable.

So how has this other version of me managed to let him go? Is it simply the shameful fact that she knows he loves her so much that she cannot truly lose him, so she risks it and pushes him away, not believing he'll go? And then it got messy, messy, messy?

I know that no matter how much someone loves you and you love them, there's no guarantee that they will always be there. And I guess the version of me who didn't lose her best friend in a horrible car wreck hasn't learned that lesson. Takes relationships like these for granted. Whereas in real life, I just don't build them at all.

I can't help but notice that she, unscarred by grief and massive loss, has also managed to forge new relationships better than I have. I don't even have any to take for granted, so informed by that one big loss that I'd rather have nothing than risk having something and losing it.

"What do you think of your life here, then?" asks Cillian, tossing another log on the fire; maybe he's not ready for the night to end either.

"Um . . ."

"Ah, you hate it."

"No, I don't!" I say, meaning it. "The opposite. It's that it's a little hard to admit, because I keep hearing about how the Meg *you* all know seems to resent all this and it sounds like that version of me wishes she had *my* life. So it feels like it'd be a little rich coming from *this* version of me to envy this life." I make a face about how confusing it all is. "It makes me feel like my soul is destined to stay on an endless, ridiculous cycle of thinking the grass is always greener."

"But what do you think of it?"

I take a sip of my beer. "Well . . . I love it here. I wish I could see it covered in snow. I feel like I'd rather experience a million blustery days here than a million sunny days in LA. And that's coming from me, who hates the cold."

He nods and doesn't say *I know*, but I understand that he does.

I go on. "I think it seems nice to know the people in town. I think the job at the shop sounds like fun. Earlier, upstairs, I had this image of us sitting up there together eating carryout and . . ." I trail off, feeling suddenly shy. "Seemed nice."

"We've done that a lot," he says. "And you're right. It is nice."

He gives me a kind little smile and I return it, feeling a flutter in my chest.

"I think the whole thing sounds"—I look for the word that really means what I want it to, and land on—"enchanting. Even the part where I never do anything more . . . I don't know . . . important. Like living could be enough."

My cheeks get hot.

"Are you not happy in your other life then?" he asks. "Being a celebrity?"

I can see that he's still, understandably, struggling with the fact that it's what I truly believe. It's like dealing with someone with dementia, where you kind of have to play into the reality they live in. Or a kid who insists their imaginary friend exists and is named Paul. You say, *Okay, sweetie, does* Paul *think you should have your entire fist in your mouth while you walk down the staircase?*

In fact, for Cillian and Kiera, it's probably *exactly* like that.

"Um." I furrow my brow in thought, genuinely having to hunt for the answer. "Look, the thing is, I don't want to sound like a nihilist. Like, 'Oh, in any given world I'm miserable.'"

"You're not miserable," he says. "You're hunting for something."

No one says things like this to me in my real life, but I have the feeling that it's because I'm not asking. When you're a celebrity, people rarely want to tell you *no*. How do you think Michael Jackson went as far as he did with plastic surgery? How did Kim Kardashian get away with wearing that Marilyn Monroe dress? Who lets Johnny Depp out of the house looking like he does? Or, honestly, who lets him out of the house *period?*

He used to be so hot.

Not the point.

The point is that people stopped telling me *no* as soon as I became a household name. The glam squad who comes over to my house does nothing but gas me up, telling me how gorgeous and perfect I am. My personal assistant, Lisa Michele, might not listen to me all that well, but it's not because she's honest and real. She's just kind of an asshole. As for my parents, I mean, they love me. And they're never getting the full story.

And when I first moved to LA, no one knew the real *me* enough to keep me in check with myself.

In this world, this other version of me is lost. But it doesn't sound like she's taking much input either. It's easy for me to see that she has a massive wall up.

I let that sink in for a few seconds and then say, "It's probably the same in my life. I guess I never really thought about it. I was so driven to claim my success, and I got it. And it's not like I was moping around like a poor little rich girl. I get that it's good! I like good champagne. I get massages all the time. I've met Cary Grant's daughter. Gwyneth Paltrow sent me a vagina candle once."

"Never thought I'd hear *Cary Grant* and *vagina candle* in such close proximity."

"That's Hollywood, baby."

He laughs, and I admire his smile yet again. Getting back on track, I say, "What I'm trying to say is that I have a good life. But I'm not happy. And I think I'm scared."

"What of?"

I consider, staring at the red-hot wood in the fireplace and letting my thumb rub against the cold of the glass. I want to tell him everything, to have no secrets from him. But I don't. I tell him some of it.

"Of getting what I wanted so badly and then losing it. Growing old. Becoming weird looking after one plastic surgery too many. Public humiliation. Becoming a cautionary tale. Getting canceled because I say something I don't know is wrong. It makes me sad to hear that this version of me isn't content, because it seems to me like she has everything."

"Maybe she's in your life like you're in hers, and she's loving it. Probably is."

He takes a deep swig and I sit straight up.

"I had that same thought. How fucked up is that?"

The last log breaks in half, crisped nearly to charcoal with its webbing of red-hot fire within it. I already know he's going to call it the end of the night.

"Can I walk you home?" he asks.

"Yeah, that would be great," I say. "I suppose you want Maureen back."

"I'll be taking her back, yes. I wondered why you didn't bring her today. She loves a good party."

"Sorry about that," I say. "Kiera did let her out tonight and took her for a walk in the rain. She'll probably stink when we get back to her."

"That's all right."

We clean everything up, he puts out the fire, and then he hands me a wad of cash.

"Oh, no," I say. "I couldn't."

"Take it," he says. "You need the money."

"Right." I take it, slowly. "Guess you're right."

"Plus, you earned it. Couldn't have done tonight without you."

"Thanks."

I grab the sweatshirt from under the bar and pull it on, feeling deeply cozy in its soft fleece. Cillian turns everything off but that one light in the corner. I get the impression it's always on, which comforts me. At the door, I find my body close to his as he holds it open for me to go ahead of him. He smells like a hint of the most intoxicating sweat I've ever smelled.

It's stopped raining, but the temperature has dropped considerably.

"What do you want in life?" I ask, feeling rude for not having asked sooner.

"I'm pretty happy," he says. "I love the pub. I like the hours; I'm a night owl. I like the folks around here. I want to travel more, but I haven't. Not much, anyway—some with you when you travel for the store. But not enough. I tell you *no* too much, I think."

I look at him. I'm not sure what to say, but I'm touched that he's identified a problem in his own behavior. Guys so often don't. *People* so often don't.

I mean, one need look no further than *both* versions of me. And how many versions of me are out there? Is it infinite? Are all versions of me this restless?

God, I hope not. Like a whiny *Everything Everywhere All at Once.*

He goes on. "I keep pouring my money into upgrades for the pub. It needed all new plumbing and electric not too long ago, so that cost a pretty penny."

"Nothing missing in your life then, except kitchen upgrades?"

His elbow grazes mine, and he says, "I think you know what I'd say to that."

I do, and my heart feels so big it might explode. "I guess I do."

We get to the front door, and I hear Maureen barking inside.

"We're coming, we're coming," I say.

I find the key and open the door. Maureen jumps around, positively beside herself. She's clearly over the moon to see what is, I have to guess, her two favorite people on the planet.

She's a little damp from her earlier walk, but somehow she doesn't reek of wet dog.

"Oh, yes, girl, I know," Cillian says, allowing her to nuzzle against his chest as if she wants to climb directly into his heart.

I can relate.

I find the leash and hand it to him. "Sorry about the whole dognapping thing," I say.

"It's okay. I like that you love her so much. You ought to; you made me get her to begin with."

"I did?"

He takes a beat.

"We got her together, really. But you were afraid of the commitment, I think. So she became mine." We both look down at her happy little face, and he says, "It was all right with me."

He looks back up at me and then his eyes drop down to my chest. He points and I look, expecting to find some embarrassing dribble of ketchup there or something, but instead I remember it's his sweatshirt.

"Oh, right." I start to pull it off.

"No, no. I just always like seeing you in my things. Probably some toxically masculine trait of mine, but"—he lifts a shoulder—"I like it."

I put my arm back through the sleeve. "I get it. I like it too."

We're standing close. I can feel the heat of his body and I long to take one step closer. I want to know how his hands feel on my skin. I get chills every time I think about when he had his hand on my arm that first night. I can't even imagine what would happen if he were to touch me for real.

"Do you want to stay?" I ask, my voice raw, loaded with a hunger for him. "I mean, even for a little while."

His eyes flit between mine, and then drop down briefly to my lips and back again.

"Do I want to?" He gives a humorless laugh. "I'm dying to. Under the worst of circumstances, I can hardly ever say *no* to staying with you."

Energy buzzes through me as I realize what might happen.

"But to you, I'm a stranger right now. I know you, but you don't know me. Or maybe I don't know you. I'm not sure how it works. I don't think it would be right."

Still, though, I feel his body move toward me a little, almost imperceptibly.

"Even if I say it's okay?" I ask.

"Even if you say it's what you want more than anything in the world."

I nod. That is what I feel right now.

I crave him so much I feel like I might burst. The places on my body that I want him to touch burn cold with his absence.

"It wouldn't be right," he says again.

I can tell this is hard for him, which only makes it hotter.

"Okay," I say, having trouble breathing normally.

We move toward each other. He puts his hand on the slope of my shoulder, sliding it up my neck, fingers going beneath the collar.

It sends shivers down my spine.

He bends and I shut my eyes involuntarily.

His lips land on my cheek, the stubble a little scratchy against my skin, his kiss soft and warm. He smells like the whiskey we had earlier and I know I would be able to taste it on his tongue.

Cillian pulls away. His eyes now have a love-drunk quality to them. I know he wants it as badly as I do. He's doing the right thing. Or what he thinks is the right thing. But I want him more than I want to make good choices.

"Goodnight, Meg," he says.

He opens the door and lets Maureen out without the leash. I stand in the doorway and watch him go. He does a sharp whistle and Maureen dashes to his heel without hesitation. Somehow, this makes me want him even more.

He turns to me and holds up a hand in goodbye. I hold one up too.

With the smallest shake of the head, he turns from me and walks out into the inky black night, lit only by the foggy moonlight and the glow of all the stars I could never have possibly seen back home.

CHAPTER SEVENTEEN

The next day at noon sharp, Aimee arrives with a box of fresh dough-
nuts and orange juice. At about twelve fifteen, Kiera shows up in
sunglasses, despite the overcast day, looking a little worse for wear.

"What are you eating?" I ask, looking at the white triangle in her hand
and her full mouth.

"Tayto crisp sandwich. You want some?"

She holds it out like a sweet dog offering its horrid, ruined toy. "Oh,
I'm . . . I'm all set."

I make a big pot of coffee while Aimee boils water for tea. I go to put
on gentle music so as not to rattle the visibly hungover Kiera, but I'm unable to withstand so much silence. The other me has a playlist called *shhh,
it's nice.* I press *Shuffle* and an acoustic, subdued version of "Blues Run the
Game" comes on.

"Oh, that's a lullaby, that is," says Kiera, draping herself over the side
of the sofa.

"I hope it's okay I invited that one," says Aimee. "I figured, the more
minds on it, the better."

We both look at her.

I look to Kiera, who says, "I like to be a part of things."

Aimee and I look at each other now, both resisting a laugh. It's our first *look* like this. The kind of exchange you have with someone when you don't need to use words.

"Of course it's okay," I say, knowing that Aimee really invited Kiera because she wanted the buffer. It would probably be too much to hang out with me alone after we evidently hadn't in so long. I don't mind at all. It's been even longer for me, except for the coffee date.

I'm surprised at how excited I am to work on this. *Brilliance* lacks the artistic exploration I thought I'd one day have if I was lucky enough to succeed. It'll feel good to genuinely contribute.

Aimee sent me the file of the existing script this morning and I read it while I waited for them to arrive. It seems fun. A dark comedy with an emotional core, though she hasn't figured out the ending yet. It's a quick two-act sixty minutes about two girls, Hailey and Lola, going back to their hometown for a high school reunion. While they're there, they decide to try to break into Hailey's childhood home—now owned by someone else—to retrieve the time capsule they hid under the floorboards when they were sixteen.

It's funny and smart, like Aimee. But, despite what a perfectionist she is, the fact that she's let it come down to the wire like this is *not* like Aimee. I want to ask how she let it happen, but I know that's the wrong thing to ask when you're in the *we have to pretend this is totally fine and doable* phase.

"Want anything in your tea?" I ask Aimee, dropping the two bags of Earl Grey into the pot she pulled out. Evidently everyone knows their way around this kitchen better than I do.

When she doesn't answer, I look behind me to see she's on her phone, looking furiously stressed.

"Kiera? Coffee or tea?"

"Coffee, please. Too much sugar, too much cream."

"Got it."

I give Kiera's to her, then bring over the tea and mug for Aimee.

"Everything okay?" I ask.

She's tapping her foot on her crossed leg, not listening. Tapping away on her phone.

I look at Kiera, who shrugs.

"Hey, Aim?" I sit down next to her.

She looks up. "Sorry. Fucking . . . crisis, ugh, dammit."

"What's going on?"

She drops the phone on the table and stares at the ceiling. "The girls have dropped out."

"The girls meaning—"

"The actors. The two leads of the show. The *only* people in the show. Basically."

"*What?* Those assholes. Let me see the text."

She gestures at her phone and out of some ancient habit, I guess her passcode—all fours—and open the text thread. It's a group text between Aimee and two girls named Rebecca and Val.

Aimee—hey so, were really sorry to do this over text, but were both way to busy getting ready for the 1 act festival coming up and the summer term is way more intense than we thought it would be . . . and tbh it seems like the show is not gonna be done in time anyway? and neither of us want that critic to see us in something that seems unfinished. Itd be like the first time he sees us in something and we just dont think its a good idea for our careers. hope u figure something out though! please dont be made at us! xx

Then:

mad*

And:

ily, xx

Those texts came from Rebecca's number, and are followed by a text from Val.

we feel so bad! Xx

On one hand, I get where they're coming from. It's insane that she's not finished the last few scenes, and without something complete, it feels unlikely that they've reached a good flow with the rest of it.

But logic is simply not what friends are for. "Those absolute *bitches!*" I say, handing the phone to Kiera, who has feebly come over. "What careers?"

"Exactly! They're sophomores!" she exclaims. She's been balled up with her knees by her chest, but now she releases her limbs, throwing her arms in the air with fury. "They're college students! They're supposed to take every opportunity handed to them!"

"Haven't they ever heard of commedia dell'arte?" I say. "Has that fancy school not *informed* them of *devised theatre*?"

"I wouldn't go that far," says Aimee. "That'd be like me lighting my hair on fire when striking a match and then calling it experimental art."

Kiera raises a hand. "I have a degree in that very thing, from that fancy school, and let me tell you, you'd have a grand chance of winding up in the history books with a stunt like that."

I want to laugh, but resist. "It's okay, Aimee, we can—"

Aimee shakes her head. "I don't even blame them. It's a shitty show."

"It's not a shitty show," say both Kiera and I at the same time.

"Oh no, it is," says Aimee, hysterical now. "I know it is, because I have good taste. And because I'm a good writer. I'm a good writer who's doing bad writing right now, and who left it until the last week to finish the play that could have changed my life."

"I can't get over the bad grammar in this, speaking of good writing," says Kiera, putting the phone down, having made her way through the text. "They're useless. Good riddance, I say."

"What was I thinking having a party? Or spending time with my children?"

"Okay, let's all calm down a little," I say. "It's a short show. You're almost done. And you're not totally out of luck."

"Uh, really, because it feels like I just lost my life savings on a bad hand in Vegas."

"Okay," I say, deciding against perpetuating the Vegas metaphor with something stupid about Lady Luck. "I'm an actress. My show is rarely done until the day we film, sometimes PAs are handing me scripts with substantial changes once I'm already in hair and makeup."

Aimee and Kiera exchange a look, and I remember I'm not Lana Lord on vacation to visit my friend Aimee. I'm Meg Bryan, their friend who is having—probably—a nervous breakdown.

"Believe me or not, but I can do this. Give me a role. You do the other one. Who better? You know it inside and out. And you were always good."

"I haven't acted in ages," she says, blood draining further from her face. "I'm completely rusty. And the costume would make me look ridiculous. Little stupid dress."

"Aimee. You kind of have no choice. You're down to the wire, the only thing you can do is have a ton of coffee, finish this script, get it to tech as soon as you can so they can figure out lighting cues, etc., and then start rehearsing with the final material. I'd say desperate times call for desperate measures, but frankly I cost a fortune these days, and I'll do it for free."

I smile to show I'm kidding, and to hopefully show how manageable and chill this all is.

"You're right. I have no choice."

"I mean." I turn to Kiera. "Unless you act."

She furrows her brow and makes a pouty face as she shakes her head slowly. "I go all stiff and sound like I'm reading a nutrition label."

"She's based on you, anyway. Lola."

I turn to Aimee. "On . . . me?"

She rolls her eyes. "Yes. Ugh. Fine. Okay. Let's figure this out. You're Lola. I'm Hailey. Let's finish this script."

Our eyes linger on each other's.

There is a jingle of a bell in the far, far back of my mind. Aimee saying she wanted to write something one day. We were both playing prostitutes—which was the word we used then, we were years before using *sex worker*—with very few lines in a stage adaptation of Guy de Maupassant's *The Necklace*, and we were sitting in the hallway in full hair and makeup. Elaborate Gibson Girl wigs and extremely flattering corsets with big skirts—and she said, *I don't think I like being onstage. I think I want to write something one day.*

Really? Like what? I'd asked.

She had shrugged. *Maybe something about friendship. There are too many romances. Plus I know nothing about love. Obviously.*

I remember us both laughing and moving on, me not giving it another thought. I think that was around when she got dumped for the first time.

I can't believe how much I've forgotten. It's startling. Even stranger is how it's still in there, somewhere. Every buried memory waiting to be excavated.

We go over the existing material, making a few changes as we go. An idea for the ending starts to form in my mind, but I'm afraid to suggest it. So I keep quiet.

For almost two hours and all of the tea and coffee, we go over every possible resolution for the characters, but nothing feels right. It's all leaving us cold. It's either too schmaltzy or too neat or too boring.

The ideas, in fact, even put Kiera to sleep. She's in her hoodie and sweatpants in the fetal position, lightly snoring from the couch.

Eventually, I realize that I have to share my idea.

I use my best acting skills to sound natural when I say it.

I gasp and grab her wrist. "What if one of them is dead? What if the twist is that one of the two girls has been dead for years?"

I have trouble meeting Aimee's eyes, but I can feel them on me.

"Which one should it be?"

"Definitely Lola," I say. "I mean, I think . . . what do you think? She's the party girl. Hailey's the nice one. She should be the one alive."

I finally reach her eyes and I crumble beneath her stare.

She knows. She knows. Immediately she knows.

"How did she die?" asks Aimee.

My mouth is suddenly very dry, so I take a sip of water and shrug. "I don't know, maybe a—maybe a car accident?"

Aimee nods slowly. Goose bumps rise on my arms and up my neck. She. Knows.

"Who was driving?" asks Aimee, her eyes boring into mine. "Tell me the truth."

My heart feels as though it's shattering into a million pieces as I respond. This has happened so suddenly I feel out of control. A panic attack threatens in my nervous system.

"You were."

There is a very, very long silence.

Aimee's lips part briefly and then her attention is drawn away from me. I see that Kiera is sitting up.

I can tell that she heard.

I look back at Aimee. "I'm sorry," I mutter, uselessly, completely at a loss for what else to say.

Aimee and I both inhale at the same time, and then she shuts her notebook and says, "I think I'm going to go."

"Aimee—"

"No," she says firmly, in what is clearly her mom voice. "I'm going. It's all fine, I need to—I—Theo's had the kids all day and I—I'll see you at the rehearsal tomorrow, yeah?"

And then she's gone.

The door shuts behind her, and then it's Kiera and me.

She looks a million times better than she did earlier, the pink having returned to her cheeks, the rheumy look gone from her eyes. She stands up and comes over to me, no hesitation in her posture as she puts her arms around me and squeezes me tight.

"Did that mean what . . . I think it meant?"

"If you think it meant Aimee died in the world I came from, then yes." I'm freezing cold from the inside out, a shiver rattling me from my core. "Aimee died. Aimee is dead."

I have never said the words out loud. I never had to. Everyone who needed to know was there after it happened. Our parents and everyone in town. I never told anyone else she even existed. I danced around it in therapy. Thusly defeating a lot of the purpose of being there in the first place.

I feel sick and cold and tired and like I will never eat again, my hair hurts and my muscles are sore and my brain is completely empty and my heart is hollow. I feel like I was just in the car crash all over again. How strange it was to hurt all over, inside and out, but have hardly a scratch on me. Hardly a scratch while Aimee . . .

Fuck.

I'm amazed when my arms manage to lift and hug Kiera back. She hugs me even harder and says, "It wasn't your fault."

"It literally was," I say. My eyes prickle with unfamiliar tears. It's been years since I've cried off-screen.

"It wasn't," she says. "It wasn't your fault, Meg."

I bury my face in the thick cotton of her soft hoodie, gritting my teeth hard to keep from fully sobbing, afraid that if I topple over into the sadness, I'll never come out. "It was," I say. "She was driving, but it was my—my fault."

"It's okay. It's okay."

I shake my head against her, not believing her words, but feeling deeply touched by them anyway. Especially because I know that to Kiera, this all must be an elaborate hallucination on my part. It must be. People don't come back to life. People don't appear from parallel lives.

I gather the fabric in my hands and she says, "It's okay, love. It's okay. It's okay," over and over again. I can't stop from sobbing now. "Cry, it's okay."

A long time passes. Somehow, without a conscious decision on my part, we go from standing to sitting on the ground; eventually I'm a puddle in her lap. I go through waves of crying and not being able to breathe and then stillness, and I know that she won't leave even when I start up again. I know she won't be annoyed; even though she jokes around a lot, I know she won't this time. Whatever this is, she's here.

An Ethiopian song I distantly know from the depths of my own playlists has come on, and with surprising clarity I remember it's called "Homesickness." Part one or two, not sure which. I don't think I would have recalled even the title if I wasn't experiencing the feeling myself then. The feeling of homesickness in a new and truer sense of the word.

It's then, with devastating clarity, that I feel almost transported back to the scene. The headlights. The stoplights changing from red to yellow to green and back again. I remember feeling that it was odd that they went on and on like that, they were on a schedule of some kind. They'd had a major role in what had just happened—the biggest, maybe, and yet on they went.

There were sirens in the distance, coming toward us, and it was weird to know they were for us. I'd never had a personal relationship with the sound before. The radio was still on. The other driver was trying to speak to me, then looked in our car and saw . . . Aimee. And so, I had looked.

She had looked unnatural and broken. Too still. Her hand was in her lap, the back of her knuckles flat against her thigh. Her hair was hanging down in front of her face, blowing a little in the impartial breeze. I noticed and considered the stupidest things. Like how she'd picked those pale-blue jean shorts to wear. That white tank top. For tonight. For this, and she didn't know. She wore socks with the tennis shoes, as if she'd ever need to worry about a blister again. So strange that she had protected herself from a little discomfort like that, but that it wouldn't matter anyway.

My eyes had landed eventually on the pink coiled rubber key chain that she sometimes stretched out to the size of a basketball and then watched shrink back down, then on the sticker on the back window, which was shattered now, that bore the name of the band Death Cab for Cutie, which she had meticulously stuck there even though it wasn't her car and her parents both hated it and thought it seemed like bad luck.

I took in the neutral buildings around us: the McDonald's that wasn't open past midnight and the gas station and ABC store nearby.

Everything I observed in that time, which was only a few seconds, seemed suddenly to be doomed and to have always *been* doomed to be a part of that moment. Omens, portents of tragedy. All pieces that had to fall into place on the march toward the inevitable, as if this scene could not, would not, have happened if she had a different key chain. The shorts were a part of it. The tank top, the shoes and socks. They were all a part of it, suddenly promoted to the ominously important positions of being The Tank Top and The Shorts and The Shoes and Socks.

Because I knew she was dead. Right away. Now I wonder if I had firm confirmation, if maybe I'd tried to shake her or something, but in my memory, it was just the strong instinct and the way her body was positioned. Or maybe a soul knows when it's suddenly alone.

Whatever it was, I knew she was gone.

Seeing her at Joy's the other day, it hadn't been simply the shock of seeing someone who had been absent. It was as if her body had reconstructed itself, bones cracking and righting themselves until she stood before me, like a Tim Burton character, back from the dead and fully restored.

My mind loops for a while on these images until it finally grows weary and slows down again.

Once my breathing has returned to normal, Kiera pushes my hair off my damp face, pats me on the back, and says, "I have an idea. Why don't you slip back into something comfy and we'll watch a little *Titanic*, eh? We can eat somethin' and have some tea. We'll watch someone else's horrible tragedy. What do you say?"

I breathe in deeply, letting the muscles in my stomach relax—or at least deflate—a little. In my real life, if I got anywhere close to feeling this intensity of emotion, I'd be jumping on the Peloton or booking it to Equinox. Or taking one of my prescribed Xanax.

It's not until I think about this that I realize that, since that first night landing in Avalon, I haven't actually had a panic attack.

Except for this burst of very real, worthy emotion, I've been okay. Despite it all.

"That sounds good," I say, wiping the tears from under my eyes and laughing at the pile of spent tissues that has accumulated on the floor beside our pietà.

Kiera conjures a fresh box from somewhere. She rubs my arm and says, "Okay, go get changed. You look far too cute for lazing. We don't have work, so nothing to worry about."

I completely forgot I had a job, so this is a good reminder and good news.

I take off the remains of my makeup, giving a sorry laugh at it streaking down my puffy cheeks, and put my hair in an efficient, comfy ponytail. When I go into the bedroom, I see Kiera has set out an outfit. It warms my gaping heart as I put on my favorite sweatpants, a cashmere T-shirt, and Cillian's Avalon Rugby Club sweatshirt. I feel a little lovesick and lame putting it on, but choose not to care.

I curl up on the couch while Kiera fusses around tidying the place up, putting on the Christmas lights.

I open the phone and go to the texts with Aimee—the last exchange being the file she'd sent, which I had thumbs-upped. I type out a few different things. *I'm sorry. I love you. Please don't hate me. Please come back.* But I delete them all.

"All right," says Kiera with a clap, once everything is done. "Need anything else? Food is on the way."

"No, I don't think so," I say. Then I get an idea. "Actually, let's light one of those candles."

She gives me a look of exaggerated shock. "One of *the* candles?"

I shrug. "What am I waiting for, you know? You only live once."

I give a puffy sniff and then we both laugh.

"Jesus Christ, and I thought the Irish had gallows humor!" She is truly laughing now, which is contagious, and suddenly neither of us can catch our breath.

When I can finally say, "Oh my God, that's awful," I get up and go retrieve one of the candles, finding a box of matches from the drawer above the cabinet to light it. It smells amazing.

"It must feel weird, me having this reaction. Getting so incredibly upset," I say. "I mean, it's not real to you. And she's clearly alive. Here."

"I feel sad for you both," she says. "Look, I don't know what's going on for you, I really don't. But it doesn't matter. There's no question that everything you're feeling is real."

I nod. "Thanks."

"Pretty glad I'm not Aimee, though. I'd be having an existential crisis if I were her. I mean, *God.*"

I exhale loudly and say, "Yeah. That's what I'm afraid of. What if the universe collapses?"

"I don't think you need to worry about that, you narcissist. Let's watch your movie, shall we?"

I snort and plunk down on the couch.

I feel myself tear up almost as soon as the Paramount logo clears the screen. The rumble, those first few instrumental notes, then the vocals start and I'm ready to fall apart. The sepia imagery begins, people waving good-bye for the last time, not knowing it's the last time. I heard that James Cameron used some real footage in that part, but I don't know if it's true. It hardly matters, it's devastating. Especially when it cuts to the inky-blue water, gently churning.

Why do I love this movie so much? I mean, besides the fact that it's literally a perfect film.

I think about it as Bill Paxton navigates the wreckage.

It always makes me cry, this movie. In real life, I never cry. I never get choked up, I never tear up. It's like I save it all up for the big catharsis. *The Notebook* too.

God, I'm basic.

A little while later, Jack Dawson has just won tickets to America in a poker game when there's a knock on the door.

"I got it," says Kiera.

She gets up and opens it. It's Cillian.

I flush and try, idiotically, to hide that I'm wearing his rugby sweatshirt.

He's holding a brown paper bag and he looks past Kiera to me. I pause the movie and wave at him. "Hi."

"What's wrong?" he asks.

"Nothing," I say, and then burst into tears.

I'm suddenly *flooding* with emotions. Were these my options? Stone-cold ice queen or *Waterworld: The Person*?

He hands Kiera the bag and comes to crouch in front of me on the floor. "What's happened?"

I look at Kiera.

"I'd say it's bad tact to go talking about it, but then again, I don't think there are rules about this kind of thing," she says.

"I don't know, maybe it's not—"

"Don't tell me then," he says. "Not if you don't want. Are you okay?"

His tone is efficient, and it lends me a feeling of stability I can't give myself at the moment.

"I'm okay," I say. "It's some . . . it's some *other-life* bullshit."

He exchanges a look with Kiera as he puts a hand on my knee. As he does, he sees what's on the screen. "Oh, fuck's sake," he says.

"You're welcome to stay and watch," I say, suddenly, through another unexpected urge to burst into laughter.

Kiera mutters something to him as she passes him with the food. I don't hear what she says, but whatever it was, he responds to me, saying, "It can't hurt to watch it a sixteenth time, I suppose."

He's brought over chicken soup with white rice and seemingly fresh bread with salted butter.

"Is this your soup, Cillian?" Kiera asks. "Must be, it's the best."

"Yeah, I made it. Had the time. Mammy made the soda bread. Don't tell her it's for Meg." He winks at me and I smile.

Kiera splits the soup into three oversized mugs and puts the bread and butter on a wooden cutting board. She opens a bottle of red wine and pours it into three juice glasses.

I sit in the middle. Kiera is on my left, resting her bowl on the armrest. Cillian sits on my right, holding his soup by the mug handle and leaning forward to eat it. I put mine on a pillow in my lap.

I feel overcome with a deep gratitude for the moment. For the out-of-season Christmas lights that are slung around the room. For James Cameron. For the embracing nature of borrowed boy clothes.

But mostly for Kiera and Cillian. Kiera heard more than I ever even told to a therapist. And she still likes me after hearing it. She came over and hugged me. She told me it wasn't my fault. She stayed with me in a way I didn't realize I needed.

And Cillian. He doesn't even know what's going on, but when Kiera asked him to come—apparently she told him it would be good if he could stop by, maybe bring some comfort food—he made food and came. When he saw that I was upset, he didn't need to hear anything about it. He was willing to sit down and watch a three-hour movie that I am well aware he doesn't want to watch for the sixteenth time.

They're here. And it doesn't feel big. It doesn't feel intense. It feels nice, right, small, cozy, real.

I blubber and when they turn to me, I say, through yet more tears, "You guys are so nice."

They exchange a bewildered look. "She's lost her mind, but it's kind of nice, isn't it?" asks Kiera.

Cillian smiles at me, then rubs my knee for a moment before returning his attention to the screen.

I try not to speak along with the movie, but when Cillian catches me mouthing Rose's line *I believe you are blushing, Mr. Big Artiste. I can't imagine Monsieur Monet blushing,* he gives me an indulgent shake of the head and manages not to seem the least bit irritated with me.

A steady stream of tears falls out of my eyes unbidden for most of the movie, and I feel that I know deeply now that the grief doesn't have much to do with Rose and Jack's fated love story. I know it's about Aimee's and mine.

It's about all of this. The real reason I'm crying is because I am already mourning this life. I am afraid that I'll have to say goodbye, and I don't know if I can live through it all over again.

CHAPTER EIGHTEEN

Moving to LA wasn't a measured decision. I didn't finish school and then drive off in an old jalopy with *just graduated* written on the back. No. I didn't move to LA at all. I *fled* to LA.

In the days after Aimee died, I spent day in, day out in a silent, furious rage. I sat outside by my parents' screened-in, chlorinated pool, staring out at the man-made lake behind their house and seething. I woke up early every morning, unrested from hours of watching the clock tick on and on through the night, then went out to one of the rubber-strapped pool chairs and baked in the sun until it hurt. My skin pulsed with the heat and the rage that roiled inside of me. I sweated out every ounce of water I drank and ate next to nothing. Even to my parents, I probably looked like I was tanning at the pool, luxuriating as if nothing had happened. As if maybe I wasn't facing it, at the very least.

They both came and asked me repeatedly if I wanted to talk. They brought me fresh juice and toasted bagels slathered in butter and cream cheese. But I was snotty and irritable back at them.

I didn't go to work, which didn't surprise anyone. At the time, I was employed at a beach club bar at a hotel selling pretzels from a hot cabinet and plasticky cheese with stale corn chips, so it wasn't as if no one could cover me or live without the service.

Then, on the day of the funeral, my mom laid out a new, dull-looking black dress with a pair of grocery-store stockings and my little black ballet flats. She left a note on them.

Meg,
I always find that, when it comes to funerals, it's best to wear something you'll never wear again. I thought you might hate this.
We love you. We're going to Aimee's parents' house to help prepare for the wake after the service. See you later. Call if you need anything. There's a hash brown casserole in the fridge.
Mom

I had stared at the note and it filled me with anger. The fury that had been boiling inside me for days erupted.

I took the dress and threw it in the trash can along with the note. I then went to my room, blasted music as loud as I could—fuck the neighbors with their probably untraumatized lives—and filled every backpack and duffel I had.

I got in my inherited Camry and started driving. I had a couple thousand dollars in my bank account from working through winter break at the hotel, the last few weeks, and what I had saved from last summer. I had enough to get to LA and rent a room somewhere, probably. I'd find a restaurant job. I could start making tips right away.

I'd lie about how experienced I was. It would all be fine.

I was in Texas before I answered my parents' calls.

They couldn't make me come back. They couldn't do anything. Over the next two days, they both tried the angry *Get back here right this instant* tactic. They tried the tearful appeal, the frank appeal, the kind appeal. Then, eventually, they gave in. They told me they loved me and let me be.

I haven't thought of it at all in many, many years, and I feel so guilty now that it makes me ache. To this day, I have no idea what kind of financial loss they took when I dropped out of college. I know they must have paid some tuition for the year I didn't attend. Not to mention what a waste the previous semesters had been. They never mentioned it. Like they never mentioned the money I constantly borrowed over the next several years as I lived not-quite paycheck to paycheck.

No wonder they aren't flitting off to the Amalfi Coast in my life. Instead of a vacation fund, they spent years bailing me out. And no matter how many times I try to send them money now, they never accept.

After missing Aimee's funeral, I never talked to anyone from home again besides my parents. I never even went back to Florida. Not for Christmas, birthdays, nothing. I made excuses about work, and then when I had the money, I flew my parents to me. That was the only way they'd accept any money from me, and only because I would book nonrefundable tickets and insist that it was a Mother's Day, birthday, or Christmas present.

My whole focus in LA became fame. Success. Changing my life so substantially that it didn't resemble the one with Aimee in it; making it so perfect that I could never again wonder if I'd made a mistake by staying in Florida with Aimee.

And that's how I ended up *never* saying her name in my new life. I could pretend she hadn't died by pretending she had never lived. If I was in this new, completely different life, it made sense that she wasn't in it.

As much as I tried to forget about her, I still often wake up with a start. If I hear a crashing sound, my heart rate spikes. I hate driving. I'm white-knuckled most of the time I'm a passenger. I gasp a hundred times a car ride. I hate the hospital. And whenever I think of her, I become heavy, my body weighing a hundred tons, as I think about how it was *my fault, my fault, my fault.*

If I had only . . .

If I had . . .

If I could have hidden my feelings . . .

If I had pretended I didn't care . . .

It obviously had not worked. I clearly never resolved my past, never really moved on.

Which caused more guilt. How dare I be unhappy with such a glamorous, charmed life?

Aimee had texted me early in the morning, the quiet vibration of the phone on the nightstand enough to rocket me out of unconsciousness. As soon as I saw her name on the phone, a fresh jolt of adrenaline coursed through me, but it was just the file of the new script, sent without comment. I had opened it and read it in its entirety, over and over until the sun started to tinge the sky dusty periwinkle and sleep took me over.

When I finally got out of bed, Kiera was gone, a note left behind again, the corner tucked under the partially burned candle.

You're a good person. Love ya, xx, K

I put it on the fridge with a magnet, and then went on memorizing lines.

They're easy to remember for three reasons: One, she wrote the dialogue in a voice very similar to mine. Two, my professional experience. And three, I am so desperate for pieces of Aimee that I consume her words the way a Hungry Hungry Hippo goes after little white marbles.

When I arrive at the Avalon Playhouse, I am instantly swarmed by feelings. It's like déjà vu, and I realize that that's what a lot of my time in Avalon has felt like. When I knew where the whiskey was, when I knew my sweatpants were in the back of the closet. When I look at Cillian. That scene I saw at his apartment. There's a sense of familiarity but no memory alongside it. I wonder if this *is* what déjà vu is. What if it's different realities bleeding through?

Somehow, that's a comforting theory.

The theater is grand and warm. Ancient and broken-in, a content wisdom in its walls. I can practically hear the echoes of all the ghosts on the stage and in the audience.

I know a lot about the theater, since it's attached to the school. Or more accurately, the school is attached to it. Both were built in a Tudor style and are surrounded by lush grass and ancient vines.

As the story goes, the Avalon Playhouse was built in the late 1500s for Queen Elizabeth I by a secret lover. No one knows if she ever visited it, and there are a lot of questions about it due to the fact that Ireland was in revolt and tensions were high with the English, to put it incredibly lightly. She was busy colonizing the place and the Irish wouldn't have wanted her around, so the idea that she had a secret Irish lover is all the more salacious. Another version of the story says that it was some psycho wealthy guy who built it for her but that she never even knew him.

Being here now, walking across the stage, I remember why I wanted to be an actor. I love being onstage. Not doing forty takes with a fussy director in a cavernous studio with my face carved into something new, depending mostly on editors to make the performance into what people will eventually see. I like the lights, the people, the hallowed feel of a theater. The specialness of existing in a moment that only happens for those who witness it.

Living in the moment. There's something to that old cliché.

I hear a door open and then a moment later, see Aimee walk in off the left wing.

Ghosts in theaters. Such a thing.

"Hey," I say.

"Did you have time to review the lines?"

I shy a little at her professional tone. I had hoped that she would have warmed back up, a hope that seems delusional now.

"Yeah, I—I learned them."

"Great. Any questions or issues?"

"No. It's a great script, Aimee."

She hesitates, and then says, "Great, let's run a few lines and see how it goes. Tech should be here soon."

"Aimee, can we talk? I'm so sorry about—"

"Meg?" she says, using that new, very adult voice of hers. "We have a lot of work to do. I can't deal with your little hissy fit bullshit. I indulged your whole interdimensional whatever for as long as I could, but I don't have time for that right now, okay?"

This sends a searing pain through my heart and I feel like a fool. "You said you believed me."

She gives a humorless laugh. "Believed you that you're from a parallel universe? One where I'm *dead* and you're *famous?* Come on. Either you're consciously trying to get some kind of rise out of me, or your psyche is begging for help. Okay? So, until you get into some much-needed therapy, let's do the task at hand, shall we?"

I'm in *therapy*, I want to whine.

"You're trying to hurt me because I told you . . . about the . . ." I can't say it. "Because of what I told you."

"No, *you* were trying to hurt *me* by saying that. And yeah, now I'm mad."

"Fine," I say, resorting to being bitchy back, since I don't know what else to do.

She pulls out a chair and then says, "Okay, flip to page seventeen, let's run those. We did the beginning enough the other day. I want to see how this flows into the new ending, then we can go back."

"Sounds good," I say. Turning to the correct page, I clear my throat and begin. "Hailey, this is stupid. Let's go to the party."

"It's not stupid; it matters to me. Here, help me up. I can't believe they still have the same lattice."

I let out an irritated exhale.

"What?" asks Aimee, deviating from the script.

"What, what?"

"What are you sighing about?"

"I was acting, Aimee."

Comprehension dawns and she says, "Oh. Right. Sorry. Go on. I can't believe they still have the same lattice."

"It's probably not even in there, and if it is, who cares? It's like, two Polaroids and some expired candy."

"Fine, don't help. I've climbed this thing a million times without you."

"Will you *stop?*" I yell, my voice echoing around the empty theater.

Aimee looks startled, but then carries on. "What are you so afraid of?" she reads.

I hesitate and then put my hands on my thighs and bend over, embodying Lola's exasperation. "I don't want to dig up the past." I laugh. "I mean, really, let's not go back there."

I stand and breathe in deeply, letting it out as my head tilts at Aimee.

"I know you're acting," she says, once again going off script. "But it's really weird to hear you saying the lines. I pictured you when I wrote them, even though I knew you wouldn't come out to auditions or anything."

We spend the rest of the afternoon rehearsing. The lines are working. They're not awkward or stilted. But there's no heart in them. There's no heart in her delivery. I wonder if either of us will be able to open up enough to make this thing real. To make it special.

It's like a modern *Who's Afraid of Virginia Woolf?* but with more comedy. The two female characters don't speak anymore, but come together for their high school reunion; ultimately, the decision of whether or not to break into this house for the time capsule becomes a metaphor for the past they can't agree to revisit. Throughout the story, they switch back and forth on taking the lead in saying they want to break in for it.

The show takes place in a backyard, and I can see that the set builders are more than halfway through with the backdrop. A velvety blue sky with holes for starry lights to shine through. They're testing the lights, securing them on the back. There's an old white wrought-iron patio set that's stunningly similar to the one Aimee had growing up.

I wonder if anyone in Avalon knows her well enough to recognize it besides me.

Theo, I guess.

We spend hours going through it. Over and over and over, surviving off of protein bars and gallons of water. The lines are deeply engrained by the time we finish, and now I can start focusing on how to deepen the delivery, work on the character. We only stop because I point out that we're no longer improving, and that we've peaked for the day and any more rehearsal runs the risk of actually making us worse.

Aimee reluctantly agrees and I try to reassure her that it's good. It's going to be good.

As we shut the lights off and make our way out of the theater, Aimee says, "Good job today."

I get the feeling she just wants to fill the aching silence.

"Thanks. The set looks great. Simple but really good. And this theater is amazing. Cooler in person."

She pauses, and I remember that she doesn't believe me anymore. It's so uncomfortable to be uncomfortable with her.

Against my will, faint memories of that last month of Aimee and me together come into my mind. We were at school, sharing a dorm room. We lived in the college residence hall, and it was a constant, miserable party we could never leave. There was always some guy playing guitar with his door open. Weed drifted around the air at all hours of the day. Someone had a cursed karaoke machine that seemed to only have the songs "Mr. Brightside" by the Killers, "Kryptonite" by 3 Doors Down, and "The Reason" by Hoobastank. The lighting was prison-fluorescent. I had saved enough money from working the beach bar that I could have lived in the nice new student housing building, but we stayed there because Aimee couldn't afford it.

A vague memory of a fight starts to gather.

We wouldn't have to live here if you had the money to move out with me, I had said.

That's so shitty, are you really going to bring up how much money you have?

You would have as much money as I do if you'd worked all summer! But you didn't, you sat around in Theo's stupid basement watching him play video games!

I suck air in through my teeth now, suddenly remembering how many fights we'd had like that. I wasn't wrong, but I wasn't right either. If I'd had my therapist back then, she would have encouraged me to break my codependent bonds and live where I wanted to. But the problem was that I wanted to be where Aimee was.

We'd been so snappy with each other that last semester. I never let myself think about it. What possible purpose can it serve to think about all the bad times? Who thinks about those once someone dies?

"See you tomorrow," she says coolly now before splitting off and heading toward her own home.

She'll go home to a husband waiting for her, kids waiting for her. A whole little family she built from scratch.

I start to walk home, rain falling in big drops, drenching me. Then I get an idea.

A very bad idea.

CHAPTER NINETEEN

Maureen and I run through the rain and I feel like a naughty kid, gleeful in my bad behavior. Now I get why the other me is always stealing this dog.

First of all, when you're sad or lonely, it's nice to have a wonderful, happy little creature who's never in a bad mood to sit there with you and . . . well, I guess, love you.

Second of all, it's an obvious ploy for Cillian's attention.

It was so easy. Seeing that Cillian was busy at the bar, I walked up the stairs to his flat and checked under his mat for a spare key. Lo and behold, there was one there, either due to magic memories translating through dimensions or simply because he is predictably trusting. I used it and went in and took Maureen back. I left behind a note.

Hope it's okay! xoxo, M

I mean if he *really* cared, he'd probably move the key. I think, deep down, he likes it. At the very least, Maureen gets extra love and playtime while he's working.

She splashes through the puddles and I do too, not even minding how wet either of us are getting. I take off my hood and let the rain drench my hair, the cool water running down my cheeks, and I feel deeply present. Things aren't perfect right now. In fact, a lot is really weird and confusing. But I feel more like myself than I have in a long time.

I think back to my birthday party, when Barry Keoghan had stood in Grayson's yard and done this very same thing. It feels like two lifetimes ago. Maybe more.

Once fully drenched and back at the cottage, I fumble for the key and then go inside, letting Maureen race in ahead of me.

As soon as she's in, she shakes the rain everywhere, which only makes me laugh.

I go to the bathroom for a towel and come back to Maureen, saying, "Come here, pup, good girl."

She obeys happily, letting me scrub the moisture out of her fur.

I feel almost drunk on well-being. I want to stay here, doing laundry and hand-drying the dishes, picking up coffee and cream from that tiny supermarket. Stopping off at the pub, rehearsing for shows in that old theater. Healing my friendship with Aimee and nurturing the one with Kiera.

And, you know, banging and then hopefully marrying the shit out of Cillian.

Maureen buries her damp head into my chest and it knocks me over. I smile, tell her she's a good dog for the millionth time, and then stand up, tossing the wet towel into the washing machine before going over to the record player and picking out an album. I choose one of my favorites, one that I always listen to with my mom: A-ha's *East of the Sun, West of the Moon*.

I open a bottle of Gamay, pouring a few ounces into a glass I've decided is one of my favorites, having a sudden wave of certainty that I pilfered it and its matching partner from a hotel where Cillian and I once stayed. Was it the place in Dingle, maybe? As usual, it isn't quite a memory.

The first song on the album is the ever-melodramatic, blindingly Norwegian, delightfully overwrought cover of "Crying in the Rain." I blast it loud and get into the steaming hot shower. I take my time, indulging in the water and not bothering to worry about the next thing I need to do. Halfway through the shower, I traipse out, cold and naked, to gingerly flip the record.

It's an everything shower. I shave my legs and underarms in that slow, careful way rarely afforded to women in a hurry. I let a goopy hair mask sit on my hair. I sing along to the music at the top of my lungs—something I weirdly have not done in years, since I'm never really alone.

When I finally get out, my skin is warm and plump. I wrap my hair in a towel and look at my reflection.

I feel a real sense of fondness for the girl in the mirror. She didn't deserve to be changed. She didn't deserve to be whittled into something *more palatable* for social media. She's a good person who deserves carbs and sugar and whatever else makes her happy.

I retrieve a bar of chocolate from the kitchen and take a big piece, tossing a sweet potato dog treat to Maureen, then relighting the cabinet candle from last night.

I build a fire in the living room hearth, and then decide to go crazy and build one in the bedroom fireplace too. It's a particularly chilly night, especially in this old house.

The fires warm the place up so much that by midnight, I'm comfortable in a big, hideous, *gloriously* soft T-shirt that says *Avalon School of the Arts* on it, no bra, and my ratty old sweatpants, my hair brushed back into a ponytail. Maureen jumps up suddenly and runs to the door, tail wagging, nose at the base of the doorjamb.

I have a feeling I know why.

I go over and open the door, hanging on to Maureen's collar. I didn't mind being wet earlier, during my coming-of-age movie moment of reconnecting with nature, but we're both clean and dry now and I'd actually like to stay that way.

I see Cillian running through the dark rain, and something deep inside me shudders. He's in a white T-shirt and jeans. No jacket. Eat your heart out, Mr. Darcy.

The light catches him as he gets closer. He gives a cheeky grin, and my heart soars.

"What dog?" I call out innocently.

He gets to the front step. "Mind if I come in?" he asks.

I move aside, and his body touches mine as he goes by.

"Sorry, didn't mean to get you wet."

I strain to keep from making a sex joke, and say only, confusingly, "Oh, it's nothing. I mean, don't worry about it."

My grip on her collar slips and Maureen starts to run out, but is stopped by Cillian's quick, sharp whistle.

Whoa, *why* is that so hot? He's like Captain von Trapp without the late-wife baggage and war trauma.

I find a dry towel from under the bathroom sink, and then ask, "So why didn't you wear a jacket or something?"

"I was in a hurry."

As I hand it to him, I look up into his eyes and see something there I haven't seen before.

My blood runs icy. In a good way.

"I feel like a right clown," he says.

"Why's that?"

He breaks my gaze and walks into the kitchen, where he tosses the towel into the washer like I did, and then opens the fridge. "Y'mind?"

He holds up the open bottle of Gamay. I gesture that he should go ahead.

He gets out the glass that matches mine.

"Did I take these glasses from a hotel by any chance?" I hold mine up.

"So you are starting to remember then?"

"No," I say, thrilled that I'd been spookily right. "I have flashes sometimes. Vague sort of memories that aren't really memories. It's kind of like being a little psychic except all I get is senses of things like that."

"Bit like déjà vu?"

My mouth falls open. "Exactly!"

He pours his wine and then leans against the counter. The candlelight sends him into even more flattering light than usual.

"So why do you feel like a clown?"

"Ah, yeah. Because I know you're not the same girl. You said as much. But you are. And somehow, it's doing my head in."

He smiles and blushes a little.

"Can I say something completely inappropriate?" I ask, the words coming out without my full consent. "Now that we're being honest with each other."

He nods.

"You look"—I glance at his body and then back to his face—"really fucking hot tonight."

That muscle in his jaw flicks and he says, "So do you."

I know I'm in sloppy pajamas, but for once in my life I don't do the self-deprecating, painfully female thing where I say, *No, no I look awful.*

I get it. I get that he sees *me*, not the clothes.

"This is so bizarre," he says. "I don't think there's a rule book for what you're supposed to do in these situations."

"Situations where your ex-girlfriend is convinced she's traveling from another dimension and therefore she doesn't know you?"

"That'd be it."

"Do I seem the same?" I ask, busying myself with a sip of wine.

He nods. "Mostly. Bit more relaxed, actually. You haven't broken up with me this week, so that's different. Though I guess, we're not together."

He doesn't say it in a mean way.

"Why do you put up with it? With . . . me?"

He takes a nip of the wine and then says, "The sex. It's really good."

This shocks me and my eyebrows shoot up my forehead as I say, "Cillian!"

"I'm only coddin' you. Not about the sex. That really is very good." His gaze is steady on me. "Very good."

I smile, my heartbeat quickening. "Yeah?"

"Yeah," he says, matter-of-fact.

I've inched a little closer. He leans on one arm, clasping the edge of the counter.

"But that's not why I put up with it," he says. "I do that because I love you, Meg."

The words make me weak. In my real life, when a man tells me he loves me—off-screen—I'm sent into a strange tizzy. It feels as though a truth serum pulses through me and I physically can't bring myself to lie and tell him I love him too. Even when it's a real relationship, and I should love the guy by then.

This is the exact opposite experience. I shouldn't love him. I don't even know him. And yet I feel more compelled to say the words and mean them than I ever have in my life.

"I think I love you too," I say, using the apologetic *I think* not to white lie, for once, but to soften the intensity of what I'm really feeling.

He nods. "It would be nice if you could talk to the other version of yourself. The one I know. Maybe put in a good word."

A smirk plays at his lips.

"I could kill her," I say, laughing. "She's screwed up a really good life."

"Nah. Figuring it out. I've made a lot of mistakes. I always try to hold you too close. The old saying about the bird."

"Or Lenny and the puppy."

His eyebrows go up and he says, "Oy, I'm not that bad."

I laugh, and then there's a long, heavy silence between us, filled by the Sarah Vaughan record I put on right before he arrived.

I change the subject. "So is the sex really that good?"

He stares at me, looking amused, and bites his bottom lip. "No one has better sex than us."

"No?"

"Mm. No."

"I bet it's only fine," I say, flirting and trying now to cover up how strangely, how intensely I want to find out. "Ya know, I mean *most* sex is *fine.*"

He hesitates, then pushes off the counter and comes toward me.

I straighten up, wetting my lips nervously and covertly. He sets his glass beside mine and then puts his hand down on the wood so that his skin barely touches mine.

His scent is intoxicating.

I've lost all my cool. I am putty.

"The key to good sex is listening to each other," he says. "You told me what you like. I know you like to be kissed here." He touches the spot behind my ear and I inhale sharply at his warmth. "I know you like to be held here." He puts one of his strong hands around my waist, pulling me barely toward him. "I know you like to be bitten here." He leans down and gently slaps the inside of my thigh.

I'm going to die.

"Seems like you listen really well," I say.

"You leave me no choice." He leans forward then, his lips close to my ears, where he whispers, "You never shut the fuck up."

I push him away by the chest, smiling and saying, "Okay, all right, very nice."

He laughs. "I'm kidding. I love to hear you talk, Meg. Even when you're saying batshit crazy things like you tend to."

My aching desire for him mingles now with a warm fondness. There's an ease between us that runs more deeply than I can reach. I can feel the importance of us. We're Cillian and Meg, Meg and Cillian. Iconic in our own private way.

I step toward him, waiting for a long moment before I reach up and put a hand on his cheek.

He leans into it, shutting his eyes, then wrapping his fingers around my wrist.

I run my own through his hair and step even closer.

He kisses the thin skin on the inside of my palm and I inhale deeply.

I don't know which of us initiates, and it hardly matters. His lips are on mine, my lips are on his, and I feel like I might explode.

He kisses me with hungry urgency, one hand flat on my back, one on my jaw. He's the best, best, best kisser I've ever encountered. And for a bit at an award show, I once kissed Glen Powell.

I love every piece of him that touches me. His slightly rough face where he hasn't shaved in a day or two, the taste of French wine on his tongue, the intensity of his desire and how I can feel it matched inside me like a magnet.

In that moment, I release the doubt I have about whether or not I do or should love him. I let go of the idea that no one can love someone after only knowing them a few days. If this whole experience has taught me anything, it's that there are gorgeous mysteries winding between us and the people we care for.

Why should I wonder if I love him when it's my very certainty that causes me to ask the question in the first place?

I pull back and say it. "I love you, Cillian."

No apologies, no soft language, no insulation, nothing to break the fall. I know he already told me he loves me, but that's not the part that scares me. It's the part where I love someone too.

"I love you, Meggie."

He looks into my eyes and I realize this is the first time I've been in a moment like this. I'm so unprotected that my nerves start to hum. It's gentleness in his eyes that tells me not to worry.

And I wouldn't, if this life were mine.

Our lips collide again, messily but in a hot way. He takes off my big T-shirt.

I pull off his damp one, revealing an absolutely *sarcastically* good body that couldn't be better if I had specifically had it made for me.

He lifts me up and takes me into the bedroom, lays me down slowly, his body over mine.

"You're sure?" he asks.

"Cillian, my flight is in two days. I have no intention of getting on it. But I'm afraid of what might happen. I'm afraid I'll never see you again." My eyes fill with tears and I blink them away. "If I wind up back in my old life and don't know what it's like to do this with you, then I'm going to lose my mind. Even more than I already have."

"Meg. We will never lose each other."

He says it with such conviction that I actually, somehow, find myself believing him.

But that doesn't mean I don't want him anyway. I'm not *that* sure he's right.

He pulls off my sweatpants, kissing me from my neck to my chest, to my stomach, all the way down to my shaking thighs.

When he finally moves my thong aside and touches me, I shudder at the substantial weight of satisfaction and relief. I feel my heartbeat all over my body as he moves with expert grace and, clearly, a well-memorized choreography.

It's not slow and sensual, it's frenzied and urgent. The kind of thing I've thought was eye-roll-worthy in so many movies and shows. *When is sex really like that?*

Now, it's like that *now*.

He seems to know how hard to grab on to my arm, my tits, my ribs, my ass, my thighs, never too hard, never too soft. He uses just enough teeth on my hip bones and nipples and ears. I'm primal, my open mouth on his cheekbone and in his hair as he puts his fingers inside me and uses his thumb on my clit.

I am obsessed with his body, desperate for the muscles beneath the skin, curious and hungry to run my tongue and fingers and everything else over the peaks and valleys. The bend of his collarbone, the soft part behind his ear, the marble of his strong legs.

I am engulfed in the smell of salt and wood and rainwater and fry oil in his hair, a combination that makes me nostalgic for something I can't place. It's so good it makes me dizzy.

I should not be surprised that he has a great dick. And maybe I'm not. I mean really, look at him. I never thought I cared about that kind of thing, for real, until that moment. And maybe it isn't the size so much as how truly *perfect* it is. The Platonic ideal. His anatomy plugs so perfectly into mine, so satisfyingly correct. Every part of him manages to touch every part of me.

I feel like we are discovering or inventing sex for the first time. It's suddenly so clear that *yes*, the motion of thrusting in and out is so that—*ohhhh*, right yes, it's for both of us. When he throbs in me or puts my breast in his mouth, I feel myself heaving and thinking, *Yes, they should write about this, there should be a whole genre about this.*

I always felt like I was doing something wrong in the past when my mind would wander, and now I know I wasn't. My mind wasn't wandering far enough. While I lay in some Echo Park bedroom letting an okay-looking Loyola alum who met Jerry Seinfeld once go down on me, I was thinking about the meter outside. When Grayson and I had sex, I thought about whether or not the hot tub heater was turned on and if my Kindle was charged so I could go out and read after. But now, my mind has found what it couldn't in meditation; I am thinking in colors and feelings and music and abstract imagery. I'm not awake or asleep. I'm experiencing something new.

And while my mind is in space, my body is fully present. Every nerve, every urge. I am following my desire like stage direction in a script. I want to, so I move on top of him. I bend over him, my hair falling in a curtain around our faces.

It's. Fucking. Hot.

It's not awkward when it's over. We lie upside down on the bed, limbs entangled, the heat of the fire warming us from behind. I stare up at the print above the bed for a long while, both of us catching our breath.

"Have I told you about that? Why I have it?" I gesture at it.

He shakes his head. "No, actually. You haven't."

"I had it on my bedroom wall when I was a teenager. Along with a million ads from magazines and printouts of celebrities. I used to stare at it for hours when I was a moody teenager, listening to Fiona Apple or Mazzy Star or Death Cab or eventually Lana Del Rey. I used to call it *sad girling*."

I feel him chuckle. "Yeah, that sounds about right."

For the first time, I'm telling him something about myself that he doesn't already know.

"Does it?"

"Well, you're not a very sad person. Restless, yes, but unhappy, no. When you do get sad, it's always a little funny like that. *Sad girling*. It's funny. Melodramatic. Anyway, you were saying."

"Oh, I don't know. I identified so much with the girl in the painting. Obviously, I was in high school so I was overly emotional about everything and I could relate to her as she stands on the outside of the presumed fun. She's alone, trapped in her own internal landscape."

"Mm."

"I thought I'd grow out of it, especially if I was the one on the screen— not in the audience, not in the hall. But instead, I've only come to get it more and more. I still kind of feel like her. Especially being here. I feel like I'm on the outside of my own life. I mean, I *am*. Outside of both, I guess."

He squeezes me a little closer.

"I think she's an usher."

"What?"

He points at the girl in the print. "She's in a uniform. I think she's bored at work. I don't know that she's upset as much as she's just . . . waiting."

I sit up and squint at her. "Huh."

A log cracks behind us and he turns to check on it. It's fine, so he pulls me closer and relaxes again.

"You're not on the outside of your life looking in. Everyone isn't off having some perfect moment and you're left out of it. You're alive right now. Whether your *real life* is back in California, or it's here, or if it's on Pluto, it doesn't matter. You're here right now. I wish you didn't feel like things were such high stakes. You can be happy, you know. Look, let's say you're right, that girl there is on the outside, yeah? Everyone's inside enjoying the film, and she's in the hall." He shrugs against me. "She could walk in. And maybe the happiness is closer than she thinks."

"It's not as simple as that."

"But maybe it is, also. It's the indecision that'll kill ya."

I look up at him and he looks down at me. I love being this close to him. I love the firmness of him.

"So do you think that . . . the Meg who lives here. Do you think she should go try to become an actress then?"

"I think she should do what she wants. I only hope she lets me be a part of it."

I think about the proposal. I had asked myself how it was possible that the other version of me didn't know how good this life is.

But now I see it, or at least I'm starting to.

She went from life with her parents in a small town in Florida, to college in a small village, and nothing more. There was no great tragedy that taught her, for better or worse, about the unpredictability of life. She is restless with the unlived life rattling around inside, never having given it a shot.

When I showed up for my *Brilliance* audition, I was in a terrible mood. I'd been dumped by some guy who thought he was the next Quentin Tarantino, I'd found a rat eating a cockroach in the laundry room of my shitty apartment building, and I'd bartended for a particularly bad crowd until two a.m. before making my nine a.m. audition. I was mad at myself for not running the lines enough, for not coming up with something creative to go in the room with. I showed up raw, real, and unprepared. And what do you know? That worked better than the overthought approach I'd been trying for years.

It's not *Which life is right?* It's that I need all of it. I needed to try to be big in LA; I could never have appreciated a smaller life without it. But it doesn't mean that that life is right forever either. And that's okay. I can lead a hundred lives in my lifetime.

I remember what Kiera was saying about celebrities, and how they often pour their whole souls into success, only to wind up hiding. I thought it sounded tragic. Maybe it isn't.

I'm not supposed to be in LA with Grayson and Lisa Michele buzzing around me. I have to change my life. Maybe the universe will be kind enough to forget me here, in this other life, but maybe it won't. The glitch could end in an instant. Life, as I know too well, can do the same.

My mind whirs, but instead of being confused and conflicted and overwhelmed, like midnight epiphanies sometimes can make me, I know the pieces are drifting into place, settling in.

I fall asleep on Cillian's chest, wrapped in a deep feeling of contentedness that I've never had in my life.

In any life.

CHAPTER TWENTY

Cillian and I fall asleep in a tangle, and I only wake in the morning when I hear him quietly shutting the front door. I curl up in the scent of our extremely hot sex, and sleep for another few hours.

Then the next thirty-six hours go by in a haze.

We rehearse from early in the morning until the wee hours. We eat cheese and crackers and protein bars and drink endless water as we sweat beneath the stage lights, running scene after scene, again and again.

The set is complete, the starry sky functional, the fake grass covers the stage, all the props are ready. It now looks so much like Aimee's childhood backyard that my heartbeat flutters when I first see the bizarre reproduction. It's both unnerving and strangely comforting.

Another memory, long buried, comes to mind as I look at the set.

Suddenly I can smell the charcoal of the grill and citronella in the air. The rattling and chirping of spring peepers and cicadas in the boggy trees and the sound of a James Taylor CD playing from the kitchen. My parents sitting at the table drinking red wine and snacking on Tostitos

chips with queso and salsa; Aimee's dad drinking beer from a green bottle, wearing an apron that said *Never Trust a Skinny Cook*, and her mom
refilling her own glass of wine and enthusiastically telling a story about
the time she got stuck overnight in the Atlanta airport and wound up
talking all night to a nice man who—she didn't realize until later—was
George Lucas.

Aimee and I were drinking pink lemonade out of unbreakable stemless
wineglasses and sitting with bare legs in the grass, tugging at blades and
talking about people at school, scratching absently at mosquito bites. Young
enough and comfortable enough with discomfort not to care about the way
the grass and bites made us itchy or the way our scratching might leave scars
on our ankles one day.

Aimee leaned over to me, pointed at our parents, and said, *Do you think
that'll be us?*

To which I remember replying, *Married?* Which sent us both into
hysterics.

We were twelve years old, preoccupied mostly by the impending birthday that would give our age a *teen* at the end, the boys in our English classes
who seemed to finally know we were alive, and the fact that Halloween was
only a few weeks away and we still hadn't decided what to be yet. We didn't
make a proclamation about our futures like sage children in a Steinbeck
novel. I think we knew, without doubt, that it *would* be us one day. We'd
grow up, we'd know other grown-ups, and we'd eat snacks, we'd like wine,
and know everything.

The memory is interrupted by the intense collision of another one.
The first and last time I went into Aimee's backyard after she died. It was
dark and quiet, almost like the frogs themselves knew to be reverent. It was
empty and vacant, the smell of charcoal and the sound of the radio long
gone. Aimee, gone.

My reverie is halted by Aimee coming in to start rehearsal, having no
idea that the set is so unsettling to me. To her, it's probably a funny little
thing to have it look like her parents' house. To me, it's time travel. A grave-
digger in my repressed memories.

We're wrapping up dress rehearsal when I say something I've been avoiding for two straight days.

"I have to point this out," I say, interrupting the second act.

Aimee gestures with irritation for me to go on. "What is it?"

"Do—I mean, I'm not trying to blow up the whole—"

"Go ahead."

"I think it doesn't work to have Hailey tell Lola that she's been dead the whole time. It's a rip-off for the audience if they end up feeling fooled by Hailey. She comes off like a punishing ghost. And it doesn't make any sense, because how would Lola not know—"

"Are you kidding right now? We can't rewrite the whole ending, Meg!"

"I know, but it isn't right."

"Meg, what the hell are you suggesting? We've got twenty-four hours. This is actually wild."

"It doesn't have to be anything substantial; it's a few lines that need to be changed. Lola should be the one to tell Ai—Hailey." I flush at the mistake. "Lola should tell her. Because at the end of the day—"

My throat tightens.

"What?" she asks, still firm and professional.

"At the end of the day, isn't Hailey a figment of Lola's imagination? Hailey doesn't know that she's . . . you know, she doesn't know. The whole thing is a metaphor for Lola to work through the fact that she hasn't accepted her friend's . . . death."

The meta-upon-meta nature of what I'm saying is definitely not lost on me. I blink away the tears, refusing to allow them to fall.

It's not lost on Aimee either. "That's awfully Lola-centric, isn't it? I mean, the whole world doesn't revolve around Lola."

"It makes more sense to me," I say. "Narratively."

She pauses, then says, "We're leaving it. Guys, I think we're done here."

She goes over to her binder and grabs it off the ground. The small tech crew move slowly toward shutting the rehearsal down.

I watch Aimee go down into the seats and collect her stuff. A wave of something hot rises in me.

A deep, unseated anger is dislodged. In the last several years, I've stopped speaking up. It's why my assistant controls my life and runs rampant over me. It's why I do all the paid ads I hate doing so much. It's why I have a PR-arranged relationship, live in a house that doesn't feel like my own; why I've gotten so much work done and lost so much weight. Because I haven't felt like I deserved to say *no* or to admit when something doesn't feel right. I've stopped trusting myself.

She's about to leave when I call after her. I might not have forever to have this fight. "Hey!"

My voice echoes around the place. Visibly startled, she turns to me. "What?"

"Don't *what* me," I say. "We need to talk."

She laughs. "What are you going to do, break up with me?"

"I need to know why you're so mad at me. Because you're my best fucking friend, and I don't understand what happened between us. I deserve to figure it out. Even if you don't feel like it."

"Meg." She looks exhausted.

"No, don't do that. You may not believe what I told you, but it doesn't even matter. We aren't talking, and we swore that we would always be friends." I hold up my pinky, gesturing for the promise we'd made. I let my hand fall at my side and stare at her in the darkness of the theater.

"Fine."

She tosses her bag down, letting her binder and books clatter on the ground as she stomps toward me. She gets right up onstage and then crosses her arms. "I'm here, you happy?"

"Yes."

She seems to steel herself. "What were we fighting about the night—the night it happened?"

I hesitate, surprised by her question. "You weren't telling me something. I was pretty sure it had to do with Theo. I couldn't get it out of you. You were being really weird at the party and then said you wanted to go home. I was afraid you were pregnant or something, but in the aut—" We both go a shade paler at the near mention of the word *autopsy*.

My stomach flips. "You weren't. I'll never know what you didn't want to tell me."

She goes paler still, and then says, "I think I might know. Actually."

My chest runs cold and I feel my body harden, bracing for impact. "What?"

What would this Aimee know that my Aimee also knew? What secret could transcend this much time and space?

"I did get into Avalon. When you did."

I'm confused, but furious understanding starts to creep into my bones before my mind can catch up.

"What are you talking about?"

"We both got in."

"Then why did you tell me you didn't?"

"I knew you'd go anyway."

It's too much to comprehend. "Wait, wait, wait. Okay, first of all, no I wouldn't, I *didn't*, in fact, I did stay at that terrible school and live in a shithole dorm with you. In my world, which you don't believe anymore."

She bites her bottom lip in a way I forgot she used to do. "I do believe you. I was mad and being mean."

I pause. "Why didn't you go to Avalon with me?"

"Because I didn't want to!" she says, her voice now the one bouncing off the empty seats and through the sky-high rafters. "I didn't want to."

"What do you mean, you didn't want to? It's literally all we talked about for like two years!"

"No, Meg, it's all *you* talked about for two years."

I shake my head. This is bullshit. "We stayed up every night talking about it."

She doesn't say anything because we both know what she'd say. Which is that I was the one who stayed up every night talking about it.

"Okay . . ." I relent. "So why didn't you tell me?"

"I knew you'd blame it on Theo. Because, yeah, I wanted to stay with him. I loved him, Meg, I've always loved him so much. Even when he was a loser idiot teenager, and now that he's not, I love him the same. I knew that you'd think I was being a dumb girl staying home to be with her townie boyfriend. I never wanted a *big life* like you." The way she says *big life*, I can tell she's quoting me. "You could never understand why or how anyone could ever want anything less than to become an icon. To become immortal." She gives a laugh joylessly.

I seethe. "This is crazy."

She nods slowly.

It makes sense. It makes so much stupid, stupid sense. I can hardly believe it, because if this is true, and if the timelines diverged when I think they did, then it means she lied in my world too. And in *my* world, it's even worse, because she let me stay home without telling me the truth.

I think of how I'm always trying to get my mom to move out of Florida. How she's always telling me that she and Dad like their life there. How I'm often angry when I get off the phone with her.

More strange, disjointed memories start to pour over into my consciousness like an overflowing bathtub, the hot water seeping over the sides.

No wonder the atmosphere was so charged after we graduated high school. Aimee acted so weird, especially once we got to college. No wonder she encouraged me to move to the nicer building without her. No wonder she got so visibly uncomfortable every time I joked about having stayed home for her. Clearly, I had been veiling my own resentments, but I'd based them on what I thought was the truth.

Every time things sucked, they double-sucked for her because she felt guilty I was there, ostensibly, for her.

"But I saw the letter," I say.

She shakes her head. "No, you didn't."

I have an image in my head of the rejection letter she received. I can see it.

But as quickly as it appears, the memory begins to go up in flames, as if I were holding a match to the edge of the letter itself.

"You never asked to see it," she says. "I think you knew. You must have, somewhere."

I feel a strange tremor run through my skeleton and I wet my lips and clear my throat. "No, that's—no."

"I kept thinking you'd ask to see it, but when you didn't, I didn't volunteer it. Obviously. Because it was a lie."

A small waft of amusement goes between us and I can't help but scoff.

"This changed my whole life, you know. That decision. That's what this whole thing is about. I think. My being here at all. I had two lives. I picked one. The one where I stayed with you. And where I lost you."

"You should have come," she says to the ground. "This is what should have happened. To me, it is what happened."

"Why didn't I? If I knew? Why would I stay in Florida with you if I secretly knew?"

She shrugs. "I don't know. I don't know if you knew or didn't."

We look at each other now, and I feel like we're two fairies trapped under a jar. Both easily apprehended because we were paralyzed with fear, too afraid to take flight.

"So this is why we were fighting?"

"I mean, it started as an argument about Theo. Then I told you the truth about my acceptance. I was so mad. I wanted you to learn to like Theo and when you wouldn't, after all this time, I snapped. Told you. I knew it would make you as angry as I was. I think my logic was that you'd see that you were selfish, you broke our deal and came without me. Which is stupid. I knew it was stupid."

"And . . . how did you end up coming here? To Avalon? If you didn't want to."

She exhales heavily and says, "I changed my mind. I realized I was making a major life decision based on fear and decided that it was a worthier thing to follow your dream than to have no dream of my own. I couldn't stay home for a guy, in the end. I figured if it was meant to be, then me leaving for an opportunity like this wouldn't mean saying no to a life with him eventually. And he wasn't really getting it together yet. The weed-smoking was a lot back then, and obviously it just *was different* then. Like a whole-ass lifestyle."

It's true. When we were teenagers, you didn't have to be a prude to think the stoners were lame. Now, in California, I don't know anyone who doesn't have gummies, a vape pen, a topical cream. . . . I could go on.

I hear her phone buzz on her stack of things in the aisle where she left them.

"That'll be Theo," she says. "I usually put the kids to bed."

"Okay."

She pauses, then says, "It is annoying, you'd think he could do it one night without me. Maybe I should divorce him."

She's kidding of course, and I laugh gratefully. "I love that guy, I think you should stay forever."

We both laugh, then when the awkward silence hits, she inhales through her nose and says, "I'd better . . ."

"Yeah, for sure."

She goes back out into the empty theater and picks up her phone, then gathers her things. She holds up a hand to say goodbye, and I hold mine up.

"Turn the lights off, yeah?" she says.

She goes through the squeaky door to the outside, and I'm left by myself.

⁓

That night, I text Cillian and he tells me that he's got a busy night at the pub. I text Kiera, too, who says she's busy but can't wait to see the show tomorrow.

I get back to the cottage, absent of all the company I've had recently, and feel overwhelmed by the emptiness.

It's not that I feel sorry for myself or panic at the idea that I have to face an entire evening alone.

No, it's weirder than that. More complicated.

In the last couple of days, I've been feeling more and more divided. Tense but relaxed. Happy but worried. As if I'm slicing into two. And I've seen enough movies, consumed enough stories, to fear what I think might be inevitable.

Tomorrow night, after the show, I have a flight from Dublin to LAX. I have no intention of getting on that flight. I would cancel it if I could, but of course my ticket doesn't exist. It's from the other reality. So why am I so afraid that the end will come and take me?

CHAPTER TWENTY-ONE

———

Aimee, I can't find the garden hose! I don't know how it went missing, but—"

One of the tech crew, the teenage barista from Joy's—who's not named Freddy and is in fact named Antony—bursts into the dressing room. With him comes the ambient sound of busy energy from outside.

He looks stressed.

"Stage left, I just saw it," she says.

He sighs deeply, putting a hand on his chest. "*What* a relief."

He rushes back out, sending this room back into silence.

Aimee and I look at each other.

"I can't do it. I haven't had any time to emotionally prepare for this. I hate being onstage!"

I'm filled with a fizzing, nervous anticipation I haven't felt in years. Knowing everyone is out there, that they'll be watching in real time. I'll hear them laugh. I'll feel them listen.

"You can do this," I say to Aimee, earnestly. "It's you and me."

The characters are us, in a way, but there's another meaning to my words. It's going to be us onstage and nothing else matters.

She exhales noisily and says, "Why did I agree to this?"

"Because it's the best thing." And the only thing, because otherwise she was big-time fucked. "You're going to be great."

"Maybe! Or maybe I'll suck!"

She sits down next to me and starts buffing her foundation into her skin with frantic energy. I finish my lipstick and then, as she overapplies blush, I say, "Okay, okay, let's calm down, let's put down the makeup. Come here, let me help you."

She turns to me, looking anxious, her eyes pointed at the ceiling, her eyebrows in a state of worry.

I blend the foundation around her jawline and clean off the blush brush with a tissue before starting to buff in the color.

It's been a really long time since I've done another girl's makeup, but I always used to do Aimee's. Even if I did a bad job.

When we were around thirteen years old and really discovering makeup for the first time, we'd experiment with it in my parents' bathroom while they watched *Survivor* downstairs. Once, we got caught using my mom's good stuff and she tried to teach us better techniques.

Then, once we were older and I was starting to get the general hang of it, I'd do Aimee's makeup before homecoming, when we were usually each other's dates. Before prom, which we both had dates for, but left early. Before the plays, even when I had the lead and she was in the background. Before our joint high school graduation party.

In college, she leaned into a more natural, clean look and lost interest in me practicing cat eyes and contouring on her.

I cringe a little now, thinking about how I had forced her to let me use her as a little doll sometimes.

The welcome music kicks on outside, dreamy 1930s jazz. It doesn't have anything to do with the plot or the show itself, but Aimee insisted that it lends a festive feel to any situation, and I couldn't argue with that.

As soon as she hears it, Aimee inhales sharply. It's almost time.

I look at the clock on the wall. Thirty minutes 'til curtain. Six hours until my flight. I just need to get past boarding time and I'll feel safe here.

"Hey," I say, smiling at Aimee and dropping my chin. "You're fine. You don't need to worry. Plus, I'm an old hand at this now. If you screw up, we'll freestyle. No one else will know."

She nods tightly. Then she says, "Meg, can I tell you something?"

I sit back. "Of course. Anything."

"Last night—last night I had a really weird dream."

"That *always* used to happen to me before a show. What was it?"

She bites her bottom lip, eyebrows tented fretfully. "We were in Florida. I was driving. I think—I think it might have been the—the . . . it was by that McDonald's. The one that closed before midnight."

Oh God.

"Shit." I feel like my heart might disconnect from my body completely. "Are you serious?"

She nods. "It was scary, Meg. I thought you weren't supposed to be able to die in dreams, but I just . . . and then I woke up."

I reach out and put my arms around her. I squeeze her, even though she doesn't, at first, hug me back.

"I don't want to believe you," she says, sniffing and pulling back. She uses a triangle of tissue to dab at her tears. "It feels impossible to accept it. It's terrifying."

"Would it make you feel better if I said I made the whole thing up?"

She scoffs. "*No*, God!"

I laugh sadly. "I wish I had."

Her phone buzzes. She reads whatever pops up, then groans and says, "The bartender didn't bring ice—dammit, how . . ." She texts back furiously.

I move away from her, feeling as though this whole world is starting to slip between my fingers like sand.

"Fifteen minutes," says the stage manager, appearing in the doorway.

"Gah!" exclaims Aimee.

"It's okay!" I say. "Look, don't think about the dream. I'm sure it was your imagination. We talked about it. You've seen movies. Your brain probably repurposed a bunch of tragic stuff and turned it into a nightmare."

She looks at me, and I look at her. I don't believe the words I'm saying. There's been too much weirdness since I've been here. Including the *being here* thing to begin with. But also the strange bleed-through of memories and feelings that I shouldn't have access to.

What if her *soul* knows? What if all our souls know things? What if that's what instinct is? What if that really is the explanation for gut feelings, intuition, déjà vu, kismet, and everything else? What if it's our souls, remembering or knowing the truths of all our other lives?

"Bullshit," she says, looking into my eyes. "You don't think it's a dream. Neither do I."

We're both silent for a moment.

"Come on," I say. "Let's get into costume."

We've been sitting here in our foundation garments—which is really the only word for this particular kind of scaffolding.

She's wears an A-line dress with stockings and little kitten heels. I'm in a chic blue jumpsuit with high pumps.

Once dressed, we look in the mirror.

Our reflection sends a chill through me.

I don't want to say that I've gotten used to being around Aimee again. I haven't stopped being amazed, confused, weirded out. I would say that I've adapted, like I have to the rest of this surreality. But this is the first time I've seen myself beside her in real life, and something about this is startling.

I don't know what I expected. That her reflection—or mine—wouldn't show up? Like a vampire? Or maybe some M. Night Shyamalan twist, where her reflection is some terrifying proof that she really is dead. Or maybe that we'd suddenly be nineteen again?

Instead, it's us. Thirty-year-old me, thirty-year-old her. Together. Alive.

Our eyes lock on each other's.

"Let's go look at the audience," I say. "Do you think the critic is here yet?"

"I don't know, I've seen *Waiting for Guffman* one too many times."

We sneak to the side curtain and look out at the theater.

"Aw, look," says Aimee, nudging me and then pointing at Cillian in the middle of front row, talking to Theo, his ankle resting on one of his knees and a beer in his right hand.

The place is packed with warm, delicious energy as noisy men clink their glasses of beer and ladies clutch their shawls close while sipping from small glasses of wine (not being sexist, that just is the situation for the most part). There are some irritable-looking teenagers and hyper kids who undoubtedly won't stay still for the performance. Including Clare and Ronan, who are in tow with Theo, playing in front of the stage. He's got a beer too and he tilts his head with interest at something Cillian says.

I feel a pang of unexpected fondness for Theo and resolve to apologize to him after the show, or at least try to talk to him. Get to know this version of him. We're staying at the theater for a little party and mingle thing afterward. I'll do it then.

Clare holds something up for Cillian to look at. He takes it and says something that makes her laugh.

"Cute," I say. In yet another life, I could see the four of us out on double dates. Having fun. Maybe her kids and . . . my own kid too. One day. A long time from now, when I'm physically capable of that kind of responsibility. When I've finished sorting out my own child- and teenagehood.

I watch Aimee's face as she looks at her family. The tender, slight smile. The softness around the eyes, which focus far off into a world with them.

It's like it recharges her. Helps to wash away the sadness she felt a moment ago, thinking of the dream. Thinking of how bad things could be or might have been.

"Do you see him?" asks Aimee.

"Who?"

"The critic."

"How would I recognize him?"

"He's the one person who isn't from Avalon—or, I guess you don't know everyone. Never mind."

"Oy, ladies," comes a voice behind us.

We both jump and turn to see Kiera.

"What is it?" asks Aimee, putting a hand over her chest. "There's a disaster, isn't there?"

"No! I chatted up that critic. We had a glass of wine and it turns out he's a young, dashing sort of character. Not the old, stodgy miser I was picturing. Maybe enough to finally steal me from my Nial spiral."

This makes me laugh, but Aimee says, "Ohmigod, ohmigod, ohmigod."

"I know, I know, I thought it would be good if you knew—I told him how amazing you two are, and how you've been friends for years and all. He looked impressed when I told him the backstory."

We both stare at her.

She looks between us and then says, "Oh, no, *God*, not everything. I just told him it's based on your own friendship. Basically. He thinks it sounds good! Seems like it's a pretty big deal he came all the way out."

"No pressure," I say to Aimee, giving Kiera a wide-eyed look of *shut! up!*

"No, no! He said he's looking for *real*. He's looking for *raw*. And he said if this show is anything like it sounds, then it'll be right up his street. I'm here to tell you good luck and remind you to give it your all. Hold nothing back. Really. I've known you both a long time. That's your issue. You're so tough, the both of you. I know that's rich coming from an Irish girl, but that should tell you something."

"Five minutes!" calls the stage manager.

"I also got him a little tipsy. Okay, break a leg, ladies. I can't wait to see the show!"

She winks and goes off.

"I'm so nervous," says Aimee.

"It's no big deal," I say, looking as cool and collected as humanly possible. "You're fine. Everyone will love it. And if they don't, then fuck 'em. But they will."

She nods. "Okay."

"It'll be great. I promise."

I hold up a pinky. After a moment, she holds up hers, too, and links it with mine. Electricity buzzes between us, coursing through my bones starting at that joint.

"Okay, okay. We got it. Let's do it."

The din of conversation quiets outside as the lights go down. Aimee and I walk out onstage, concealed by the curtain, and take our places.

A wave of adrenaline goes through me. I take a deep breath. The curtains open. The spotlight lands on Aimee and me.

Showtime.

CHAPTER TWENTY-TWO

—⁓—

hat's not why! Okay?" I say the line loud and firm but allow the despair to come through. We're almost at the end of act one. It's gone well so far, but I can sense that the audience isn't particularly moved. "Please, if we're going to this stupid reunion, then let's go. Let's go now."

It's the scene where Hailey is about to tell Lola she's a ghost.

Aimee, as Hailey, looks at me from across the stage with her arms crossed. She comes over to me and lightly smacks my legs off the chair so she can sit.

When she does, she leans forward and whispers so that no one else can hear, "Do it your way."

"I'm sorry, I'm not trying to be a drag," I say, loudly, ad-libbing, then whisper under my breath, "*What?*"

She must be noticing the lukewarm response in the room too.

"End the scene your way. You were right, it should be Lola who tells Hailey." She says it quickly and quietly before going back to projecting, standing and walking a few feet away to say, "Tell me why you're so scared of going in to get this stupid time capsule. I know it's not the breaking-and-entering part; you stole enough vibrators from Spencer's Gifts to prove that crime isn't the issue here."

The audience laughs in surprise, even though I doubt they have Spencer's in Ireland. I laugh too, taken off guard by the freestyle.

"You're right, it's not the crime part." I stand also, then let the smile fade as I briefly rub my own shoulders awkwardly before letting my arms fall to my sides. "Hailey, there's something I have to tell you."

She pauses. "Okay, what?"

This is so risky. Especially considering how dark things got in the dressing room. I don't want to think about it. I don't want to remember it. I've never allowed myself to remember the accident as thoroughly as I fear I'm about to. Not even the other night with Kiera.

"Do you remember driving back from that party? We were in your dad's car. Leaving that guy Sam's house."

Aimee's jaw sets bravely. "Yeah."

"Do you remember . . . what happened?"

The room goes tense for the first time. It's funny how you can tell.

"What do you mean?" she asks. "We were listening to music and you were being—"

"We were fighting. But do you remember on the corner of"—my gut roils—"Mangrove and Ponce de Leon . . ."

A hand goes to her mouth slowly. "There was an accident." She looks scared of her own words.

"Yeah," I say. Then, all at once, "Hailey, you've been dead for over a decade."

There's a unified gasp from the audience, and then, after the perfect amount of time, Aimee storms offstage. She has to; since we changed the lines, no one knows that it marks the end of the scene, the end of the act. Luckily, it works narratively.

As soon as she's gone, I let my chin fall to my chest. I crouch and cover my mouth, with a thousand-yard stare into the wings.

I hear Aimee whisper-shout, "*Curtain! Now!*" to the crew member, and at her word, they shut the curtains on me, marking the time for intermission.

The lights go down as they do and the theater erupts in applause.

I step offstage, feeling a little nauseous.

At the best of times, I used to feel weird onstage. The excitement moves through the body, churning and agitating and vanishing and appearing again, as strong and unpredictable as an angry ocean.

I wasn't worried about tonight, for the most part. We got to a pretty good place in rehearsals. It was kind of the equivalent of cramming for a test versus steadying the whole semester—it's all fresh.

But now that we're changing it on a dime like this, it's basically experimental theatre. I'll have to talk about what happened. Out loud. For real. For the first time in my life. I've barely thought about it to myself until the last few days.

In the wings, Aimee is texting and talking on her walkie-talkie furiously, making sure everything is in place. She's mentioning missed cues no one noticed and worrying that the mic is picking up on the creaking of the floorboards. She's telling them to pay attention, because things are going to be unscripted.

It's a bold choice, and the shocked looks on the weary stagehands' faces show it. But Aimee doesn't back down.

Through a crack in the curtain, I glance covertly out to the front row, where I see Theo is returning from the bar with two beers while Cillian watches the kids.

I swear to God my previously mute ovaries scream at the sight of him smiling and talking to Clare, who now has a hand on her hip and is confidently yammering about something.

I shut the curtain and step away, looking at the set onstage.

We used to sit out in Aimee's backyard for hours. She had an old house from the 1920s, where my parents had a new build. My house was all mosquitos in hose-water-drenched grass, cool tile flooring, fresh paint.

Aimee's house had crank windows and real wooden floors, paneled walls in a galley kitchen. The backyard was lush and filled with flowers I never saw anywhere but there. It smelled like honeysuckle and dew. The back had a lattice with ivy and morning glories and we used to sneak out by climbing it. Of course, when we snuck out, we usually only sat in the backyard. In retrospect, we were kids who wanted to be bad but never really got into trouble. Her parents probably knew. But she sometimes would sneak out to see Theo, and they went all over town.

"Water, babes?"

I turn to see Antony holding a big bottle of water.

"Thanks," I say, taking it.

"No problem."

He then runs off to deal with some other crisis no one in the audience would ever notice.

I think about Theo and Aimee again. When we were in high school. Once they started dating, they were inseparable.

It did make me jealous. Aimee was right. She hadn't outright said it that way, but that's what she meant.

I had some crushes back then, obviously, a boyfriend or two, but they were dumb boys. A way to get kissed for the first time or not show up to prom by myself. She had that *first love* with Theo, and I didn't, so I couldn't understand it.

The truth is, in high school, no one wanted to date me. Probably because all I did was hang out with my best friend and scream-sing "Ordinary World" by Duran Duran in the car with my mom.

The truth is, I was jealous that Aimee had a boyfriend. Jealous that he hadn't liked me.

The truth is, I got work done and lost all that weight because I didn't want to look at myself. I wanted to be someone new. I wanted to be chosen and accepted.

The truth is, ever since the car accident, I have been hiding.

The truth is, Aimee is dead. I saw her die.

This has never hit me like it does in this moment. Even the other day when I collapsed in Kiera's lap. It's like that moment walked so that this one could run. My ears ring and my heart races alarmingly fast. Everyone around me seems like part of an even different reality. I feel like I'm dying; my brain is emitting that drug, maybe that's what all of this has been.

It's a panic attack. My first major one since I arrived.

They happen when I feel out of control. That's what Cillian said that first night.

I don't think I would have understood it a week ago, but yes, I *do* feel out of control right now. I'm unraveling a ball of certainty that I am not sure I can rewind. I'm accepting what was unacceptable, and I'm afraid of what it'll mean. Will it make all of this fall away? Will it send me home?

Will it make the rest of my life unlivable?

I need to breathe. Around me people move and talk efficiently as if I'm not experiencing an emergency.

In, two, three, four. Hold, two, three, four. Out, two, three, four. Hold, two, three, four. Then again, in . . .

My heart rate slows and I'm starting to be able to hear and see normally again.

If the panic attacks are about feeling powerless, then no wonder I've had so many. I've never had an ounce of control. In LA, I don't have power over the hours of my day, the money in my bank account, the way I look, what I say, what I eat—anything.

Or I do have control, but I haven't been taking it.

"Okay, you do the first line, and we'll go from there," says Aimee, appearing suddenly at my side. "Try to keep it close to the script where you can for the lighting cues and all, but do whatever's best."

Her happy face makes me want to cry. "Aimee—"

"Do it," she says.

"I don't think I can do it. I can't talk about this—"

"We have to do this. Do it for me."

She stares at me hard and I feel how deeply she needs it. But why in front of everyone? Why in front of an audience?

And yet, somewhere in me, I feel like I understand.

Onstage, we can't run from it. Onstage, it's easier to face, as if it's not quite as real.

"We'll use it," she says. "You and I have trouble being vulnerable. It's like Kiera said. We're tough. But you never had trouble onstage, did you? You're so much more confident when you're acting."

I don't get a chance to answer her, because a moment later the bell rings outside and we hear people start to get back to their seats.

The theater begins to quiet as the lights go down, and Aimee whispers, "*Places!*"

I stand on shaky legs and go to my spot.

Aimee stands in hers.

The audience is completely still, waiting for the resolution of the cliffhanger we left them on.

The lights rise. Someone coughs.

"Do you remember now?" I ask, as Lola.

"Tell me what happened," she says. I can see that she's fighting back the emotion—she's unblinking, face unmoving. "What happened, Lola?"

I grit my teeth and tell her.

"We were fighting. We were at the party and you didn't want to be there. I was having fun, but you weren't. You wanted to get home to go meet—your boyfriend." I rub my face with both hands. "Your boyfriend—Leo." Oh my God. So uncreative. The *Titanic* and Theo of it all. "I was mad at you because you were always ditching me for him. You were always ditching *everything* for him. And he was such a jerk and such a loser—sorry."

I feel guilty, knowing that Theo might piece together enough to be hurt.

She gives one clipped shake of the head. "No, go on."

This is the worst. The actual worst.

"I—well, it was my fault," I shut my eyes and then blink a few times before going on. "I was screaming at you. I was nineteen, I had zero handle on my emotions back then. And I was yelling at the top of my lungs. I felt like you weren't, I don't know, you weren't *hearing* me. I wanted you to listen to me for once. You wanted me to be quiet and—"

How much do I actually have to tell her? Do I have to confess to everything?

I ground myself and then go on.

"You told me to be quieter, but you were screaming it at me too, so I cranked up the music as loud as I could and I wouldn't let you turn it down. It was only a few seconds but someone ran a red light and we didn't . . . we didn't see them coming."

"And then . . ."

The pause is heavy.

"You . . . d-died instantly."

I resist the visuals entering my mind. Her body in that awkward, unnatural position. The mangled driver's-side door. The almost undamaged car that hit us. The driver's anguish.

"I remember now," says Aimee, starting to cry, trying to keep the tears at bay. "It was raining."

This is true. And I haven't told her this part. I hadn't *remembered* that part. God, it was pouring, how had I forgotten that?

The scene plays out again in my head: the winds were rushing, her hair blew not in a breeze but in whipping winds that cycloned through my open passenger door and her shattered window.

I could see the reflection of the stoplights and the headlights and the red and blue from the sirens on the wet asphalt.

"Yes," I say. "How did you—"

Aimee looks at me, and I see that she realizes too that it's the truth. "I don't know. I just . . . know."

"I'm so sorry," I say with a shake of my head. "I wish I'd been quiet. I wish I'd shut up for once in my life. It was none of my business what happened with you and Leo," I say, remembering *not* to say *Theo* in the nick of time.

She stares at a spot on the ground, and asks, "What was the music?"

"What?"

"The music. That you blasted. What was it?"

"Oh. Actually it was . . . *Revolver*. The Beatles. 'She Said She Said.'"

She laughs once, then sniffs. "The lyrics."

I nod. *She said I know what it's like to be dead.* The foretelling of that song had made me sick with irony. I never told anyone that detail. They didn't need to know.

"I haven't been able to listen to that album since. Which sucks," I say, trying to lighten the mood, "because it's good."

She laughs too. She sits down at the table and says, "I think you got it wrong, though."

"What?"

"The accident—I don't think you remember it right."

"I—what do you mean? It was my fault. We would have heard the other car coming if—"

"It wasn't. Remember? It wasn't your fault."

She stares at me. I can see a frightened honesty in her eyes and I feel weak. The audience is tense.

"No," I say. For the very first time, the real images of what happened that night start to flash in my mind. "No!" I scream now.

"You have to face it," says Aimee. "You have to. You never did, did you? You never think about it. You said so."

The images are rolling in now, unstoppable. The memories driving toward me at a hundred miles an hour, Ringo's crashing cymbals scoring them. The music had kept playing even once I climbed out of the car. It was "Good Day Sunshine," blasting relentlessly as I stepped over broken glass. I had called her name and she hadn't moved. Over and over and then I had gotten back in, my knees on the seat. When I shook her, she moved like she was made of rubber. I was cold all over as I stepped back out of the car, and that's when I'd noticed all the silly things. The socks. The gas station.

"I was a terrible driver. Especially in the rain. Remember that time I backed out of your parents' driveway and hit the neighbor's car? That wasn't even a thunderstorm. That was light rain."

"I'd—I'd forgotten—"

"Or the time I rear-ended the guy at Steak n' Shake?"

There's a small ripple of laughter from the audience. They're asking for permission to find humor in the tragedy.

I give them a joke.

"That was meaningless sex," I quip, even though my soul feels like it's slipping out through my bare feet. I kicked my shoes off in the last act.

They laugh again, a laugh of relief, but I can tell they're in this with us.

"Very funny," says Aimee. "But M—Lola, are you sure someone hit us because they went through the red light? Weren't *we* the ones to go through the red light?"

"Of course it—right? Wait, no . . ."

Aimee, look out—AIMEE!

My own words come screaming back into my head.

I gasp, putting both hands to my chest. I can hear the words as clearly as if they were being screamed in my ear.

AIMEE!

"And I was the one to turn up the music," she says. "Because I was trying to drown you out. I didn't want to hear it. Did I?"

My hands are shaking. My body lowers to the ground, my fingers reaching for the plastic grass. My ears are ringing. Everything feels very far away.

No, stop talking, stop—no, I don't want to hear you speaking right now, I want to—Meg, let go!

Aimee's voice from the past comes to me as clear as a bell.

She hadn't let me turn off the music. She had cranked it. That's why I was yelling. *That* was why I was screaming at her. I was yelling over the music.

"Oh my God," I say quietly. I don't project enough, but the whole theater is so silent that they can hear me.

I remember now, how she slammed through the red light, accelerating as she did. She could get so livid back then. And then the other car had driven straight into her side.

"I'm the only one who knows," she says, her tone softening. "I'm the only one who was there. And since I haven't been here to blame, you blamed yourself. But it wasn't your fault. Neither of us were perfect. We were doing our best."

There's a long silence.

It doesn't make it easier that she had fault in it. It doesn't make it hurt less. But it's the truth, and that's important.

Tears roll down her face and I feel myself burning hot with feelings that have been locked away for years. I let out a sob and then laugh before saying, "I love you so much."

"I love you too."

"I miss you all the time." I can barely get through the words. "I don't talk about you because it hurts so, so much—it's not because I don't miss you, it's not because I don't care anymore." My throat is tight and my nose is so congested I can't breathe through it. "It's because I'm afraid that if I admit how sad I am, I'll never be okay again."

My breath comes in sharp staccato.

She nods, then kneels on the plastic grass in front of me, reaching out and pulling me into her. "I know that."

I hug her back. Hard.

No matter what is going on here, I am certain that the arms around me right now, the hair I'm burying my face into, the scent of her skin—it's Aimee.

No one will ever be able to tell me that this moment was not real.

Both of us start to catch our breath and I become vaguely aware of the sniffles coming from the audience.

We break apart and I see the way the stage lights hit her skin. I can see her every tiny pore. I can see the lighter tips of her eyelashes where I missed putting mascara.

She looks offstage and gives an almost imperceptible nod. A cue.

I cover my eyes for only a moment and look up when I hear the back door of the set opening. Antony appears in the doorway. His bit part.

"Can I help you?" he asks.

I stand, blinking, and then say, "Sorry, we were—"

But Aimee has vanished from the stage.

I look into the wings and am relieved to see she's still there. Both of her hands are on her chest, and her face is blotchy and red, but she's smiling encouragingly.

"My friend used to live here," I say to him now. "I'm in town for a re-union and I haven't been back since . . . since she died."

More sniffles in the audience.

"Oh. I'm so sorry." He looks behind him. "My wife just made dinner. Would you like to come in?"

I hesitate, then walk through the door.

CHAPTER TWENTY-THREE

The crowd erupts outside and Antony pats me on the back. That's it, that's the end of the show. Experimental as hell to dissolve into metaphor for the entire second act, but it was powerful. Sometimes that's all it takes. Hopefully the critic sees it as daring and not . . . a complete disaster. Which it sort of was, but also it *was* kind of daring.

"Bruv," Antony says, holding his hands up, "that was amazing. So weird! You were on fire."

I hold my own hands out, and let him smack them.

"Thanks, you too."

Suddenly there are arms around me, and I know it's Aimee before I turn to look.

"You were so good!" she says, pulling back and holding me at arm's length to look at me.

"Curtain call!" the stage manager yells, then gestures like a furious crossing guard for us to go, go, go.

Antony goes out, the audience doing a general, ambient round of applause for him.

I go out for my bow. People start to stand and cheer.

I look back for Aimee, stretching my hand out toward her and stepping out of the center so she can bow as director, writer, and star.

The crowd roars for her.

When we do the final bow together, I look down in front and see Cillian. He's beaming at me, clapping hard and loud. He stops and puts two fingers between his lips and whistles loudly.

Of course he can do that. Who knew I was so into hot boy whistles?

The curtains close eventually. Antony steps off into the wings, making exhausted sounds, as if tonight was a lot for *him*, and I'm left alone onstage with Aimee.

"I meant what I said," she says. "The dream was so vivid."

"I never told you it was raining."

"I know. I know. I saw it all. It came out of nowhere but I swear I remembered or knew or . . . something. Like how you know that none of this is *your* imagination." She shrugs, at a loss.

"This is a lot."

"It's a lot. And I'm sorry, Meg. I've been such a bitch. It's, you know, we haven't talked much, and then you suddenly start telling me I'm *dead*, I mean, this is all such unknown territory. I believe you, but believing you means accepting something really, really hard and scary."

"I know, I know. There's no right way to do this. I'm so sorry, so mad at myself that I never let you be with the person you loved without complaining. It's not my business. It's not."

"No, but that's what friends are for! And it did help. I mean, when you left and I was alone with him in Florida, I knew he wasn't getting his life together. It was your voice in my head that told me to choose myself. It was sort of an *If you love something, let it go* situation. I did, and it worked out. I couldn't have done that if you'd been blindly supportive."

"But I was jealous, too, in a lot of ways. You were right. I'm sorry."

"It's okay! It's okay, Meg. I'm here. I know I'm . . . gone . . . in your world. But I'm here. And I'm not going to spend even a second taking that for granted again. Here, I have my k-kids, and . . ." A wave of heavy tears flows through her and she covers her face. "I . . . I love them so much. I'm so in love with my life. There's no life for me but the one I have now. I belong here. No other world would be right for me."

I breathe deeply and I swear, it may be the first real, satisfying breath I've taken in eleven years.

Since arriving in Avalon, I've remembered more and more about Aimee. But I've also remembered more about myself. Like how I used to be loud and obnoxious and annoying, like I was in that cringey video of me bothering Aimee at school, and how I'm glad I'm not anymore, but how maybe it's a shame—and perhaps even *more* annoying—to tiptoe all the time. I remember now that I really loved the crap junk food my mom let me have every once in a while. I remember lying on the tile floor of my house in the thick of summer, unconcerned with the fact that it may be dirty, Aimee and me both with our tanned legs in the air, matching anklets on our matching bug-bitten ankles and chipping pink nail polish on our toes, a Fruit by the Foot in each of our mouths, turning our teeth purple. I remember borrowing her T-shirts for sleepovers and asking her mom if she had anything for a stomachache. I remember flumping down in the recliner in the living room at my house and begging my parents to let me invite Aimee over.

We used to ask our parents for the privilege of washing the cars so we could play in soap and hose water on a sweltering afternoon. We would hop from foot to foot on the hot blacktop as we waited in line for Good Humor bars from the ice cream man. I would lie down on school nights on top of my sheets with my blue plastic fan blowing on me until I fell into a humid sleep.

I used to do my homework in the backyard. I used to spray *I Can't Believe It's Not Butter!* on already-buttered microwave popcorn. I constantly begged for gum at the checkout line at Publix. I used to read time-travel romances in the hammock in the backyard. I used to watch *General Hospital* with my mom. I used to write down the lyrics to my favorite songs and slide them into the plastic cover of my binder for school.

I didn't just block out Aimee when I hid from the memories of my past. I blocked out myself. I let my old self die with her. But I didn't need to. I shouldn't have let her. No wonder I'm unhappy in my life in LA. I have no idea if it aligns with who I am, because I abolished all the versions of me that existed before I ran away and started pretending.

Literally. For a *living*.

I feel awash suddenly with all the things I'd forgotten how to feel. Warm hose water on my feet and the metallic smell of damp concrete where the water leaked at the faucet, sunburn on my shoulders, the sting of sour Skittles on my tongue, the pinch of the chain from the swings at the playground, the scald of bare thighs on the hot back seat of a Toyota Sienna that had been baking all day in the sun. Being told to be quiet for singing too loudly by myself in my room and feeling embarrassed. The delight at getting to pick out some kind of treat on a boring errand with one of my parents. Something like Reese's Cups at Home Depot. The ecstasy of seeing my name at the top of a cast list on a bulletin board. Being happy and moving instantly into a jumping hug with my best friend, no self-consciousness.

The achy pain of the mono that got me out of school for three weeks in sophomore year of high school (not all bad). The devastation of *not* being cast in a show. The furious boredom of a grounded Friday night. The biting flies that swarmed in the late afternoon at the community pool where we sometimes went to hang out with friends. The searing truth of a torn-open, skinned knee from crashing my bicycle into a parked car.

Yes. A parked car.

That's not the point. The point is, I'm clearly having a significant breakthrough.

I knew, of course, that I had blocked Aimee out and that it wasn't healthy. But I hadn't understood or considered exactly why. It hadn't occurred to me that I had hidden more than the death and grief from myself. I didn't want to remember who Aimee *or* I had been back then, because we had both been doomed. It was too painful to remember them as they were, those happy, sometimes sunburned kids with devastation lying in wait for them.

But pretending changed nothing. It gave me even less of what I missed.

"Let's go join the party," says Aimee. "I'm alive. Might as well have some fun."

I laugh, tears still brimming my eyes. "Right."

We walk together offstage, hand tightly in hand, and then out into the empty hallway beside the entrance to the auditorium.

"I'll be right in," I say, riding my instincts, having a strong compulsion to take a moment to breathe before going in to see everyone.

She smiles warmly at me. "Okay. I'll see you in there, yeah?"

"Yeah," I say. "I just need a sec. I'll be right there."

She nods, gives my hand a last squeeze, and then we let go at the same time.

She opens the door, releasing an audial waft of festive fun.

I don't know why I want to be alone. Right now, everything is as it should be. I have a deep sense of order inside me, an optimism about the future. An assuredness that things will never be as hard as they once were. I guess I sort of want to be alone with that for a second.

I sigh, basking in the bone-deep relaxation I feel. I've never felt this way. I've been a live wire of denial and gilded, hidden emotion for years and years. For as long as I can remember.

I breathe in deeply, then exhale.

That's when I notice the silence. It's absolute. Unyielding. Empty.

I strain my ears, listening for the laughter on the other side of the door. Listening for the yearning vocals of Nat King Cole's "You Stepped Out of a Dream" through the wall, as I'd been able to hear a moment ago.

But there's nothing.

I move toward the door and press my ear to it, unwilling to open it quite yet.

It takes everything I have to open that door. When I do, I'm met with darkness.

The theater is empty.

CHAPTER TWENTY-FOUR

N o. No. No.

This cannot be happening.

I walk into the theater, almost expecting four hundred people to jump out and scream, "Just kidding!"

Of course, they do not. They are gone.

It smells different. Dusty. Musty. Like the room hasn't been used lately.

There's no sign of life anywhere.

The bar is gone. The kids in front of the stage are gone. Cillian is gone. No Kiera chatting up a critic. No crowd.

And the set—the set is gone too.

Oh my God.

I back up into the hallway again, fingernails digging into my palms, unwilling to believe it.

Maybe they all left? I must have not noticed the dust before?

Hello, denial, my old friend.

I know, in my heart, that at the very least, breaking down that bar would have taken longer than this. I worked too many catering events not to know that. And the set. It couldn't disappear. It was simple, but it would take at least a day to strike.

I go back out into the hallway, then crash outside into the night. There's no one out here. Only an empty road. Quiet fields. Sleepy houses, none with lights on. No smoky, green smell in the air.

It's like the place has been abandoned.

For once, the sky is dark. Starless.

I tear down the road, running toward the pub through the deafening noiselessness and past every closed business, afraid of what I'll find. My footsteps echo strangely.

The pub has no lights on—not even the amber lamp—and the doors are locked. I bang on the door anyway, as hard as I can, and then stand in the middle of the street and scream for him.

"Cillian!"

Nothing.

Nothing.

Nothing.

"*Cillian!*" I spin in a circle and scream, "*Kiera!*" Then, finally, "*Aimee!*"

I realize then that I don't have my phone. I can't even try to call anyone.

I run as fast as I can back down the street again, my still-bare feet growing colder against the chilly, slightly damp ground.

I run to Aimee's house, where so recently there had been a lively party. A party where I had so confidently drifted through the scene as though it could not be stolen from me. What was wrong with me? How had I not hung on to every stupid second like it could be taken away?

This is exactly what it felt like when Aimee died, when I wondered how I had not smothered her with appreciation. How had I not held her and never let her go and loved her all the time?

How had I simply *had a cider* and *walked around chatting* like a few days later it might not all be over? I knew it might be. I feared it would be. And yet I kept living.

How dare I?

I know there's no one there, but I pound on the door anyway. I let my forehead land against it, flatten my palms against the wood, and then turn and look out at empty Avalon.

It may as well be a movie set.

Eventually, I have no choice but to return to my home base.

From the outside, the cottage looks the same as ever, and I feel a moment of hope lift inside me as I go through the swinging fence door and then run up the path to open the door.

It's locked.

No.

I remember the lockbox and put in the code. Zero, six, one, nine. Easy to remember. June nineteenth was the day of the accident. Right before my birthday.

It opens—more hope—and inside I find the house key.

I fumble with it and then go to the door. My hands are shaking so badly that I can't open it at first, even dropping the key and having to find it in the grass again before finally fitting it in the lock and opening the door.

My heart nearly stops when I get inside and see my suitcase—*my* suitcase—in the foyer. My carry-on on the floor beside it.

They're the ones I packed in a hurry back in LA. The ones I got sent for free and had to post about with a bunch of insincere hashtags and an offer of 15 percent off with the code LANA15. The suitcase with the zipper that tore the first time I used it when we took a flight to Georgia to shoot a special episode of *Brilliance*.

I let the door fall shut behind me and I stare at the suitcase. On the table, I notice my phone. My real phone. I pick it up and see a picture of Dido as the background. Though I can barely see the picture because there are about a trillion missed notifications.

It is all undone.

I hear the sound of tires on gravel outside and know what I will see when I open the door.

A taxi. Its glowing sign diffused by the fog that's descending upon the nighttime.

The driver gets out.

"You call a taxi to Dublin, ma'am?"

"No!" I scream immediately. Then I say, "Wait one second, I'm—I'm sorry."

He climbs back in, like this happens all the time.

I pick up my phone and google *Lana Lord*.

A slew of articles comes up. News about the finale. News from an unreliable source suggesting Grayson and I are expecting because of yet another unflattering picture taken of me at Sushi Park.

The taxi honks once outside, politely.

I google Aimee's name. Nothing much comes up until I add the name of our hometown at the end.

Her obituary.

"No, please," I say out loud, fighting back soul-deep nausea, asking whatever forces to please have mercy and not take it all away. "Please, please," I whisper.

I shut my eyes hard and then open them again, hoping that the place will be different again, back to my new normal. But no. In fact, I notice that it's not even the house I got to know. Not really.

I glance around, noticing the little signs for which light switches to leave flipped and what not to throw down the toilet and where to find extra towels and firewood.

It's a true rental house now.

The taxi horn goes again, this time less patiently.

I know what I have to do, but I don't want to. I want to sit in the middle of the floor and never leave. Never. I don't care. I'm not leaving.

But almost as if I am not in control of my body, I find myself going to my suitcase, pulling up the handle, and dragging it outside.

"Sorry!" I call to the driver. I feel fluttery and panicky and strange as my body goes through the motions of locking the door and replacing the key where it belongs.

I can't leave, I can't, I can't. Maybe if I simply stay, it'll all go back to how it was in the morning. Maybe it comes and goes. I can deal with that. I can't deal with it being over.

But no. I know it's over.

I get in the back of the taxi as the driver puts my things in the trunk.

I look out the window at the cottage, knowing in my heart that it's different. It's changed. Avalon has changed. Everyone is gone.

Everyone is gone but me.

"How was the trip?" asks the driver.

I bite the tip of my tongue to keep from screaming. I cannot bring myself to say more than, "Good. Thanks."

"All right," he says. "It'll be about an hour ride, ma'am, so settle in. I'll let you know when we're getting close."

I nod, feeling like an injured little kid, and say, "Okay."

I stare outside, watching it all go by.

My eyelids start to grow heavy, and I don't know how long it takes, but somehow, I fall asleep.

I dream that I'm running around Avalon, as I had been, but that when I get to the pub and bang on the door, the sound is thin. Not timeworn chestnut as hard as rock, but thin plywood. The pub isn't real, it's just a painting.

Desperate, I lean against a tree, only to have it fall over too. It's hollow.

I look up, expecting to see the moon, but find tracks of lighting.

The grass is plastic, like that on the stage tonight. The fog pumps from a machine at my feet. The wind comes from a fan.

It's like that scene in *The Truman Show* with the stairs leading to the door through the sky. All of the life that felt so real, turning out to be something synthetic, something created.

In my dreams, I see Avalon as if it were an empty soundstage.

Nothing more.

CHAPTER TWENTY-FIVE

I keep my Dodgers hat low and my sunglasses on as I move through LAX. I'm recognized by a few people anyway, who whisper and point, and I fend off some who dash up, taking pictures of me or filming themselves with me as they ask if I really am pregnant, ask if I know the twist of the next Marvel movie Grayson is going to star in, and ask where I've been.

I go through the delirious motions of arrival. I wait in the long bathroom line, and, like many weary travelers, I see a sallow reflection I barely recognize, but in my case it's uniquely unfamiliar.

I'm back to reality.

Thinned nose. Sharp collarbone. Plump lips. Never has a girl been so disappointed to see that she's twenty pounds thinner.

I wait at the baggage carousel, get my suitcase, and then wait on the curb for my driver to arrive.

I get in, thankful to find the back of the car empty—no Lisa Michele here to talk my ear off about some horrible new infrared beauty product or whatever.

It's sunny and bright, warm with a cool breeze. The car drives beneath blue skies with wispy white clouds. Sparkling green palm trees wave in the morning sun. The traffic is slow-moving because of the hour, but I don't care. I feel empty. Like someone took an ice cream scooper to my insides.

The driver swears at the people who cut him off, lurching from lane to lane.

I realize, at some point, that I'm not tense. I'm heartbroken, but I'm not electrified with fear like I usually am in the car.

Instead, I feel shrouded in grief. The loss of Cillian. The loss of Kiera. The loss of Aimee, all over again.

I hadn't even gotten to say goodbye.

I hadn't had a real last moment with Kiera.

I never made up with Cillian's mom, apologized for breaking her son's heart and explained that my own heart was broken too.

I never met bloody Kay Donahue, tried her soup or listened to whatever gossip she'd have to impart.

I never thanked Cillian's dad.

I forgot to tell Aimee about all the friends we had in high school and what they're doing now, in my world.

I never got to tell Cillian all the ways he made me feel. Because there's not enough time on earth for that.

It's so incomplete. It's as if my favorite show got canceled without wrapping up all the storylines. But that's what grief is, isn't it? Expectation and resolution slashed, leaving unfinished conversations behind.

Will it feel like this forever now? It can't. I can't.

These thoughts remind me uncomfortably of those days after Aimee died. I couldn't make sense of the loss. It didn't *make* any sense. I kept thinking I could use logic to talk my way out of the reality I was suddenly facing. The reality being that I would simply never have back the happiness that had fallen through my fingers and shattered on the ground beneath my feet, the shards of it lodging into my skin, past the calluses, and making me bleed.

Despite the traffic, we're back at Grayson's house sooner than I'm prepared for. I melt unhappily out of the back of the car and walk up the driveway.

I don't get inside before I hear the jingling of her collar.

Dido comes running toward me.

The one silver lining to all this.

"Oh, Dido," I say, feeling my love for her spill out all over the temperature-regulated concrete we stand on.

I drop to my knees and greet her, kissing her a million times and taking in her familiar scent.

I go around the back, Dido staying right at my heels, unwilling to leave me. I leave my suitcase on the porch and walk through the enormous open doors that lead to the living room, where I see Grayson sitting in front of an absolute cornucopia of junk food. I may be in a state of misery and confusion, but even I can tell that it's a pretty hilarious amount of trash.

He sits up, and I see that he's eating cake straight out of the butter-yellow Porto's Bakery box. Really committing to the weight gain thing. I wonder if he's choosing to forget that they could do it with prosthetics.

On the screen before him I see that he's watching *Charade*.

"Babe!" he says. "Welcome home! How was it?"

Babe. More confirmation that I'm me again. Whatever that means.

"It was good," I say, obviously not even getting close to the truth. "Looks like the carbo-loading thing is going well."

"I know, right? Look, I've got the belly goin'," he says, pointing at what is inarguably still a very lean abdomen. "Watching some Hitchcock."

I glance at the screen. "This isn't a Hitchcock movie. Stanley Donen directed it."

Grayson looks at me, confused, then back at the screen.

I sigh, go to the fridge, and pull out a bottle of green juice from Pressed Juicery. I always feel depleted after a flight, but obviously, this time, I feel weirder than ever.

"I'm going to sit by the pool for a bit," I say. Apparently melancholic sunbathing is my go-to activity when grieving.

I go upstairs and put on my bikini, feeling startled once again by my slimmer physique, my unfamiliar face. Dido pants beside me.

I stop at the freezer on my way to the pool and pull out a tub of Grayson's Van Leeuwen ice cream. I grab a spoon, but don't bother with a bowl, and leave the green juice behind.

I sit outside, eating the vanilla ice cream in the warm sunshine, in a beautiful life that no longer feels like my own and that maybe never did. I look up Cairdeas Pub and only find results related to the two words individually. When I type in *Avalon* at the end, I still get nothing relevant. Avalon has different businesses than the ones I would recognize.

I do this with every imaginable combination of things I saw and experienced there. Looking for the needle in the haystack that tells me what I found was real.

But I find nothing. I knew I wouldn't.

How can it be? How can *any* of it be?

I hate myself for the fact that it's all already starting to fade away like some vivid dream I swore I'd never forget. The same thing that happened when Aimee died. She already felt like a memory, even a few days later. My mind adapting too fast to the new reality. How quickly the past tense needs to be employed.

I sit out there until the ice cream is completely gone and the wind turns too chilly. Then I go inside and find Grayson, now watching *Vertigo*.

"Hey, Grayson?"

"Yeah, babe." He doesn't take his eyes off the screen.

"I think we should break up."

His face falls and he turns to me, sitting up. "No, really? Why?"

I shake my head. "It's not right. This isn't real."

He lets his gaze fall to the floor and then shakes his head. "Man. That's a bummer."

"I think you're in love with Elsa. You should ask her out."

"Oh, come on, is this about that again? I've told you—"

"No, no. I'm not accusing you. I believe you. I believe you didn't cheat on me. But I think you love her."

He furrows his brow. "What happened, Lana?"

"My name is actually Meg. I know you know that, but . . . yeah, that's my name."

"I know, I—you introduced yourself as Lana, you introduce yourself as Lana to everyone. I thought that's what you wanted."

"It was. It was. But. I'm Meg." I lift my arms, then let them fall against my lean thighs.

He nods and then stands, crumbs falling off of him. "Nice to meet you, Meg."

He cocks a little smile, and it melts me a little. He's sweet. If dumb. Gorgeous, if completely unattractive to me.

"Yeah. Look, I'm not mad at you. You didn't do anything wrong. You're actually really great. Especially for an actor," I say, giving him the hint of a smile back. "But we were set up to be together, and we were lucky we actually liked each other. It worked for a while."

"I understand. I'm really disappointed about this, but . . . I mean, I can't change your mind?"

"I know what real love feels like, and this isn't it. We both deserve to find it."

He looks really serious for a moment. "Okay."

"Okay. Well." We both seem to think I'm going to say more, but then I don't, only, "Well, I'll see you."

And then I go upstairs, find one of my overnight duffels, and pack it with the things I like, grabbing the boxes that hide my personal things. I fill a backpack with some clothes.

I throw on my sweatpants and a sports bra, tie a sweatshirt around my waist, and then go through the bedroom closet, looking for my tatty old Hopper print. I find it rolled up with the hair tie.

I grab Dido's favorite toy, leash, food, bowl, and dog bed.

I don't see Grayson again on my way out to the garage, where I unlock my big, stupid, ostentatious Land Rover and get in, tossing my bags and Dido's in the back and letting Dido jump in after them onto her bed. I go back for the suitcases I'd packed for Avalon and never reopened, then decide to leave them. I can't look at them. I don't care about anything inside.

I'm leaving California with less and more than I came with.

I start the car, open the garage, and peel out, knowing that it's the last time I'll ever be here.

I don't know where I'm going when I start driving, but by the time I hit the 10, I do. At the next traffic slowdown, I type in my parents' address and settle in for the forty-hour drive.

I put on the *Revolver* album, roll the windows down, and drive away from the sunset.

CHAPTER TWENTY-SIX

Florida is as hot and humid as an Equinox steam room.

In the mornings, I lie by the pool with a paper towel wrapped around a bagel with cream cheese, happily eating carbs and drinking sugary bright orange juice my mom bought at Publix. In the evenings, I drink inexpensive Trader Joe's wine—out of a juice glass—and sit on the back porch with my parents while my dad grills burgers to a Crosby, Stills, Nash & Young album. They have the neighbors over one night, and we play a lively game of Trivial Pursuit. No one cares whether I'm famous or not, they still tease me for forgetting the lyrics to the national anthem.

They are not the kind of parents who kept my room the same, like some strange shrine to the past. Years ago, my mom asked me for permission to put some things of mine in storage, then eventually told me she painted the room; then one day, it became what it is now. A nice, simple, comfy guest room with L.L.Bean percale sheets. A room that doesn't resemble the one I grew up in.

I can't believe it took me so long to go home again.

It's not until Friday afternoon that my mom finds me by the pool and asks if we can talk, and I can see it's something important.

I sit up, preparing myself for bad news; if she tells me she has cancer or something, I'm going to drive the Land Rover into the swamps of Alligator Alley.

Although, it's a Land Rover, so it would probably be fine.

"What's up?" I ask.

"Well, honey, since we didn't know you were coming, I made plans for this weekend. I can cancel them if you want, but—"

"Oh, no, Ma, do whatever. I'm fine."

"Tonight I have plans to do dinner with Jenny. Your dad has dinner with Joe, and I do dinner with Jenny. It's a little routine we've gotten into. Sometimes we all do something together, but tonight it's us girls."

I nod slowly as comprehension dawns. "Ah."

Again, I think about how many times I tried to get my parents to move because I thought they needed some other kind of life. Even though I didn't have my own figured out. Probably *because* I didn't have my own figured out.

"You are welcome to join us, and in fact, I think it would mean a lot to her. To me. To you. To all of us."

I haven't seen or spoken to either of Aimee's parents since the night we left for the party. When Jenny tossed Aimee the keys and said, *Drive carefully, sweetie.*

Now that I remember it was raining, I remember that she actually said more after that. I mentally squint to find the words.

Drive carefully, sweetie. It's supposed to rain later. Maybe let Meg drive?

Mom! had been Aimee's only reply and last word to Jenny.

I stare at Dido, who is happily basking in the sun.

Then to my mom, "Okay. I'll come."

Three hours later, I'm showered and covered in aloe lotion after underestimating the power of the sun—for five days in a row—and wearing a borrowed matching set of what my mom calls her *loungewear* to go over to Aimee's parents' house.

"I don't know why I'm so nervous," I say to my mom as we drive down familiar, half-forgotten roads in her years-old SUV.

"It's natural," she says with a shrug that puts me, strangely, at ease.

Pulling up to the house makes my heart skip several beats in a row, my nervous system well aware of the last time I was here.

Thirty-three Blue Daze Lane. There it is. Aimee's house.

The house looks so similar, and yet the differences are startling. Time has worn the place into something new. Something more settled. The flowers and trees around the house are bigger and older now, making it impossible to think I was only here yesterday.

It's then I realize that the set that was built for Aimee's play was mimicking a version of this house that hasn't existed in a decade. Like she didn't truly know how much it had changed.

As if she hadn't been home in so long. As if her last memories were of the house when she was nineteen too.

The realization gives me chills. It's like she was a ghost, only knowing what she knew when she died. And hadn't she been, in a way?

I think of Cillian and Kiera and Maureen and have to shut my eyes hard to stop from crying.

Jenny comes out of her front door in a kaftan, looking breezy and comfortable. My mom told her I'd be coming, so it isn't an unpleasant trauma surprise party.

When she sees me, her face breaks into a comforting smile and I realize that I have really, really missed her.

I walk right up to her and hug her. Having had my arms around Aimee only a few days ago, I'm vividly aware of the undeniable similarities between them. I squeeze her once, hard, and then let go.

"Come on in, ladies," she says, not immediately putting a spotlight on how long it's been since I was here and under what circumstances I left.

She's not attaching *importance* to every second in the way I feared, and I relax as I walk inside.

The house, of course, has the same bones that it did when I last saw it. The counter in the kitchen that leads to the small dining room. The living room that takes a step to get down into. But things are different too.

I guess I'd expected . . . well, a time capsule. The same busy bulletin board with Post-it notes, an out-of-date calendar, and an irrelevant business card for Aimee's old orthodontist. I'd been expecting the place to match exactly with my memories, like two negatives held up one behind the other.

But it's not the same. I realize now that most of the furniture Jenny and Joe had back then was probably inherited or thrifted. They didn't have a lot of money, and they were fairly young parents, which is the kind of thing kids don't notice. Most people in their twenties and thirties, despite what the internet wants us to believe, are living in houses built out of the things they can find that work. They're not usually *curating space*, like influencers want us to think they are.

Now, it's a clean, mid-century style and it's perfect for them.

The windows have been replaced with new ones, which probably make the bills lower and the house quieter. I remember being told to quiet down constantly when we were out back and they were trying to watch *The Bachelor* or whatever inside. I have a brief fantasy of being here together, grown, with our moms, and having wine, sitting outside the thick new windows.

The dining room table is clean and white, instead of the oak one where I used to sit and eat spaghetti. The couch is pale yellow with spindly, angled legs instead of the big, overstuffed one they used to have. The kitchen has new, updated appliances. The wood paneling is bright, painted clean white.

Jenny clearly kept living. Kept growing. Kept evolving. She didn't freeze in time. I think I feared that everyone here had. That no one else had the ability to change but me, so coming home would be a frightening step into the past.

But it isn't.

At first, it's small talk about what I've *been up to*. She told me she's watched the show and thinks I'm *just marvelous on it*.

When Jenny finishes making the tacos, we eat and chat about how good they are, and then—after the third margarita hits—I bring up the elephant in the room, even though I'm the only who can see it.

"So I had a crazy time in Ireland."

That is what I lead with. A bewilderingly blasé start to a story that neither of them are going to believe.

For the next half hour, I tell the moms what happened in Avalon. They exchange a few looks here and there, and I push through.

"I know it sounds crazy," I say. "It was crazy. And I don't know what the hell it was, or how, but I'm telling you, it happened."

I'm very clear about the fact that the internet results changed, that my face changed, that nothing was as it is in reality. I don't want to raise hopes that maybe there was a mistake and Aimee is actually living in Ireland somewhere after pulling off the crime of a lifetime, faking her own death.

When I finish, I'm not sure what they're going to say. I'm not sure if my mom is going to apologize for what I've said, if Jenny is going to change character completely and slap me across the face and accuse me of terrible lies.

"You know, *this* is going to sound crazy," says Jenny, stirring her drink with her straw. "But I believe every word you said."

My mom looks patient and kind as she nods at Jenny and says nothing.

"You do?" I ask.

"Yes. I do. There's a ton of research on quantum science lately. I was listening to an episode of *Radiolab* that went into this kind of thing the other day."

"Oh my God, Aimee said the ex*act* same thing when I told her. Almost verbatim! And that's proof in itself, because God knows I don't listen to *Radiolab*."

She gives me a polite smile and says, a little cryptically, "I wonder."

Then something occurs to me. "Jenny, did Aimee get into Avalon?"

Her eyes are wide now, fractured with pink. "Yes, she got in. It was awful, her lying to you like that. We tried to tell her to trust you with the truth, but she wouldn't do it. We couldn't make her, and it didn't feel like our place."

I'm relieved she knows, and it feels like the last puzzle piece truly put in its place for me to see the big picture. "So she got in. She really did."

"I'm so sorry, sweetie. I never wanted to tell you after she was gone."

"No, no, I'm not mad. It's sad. I wish she'd known she could trust me, and I should have been trustworthy not to blow the whole thing up because she didn't want what I wanted. And I should have done what was right for me. If I had . . ."

It hangs between us all.

Jenny reaches across the table and puts a hand around my wrist. "It's not your fault, Meggie."

A sudden howl of emotion races through me like a wicked wind as I look at her, see that she means it, and then burst into sobs that feel so deeply rocking that they scrape against my insides and threaten to burst me like a balloon.

But I'm there with our moms. They're making sympathetic sounds of understanding and my mom's hand is on my back, moving in slow circles, and Jenny is holding my hands and not pulling back as I grip her as tightly as you might a cliff face if you were suspended a hundred yards in the air with no rope.

I cry, and I cry. I sound like a child, I sound like an animal. I can't breathe, my stomach aches and cramps, my chest threatens to crack, my face swells like I'm seconds away from anaphylactic shock.

—

And then, eventually, like the ocean eventually does after even the worst tsunami, my waves begin to calm. From tidal swells to soft ripples against the shore. I have this sense of certainty that I had finally touched the bottom of the emotion. I now know the depth of my pain and, finally, I can begin swimming toward the surface. I never need to go that far again.

I can eventually breathe.

They even eventually make me laugh.

When all has settled again, Jenny sniffs and bites her bottom lip. "Maybe I'm a hopeful mom who misses her daughter"—she smiles bravely through the tears—"but it makes me feel good to imagine she's out there somewhere. Leading a different life."

My mom says, "It's a big, unknowable universe, isn't it?" She gives Jenny a squeeze on the arm and says, "I think it might be time for another round of margaritas."

⁓

On the Uber ride home that night, I say, "I'm sorry."

"For what?" asks my mom.

"For trying to get you to leave Florida. It's none of my business to tell you where *your* place is. I'm sorry I tried to."

"Oh, it's okay. I know. Thank you for saying something. I appreciate it. I really am happy here. I have everything I need."

"Good. I'm glad." I look out the window for a minute. We drive past all the low houses that seem the same as one another, but for the little windows with golden glows inside revealing different lives. Different cars parked outside. Grill smoke coming up behind some, teenagers in bikinis sitting out front of some, kids playing out front of others.

The song on the radio changes to Freddie Mercury's cover of "The Great Pretender."

We pass the place where the End of Summer Carnival is held every year. Where the fortune teller gave Aimee and me our destinies. The field is empty now and so much smaller than I remember. Just off a small road near a Publix grocery store and the Tex-Mex restaurant where I spent my sixteenth birthday. We're only a few miles from the intersection where the accident happened. I bet that's also smaller than I remember.

"How did you know this was the right place for you?" I ask.

My mom laughs. "My best friend is here."

She doesn't seem to think much of her comment. She looks out the window too, in one of those cheerfully unappreciative moments we all have where we aren't thinking about how it all might be taken away and instead we're just living in it.

My eyes well up with tears and I nod. "That sounds like a pretty good reason to me."

EPILOGUE

The restaurant is loud and festive, and everyone looks their best. It's the season for maraschino-cherry-red lipstick, sparkling jewelry, and pretty clothes hidden under big, warm coats. It's Christmastime in London, and everyone was right when they said it would be magical.

I quit *Brilliance* a week after returning home to Florida. A week after that, I saw that the show had been canceled. According to *Vulture*, which did an in-depth article on the rise and fall of the show, it's because of my departure, but I know it's not.

Not that I'm not going to let everyone else think that.

I ended up staying in Florida for a few months with my parents, slipping surprisingly easily back into the role of being a kid, complaining about being asked to do laundry and dishes, sunbathing all day, eating chips and dip as a meal. I watched movies with them, my mom saying "Oh, for Pete's sake" every two seconds whenever we watched something too artsy, my dad reliably falling asleep every time we watched a rom-com. I ran errands I didn't feel like running. I went over to Aimee's parents' house a lot, and they came over too. We grilled and I drank wine with the grown-ups, like I thought I would one day.

I took some time to consider where I wanted to be next. I knew I needed a break from LA and all its milk substitutions, but I didn't know where to go. I wound up having my agent set up a bunch of auditions and send off tapes to different directors, but without telling her, I also reached out to a few theatre companies. I got an audition with Les London Players for a play called *With a Ribbon*, a holiday show that calls itself a cross between *Love Actually* and *It's a Wonderful Life*.

And lo and behold, I got the role I wanted!

It stars three sisters and I'm the youngest. There's an ensemble of truly hilarious people, and the show itself is funny and heartwarming.

As soon as I showed up on the first day, I knew I had made the right choice, and I felt truly honored to have been cast. The other actors were excited and enthusiastic, all with the attitude that we, as a community, would be building something together. No one seemed to even care how big or small their role was. Everyone was in high spirits. I became friends with all of them, meeting their equally wonderful partners or, if unattached, hearing about their bad dates. We went out for spicy curries on chilly nights and drank cheap beer—me remembering always that I do, now, like lime pickle and never skipping the naan.

For the holidays, the streets near my little rented flat have twinkling lights and banners on the lampposts advertising *With a Ribbon* and *The Nutcracker*. I have a new favorite coffee shop and I've learned that I hate Marmite but love tea with cream. Dido—the dog, not the singer—is with me, and she trots happily along the wet streets with me when we do our morning and evening walks, as happy in London as she was in Florida as she was in LA.

She would have loved Avalon, too, I think. She would have loved Maureen.

I feel an immense sense of loss after Avalon. But I also feel free of the unbearable weight of unacknowledged grief that I've been traveling with for years, and that has offset some of the pain. And when it hurts, I let it hurt.

I am myself, right now. I am not hiding from the version of me who once was. I'm the girl from Florida who, to this day, has permanent tan lines. I lost my best friend in a tragic car accident.

After meeting Cillian and Kiera, I believe in love in the way I used to when I stayed awake at night, with or without Aimee, dreaming of what it might *someday* really feel like. I believe that good, wonderful people are out there, waiting to be met. Losing Aimee didn't mean I've lost the chance at true friendship. It only means I lost Aimee.

But I hadn't needed to lose everyone. I didn't need to become an island. I have my family; I have Aimee's family. I have these new friends in London. It's *not* impossible to meet new people and grow to love them as much as I loved Aimee. No one will ever replace her. But there are people out there who I can love and like in new ways. And if my little brush with surreality proved anything, it's that there are infinite lives and possibilities. Aimee isn't nothing now that she's gone; her loss doesn't need to be a black hole or even a blank space. She just isn't here.

Out of all the lives I might have, I believe I can make this the one that feels right. I simply have to build it. Nothing as simple as fame could give me what I need. What I need is to be around people I care about. To let people love me. To have small moments, knowing that they're the biggest ones, and not ignore them because I'm too busy looking way off in the distance, either future or past, for some imagined thing.

I'm not here waiting for life. I'm in it. It's happening *now!* Look out!

I'm out to dinner at a restaurant called Home with the entire cast of the show. The dinner was a surprise put on by Nelle, who plays one of my sisters. I told her—well, over the last few months, I've told all of them—about Aimee. I've cried about a hundred times—it's really my new thing—and they've been so nice about it. In fact, it's kind of become one of the running jokes of the show that we're here to put on a good performance, yeah, but we're also here to work through some trauma.

Tonight is Aimee's birthday. Nelle asked me to dinner to commemorate it, and when we got to the restaurant, all my new friends from the show were there at a big table with balloons to celebrate.

"I'm so glad it's a good surprise," says Nelle. "It seemed like such a banging great idea, and then I was horribly afraid it would be like a living nightmare showing up to see fifteen people on a night like this."

I had mentioned to Nelle that I wanted to start doing something every once in a while to remember Aimee, even if it means getting junk food and watching a fun movie on her birthday. I don't want to do the intense grief thing of growing morose on every birth-and-death-day. Not at all. I don't want some annual memorial with heavy words and thoughts. I just want to remember her whenever I can, big or small.

I laugh, shaking my head. "No, your instincts were right. It feels good to do something fun and"—my chin weakens and my throat gets tight—"I sat with it alone for so long, it's nice to do this. *She* would hate this, but I love it!"

The few people listening laugh, and so do I.

The night is so fun. There's a live jazz band in the restaurant playing old holiday standards. We've gotten dozens of oysters, fried calamari, bread and butter, and prawn cocktails—which are a lot different than shrimp cocktails in America, possibly not for the better—and bottle after bottle of champagne.

This is exactly what I want. To be around good people and have a nice time, laughing a lot. Giving something like her birthday a little happiness and festivity. She always hated that it was so close to Christmas, but for me, I think of it as a way to ensure that every year, the world decorates for her.

After dinner, we all say a long, chatty goodbye on the cold, snowy (yes, snowy!) sidewalk outside the restaurant, making excited comments about the upcoming performances, which start in a few days. Then Nelle, myself, and a few others decide to keep going and head to a nearby pub.

The place is cramped and cozy, reminding me distinctly of Cairdeas Pub, which I've imagined would have been almost *too* adorable around the holiday season.

It's decorated with delightfully tacky tinsel, garlands, and colorful lights. There are ugly sweaters everywhere and there's a drunk Santa in the corner with his fake beard pulled down beneath his chin.

I squeeze up to the bar to order us a round of beers, insisting that I'll get them while the others go to a table.

The bartender comes over and I order a round of five Guinnesses. He nods and goes off to get them, and then, through the din, I hear a voice.

"Christ on a bloody knitting needle, I've been waiting fifteen minutes for a pint!"

I know that voice.

I look around and see, two people down from me, the most distinctly familiar face. Freckled. Bright blue eyes.

Kiera.

I stare at her and she sees me. The moment of recognition from her makes my heart nearly stop as she points and says, "Feck, it's you!"

I stop short of saying her name as she squeezes past the people between us and says, "You're Lana bloody Lord, aren't you?"

Of course. The look of recognition isn't because I'm Meg. It's because of TV.

But that doesn't explain it. How is she *here?*

I nod, speechless, and she says, "I wondered how you got a drink so fast. What are you doing in London? Please tell me that *Brilliance* is coming back for another season."

I shake my head. "No, no. It's over."

"Damn," she says.

"I'm here to do a play," I say, so stunned by her presence here that my voice sounds strange to my own ears. "Sorry, what's your name?"

"Kiera," she says, solidifying my feeling of relief and joy.

I look past her and see that Nelle and the others are still there, at a round table nestled in the bow window. I glance at my phone and see that it's still mine. My life is still my own.

"Sorry, I'm sure you're very busy and—" she says, seeing me look at my phone.

"No! No, I'm not! I'm—did—would you like to join my table?"

She smiles. "You gotta be kidding me. Can I tell you something?"

"Yes, what?" I ask, urgently. The bartender comes over with the beers and I say to him, "Get her anything she wants."

"I'll take one of those." She points at the Guinness I've ordered. "Actually, could you make it two? I've got a friend here, I'm happy to pay for it—"

"No." My heart is going to literally explode. Who is her friend? Could it be someone else from Avalon? Could the universe really be that kind? "On my tab, please."

Could it be Aimee?

I wish it for a second, and then know in my heart that it won't be.

"Truth is that my pal is never going to believe it's bloody *you*. He made me fetch the drinks, says I owe him, which of course I do, as I'm the one who made him come out with me and he does me favors all the time, but when he sees that I've met *the* Lana Lord, his eyes are going to fall out of his skull. He didn't mention you were in a show here, he's going to be shocked."

The bartender puts the beers on a tray and sets it on the bar. I hand over the cash.

"I've known him since I was a kid, and I got him into watching *Brilliance* with me, and I swear to you, he's your biggest fan. Not that he'll admit to liking anything all that much. And of course he hates the show, but that's how you know he loves you."

I am actually unable to speak as I hang on to her every quickly spoken, heavily accented word. I don't dare get my hopes up as I take the beers over to our table and she goes off to get her friend.

"You look like you swallowed a blowfish. Are you okay?" asks Nelle.

I nod quickly. "I'll explain later."

I have actually told Nelle about the whole Avalon thing. As a believer in psychics, reiki, tarot, past lives, and just about everything else, she completely bought it.

I rise to my feet without meaning to when Kiera comes back with him in tow.

He flushes when he sees me.

"Cillian," I say, my voice a whisper.

"*Cillian?*" says Nelle beside me.

Kiera comes over and says, "Hiya, I'm Kiera," to everyone, then to me, "Lana, this is Cillian."

He holds out his hand to shake mine, giving a tight-lipped, embarrassed smile.

"You're as scarlet as a radish," I say, using his expression.

He nods. "Nice to meet you, Lana."

"Actually, it's Meg," I say.

Nelle has stood and is watching the whole scene play out before her with wide, glitter-lined eyes.

"Don't mind him," says Kiera, "he's only in love with you. He's watched all of *Brilliance* . . . how many times is it now?"

He flushes even deeper and cracks a small smile. "It's a good show."

"No it isn't," I say, with a smile back.

We all sit down, Kiera expertly arranging so that Cillian and I sit next to each other.

I have grown used to the surreal in the last few months. Or maybe in the last decade, since I lost Aimee. My whole body is in invisible shivers as I revel in the unbelievable situation I find myself in.

"Do you ever get déjà vu?" asks Cillian, leaning a little closer to me. His voice is quiet enough that only I can hear him, but it's as clear as a bell. As if we've sliced the air around us and created a place for us.

I nod, my eyes latched on to his, an irrepressible smile at my lips. "I do."

"Me too," he says. "I'm having it now."

"So am I."

His eyes hang on mine and we both smile again.

Sometimes I feel like my memories are less like a library filled with detailed volumes of moments lived, and instead, every moment is an atom in the air around me. The past is what I breathe, it's what keeps me alive. Aimee. Avalon. Childhood summers. The remembered adrenaline of a night onstage. It's all there, around me, all the time, enigmatic and abstract.

I feel immensely grateful as we sit there at the pub, as my knee leans lightly against Cillian's and my finger absently runs up and down the condensation of my glass, and as cold air comes in through the door beside our table and we all cheerfully lament the icy gusts. I laugh with an open mouth and talk a little too loudly; I joke freely.

I don't try to protect the memory of tonight from tragedy by pretending it isn't lovely, and I don't cherish it so hard that I smother out its spark. I don't question the magic or panic that what I love is slipping through my fingers, or that every good thing will one day be cast pale against the darkness of future catastrophe.

Instead, I have a good night. I get kissed in the snow. I eat chocolate in bed. I make plans for tomorrow.

ACKNOWLEDGMENTS

It always baffles me when I see people panicking over who to thank when they accept their awards, but actually—remembering everyone is hard!

Firstly, I have to thank the two people who help the most when I write a book: my mom, Beth Harbison, and my partner, Richie Costales.

It is infinitely easier to stay motivated to write every day when I know I will be able to call my mom and read her the chapter I just finished. I know she'll give me good advice, calling out things that might need changing, but mostly—because she, a writer too, understands how vital it is to remain encouraging at this stage—she laughs in all the right places, says when it's a great line, and when I reach the end, always says something like, *Is that it? I want to keep reading, go write more!* Not to mention that I owe her my career, my life, and probably some money. It was she who—when I was nineteen—told me my first book was good, and then printed it out for her agent to read. I would have none of this if it weren't for her daring.

The other most deserving of my gratitude is my beloved partner, Richie. At the end of his long workday, he always enthusiastically agrees to hear my new chapter and then patiently responds as I ask for more and more praise. He is a brilliant brainstormer who will happily devote a precious weekend afternoon to my scrambled, abstract ideas and not only put up with the manic waves of my ennui and frenzy, but help me find clarity in the madness. He also watched *Titanic* in theaters with me not too long ago, and bless him, when it comes back around, I know he'll do it again.

It's also Richie who took me to Ireland, and who is nice to me every time I whine, "I miss Ireland," like I was raised there and then torn from it by ship.

I guess I'll acknowledge my brother, who is my best friend, but only for being generally great and not because he did *anything* to help me with this book. At the time of me writing this, he has STILL NOT READ IT DESPITE BEING ASKED FOUR THOUSAND TIMES. He's an incredibly smart musician and storyteller, and the book probably would have been at least a little better and/or easier with his advice. If he ever *does* get around to reading my little story, he will see that he has been publicly shamed. Love ya, Jack! (Can you all go listen to Thalo on Spotify so he gets rich and famous and has time to read again? Thanks ♥)

Sallie Lotz, my fabulous editor. I liked her right away. After our first call, before I'd decided which publisher to go with, I received a letter from her. It made me feel energized and seen, and I think I knew right then I wanted to work with Sallie. It was so meaningful to see her thoughtful notes in the margins that were not only corrections and suggestions, but also comments like: *same!* and *IT ME* and *love this!!!* plus heart emojis whenever a dog was on the page. It's not a given that an editor will mention the good stuff, and it meant the world that she did.

Thank you to Annelise Robey, my agent who has been with me ever since my mom printed out that first draft of *Here Lies Bridget*. I can only imagine what a roller coaster it was to hear and read every meandering creative idea I had as a teenager, throughout all of my twenties, and to this day. This book exists because she called me after business hours to respond to the idea I'd sent her for this, saying, "Yes, that, write that!"

The delightful Logan Harper, who joined the force at the agency for getting this book published, and Amy Shiels, the glamorous Irish actress who made time to read an early draft of this book and verified all my Irishisms and therefore (hopefully) protected me from looking like an absolute *eejit*.

Thank you to Taryn, Tris, and Sarah, my dependable early readers. To Emily, who is always there for an unexpected hour-long call about buried trauma.

I want to thank Tarot (my own perfect black Lab), DoorDash, sherry hour, champagne consumed out of glasses stolen from the Ace Hotel in Palm Springs, noise-canceling headphones, *The Holiday*, James Cameron, justified meals out to celebrate minor accomplishments along the way, the *Off Menu* podcast for all its neatly organized restaurant recommendations sorted by region (Tigh Neachtain in Galway was a highlight), candle service, and the people I chatted with in Ireland, especially the bartender in the amazing city of Dingle who had me hop behind the bar and pour Guinnesses for customers after I told him I was a bartender for most of my adult life.

Also his nephew, who was a dead ringer for my late father, and the smart, funny farmer who sat at the bar through the lock-in with us.

Lastly, I have to thank Kiera and Cillian, characters in supporting roles who came to me so fully realized that I looked forward to spending time with them every day of this process.

Okay, gotta go, have a whole new book to write. Thank *you*, reader, for making this career possible. You're literally the best.

OFFICIAL PLAYLIST FOR
THE OTHER SIDE OF NOW

1. "Where or When," Peggy Lee and Benny Goodman

2. "It Never Rains in Southern California," Albert Hammond

3. "Funeral," Phoebe Bridgers

4. "Anti-Hero," Taylor Swift

5. "Who Let the Dogs Out," Baha Men

6. "I'll See You in My Dreams," Django Reinhardt

7. "Looking Back," Nat King Cole

8. "Hounds of Love," Kate Bush

9. "The Melting of the Sun," St. Vincent

10. "Lightning's Girl," Nancy Sinatra

11. "I'm Old Fashioned," John Coltrane

12. "Boy and Girl," Unloved

13. "The Rainy Day/The Grand Canal (Reels)," Paul Brady, Tommy Peoples, Matt Molloy

14. "She Moves On," Paul Simon

15. "Blues Run the Game," Headless Heroes

16. "Homesickness, Pt. 2," Emahoy Tsegué-Maryam Guèbrou

17. "Crying in the Rain," a-ha

18. "Out of This World," Sarah Vaughan

19. "Better Version of Me," Fiona Apple

20. "Into Dust," Mazzy Star

21. "Soul Meets Body," Death Cab for Cutie

22. "Anywhere Like Heaven," James Taylor

23. "Any Time, Any Day, Anywhere," Lee Wiley

24. "Ordinary World," Duran Duran

25. "She Said She Said," The Beatles

26. "You Stepped Out of a Dream," Nat King Cole

27. "Here, There and Everywhere," The Beatles

28. "Carry On," Crosby, Stills, Nash & Young

29. "The Great Pretender," Freddie Mercury

30. "Skating," Vince Guaraldi Trio

31. "In My Life," The Beatles

32. "Better Now," Thalo

ABOUT THE AUTHOR

Ellyn Jameson

Paige Harbison is the author of three young adult novels, the first of which was published in 2011 when she was just nineteen years old. More recently, she's worked on several celebrity projects as a ghostwriter. *The Other Side of Now* is her adult debut. A woman of many talents, she also is a visual artist, records music with her brother (band name: Thalo), hosts and produces the podcast *Nameless Best Friends,* and has a solid social media presence, amassing millions of views on her one-minute movies. She lives in LA with her partner, Richie, and their dog, Tarot.